TEMPTING FATES

Meagan Spaid

To all best friends everywhere-
Without you, we would be nothing.

To Jackie and Makayla-
Without your patience, kindness, love, and your belief in me,
even when I felt like I was failing and my world was falling apart,
this book would still be sitting on my computer, unfinished.
I love you both.

CONTENTS

Loch Vanhir
Reynardsville
Springfield
Riverdell
BRUNHOLL

Unexplored
Everridge
Unexplored
Rotmuth
Ber

WARNING

If you have read the first two books, then you may know where this page is going. If not, then buckle up, because this is going to get rough.

This book is not for the faint of heart. Some dark and heartbreaking topics are explored inside these pages. For example, all of my characters have gone through some form of abuse, physical and emotional. As such, they respond in various ways to their traumas, some healthy, while other responses, not so much.

So, without further ado, if you can not handle: Emotional and physical abuse, torture, talk of death, murder, and other forms of violence, this book may not be for you.

PROLOGUE

MATTY

A strong wind blew across the dry landscape, rustling the sparse vegetation and kicking up dust, making it hard to see further than a couple hundred feet. Standing on the side of a large, empty field owned by his dad, his hands on his hips, Matty surveyed the land he'd helped plow earlier that day. The plow, still covered in dirt, sat on the hard-packed dirt road leading to the field, the old ox he had used to pull it still tethered to the contraption, his sides coated in a fine layer of sweat that was collecting dust and flies.

The freshly turned dirt of the field was a rich, healthy brown, and the smell... Matty took a deep breath, inhaling the familiar scent, his body relaxing as a faint smile flickered across his face, but only for a moment. The smell was rich and earthy. He hoped that it meant that the wheat they would plant by the end of the week would do well and yield an abundant crop. They needed it.

Surveying the field one last time, he turned on the spot while dusting his dirty hands off on the sides of his pants. Not that it helped much. His pants were as dirty as his hands and they came away just as filthy, dirt gathering in the creases of his palms and getting stuck in his nail beds. He snorted, amused but not surprised before he scanned the dusty horizon.

His eyes came to a stop on a dark spot in the distance. A collection of dark rectangular shapes. A city. Springfield, to be exact. His hometown.

Springfield was a small city if you could even call it that. Matty wouldn't. More like a village. Only a few people lived within the city's limits while the rest resided on farms much like the Claery's own spread of land. And there were only a handful of businesses. Hardly worthy of being called a city, he thought. Some people, mostly visitors and those who knew it well, called Springfield a lawless spread of humanity because if truth be told, Matty had to admit that wasn't far from what it really was. Rules didn't apply here. And the only thing keeping the town together was the need to survive. You couldn't do it alone. Not out here. Not when the closest human city was miles away.

Springfield was growing quickly, though. Land had opened up to settlers an hour or so north of Springfield by horseback. In the mountains that loomed in the distance, to be precise. Land, cheap land, attracted people of all sorts. Young ones looking to make a name for themselves. Those that were escaping the law were the other main culprits. Prospectors and miners made up the rest of the bunch. And they all stopped in Springfield on their way up. Some stayed, liking Springfield, though those were far and few in between. Most kept moving, the drive to succeed, to make a name for themselves, was too strong to resist.

But growth was growth, and Matty wasn't going to complain. It meant bigger and better things were coming, or so he hoped. Word around town was that a news office was finally opening up right there on main with the rest of the businesses. He bit his lip anxiously. He was more excited about that than he cared to let on. More than he should because he could write quite well if he did say so himself. Perhaps, if he was lucky, this was his chance to get away from the farm. His first step in the right direction. His first step to freedom. He'd get out of this hell hole yet. Just like his older brothers.

But...

Matty's eyes scanned the dark spot that was Springfield as he hesitated. His stomach twisted nervously, making him nauseous. If he got a job at the news office, then he'd be closer to a certain girl he'd grown up with. The daughter of a family friend, Clara O'Donoghue. If he was being honest, he wanted to be closer to her. She was a bright ray of sunshine with her easy smile. And her sheer will. He'd never met someone as determined as her before in his life. It was admirable. If she put her mind to something, well, he wouldn't bet against her. Not now. Not ever.

But if he took a job at the news office, he'd be able to look out from the office window. If he was lucky, he'd get to catch a glimpse of her as she walked from her family's apartment above the general store to her pa's bar that she currently tended.

Matty's heart sank, not even seconds later, as he thought about sneaking glances at Clara. Unfortunately for him, she was the most eligible young woman in the whole town, and because they were family friends, he had the privilege of knowing her well. He'd even say that they were friends. Good friends. Or they had been. Since she'd taken over her father's bar, she'd become a bit more recluse. Matty wasn't sure if that was because she didn't have time for him anymore, or if it was because she was genuinely cutting him out. Or worse... She was already being courted by someone else. The thought made his heart pang painfully. Gritting his teeth, he hoped that wasn't the case.

If only he could get her alone so he could ask her. Or, well, that would be too awkward. For him, at least. Even if he did get her alone, would she even answer him? Matty wasn't sure. Perhaps... No. He shook his head. He wouldn't ask his dad to find out for him. He already knew how that would go. His dad would go to Clara's pa and ask for him. Then he'd try and arrange something for Matty. But that wasn't how Matty wanted his potential courtship with Clara to go. He wanted to take his time, wanted to woo her if he could. Taking her out to the farm to show her the baby animals, having dinner with his family, and then spending the evening on the wrap-around porch, snuggled up together on the porch swing while they discussed their future sounded like heaven. Taking her to one of the shows at the theater, holding her hand under the table, and flashing her a sweet smile or two between acts. Meeting her at her pa's general store and sneaking into the backroom for a few stolen kisses. Why would he ever pass that up? No, it would be best if he didn't say anything at all to his dad.

Speaking of his dad... Tearing his gaze away from the city in the distance, Matty turned his attention to his parents' house. His muscles tensed as he surveyed the farmhouse. It was a whitewashed two-story building with a wrap-around porch. He'd spent countless evenings just sitting on the porch swing, listening to the crickets chirp as he gazed out over the farm and up at the stars. It was peaceful. The best part of the day. But just behind that peaceful façade were his parents.

Mrs. Claery was a happy-go-lucky woman. Very tender-hearted. And, truth be told, Matty took after her in more ways than one. The one that mattered, though, was the tender heart he'd inherited. His dad, Mr. Claery, on the other hand, was a hard man to read. He had a nasty temper that he didn't let anyone but his family see. Matty had been on the receiving end of his temper one too many times and he wasn't keen on being in that position again anytime soon. He was also hard on his sons. A little too hard. He expected perfection. It was no wonder that Matty's two older brothers had fled as soon as they'd been able to. Matty was determined to do the same.

Matty chewed on his lower lip as he continued to stare at the farmhouse, his eyes no longer focused. He had yet to tell his parents that he wanted to head into Springfield permanently, that he wanted to pursue a career outside of farming. He already had an idea of how that conversation would go. His mom would be stunned, to say the least, but she would also be quite happy for him, of that he was certain. Mrs. Claery had always made it clear to Matty and his brothers that if they didn't want to take over the family farm later, then she would support them in their endeavors.

His dad, on the other hand, would be a different story. Matty gulped nervously, already sensing the storm brewing on the horizon. Shaking his head, he decided that he would have to wait until his dad was in a good mood. At that point, he would have to be very careful about what words he used. One wrong word, one sentence taken out of context, and he could already feel the back of his dad's hand as it collided with his face, sending him stumbling back into the kitchen wall.

Stuffing his hands in his pocket, Matty let out a deep breath and started trudging toward the house and the barn rather reluctantly, his feet kicking up the dry soil and causing little dust clouds. Behind him, he could hear the ox and the plow following slowly behind, ready to be cleaned up and tucked into the comfort of his stall.

Matty wasn't sure when he'd tell his family, but it would happen sooner rather than later. He wanted to get off the farm. He wanted to be closer to Clara. And if Clara wanted nothing to do with him, then when his career as a journalist took off, he'd move to a bigger city. There would be plenty of potential love interests there. Or so he hoped.

But that's only if Clara gave him his heart back.

Matty would never live the life of a small-town farm boy again. Not if he could help it.

CHAPTER 1

ALICE

The wagon creaked as it crossed the frozen snow- and ice-covered ground, getting stuck temporarily in frozen ruts from previous travelers and natural divots and holes every so often, causing everyone in the wagon to jerk and groan. Their travel-worn bodies were starting to hurt from the cold as well as from the harsh movements. Shifting on the hard wooden bench she was sitting on in the back of the wagon, her back pressed against the side of the bed, her head bent forward and her chin tucked down with her quilt pulled over her head for extra warmth, Alice exhaled. She could see her breath coming out in white puffs, clouding her face and her vision as she peered out over the sparkling, white world that winter had gifted them, or rather cursed them with. She clutched her heavy quilt tighter around her as she shivered. Next to her, Mirabel Blake, her best friend, and soon-to-be sister-in-law if they survived the journey west, shivered as well.

Alice's teeth chattered as she glanced over at Mira. Just like Alice, Mira's long hair was pulled back into a braid, loose hair escaping and framing her face as she huddled under her own thick quilt. Her cheeks and the tip of her nose were rosy, and every few minutes, Alice could hear her sniffle, the freezing temperatures having made hers and everyone else's noses run.

It was miserable. She was counting down the days until they reached civilization again. A soft, warm bed and a hot bath sounded heavenly.

Actually, heavenly was a bit of an understatement, but she wasn't sure what was better than heavenly. She just knew it existed. Somewhere.

"You good, Mira?" Alice asked through her chattering teeth, her voice hoarse from having to shout over the sound of the creaking wagon wheels and the wind. How she wished they had a canvas top for the wagon. It would be deafening inside the back with it on, but it would shield them from the wind, allowing them to warm up a bit.

Without thinking, she tugged the blanket even tighter before scooting her frozen body closer to Mira's to see if they could help warm each other up. Her hands were so cold at this point that they were nearly painful. Just letting go of her quilt to stretch out her fingers made her want to cry out, but that would do her no good. The tears would freeze on her cheeks as soon as they escaped.

"As good as I can be, I suppose," Mira gritted out, a miserable expression on her face as she gazed out over the frozen landscape. All they could see for miles was frozen snow that glittered in the dying sunlight as the sun started to dip below the horizon, causing the temperatures to drop further. "We should be stopping for the night soon, right?" A hint of hope laced Mira's voice as she continued. Alice watched as Mira glanced over at Xander, Mira's brother, and Able, Alice's brother, for confirmation.

Xander was the first to answer, letting out a quick huff of air as he ran a hand through his long golden hair, mussing it. He glanced at the two girls, his face unreadable as he surveyed them. "Yes. Soon," he grunted before turning away, his green eyes narrowing on a spot on the horizon. Alice, following his gaze, looked at the same spot. A copse of trees, or what she hoped was a copse of trees, looked like it was a few miles away. If they could make it there before dark, the trees would hopefully provide some relief from the biting winds that kept tearing through the valley, chilling them all to the bone.

"Think we can make it?" Alice asked Xander after a minute, her voice quiet but still loud enough for him to hear.

Xander turned his attention to Alice, his expression softening slightly. A ghost of a smile tugged at his lips, but just as quickly as it came, it was gone. He jerked his head once, nodding. "I think so," he murmured, his deep voice hoarse. "As long as the path there isn't terrible, we'll be just fine."

Alice nodded her head in return, still studying Xander. Alexander Blake, or Xander, was Mirabel's older brother. He also had a twin, Ronan, who had been one of Alice's close friends for a long time. Or he had been until he had pushed her away a few years back, stating that he could no longer be her friend and that he didn't want to hurt her. It had soured Able's opinion of the other Blake twin, but that hadn't stopped Alice from trying to remain friends with him, though her efforts had fallen short. She hadn't seen Ronan snapping and killing Mirabel's mate in a freak accident before fleeing west coming at all. In fact, it had taken her by surprise. It had also hurt, not being privy to what was going through his head at the time. At one point, she would have known. But now... Ronan was nothing more than a stranger to her. That fact still irked more than she cared to admit.

But that's where Xander came in.

Again.

Back when she was still a teenager, Alice had had a rather large crush on both the Blake boys, just like all the other females her age. They were both tall, well built, came from a good family that had quite a bit of power at its fingertips, and they were both extremely good-looking in their own way. Xander was the dream, looking like a literal god with his long golden hair, bronzed skin, and striking green eyes. His mischievous half-smile that he would flash when he knew he was in a bit of trouble could make just about everyone swoon, herself included. Ronan, on the other hand, was the mysterious outcast that most of the others her age had avoided, simply because no one wanted to get on Mr. Blake's bad side. He had a mop of curly black hair that fell into the same striking green eyes, and flawless ivory skin that made him look like he'd been carved out of stone. No one knew what he had been up to. He hadn't talked much, preferring to hang out in the back where he couldn't attract the wrong kind of attention. But he was kind, and he had always taken the time to listen to her.

She hated to admit it, but she had tailed both everywhere.

Then, one afternoon, Xander and his group of friends had decided to play a little game of truth or dare. She should have known then that it would lead to nothing but trouble. Those games always did. She hadn't wanted to look weak in front of Xander, her brother, and their friends, so she had participated, taking a dare that would forever change her life. She had let Xander mark her, effectively claiming her as his mate. But it was harmless, or so they all thought. They weren't full-fledged adult shifters, after all. The venom that was injected during the claiming process wasn't supposed to be present. Or that's what the adults had told them growing up.

They'd all been wrong.

The process had been painful. She remembered wanting to cry and scream. And gods, the sheer amount of blood. Her face paled at the memory. It was pure luck that they had figured out how to stop it – one swipe of Xander's tongue across the bite. She'd be dead and six feet under the ground if it hadn't been for his saliva, sealing the bite closed and administering the antivenom.

After that, she'd forgotten all about that, pushing the memory as far back into her mind as possible. No one wanted to remember a stupid mistake that could have ended up killing them. It was embarrassing. She should have known better.

It wasn't until Alice had started searching for both Mirabel and Ronan after the death of Mirabel's mate and Mirabel and Ronan's subsequent disappearances, that she started getting close to Xander again. Or rather, she'd started using Xander for information. She'd let him bed her, and in exchange, she'd get a piece of information that would hopefully get her closer to unraveling the mystery of her friends' disappearances. During their time together, both of them had realized that maybe, just maybe, that marking they'd done years ago had actually worked. She was Xander's mate whether she liked it or not.

Not that she was complaining. There were worse males she could have been paired with. However, she was still coming to terms with the idea that she had a mate, that she'd been claimed already. It was surreal to her.

She'd adjust. Eventually.

"Everything okay, love?" Xander asked, his brows furrowing slightly as he watched Alice studying him, his eyes roving over her curly hair and ocher-colored skin before lingering on her large brown eyes.

Jerking slightly, Xander's words dragged her out of her thoughts. She flushed slightly, her dark skin pinking up just enough to be barely visible, and nodded.

"I was just thinking."

"About?" Xander arched a brow at her curiously. He always seemed to want to know what was on her mind, a far cry from the Xander she had grown up with. Alice wasn't sure if she liked that or not, though she had to admit that it was nice to have someone to talk to who actually listened.

"Us," she replied simply as Able Kumar, her brother, scoffed from his position on the bench seat next to Xander, his hands clutching the reins a bit tighter, his eyes never wavering from the spot on the horizon.

Alice turned her attention to Able before either she or Xander could respond, hurt flashing in her eyes.

Able was her older brother and he had always looked after her. He was her protector, her shoulder to cry on, an ear when she needed to vent. But now… Alice's gaze hardened slightly. She wasn't sure if he was more upset that she was mated to his best friend, if it was because Xander had once had a reputation as a notorious womanizer, or if it was because he felt like he had been replaced. Hell, it could be a combination of all three, she realized, her gaze softening back up.

"Able," she sighed, sagging against the side of the wagon bed in defeat. She was in no mood to fight. She didn't have the energy for it.

Her hand trembling with cold, she reached out and brushed a strand of his dark curly hair, similar to her own, behind his ear before fixing his woolen cap, covering his ears back up. His dark brown eyes widened at the gesture, but then they softened, the corners crinkling as he gazed back at her with a hint of a smile.

"I still don't like this," he said under his breath in reply a second later, his gaze still soft.

"And we've noted that already," Mira said, her voice a bit dry as she piped up finally from her spot behind Able, her body still pressed up against Alice's. "Look, Able, none of us saw this coming. I would have preferred she be Ronan's mate, if I'm being completely honest. They were always good friends. More compatible in my eyes. But she has the bond with Xander, and they acted on that unknowingly years ago. There's nothing we can do about that now. We just… we just have to learn how to live with it and accept it. Be happy for them. The gods know there isn't going to be much to be happy about with everything going on right now."

Eyes widening in surprise, Alice's jaw dropped as she listened to Mira's reply to Able. She had never thought that Mira hadn't been happy about her mating with Xander, but here it was. Straight from the horse's mouth. She wasn't sure whether she should be happy or upset or disappointed or... She shook her head slightly, clearing her mind. It didn't matter. Not really. Like Mira said, there was nothing any of them could do about it now.

Peering at Xander out of the corner of her eye, she could see a similar expression on his face. There was more there, some sort of emotion in his eyes that she couldn't quite place. But it was definitely directed at Mira. Her brows knitted together as she tried to figure out what emotion it was, but then let out a soft breath and decided to let it go. If he wanted to talk about it later, he would tell her when they curled up together for the night, huddled together for warmth and comfort.

Her eyes darted back to Mira, her lips pursing slightly. Alice couldn't lie, she felt a little betrayed herself. And then her mouth fell open into a small 'o'. She glanced back at Xander, realizing what emotion was flickering behind his bright green eyes. Betrayal. He had been taking care of Mirabel since she'd had to go into hiding to avoid her marriage to her mate. He had been her only source of comfort, of protection, of, well, anything, and here she was telling him she didn't approve.

His heart had to be broken.

An uncomfortable silence followed as Alice's eyes darted between Xander and Mira. Even Able could sense the tension and wisely chose not to say anything more.

Finally, Alice cleared her throat as she eyed the copse of trees they were heading toward. "We should be hitting the last town before Springfield tomorrow. That means we should be in Springfield in about a week. But..." she hesitated, not sure if she wanted to voice her opinion or not. Biting her bottom lip, she took a deep breath and decided to go for it anyway. It needed to be said. "I don't think that all of us should go into Springfield.

It's a human outpost, yes? If they support the king and his actions against shifters, we could be walking into a trap."

"I agree," Able grunted almost immediately, making it clear that he, too, had been thinking about their imminent arrival. "I can go in if you'd like. I won't stick out nearly as much as Xander."

"Bullshit," Xander retorted with a soft snarl. "You're just as tall. Humans are tiny compared to us. We'll both stick out like sore thumbs. Don't be stupid."

Alice groaned softly. He wasn't exactly wrong, which meant that left either Mira or herself. Knowing Xander and Able, they had a snowball's chance in hell of being allowed to go into Springfield without them.

"So what do you propose?" Mira asked, worry lines creasing her forehead. "One of us still has to go in to check for Ronan. This was where he was supposed to be."

"If he was smart, he would have gotten the hell out of there," Able commented. "Humans just aren't safe to be around right now, as much as I hate to say it."

"And we all know that Ronan is on the smarter side," Xander added. "Book smart, at least. But this isn't a situation that he'd misread. It's plain as day. The humans are waging war against the shifters. End of story. Staying anywhere near them is a hazard, one even Ronan wouldn't risk."

"I hope you're right," Mira murmured, adjusting her quilt around her. "If something happened to him, I'd never forgive myself. It's my fault he had to flee."

"Nonsense." Xander shook his head, rolling his eyes at Mira. "It wasn't your fault, and you know it. He didn't have to kill Michael, but he did. This is all on him."

"But..." she started to protest.

Xander shook his head again, giving her a stern look to silence her. "It's not your fault."

"So what are we going to do then?" Alice asked as Mira pouted at Xander.

"Honestly? I have no idea," Xander sighed, running his hand through his hair yet again. "There are so many ways that even just getting close to Springfield could go wrong. We could be spotted and chased out. We could be snuck up on and killed in our sleep. We could be captured." He turned to look at Alice, his eyes meeting hers, worry and concern for her safety filling them. "Our best bet right now is for one of us to get close enough to sneak a peek at what's going on there. If we don't see any shifters, I think that's our sign that he got out and fled north to the lands I'd told him about. It's what I would have done. If there are shifters, well... I guess we're going to have to start asking around, aren't we? Hopefully, someone will have seen him and can point us in the right direction."

CHAPTER 2

CLARA

The temperature was frigid. It hurt. It made those standing outside, spectating the current stand-off going on in the middle of camp wince as they crammed their hands into the pockets of their coats or stuffed them under their armpits, hoping their fur-lined cloaks would be enough to keep them warm. Noses ran, lips were chapped, and snow clung to eyelashes.

And the noise. The wind howled as if someone had done it wrong and it was angry at the world. It rattled tents and tore at clothes. It chilled already frozen bodies even more.

And yet they stood there, Clara staring at her long-lost grandmother for the first time in over a decade. She'd thought her grandmother was dead or long gone. She'd gone searching for her, hoping to get answers. Nothing. Not even a shred of evidence that her ma's family even existed.

But there she stood across from her, the short distance feeling like a vast ocean.

Clara had never hated anyone more as the memories of the woman she hadn't been able to remember up until this point came flooding back.

As the snow and wind continued to howl around them, seemingly cutting them off from the rest of the world as they turned to face each other, Clara gazed up at Warren, memorizing his face. The dark eyes she had come to love with his long lashes currently catching thick snowflakes; the puckered scar running down the side of his face that marred his good looks but still didn't detract from them, instead making him look more dangerous; his long auburn hair tied back into a loose ponytail but was coming loose, the strands flying in the wind. She would never get tired of looking at this male. There wasn't enough time in the world for her to spend with him, or that's what it felt like. She was about to tell him so when she noticed fear flash in his eyes as he leaned closer to talk to her.

"Clara?" he whispered, his voice catching in his throat, causing Clara's heart to break at the sheer pain she heard there.

Her breath caught in her throat as well as the emotions she was trying to hold back started to force their way out. Tears filled her eyes, clouding her vision, making it hard to see Warren clearly. Her chest constricted painfully. She felt heavy. So very heavy. As if someone was sitting on top of her.

Blindly, without thinking, she stepped forward and buried her face in Warren's chest just as the tears in her eyes started to fall freely down her cheeks. This was too much. She couldn't do this. But this felt right, going to the one person who had proven he'd come for her over and over again, the one person who loved her despite everything else. He was her comfort. Her was her support. And she needed him. Desperately. Her hands grasped the front of his coat, holding on for dear life.

Out of all the people that had to find them, why did it have to be her grandmother?

"Don't let her take me," she whispered into Warren's chest as his arms wrapped around her instinctively, bringing her closer. His embrace was warm, comforting, and safe. As long as he held her close, she was sure that nothing bad would happen to her. Or so she hoped. It wouldn't be the first time fate had laughed in their faces. But they always managed to overcome the curve balls that had been thrown their way. They would overcome this one as well.

Hopefully.

She had to stay positive. But gods was it hard.

"I won't," Warren whispered back to her, one hand coming up to the back of her head and stroking her dark hair lovingly, his fingers tangling in the strands. "Not even death could keep me from you. She has no authority here. This is our pack, little fox. Mine and yours. We can tell her to leave and no one would blink twice. Except for maybe her. But who cares, right?"

Clara sank into him, letting his words wash over her, comforting her. He was right. He was always right. Or almost always right. But in this case, he was definitely right.

"Clara, I said come along," Mrs. Reynard's voice cut through the frigid air like a knife, making her flinch, the spell Warren had created, the warmth and security he was providing just by holding her and speaking so gently to her, broken.

A small sob caught in her throat as she buried herself further into Warren's chest. "Please, don't let her take me. She had her chance..." Clara trailed off as the memories of her few encounters with her grandmother came back to her once again.

"What did she do, love?" Warren asked quietly, concern filling his eyes as he grasped her chin gently between his fingers and tilted Clara's face back so that he could meet her eyes. "Did she hurt you?"

Clara gulped. "No," she whispered. "Not... No." She tried to shake her head, not sure how to explain what had happened, her words failing her, but he held her firm in his grasp, never taking his eyes off her.

"Then what did she do?" Warren asked again, confusion now mixing with his concern. "I can't help if I don't know. I need you to talk to me, little fox."

"The first time I met her, I was small. I'm not sure how young, but..." Clara took a deep breath, her eyes growing distant as she lost herself in the memory once more, despite how painful it was. "She came to see my ma and me. She was worried that I was human. If I'm remembering correctly, she tried to talk my ma into taking me to Reynardsville and leaving my pa. The second time, I was a bit older. Not by much, mind you. She essentially had the same conversation with my ma again, and when my ma refused, she called me a filthy half-breed. She never hid how much I disgusted her. I was unnatural in her eyes. Not worthy of being a Reynard. Not that I care much if I'm welcomed as a Reynard or not. They didn't want me... I still don't think they really want me. I don't want them if that means anything. They mean nothing to me. Gods, that sounds horrible."

"She called you a... a filthy half-breed?" Warren's voice took on a dangerous edge as his eyes darkened, his temper starting to flare. "Yes, you may be a half-breed, but you put most of the pure-blooded shifter females to shame. You pull more than your weight and I have no idea how I'd run this pack without your help. Half-breed, gah. If she calls you that again, so help me..."

"There's more," Clara said, her voice dropping in volume, cutting him off and startling him.

Glancing down at her, his mouth still half open, he raised his brows at her. "There's more?" he repeated in disbelief. "What do you mean there's more? What else did the bitch do?"

"Clara! Come here," Mrs. Reynard's voice rang out again, accompanied by an impatient stomp of her foot.

Clara's brows shot up in both disbelief and amusement. Had she just witnessed the leader of the Reynard pack and Reynardsville, a grown woman, stomp her foot as if she were a teenage girl throwing a tantrum? She bit her lip as her eyes darted back to Warren's, taking a deep breath before forcing herself to continue explaining.

"She knew that General Claery was after us. She wrote my ma a letter begging her to come home. Told her to leave me behind and that if I didn't survive, she could always have more children later with a male more suited to being her mate than my pa," Clara said rapidly, spitting it out as fast as she could as if she was worried that she'd run out of time or chicken out if she didn't get it all out now. "Obviously, my ma didn't leave me and my pa because General Claery ended up killing her. We both know that. But it wasn't as soon as my grandmother had anticipated. My ma didn't die until a few years later so she had plenty of time to fix the situation if she was actually worried. But no, she... my grandmother never asked if we needed help or if we wanted extra protection, something she could have easily arranged. No, all she did was write a letter and beg. That was it. She doesn't really care. She's proven that repeatedly, time and again."

"Clara, so help me, get your hands off that filthy wolf and come here," Mrs. Reynard shouted, getting progressively louder. "We have to go. We don't have time to waste. Reynardsville is preparing for the general's forces, and I would like to be back home before my subordinate closes off the city. It would make it incredibly difficult for us to get inside, as you can imagine. Now come along."

At the same time, Warren rolled his eyes, lowering his voice even further. "Don't worry about your grandmother. I'll take care of her and her "friends" over there. Just stay behind me. I won't let her take you, do you understand?"

Clara hesitated. She didn't necessarily want Warren to fight her battles for her, but in this instance, she didn't stand a chance. She didn't know how to fight to save her life unless you counted jumping into the occasional bar fight to break it up. She'd swung a few punches, but battling drunk human men and sober male shifters were two different stories. She'd have her ass handed to her faster than she could beg for mercy. Besides, she'd only hurt herself by trying to resist if things got physical. No, for once, she would listen completely without complaint. She would follow all of Warren's instructions, especially if that meant she could stay where she was wanted, where she was loved, where she felt like she belonged.

"I understand," she murmured, wiping her face with the back of her sleeve, drying the tears that felt like they were starting to freeze on her cheeks.

"Good girl." Warren pressed a kiss to her forehead before crushing her against his chest in a tight embrace once again.

Clara melted against him, taking deep breaths as she inhaled his scent, the various smells that made him who he was soothing her.

"That's my good girl," he murmured, kissing the top of her head this time, his nose buried in her hair. "Just stay calm. Let me handle this."

Nodding silently, Clara stepped back as Warren released her rather reluctantly. Hovering just behind him she reached out and fisted her hand in the back of his coat, feeling the need to touch him for comfort. She swallowed anxiously as she heard her grandmother huff in frustration.

"By the gods, Clara, why can't you just follow simple instructions? I told you to come here. We have to go," Mrs. Reynard said, the irritation in her voice growing by the second. Around her, her group of fellow shifters shifted uncomfortably, though a few crossed their arms, their muscles visibly flexing underneath their coats, making Clara's unease grow. If it came down to a fight… No, she shook her head, cutting herself off before her thoughts got too out of control. She couldn't think like that.

"She's not going with you, ma'am," Warren said, his deep voice booming across the small area, interrupting her train of thought. Authority dripped from his voice and confidence oozed from him as he spoke. Mrs. Reynard's eyes widened in response, but whether from shock or irritation, Clara wasn't sure.

Silence fell as Mrs. Reynard opened her mouth to respond and then shut it once more, as if she were thinking about what she wanted to say, especially now that more members of the Loch Haven pack were joining the crowd to see what the fuss was about.

A warm, calloused hand gripped Clara's elbow gently, startling her as she clung to Warren while she continued to watch her grandmother carefully.

"It's just me," Marcus whispered behind her, his voice low and soothing. "Relax. I'm just here to make sure no one else tries to sneak up behind you."

Feeling like her heart was going to burst from her chest from how hard it was pounding, Clara gulped and nodded, forcing herself to relax. She was safe. Warren and his family wouldn't let anything happen to her. But… She shook her head again. They'd had no control over the situation when General Claery had attacked their last camp, kidnapping her and almost killing Warren. If it hadn't been for Ronan coming to her aid and Marcus's skills at healing, Clara wouldn't have escaped General Claery and Warren wouldn't have healed enough to come fetch her from Reynardsville.

This whole situation was different, she reminded herself repeatedly. She wasn't going to get kidnapped. Warren wasn't going to get run through with a poisoned sword this time around. Everything was going to be okay.

"You have no claim over the girl," Mrs. Reynard said finally, taking a step toward Warren, as if trying to intimidate him even though she was about as tall as Clara, meaning she was tiny compared to Warren, her group following a few paces behind her. "She is my flesh and blood. You are but a potential mate. There will be others within our pack. Someone more suited for her. A fox."

"No claim?" Warren scoffed as Clara stiffened at her grandmother's words. If she truly believed that then... Her train of thought was interrupted by Warren as he reached behind him, grasping Clara's arm before dragging her out from behind him. Bringing her back against his chest, one arm wrapped around her waist, he used his free hand to tug her collar down, exposing the bite mark on her lower neck, showcasing his claim on her, marking her as his mate. And then he tugged his own collar down, exposing Clara's claim on him. "She's mine," he growled, his tone menacing.

Mrs. Reynard stumbled back a step, her eyes widening in shock as her eyes darted between the two marks. "You didn't..." she whispered in horror. Her gaze then flicked to Clara, her eyes searching her granddaughter's face. "How could you?"

"How could I...?" Clara started but was cut off again by Warren pushing her behind him once more, Marcus's hand quickly wrapping around her arm as he stepped up right behind her, protecting her.

"Don't speak to her," Warren gritted out. "You are not welcome here."

"But... I... You can't..." Mrs. Reynard spluttered, trying to look around Warren. "You can't... Let me speak to her. This should be up to her. Let me talk to her, grandmother to granddaughter. I can make her see sense. And if I can't, then I'll leave. But I can't just leave. Not when I've come so far. Let me see her. I can't go back empty-handed. I... Please."

"No," Warren said firmly. "You've done... Well, you've not done enough, but at the same time, you have done enough. Enough damage, that is. You've hurt her. I won't let you near her again."

"You don't understand," Mrs. Reynard said in frustration.

"What don't I understand?" Warren snapped. "Because from where I'm standing, everything is looking pretty clear. You didn't want Clara because she's a half-breed and you never hid your disdain. You had the opportunity to provide some form of protection for Clara and her ma back in the day, and you didn't take it. Her ma's death is on your hands. And if it wasn't for me, Clara would be dead as well. So please, explain to me what I apparently don't understand."

"She's my heir," Mrs. Reynard said, flinching at Warren's words, not bothering to deny his accusations.

Silence fell once more at Mrs. Reynard's words. Warren stiffened, not expecting that. Clara, on the other hand, took a step back, bumping into Marcus, her eyes wide in shock.

"Clara is my heir," Mrs. Reynard repeated, her voice quiet but full of regret. "Mara, her mother, was my only child. She would have taken over for me if she had lived. Since she didn't, Clara is now set to take my place when my time comes."

CHAPTER 3

WARREN

"Take Clara to our tent. Now." Warren met Marcus's gaze as he gave the order, not looking down at Clara at all. He could already see the shock on her face as her grandmother's words registered with her. She was also shaking as she drew her cloak more closely about her as if that would provide a little bit of comfort as her world was flipped upside down once more. He knew his own had just gone a bit topsy-turvy.

Marcus simply nodded, his hand still wrapped around Clara's arm. Tugging her gently, he pulled her toward him, wrapping his arm around his shoulders. Allowing Marcus to pull her close, Warren watched as Clara clung to his cousin for comfort, his heart warming, if only temporarily given the situation.

It was good to see Clara turn to his family, to trust them enough to keep her safe, to rely on them. It meant she was accepting her place as his mate, as part of his family. It was what every male shifter hoped for when they took a mate. It made life easier.

His gaze dropped down to Clara again as he watched Marcus start walking her back, taking small steps as they navigated the snow together, careful to not let her slip and fall.

"Don't let anyone except our family in," Warren called after Marcus, his voice grave. He had a feeling that if he left Clara unattended for even a second, her grandmother would send one of the males from her entourage in to nab her. Marcus apparently felt the same way. He hadn't had to ask Marcus to box Clara in between the two of them as they confronted her grandmother. No, instead, he had simply acted. For that, Warren was incredibly grateful. It wasn't every day that you were blessed with family members who just got you, that could read a situation and would react accordingly, that would have your back no matter what.

With everything that had happened in the last year or so, Warren felt incredibly blessed to have a family like his.

Still carefully leading Clara back, Marcus raised his free hand briefly to show that he had heard Warren. Warren watched for a few more seconds, noting the way that Clara's cheeks and nose had turned red from the cold and that her nose was running; that snow was gathering in her hair, turning her dark tresses white; that her lips were starting to turn purple. Regardless of whether Mrs. Reynard was here or not, it was a good thing that he had Marcus taking her back inside. She needed to warm up. They all needed to warm up. The cold was relentless and unforgiving and the last thing he needed was for her to get sick because she stood outside for too long.

His face hardening, he tore his gaze from his better half and turned toward Mrs. Reynard. Like Clara, her nose and cheeks were quickly turning red. Her dark hair was also coated in snow. But her eyes flashed angrily as she watched her granddaughter be led away.

"Bring her back," she snarled at Warren, her hands clenching into fists, shaking slightly from the anger coursing through her body. "I need to take her home. I don't care what sort of claim you have on her. That can easily be broken. We both know it."

Warren flinched at those words. They made him want to turn around and go grab Clara, to hold her in his arms and never let her go because Mrs. Reynard was right. He did know that his claim on Clara could be broken. As much as he wanted that mark to be permanent, he knew that if another male laid his claim over his own, Clara would no longer be tied to him. The thought tore him apart, his chest constricting painfully. It was one of the reasons male shifters guarded their mates jealously, much like the dragons of lore guarding their treasure hordes. No one was allowed to touch, to feel, to enjoy. You were lucky if you were allowed to see, to have a conversation with a claimed female.

They were precious above all else.

Clara was his and no one would be taking her away from him. Not today. Not tomorrow. Not ever.

"She would have to consent," Warren said in reply, his tone biting as he stalked closer to Mrs. Reynard, his hackles rising in anger. "And that you do not have. She claimed me back, fox. I think we both know where her loyalties lie."

Mrs. Reynard's face darkened at Warren's words, shrinking back as he approached her. Like Clara, she wasn't very tall, maybe five foot five at most. Warren, on the other hand, stood closer to six foot six. There was even a chance that he was taller than that. It had been years since he'd been measured and there was a possibility he had grown another inch or two. But who was counting? And who really cared?

Standing in front of Mrs. Reynard, towering over her, his eyes dark and menacing, he made an imposing figure, and he knew it. It took all he had to fight back the smirk that threatened to break free. He needed to stay cold. He couldn't show any emotion except the pure rage that filled him at that moment.

"You were simply the first shifter that paid her any mind," Mrs. Reynard said dismissively after a few minutes, her voice shaky, betraying how nervous she was despite her cool words.

"Wrong," Warren purred, leaning in, his smirk finally breaking through. "She had a handful after her. But I made sure I was the one she paid attention to." He took a deep breath as he leaned in even further. "And gods, her smell. It could drive a man crazy. The amount of potential there... I knew I had to have her. So, I did what I had to." He was now almost nose to nose with Mrs. Reynard, his ire flickering in his eyes, plain for her to see. "And when I found out that General Claery was after her, I took care of her. I got her out of Springfield. I took her somewhere that should have been safe. And when she was taken from me there, as soon as I was well enough, I hunted her down to bring her back. I did give her the option to stay in Reynardsville, though. I've always given her a choice, because, while I did take her by force to keep her safe, I would never force her to stay. I want my mate to love me back." He snorted softly as the memory came back, how he had felt awkward asking if she wanted to return with him, how his anxiety had shot sky high as he waited for her response, and how it had ended with them stripping each other's clothes off and joining together once more. He leaned in further, his nose now brushing Mrs. Reynards, his expression smug. "Do you want to know what she did in response to my offer? She chose to stay with me, and gods, I won't forget the way she felt wrapped around me that night. Not ever. It was one of the best nights of my life. And now I'm going to give her everything she's ever desired because that's what she deserves. What have you ever done for her?"

Mrs. Reynard's jaw dropped in response to his little tirade. It looked as if she wanted to call him a liar, wanted to tell him that he was wrong, that Clara was nothing to him, that she belonged with the Reynard pack. But she couldn't. Not without looking like a fool. No, Warren knew her kind. She prided herself on being quick and cunning, embodying the better-known traits of her animal, the fox. He would even bet that she was also a thief and a liar when needed. Manipulative, if the need arose. But if there was one thing that Mrs. Reynard detested the most, as a supposedly strong leader, that was being made to look like a fool. And everyone knew it. Her own pack. The residents of Reynardsville. The shifters in the region.

One of the hazards of being one of the most well-known shifters in the north-western part of the kingdom, you had no secrets.

Warren stepped back, crossing his arms over his chest as he watched her jaw work soundlessly in satisfaction. He was almost curious to see how she would respond.

"I need her," Mrs. Reynard said finally, her voice hoarse. "I don't think you understand how dire my situation is right now. I thought I had more time to find someone else to take over for me, but I don't. Not with the war starting back up. I. Need. Her."

"Wrong." Warren shook his head. "You don't need her, you old hag. You only came searching for her when you heard that there was a fox spotted outside of Reynardsville with a wolf. We certainly didn't hide as we made our way back this way." Warren shifted back, putting space between them, tilting his head to study Mrs. Reynard better, gauging her every reaction, noting how her eyes had widened almost imperceptibly. "No, what I think happened is this: you went to Springfield when you heard the rumors that she was to be married off to the general's son. That, of course, couldn't happen. Not if there was a chance that Clara could still shift. So, you wanted to stop the wedding. But when you got there, you soon realized that she'd gone missing. I'd taken her for her own safety and for my own selfish reasons, but those are neither here nor there at the moment. From there, I imagine you heard about the general raiding a shifter camp, putting two and two together. You presumed her dead. How am I tracking?"

Mrs. Reynard swallowed nervously and nodded slightly, letting Warren know that he wasn't far off in his assumptions so far. A small grin tugged at the corners of his mouth in satisfaction.

"From there, you went back to Reynardsville and prepared your pack," Warren continued, now tilting his head the other way, the muscles in his arms flexing as he shifted his arms. "I imagine you've already got a successor set up. A distant niece or nephew. But Clara would be preferable because she's of the Reynard line, your husband's line, no? Your niece or nephew is not. But they would do in a pinch."

"I... I... You're not wrong," Mrs. Reynard whispered as the wind picked up, blowing more snow into their faces. She flinched as the frozen flakes hit her skin, stinging her already painfully frozen cheeks. Warren didn't bat an eye.

"But then, as previously mentioned, you heard about the fox and the wolf and just had to track her down to see if it was Clara." Warren shook his head in disgust. "You couldn't have left her alone, could you? She's been through enough. She's lost her mother, was betrayed by someone she thought she could trust, lost her father, got kidnapped twice, and was taken advantage of by another person she considered a friend... I could go on, but I won't. I think you get the picture. She's tired. She's done. Let her rest. Don't drag her into your political nonsense. She doesn't want it."

"But... I..." Mrs. Reynard stammered. "I understand all that, but she might be the key to uniting Reynardsville again. Things are falling apart because I have not done my job well. If my husband were still alive...but he's not. And there's no point in wallowing in the what-ifs. The fact of the matter is the pack needs a strong leader to unite them. That leader isn't me."

Warren's brows shot up, almost disappearing into his hairline. Had he just heard what he thought he'd just heard? Had Mrs. Reynard just admitted that she was failing in her position of alpha of the Reynard pack? There was no way. He had to be dreaming. But no... He had heard her correctly. Judging by the silence that had fallen among the rest of the shifters in both his pack and hers, they'd heard her perfectly as well. Going off the expressions on their faces, they were equally stunned.

Warren took a step back, now unsure what to do. He still wouldn't let Mrs. Reynard take Clara away from him. Clara was happy here. Content. It wasn't his place to uproot her once again to appease someone else, especially when that person meant next to nothing to Clara. But maybe, just maybe, he could talk to Clara, and let her know the full story. From there, he would let Clara make her own decision. It was the least he could do. Though, as he chewed on his tongue, he already had an idea of what Clara would say. And he imagined her response would be quite colorful. She wasn't shy about cursing him or anything else that had angered her.

Running a frozen hand down his face, he groaned softly. Clara was going to kill him for this.

"The pack tent is this way. It's late and I don't want to send you back home in this storm. Good way to get yourself killed," he sighed, his voice still hard. "You can head out in the morning, or whenever this storm lets up."

"But Clara..." Mrs. Reynard protested, following behind Warren as he turned on his heel and started stalking toward the pack tent, not bothering to look behind him to see if she was keeping up. Whether she stayed in the pack tent or not was of little consequence to him. He didn't care. He just didn't want frozen corpses in the middle of his camp. That would be an instant mood killer. He'd offer a smaller tent and relish in how uncomfortable it would be for the Reynardsville group, but they didn't have any extras and the pack tent was the only tent large enough to house all of them. It just meant that any pack business would have to wait until they left. But they could handle that. Right? There was nothing too pressing that needed immediate attention. He was sure of it.

"I... I will talk to her," Warren muttered. "I will give her the straight facts, nothing more. But if she asks for my opinion, as her mate, I will give it to her."

"Let me talk to her then," Mrs. Reynard begged, hurrying behind him, her voice pleading as she struggled to keep up in the deep snow. "I'm sure that if I..."

"She does not want to talk to you," Warren cut her off brusquely. "In fact, she's not pleased that you are here at all. If it were up to her, she'd kick you out of camp before you could even finish a sentence. She blames you for her mother's death."

"She..." Mrs. Reynard choked, her voice becoming thick with emotion. "You take that back."

Warren turned to look at her, his eyes flashing angrily as he regarded the older female.

"Why? I won't lie to protect your feelings, fox," Warren grunted. "My mate is my world. I would kill for her. And. You. Hurt. Her. So, in my eyes, you are worse than the scum that fills the dark reaches of this very earth we live on. If I were you, I'd watch what you say next. I've already got one shifter on my shit list for hurting her. I'll gladly add another. Understood?"

Mrs. Reynard took a step back, her eyes widening slightly. Finally realizing she had no actual authority there in the mountains, she nodded slowly. This was Warren's turf, and she knew it.

"Good," Warren grunted, turning back around and leading them the rest of the way to the tent. As he watched the Reynard pack enter, he reached out, snagging Mrs. Reynard's arm before she could head inside. "Let me make one more thing clear, fox. If for some reason Clara decides to go with you, you will not harm a hair on her head. If she comes back to me with so much as a scratch, I will have your head."

"Are you threatening me?" Mrs. Reynard's voice grew colder as her eyes hardened. She still seemed nervous, but the threat of death had steeled her nerves somewhat as if she were used to being threatened. This was something she apparently knew how to handle.

"No, ma'am," Warren growled. "This isn't a threat. I don't make threats. I make promises. And I keep those promises."

CHAPTER 4

Clara

Clara stumbled into her and Warren's tent, her frozen feet catching on one of the many furs littering the fur, sending her flying forward, her arms windmilling as she tried to catch her balance. She could have sworn she had placed them far enough away from the entrance, but then again, she wasn't usually so upset that she wasn't watching where she was going. She was more careful than this, more clear-headed and aware of her surroundings, not numb with fear for her future and rage at her grandmother's unwelcome appearance.

Glancing around the tent, she looked for something to do to keep her hands and mind occupied while Warren sent her grandmother and her entourage on their way. The crates containing all of their belongings lined the wall to the left of the fire, organized by the items' purpose and how often they were used. Opposite the entrance, a small wood table with two chairs on either side graced the far wall. Her project basket lay on the ground next to her chair, yarn spilling out the top, a pair of knitting needles and a small ball of yarn set on top of the table from where she had left it earlier that morning after finishing darning a sock. Along the wall to the right of the fire, Clara had placed their other furs and blankets they used to keep them warm at night but didn't need during the day, all neatly folded and stacked on top of a spare crate to keep them off the ground to keep them as clean as possible. She huffed slightly as she glanced at the fire, noting that the dishes from breakfast were still drying on a rack next to the fire.

She'd done all her chores already. There was nothing for her to do unless she wanted to work on one of her many projects, which wasn't a bad idea if she thought about it. However, her hands and the rest of her body were still rather frozen. That would make needlework rather difficult. She'd learned that the hard way a few times already when she'd accidentally poked her finger, drawing blood. She wasn't keen on repeating that experience.

With another huff, she dropped down onto the fur closest to the fire, curling her legs up underneath her as she situated herself. Glancing over at the entrance as she held her numb hands out to the fire to warm, she noticed Marcus standing just inside, the flap propped open slightly so he could keep an eye on what was going on outside the tent. Clara's brow furrowed as she studied his expression. It was hard, his eyes cold but alert as they scanned their surroundings outside. His body was tense, his muscles taut, as if he were ready to leap at whoever walked through the entrance.

"I don't need you to babysit me," she said after a few minutes, her voice loud in the quiet tent, louder than she had intended. She flinched slightly at her volume as she wiggled her fingers, the feeling starting to return, an unpleasant tingling sensation spreading through her hands.

"I don't care if you think you need a babysitter or not," Marcus replied, his voice harsh, his eyes never leaving the landscape outside. "Warren asked me to keep an eye on you while your grandmother is here. I don't intend to disobey him. He'd have my head, especially if something happened to you. Neither of us trusts your grandmother. No offense."

"None taken," Clara grumbled, understanding a bit better why Marcus hadn't left yet. She, too, had an idea that her grandmother, or one of her grandmother's party, would try something before they left. The male who had stood closest to her had given her a bad feeling, one that made her hair stand on end. She only hoped that they would leave sooner rather than later. Being babysat for the next twenty-four hours or so did not appeal to her. She liked her privacy. And it would make her time with Warren either non-existent or very awkward. She was leaning more toward it being non-existent. Putting on a show for his family was not on her to-do list ever.

Silence fell as Clara turned her attention back to the fire, watching the flames flickering, the sounds of the wood crackling filling the tent. The sound was comforting as Clara reached behind her for a blanket and wrapped it around herself, trying to both warm herself up further and comfort herself.

Running her fingers over the roughly hemmed edge of the blanket, she frowned, her brows furrowing. Whoever had made the blanket hadn't been overly skilled with a needle, but the stitches were strong. Perhaps if she got time sometime, she'd fix the hem, she thought idly. Until then, it would do. She wouldn't complain.

As she ran her fingers over the rough stitches, the entrance blew open, letting in a gust of cold air and snow. And with that gust of cold air, Benji and Luca, Warren's younger brothers, swept in. Both were coated in snow and looked less than pleased. Both of their eyes quickly swept the tent before landing on her, their gazes dark. Finally, Benji's shoulders slumping, he made his way over to Clara and plopped down beside her, shaking snow out of his hair and getting her wet again. Luca, on the other hand, took a seat at the table, shucking his coat off and draping it over the back of the chair, his eyes repeatedly scanning the tent, as if worried someone would break through the thick canvas.

"You okay, Clara?" Benji mumbled, glancing at her briefly, ever the sweet one as she gave him a dirty look, brushing off the snow he'd sprayed her with.

"Sort of," she breathed after she was sure she'd gotten most of the snow off her, not sure how to describe how she was feeling exactly as she glanced at the youngest Slora brother.

On one hand, she was still stunned for a multitude of reasons. Her grandmother, of all people, was here at Loch Haven. That shouldn't be possible. Loch Haven was supposed to be unreachable. Safe. And then, on top of that, her grandmother claimed that she, Clara, was her heir. What kind of nonsense was that? Who would put a half-breed in a leadership position, particularly one that knew next to nothing about shifter politics beyond what she'd picked up from her mate and his family? She wouldn't. That was pure stupidity.

On the other hand, she was angry. How dare her grandmother show up after not caring for so many years? If she was truly important to her grandmother, shouldn't she have come to get her before Warren had found her in Springfield? She'd had ample opportunities to do so. More than a decade if Clara thought about it. But no, she had left her there with her pa, not that Clara was complaining. Those years with just her pa had been amazing. She wouldn't trade that time for anything in the world. But her point still stood. Her grandmother could have come for her at any time in the last decade. Instead, she had opted to wait until the last minute when she didn't have any other choice but to do so because she was desperate.

Her grandmother had no right to demand anything of her and Clara had all right to refuse.

Benji watched her as her emotions warred with each other behind her eyes, his concern growing. And then he simply nodded, as if understood at least a bit of what she was going through.

"You have every right to be upset right now," he murmured under his breath, reaching out to wrap an arm around her, lending her his strength and comfort.

"Agreed," Luca spoke up as he drummed his fingers across the tabletop impatiently. "If I were you, I probably would have punched her already."

Clara snorted in amusement. "Trust me, if I could get away with it, I would probably do just that. I have no feelings for the woman. I won't take any offense whatsoever if you really did haul off and punch her. I might even applaud you and I can guarantee you'd be my new favorite person."

Luca barked a laugh, nearly falling off his chair, as Benji sniggered quietly beside her. By the entrance, Marcus glanced back at them before rolling his eyes.

"Let's not hit your grandmother, even if it's rather tempting to do so," Marcus grunted. "That could cause more problems than we're willing to deal with right now. The Reynard pack is rather powerful while our pack isn't at full strength at the moment. And we probably won't be at full strength for quite a few years while we build up our community here."

Luca rolled his eyes back at Marcus as Richard walked in, silently observing the situation.

"You're no fun, Marcus," Luca griped as Clara snorted in amusement again. Marcus wasn't wrong, but neither was Luca.

Richard shook his head at Luca, crossing the area and sitting down in the chair opposite Luca. "That's already been established," he muttered. "Marcus is the killjoy. Tell us something we don't know."

Everyone burst out laughing at that except Marcus, who scowled.

As Clara calmed down, she glanced over at Richard. "What's Warren doing right now? Is he still talking to my grandmother, or has he sent her on her way?"

Richard pulled a face, not meeting her eyes as he thought about how to answer her. Clara's heart sank. She wasn't going to get the answer she was hoping for.

"The storm is getting worse, so Warren has offered you grandmother and her pack use of the pack tent for the night, or until the storm lets up," Richard said slowly, choosing each word carefully. "Once it's safe for them to head out, he plans on making sure they leave. He should be joining us in a few minutes. He can explain the situation better than I can. And I believe he has a few other things to say as well. Just... just hear him out before you get mad."

Clara frowned, her brows knitting together as she studied Richard for a few minutes. Hear Warren out? She usually listened to what he had to say, good or bad. What would make this situation any different? The Reynard pack was being offered shelter from the storm and then they'd be leaving. It was that simple, wasn't it? However, instead of responding verbally, she simply nodded, tightening her grip on the blanket wrapped around her, pulling it closer. Richard, seeing her nod, visibly relaxed a bit, as did the rest of the group.

Not even ten minutes later of awkward silence broken by the occasional cough or comment, Warren walked in, a weary expression on his face. His eyes instantly found Clara and he made a beeline for her. Sitting down next to her, he wrapped his arm around her shoulder, pulling her against him and away from Benji who quietly scooted back to give them space.

"I'm so sorry, little fox," he murmured, burying his nose in her hair as Clara sank into him.

"It's fine," Clara mumbled back. "It's not like either of us thought that she would show up here of all places."

"That is... true," Warren said slowly, nodding his head before pressing a kiss to the top of her head and straightening up a bit. Then he took a deep breath, his grip on her tightening as he let it out slowly. "But... There's more, love."

Clara stiffened. "What do you mean there's more?" She looked up at him, studying his face. His eyes had softened as he gazed down at her, and they were filled with sorrow and regret as if he felt bad for what he was about to tell her.

"Your grandmother does have someone else to take over if you do not agree to go back with her," he prefaced. Rubbing the back of his neck, he took a few seconds before he continued. "However, she wanted me to tell you that the reason that she wants you to go back with her is..." He paused again, swallowing audibly. "She believes that you can unite the Reynard pack and, in turn, Reynardsville. They have been divided since your grandfather's death and your grandmother has admitted that she is not the leader she thought she'd be. She has admitted that she cannot unite the pack, that she is to blame for the divide and the mistrust."

"Why me?" Clara protested, leaning away from Warren in shock. "I'm barely a shifter at all. I know nothing about this way of life except what you've taught me in the last few months. Me lead? Is she insane?"

"It's because you are of Reynard blood," Warren sighed heavily. "Her cousins, those that she has been contemplating as possibles replacement, are not of Reynard blood. There is a possibility that letting a non-Reynard take over could cause the division to become worse."

"That's a load of bullshit," Clara muttered under her breath. "The residents don't follow the Reynards anymore because my family has apparently proven to be nothing better than conniving, manipulative bastards. The residents of Reynardsville can't trust them. Me coming into the picture will not fix that. Nothing will. The damage has been done. And, if I had to take a guess at why the pack is divided, I'd wager that it's because of this behavior. The side pulling away are like the residents of Reynardsville. They don't trust my family. End of story. I can't fix that."

"I…" Warren started, a bit surprised at Clara's little rant though he had expected it.

"She's right," Marcus grunted, surprising them both. "Clara can't fix years of deep-seated mistrust. If anything, her stepping in might make it worse. Especially if she decided to take on the mantle of Reynard."

"If she decided to go back, I'd advise leaving that surname behind for good, not that it was her surname to begin with," Richard added. "When you brought her back to the pack, she was an O'Donoghue. With your mating, she's a Slora. She could technically present herself as either to the public."

"That's not a bad idea," Warren agreed slowly as he mulled over both Marcus's and Richard's words. He glanced down at Clara, who met his eyes.

Slowly, Clara shook her head. She didn't want to go, period. Leading a large pack was not her idea of a good time. As she'd pointed out already, she had no experience with that. She wasn't a full shifter. She didn't understand that lifestyle. She'd just make a mess of things.

Warren took a deep breath and nodded, a look of understanding on his face as he surveyed Clara's face.

"I don't want to do that. Let the pack fall apart. It might be for the best," she murmured, explaining her reasoning. "Sometimes, those that have been in power for as long as my family have been have lost touch with reality. They have become disillusioned. And like any living and breathing entity, it must die eventually to make way for something better, something that will benefit society in a way the old one did not. Times are changing. It's time for something new."

CHAPTER 5

WARREN

Warren's eyes widened and his jaw dropped in surprise as he looked over at his tiny mate sitting next to him, stunned by the words that had just come out of her mouth. Had she really just told him that she thought it was a good thing for the Reynard pack to crumble and fall apart? That it might benefit the Reynard pack and Reynardsville to let someone else step up and take the reins? No, he must have misheard. There was no way that she had just said that.

He shook his head as if to clear his head. He must have misheard. There was no way. Clara's suggestion was insanity. That's all there was to it. It was insanity. She didn't know what she was talking about. Let a pack die... He shook his head again, looking away from Clara and over at the fire warming their large, cozy tent.

To someone like Warren, who had grown up as the eldest son of the pack leader, who had watched his parents sacrifice themselves for their pack, letting a pack fall apart like this was unheard of. The pack came first. That had been drilled into his head ever since he had been a small boy, not only by his father but by his grandfather, too. Sure, he'd had his moments where he had been against stepping into his father's shoes and taking over the pack. It had been something that, as a young male, he had not wanted to do. He hadn't felt worthy. Hell, he still didn't feel worthy half the time. But he had stepped up into the role anyway. He hadn't had a choice. Not really. However, if he had really wanted to, he could have forced one of his younger brothers to step into that role. He could have even asked one of his cousins to take over in his stead. He could have also walked away, leaving his family to pick up the pieces. He'd had plenty of opportunities to do so and had even thought about it a number of times.

But the pack came first.

The pack was like his family. They'd had his back more times than he could count over the years. And now he had theirs. Warren would do just about anything for them at this point. It was his job. To lead. To care for. To protect.

And his mate, his equal, was going to throw her pack away. He knew she was scared. He knew she didn't know what she was doing. He knew that she was likely overwhelmed. He could see it on her face, in her eyes. But she had him and his family. They wouldn't let her fall. Besides, this was only temporary. She just needed to go long enough to help. If she could even help, that is. He had to acknowledge that there might be a chance that the Reynard pack was too far gone to help, of course. But they had to see for themselves first before they just walked away.

"Cl-Cl-Clara..." Warren stammered finally, his jaw going slack as he continued to stare at her. "I don't think you know what you're talking about, little fox. Do you know what would happen to your grandmother's pack, your family's pack, if you let them crumble like this?" His voice was hoarse as he asked her that question, his mouth dry.

"They'd form a new one..." Clara said slowly, giving him a look that told him that should be obvious, shouldn't it?

Warren's eyes widened. Oh, how little she knew. He'd not done a good enough job teaching her about pack dynamics yet. He'd have to remedy that, and soon.

"Clara... when packs fall apart, they don't always form new packs. I mean, that's the obvious solution, I know, but that's not how it works," he tried to explain, his mind going a mile a minute as he tried to figure out how to word his explanation in a way that she would understand. "So, when packs split, or crumble, like your grandmother's pack, the likelihood of them forming a new pack is slim to none. They are too divided to be united under a new banner if that makes sense. It won't matter who tries to step in to unite them once they've fallen apart like that. There's very little that would make them band together again. Instead, they'll branch off into smaller packs. Weaker packs. And they'll elect their own leaders."

Clara listened in silence, which Warren was grateful for. He was glad that she was listening to him. It made it easier for him to retain his train of thought without getting distracted. But inevitably, he knew she would have questions. And he was right.

"And that's a bad thing, why?" She arched a brow at him in question, still not understanding. "I mean, up until I said I didn't want to go and that I didn't care if it fell apart, you were fine with me not going. You said you'd keep me safe here, that we could tell my grandmother and her gang to leave. But now...? I'm confused, Warren."

With a groan, Warren rubbed at the scar on his face. This was becoming more complicated by the second, his desire to keep her safe and happy and his upbringing to lead, to take care of the pack, warring with each other. Taking a deep breath, he looked down at her, studying her face.

"If it were any other pack, I don't think it would matter much if they fell apart like that," he admitted, his cheeks flushing slightly, the words ashen in his mouth. "However, your grandmother's pack isn't any old pack, understand? They're the Reynards. They run a whole damn city. And that city happens to be the shifter capital of the kingdom. If the Reynards fall, it will plunge that entire city into chaos. It will devastate the shifter community, especially with the war starting."

Clara herself groaned. "Look, while I was in Reynardsville, it looked like the Reynards weren't even in power anymore. There were no signs of them anywhere. The old city hall was abandoned. The townhomes they used to live in, according to an old family friend, were also abandoned. The Reynards abandoned Reynardsville. And the residents know it. They don't even consider the Reynards to be in power anymore either. Honestly, if you ask me, it looks like it's too late to save the pack. So why bother trying?"

Clara hugged her knees to her chest, wrapping her blanket closer around her, staring into the fire as she finished her little speech. The whole tent fell silent, staring at Clara in shock. And if Warren had been shocked before, he was downright flabbergasted now.

"You don't mean that?" Marcus whispered from his position near the tent entrance. "You don't mean that, do you?"

Benji shifted uncomfortably from his position on the other side of Clara, looking away from her and not meeting her eyes.

Warren shifted as well, not sure whether he should be appalled or if he should scold Clara for her ignorance. Finally, he decided to do neither. She didn't know better, after all. She had been raised human. How could she know? It wasn't until he'd found her in Springfield a few months back and then kidnapped her to keep her safe that she'd found out the truth of what she was. He needed to be gentle with her. It was a lot to take in, stepping into a whole new society, especially when you didn't know the first thing about it except the rumors you'd grown up with.

"Little fox," he murmured, reaching his arm out tentatively and wrapping it around her shoulders, pulling her back into his side. He let out a deep sigh as he tried to figure out how to explain what he wanted to say next. "Packs are like family, yes?"

Clara nodded. It was one concept Warren knew that she understood. His own pack, the Loch Haven pack, had quickly accepted Clara as one of their own, welcoming her with open arms. They treated her as if she had been a member all her life, aiding her when needed. And she'd already made a few fast friends with other females her age. It was a far cry from the lonelier life she'd lived in Springfield with her pa.

"Alright, so say that our pack here ran a city," Warren started slowly. "How would you feel if the Sloras, us, stepped back and stopped ruling?"

"What? Stepped back? You would never step back. You've always told me that the pack comes first, that they're your family, that you have to take care of them." Clara frowned at him in confusion. And then her eyes widened as it hit her. "Oh gods, you're saying the Reynards never stepped back because the city is considered part of the pack by extension, so the city is "family", aren't you?"

Warren nods. "I am. I don't think they stepped back, no. My guess is that they knew that they were causing more trouble than necessary by staying in the city, so they moved to a safer location outside of the city where they could conduct business instead. By doing that, they would need a person still in Reynardsville to help rule. A spokesperson, if you will. Or a proxy. One that the city wouldn't automatically connect to the Reynards, one that the city would follow without resentment."

"That... that actually makes a lot of sense," Clara mumbled a few seconds later after digesting that bit of information. "The shifters I met, the ones that could tell that I was a fox, they weren't kind at all. Apparently, all foxes in the area belong to the Reynard pack, so they assumed that I... Oh gods." Clara's eyes widened as she let go of her legs and stretched them out. She turned to Warren, her eyes widening even further. "One even tried to kill me for being a fox, for being a Reynard. They hate the Reynards. The Reynards left for their own safety…"

Warren remained silent as he continued to watch Clara put things together, the shock, the horror, and the despair rolling across her face in quick succession.

"If the Reynards are like how your family is, they truly are still ruling, or leading, or whatever you want to call it, but by proxy… if they fall… the city will fall into complete chaos, won't it?" she finally whispered. "And with the war, if the city falls, all those shifters will be like sitting ducks, ripe for the taking. I… I… I have to go, don't I?"

"I think it might be wise, yes," Richard interjected. "We can't afford to lose Reynardsville. If Reynardsville falls, then all the shifters in the mountains, including us, will be cut off from food and other supplies until we can find another source. With it being the middle of winter, I'm not sure if we'd be able to find another source very quickly. We'd starve."

"I don't know the first thing about leading a pack," Clara protested weakly, turning to Warren, her gaze pleading.

Warren's heart melted a little at the sight. She wasn't necessarily wrong. She didn't know how to lead a pack. And she didn't have the time to properly train to do so at this point in time.

And then a thought struck him, his eyes lighting up. Reaching out, he caressed her cheek, his calloused fingers rough against her silky skin. Clara, enjoying his touch, closed her eyes and leaned into his hand, a soft sigh escaping her as she sought comfort from him.

"I know that look," Luca sighed, watching Warren closely, his sharp eyes not missing a thing. "What are you planning, brother?"

Warren hesitated a moment, not sure how his family would take his suggestion. Taking a deep breath, he decided to just go for it.

"Clara doesn't have to go alone," he said slowly, carefully, his eyes flicking around the tent, lingering on each of his family members before settling on Clara once more, studying her soft, sweet face, committing the details of that moment to memory as he let his words sink in.

Not even seconds later, everyone's heads whipped up and over to Warren, a mixture of emotions on each of their faces. Clara looked hopeful. Benji looked shocked. Luca looked amused. Richard looked concerned. And Marcus... Marcus looked disappointed.

"What do you mean?" Marcus asked hoarsely.

"She's my mate," Warren said simply, as if that were obvious, which it was. Males never let their mates out of their sight for very long. This situation was no exception. It would drive him absolutely insane to have her that far away from him, and that distance caused more than just worry. Some concerns had also popped up that he wanted... No, not wanted, needed to address. "Being her mate...I have to go with her. And look, we all know that her grandmother will try and get someone else, a fox more than likely, to place his claim over mine. On top of that, despite the fact that she'll be with family, she still doesn't know them very well. She doesn't trust them, not that I blame her. Her grandmother hasn't proven to be the most trustworthy. Then, Reynardsville is quite dangerous, especially right now. I can't let her go alone. I have to go with her. By doing so, she also gets to take advantage of my knowledge of shifter society which should help her as she tries to step in to take over the Reynard pack."

"But the pack..." Clara trailed off, looking up at him in concern, her eyes searching his face to see how serious he was about his new plan.

"Loch Haven has Marcus, Richard, Luca, and Benji. They've done a pretty damn good job at leading the pack when I haven't been available to do so," Warren reassured her. "I am not abandoning them. Right now, they are safe and they are taken care of. But you will not be, so my priority is you, little fox."

"But..." she started to protest.

"Let me do this for you," Warren murmured, drawing her closer. "Let me help you. Let me protect you. Let me love you. We've been separated for far too long where I thought you might be dead. I just got you back. Don't make me go through that again."

His voice became more pleading as he continued. He knew that he was being a bit manipulative as he tugged on her heartstrings, but it would do the job. He just knew it. And sure enough...

"As long as everyone else is okay with it, then... I would appreciate it if you came with me," she murmured, her eyes hopeful as she glanced around at Warren's family.

"I can't say I like this," Marcus grumbled, "but I understand. I truly do. And you're right, Warren. The pack is doing alright right now. We can take care of them while you take care of Clara."

With a rueful grin, Benji reached over and clapped Warren on the shoulder. "Keep her safe, brother. I want you to bring my little sister-in-law back home, you hear? She's too sweet to not bring back. We'd miss her more than I care to admit."

"We'll come back. I promise," Warren smirked. "Now we just have to go tell ole granny dearest about Clara's decision and the slight change of plans that include me."

CHAPTER 6

RONAN

Ronan's boots scuffed over the uneven cobblestone street as he meandered toward Zeke's house, home of the Romulus Pack in Reynardsville. The streetlamp behind him flickered, making the shadows around him dance which made him uneasy. Or more uneasy than he already was. The street was mostly empty at this time of night except for the few drunks who were still wandering around looking for another drink or some trouble. Most decent shifters, on the other hand, had already gone to bed, needing to get a good night's sleep before getting up with the sun to go about their days once more. Or they would be.

However, things had changed. Things had changed a lot. And not for the better.

As he reached the other side of the street, Ronan stuffed his hands in his pockets and let out a deep breath, thinking back on everything that had happened since he had set out for Reynardsville a couple months ago. At first, it had been a simple rescue mission to make sure that Clara O'Donoghue, the half-shifter he had sniffed out as a potential mate when he had least been expecting to, was still alive after being kidnapped by the shifter, Warren, and then kidnapped and tortured by General Claery. He had felt it had been his duty to make sure she made it to where she was going safely after all of that, as well as having some personal interests in making sure she was alright. The journey had inevitably turned into a quest to make Clara his, but that had failed miserably. His cheeks flamed red at the memory in both shame and embarrassment. He was no better than any other male shifter out there. He'd seen something he'd wanted, and he'd tried to take it. Forcefully.

Ronan had been so close to having her, so close to claiming her as his, being able to keep her as his own. He would have spoiled her and treated her like a queen, but then Clara had done something he hadn't thought possible while he was in the process of trying to mark her. She'd used the very dagger he'd given her for protection on him. Not that he could blame her. He'd be the first to admit that he was actually rather proud of her for doing that. It had shown him that she was learning how to think and act like a shifter rather quickly, that she would and could defend herself. Not that he'd seen that at the time. No, he'd been too upset at both their actions, too worried that she'd get herself hurt, too anxious about, well, everything.

Ronan had then followed Clara into Reynardsville to offer her some sort of protection. He knew exactly what kind of males she'd run into in such a large city when they sniffed her out and realized she was without her mate. They wouldn't hesitate to do exactly what Ronan had tried, but the difference was that they wouldn't be nearly as gentle as he had tried to be. They could care less about how she felt. She was a pretty fox wandering the streets alone. Nothing more, nothing less.

Trying to protect Clara had lasted less than twenty-four hours.

Coming out of the old city buildings, a thin cut on her neck, looking a bit shell shocked, she'd stumbled right into him after running off earlier that morning. Instead of falling into his arms like he had hoped she would, she had instead taken his heart and stomped on it, crushing him before fleeing, heading back into the mountains to find her mate who had started the whole mess in the first place. If Warren had just left her alone... Ronan shook his head, his mind going back to the last time he had seen Clara. He'd never been told off so thoroughly before. It had stunned him as his world came crashing down around him.

From that moment on, Ronan had turned to alcohol to help him cope, not anticipating Clara ever rejecting his offer so harshly. It was the only way he could drown out the pain that he'd felt. It had been like someone had taken a knife and shoved it straight into his heart before twisting it for added effect. So, from sunup to sundown, he'd essentially lived in the pubs and taverns littering the city, drinking whatever he could get his hands on. At the end of the night, he'd stumble back to the inn he had been staying at, praying he actually made it back.

That was how Zeke and the Romulus Pack had found him, drunkenly walking back to the inn and getting on the bad side of some lion shifters simply because he'd walked right into them. Zeke had taken pity on Ronan almost instantly. Ronan wasn't sure if it was because he looked like a sorry mess or if it was because he knew Ronan was a wolf as well. A wolf without a pack to be precise. Either way, Ronan was glad he had. Zeke had given him a purpose, and tonight, that purpose was to patrol the streets, making sure nothing untoward was happening. So far, the only thing he'd come across had been some teenagers trying to sneak out to do what teenagers do best: get into trouble with the other sex, drink copious amounts of alcohol, and get into their fathers' best tobacco.

Huffing a laugh as he thought about the stunned look on the teenagers' faces when he'd caught them, Ronan paused, looking around the street once more for good measure, his eyes lighting on a crumpled-up newspaper wrapped around one of the light poles. With a heavy sigh and shaking his head, Ronan walked over to the pole and pulled the newspaper off it. As he was going to crumple it further and toss it in the nearest trash bin, he paused, the words catching his eyes.

Amid Rumors of War, Are the Reynards Actually Coming Back?

It has been ten years since the beloved patriarch of the Reynard Pack passed away due to health conditions, and since then, the Reynard Pack has slowly disappeared from the public eye. The matriarch, Melanie Reynard, gave no reason for pulling her pack out of Reynardsville at the time, but rumors stated that she was grieving not only the loss of her husband but the loss of her daughter who had gone rogue and had been killed by General Claery himself.

Two weeks ago, Melanie Reynard and a small host from the Reynard Pack were spotted heading northwest into the mountains. Rumor has it that Melanie's deceased daughter had a daughter of her own, and that she, like the rest of the shifters south of Reynardsville, had fled into the mountains. Curious to find out whether the Reynards are simply going to investigate or are going to bring this lost family member home, we reached out to the Reynard pack delegate within the city.

"Mrs. Reynard has indeed gone into the mountains to bring her granddaughter home," Mr. Weatherby, the Reynard delegate, stated after yesterday's council meeting. "She received word that her granddaughter, Clara, was alive and well, living with a pack up near a secluded mountain lake. After missing the opportunity to bring her home the last couple of times she'd gone to retrieve the girl, Mrs. Reynard did not wish to waste this opportunity and took off rather quickly. We, as a pack, are hoping that she brings the girl back."

Ronan stopped reading, blinking in surprise a few times. Had he read that name right? Clara? Surely he had to be seeing things. He scanned the statement from Weatherby again. It definitely said Clara, but that couldn't be his Clara. It just couldn't. It was a common enough name, right?

Footsteps sounded behind him as he reread the first half of the article again, looking for anything that would give away who this Clara really was. A heavy hand covered in tattoos landed on his shoulder, the scent of cigarettes giving him away.

Maddox.

Ronan turned to look at the massive wolf shifter next behind him. Maddox, his usual cigarette dangling from his lip, studied Ronan, concern flashing behind his dark eyes. Letting go of Ronan, he ran a hand through his closely cropped curls, his lips curling down into a frown.

"You alright, Ronan?" he grunted, taking a drag of his cigarette before exhaling slowly. "I saw you pick up that paper and then go sort of rigid. Not normal behavior, especially with you."

Ronan, realizing how tense he was, forced himself to relax a bit and failed miserably. He grimaced as he finally wadded the paper up and tossed it into the trash bin near a tavern on the other side of the street. Returning to Maddox, he bummed a drag off his cigarette, holding in the smoke for a moment as he let the nicotine and tobacco soothe his nerves before exhaling.

"I, uh, wasn't expecting to see the headline that I did," Ronan admitted heavily after a minute, his voice a tad hoarse as he scanned the street, unable to meet Maddox's eyes.

"Which one?" Maddox's frown deepened as he stared at Ronan, his concern and now confusion growing.

"The one about the Reynards coming back. I thought the city had kicked them out," Ronan stated as they started walking back to Zeke's place once more.

"Where'd you hear that?" Maddox chuckled dryly. "Nah, the Reynards weren't kicked out. They should have been, honestly, but they left before things could get worse. Or so I was told. You'd have to ask Zeke for the full story. I only know the basics."

"But... This... Do you know anything more about the news? Do you know if the Reynards are actually coming back?" Ronan asked, his voice a mix of eagerness and anxiousness.

"Um," Maddox hesitated, studying Ronan for a few more seconds before answering. Finally, he nodded, his shoulders slumping. "Yes. The Reynard matriarch has been looking for her granddaughter for months now. Guess she grew up south of here in Springfield, or something like that. Half human. But the girl disappeared before they could retrieve her. They've been looking since. They're growing... anxious. Especially with the war. They don't want to leave the pack or the city leaderless, and from the way they're talking, she's their only hope. Bullshit, if you ask me. There are others that can..."

Ronan held up his hand, stopping Maddox before he could go any further, his description fitting his Clara almost to a tee.

"Where did you say the girl was from?" he half whispered, running a hand through his curly mop.

"Springfield. Her dad is human. Or so I was told," Maddox replied, now wholly confused. "Why?"

"You know that girl I was worried about? The one I was escorting?" Ronan asked, his voice dropping lower.

"You mean the girl that you're head over heels in love with?" Maddox corrected, having heard about Clara multiple times at this point.

"Yeah." Ronan grimaced at the correction, mentally kicking himself for not being able to keep his feelings for Clara to himself. "That's the one."

"What about her?" Maddox finished his cigarette and dropped it onto the street, crushing it beneath his boot. Ronan rolled his eyes at the act, watching as the cigarette butt slipped in between the cracks of a few loose cobblestones.

"That fox that met up with the wolf outside of town before you met me, the one you mentioned seeing," Ronan explained. "That's Clara. Clara is a half-human fox shifter from Springfield. Her mom was Mara Reynard."

Maddox's eyes widened and his jaw dropped in disbelief. Staring at Ronan for a minute, his jaw worked soundlessly. Finally, he cleared his throat and tried again. "Wait... You mean to tell me that your girl is the Reynard brat everyone is searching for?"

"That's the one." Ronan nodded wearily as they both turned and started down the street toward Zeke's house once more. "I didn't know who she was when I met her. All I knew was that she wasn't human, that she had no idea, and that she needed protecting. I failed on all counts. The male I was trying to protect her from took her anyway, told her what she was, and claimed her."

"That wolf that met her that night, the one with the red hair..." Maddox trailed off, his eyes widening in realization. "He's the one that kidnapped her?"

Ronan nodded again. "The very one. And I gave her an out, but she chose not to take it. Chose to stay with him. I don't know what she sees in him. I really don't. But if her family is determined to get her back, well, I don't know how much time left she has with the male."

Maddox snorted in amusement at Ronan's words. "The Reynards are elitists. They'll have another male fox or two lined up for her as soon as they get back. Poor girl is gonna have to go through the whole claiming process once again."

Both males shuddered at the thought.

"I do not envy her," Ronan admitted.

"Does that make you mad?" Maddox asked after a minute as they reached the front door of Zeke's, his voice hesitant, knowing this was a touchy subject for Ronan.

"Does what make me mad?" Ronan asked, having an idea of what Maddox was asking, but wanting to be sure.

"Does it make you mad that another male is going to get a shot at her and it's not you?" Maddox clarified.

Ronan hesitated, not sure how to answer without sounding like an entitled brat. Truth be told, it did make him mad. He had offered to claim Clara himself, had offered to protect her, had offered to take her wherever she wanted to go, somewhere they could hide out for the rest of their lives where no one else could find them if that's what she truly wanted. But she had refused. Over and over again.

Ronan held the door open, the sounds of the rest of the pack echoing down the hall and out the front door to them, along with the smell of some sort of warm soup and fresh bread. Ronan's stomach rumbled as he continued to debate internally on how to answer Maddox. He wanted to be truthful, but at the same time, he didn't need Maddox's sympathy. He didn't want to be judged. Put simply, he'd been rejected. He needed to move on.

Gods above, he told himself that multiple times daily. Easier said than done at this point, but it was a work in progress and he wasn't about to give up anytime soon.

"Yes," he finally said with a long-suffering sigh. "I'm quite upset. If she... No. I don't need to wonder about the what-ifs. That'll just cause more pain." Ronan shook his head. "She made her choice and I tried taking that choice from her. I learned the hard way that I can't do that again. Frankly, she hates me now. My only saving grace at this point is that I'll never have to see her again."

Ronan moved to step through the front door but was stopped by Maddox's hand on his shoulder once again.

"I really wish I wasn't the one that had to tell you this," he sighed deeply, his brows furrowing as he met Ronan's eyes. "If the Reynards are successful at bringing Clara back with them, they'll be in the city. And they'll be going from scout camp to scout camp. I hate to break it to you, but I can almost guarantee that you'll be seeing her again. A lot."

Ronan froze, the blood draining from his face as his heart started hammering in his chest. His stomach twisted and he thought he was going to be sick. He grasped the door frame to steady himself.

Clara was coming back to Reynardsville. She was going to be leading the city. She was going to be out among the troops, inspecting and helping with training. He'd be coming face to face with her again sooner rather than later. It was all that he wanted but didn't want at the same time. He needed to apologize, to beg for forgiveness once more. But he wanted to do it on his own terms, not in front of everyone else, making a damn fool of himself. But then another thought popped into his head.

Would she even let him apologize for his actions?

"This isn't good," he whispered as his grip on the door frame tightened. "I can't see her."

CHAPTER 7

MATTY

The frozen morning was still and quiet as the sun rose over the tree line on the horizon. The only sounds to break through the quiet air were the grumblings of the soldiers getting up and ready to move yet again. Matty, standing at the foot of his new wife's private wagon, watched his company slowly climb out of their tents, rubbing their arms and hands together for warmth, before slowly pulling their tents down, their movements stiff from the cold.

Matty himself was cold. He had spent the night in a tent next to Kitty's wagon, preferring to sleep outside rather than with his wife. It wasn't that he didn't like his wife, who happened to be King Augustus's oldest daughter, but he couldn't stand her except in small doses. She whined and complained about everything. The wagon was too noisy. She wasn't comfortable enough. The ride was too bumpy, and her rear was starting to get sore. She was cold. The weather was dreadful. The food was lackluster. She missed her family. And so on and so forth. Her complaints were starting to get on his nerves.

Glancing over his shoulder at his wife's wagon, his face hard, he shook his head. "What were they thinking sending a girl like her out to Springfield with me?" he grumbled under his breath. "The king is mad if he thinks Kitty can handle this. She'll be the death of me yet."

Still shaking his head, he stuffed his hands into thick leather gloves lined with fur and started rolling up his sleeping mat before breaking down his tent. As he worked, he heard canvas rustle behind him followed by a miserable whimper. Glancing over his shoulder, he raised an eyebrow at his wife.

Kitty Claery, formerly Princess Catherine of Brunnholl, was small and delicate, every bit the princess she was born as. Her long black hair was pulled back into a low chignon at the base of her neck and her fair porcelain skin was tinged pink from the cold. Her eyes were a light blue, the same as her mother's, the queen. She was stunning, but at the moment, her lips were pulled down into a small frown and misery filled her blue eyes.

"You should stay inside," Matty grunted, brushing a lock of blonde hair that had fallen into his eyes back into place. "It's too cold out here for you, Kitty."

"Don't remind me," she replied with a small whimper. "I don't know how you manage to sleep out here night after night. You could come to bed with me, you know. It would be warmer for the both of us."

Kitty took a step down from the wagon, coming closer. Matty stiffened slightly. The last time he had been this close to Kitty, he had grabbed her by the hair and dragged her to the priest to be wed. An irrational decision, one he deeply regretted, but he had been so angry with her for baiting him that he had acted before he could stop himself. And now, for better or for worse, he was stuck with her.

His wife.

The words were ashen in his mouth. This wasn't how things were supposed to have gone. He'd had plans. So many plans. And all of them had gone down the drain thanks to a couple of shifters and his father.

He wasn't bitter at all. Nope. Not one bit. Or that's what he kept telling himself. Maybe if he said it enough, he'd actually start believing it.

Matty closed his eyes and took a deep breath, willing himself to relax before he turned around to face his wife, watching her carefully.

"I mean it, Kitty. It's too cold out here for you. Go back inside," he ordered her, his voice stern.

Kitty's face darkened, her eyes filling with tears. "I'm lonely," she whined. "I know you don't want me around, but I'm here. The least you could do is treat me like a human rather than some inconvenience. I have feelings, you know. I didn't ask for this either."

Matty flinched. Then he closed his hazel eyes again and took a deep breath, steadying himself. He wanted to snap at her, to tell her that she should have stayed back at home in the capital, Rotmuth. She would have been safe and warm there, surrounded by her family. She would have had all the support that she needed and wanted. But instead, she was here all because her father, the king, had insisted. And because Matty had acted rashly and had married her out of anger.

He kept his eyes closed for another few minutes, trying to calm himself further. If she were Clara, he told himself, he would have been in that wagon with her every chance he got. If she were Clara, the moment she complained of any discomfort, he would have done anything to try and make things easier for her. Not that Clara would have complained. Hell, Clara would have insisted on riding on his horse with him rather than hiding in the wagon with nothing to do. But that was just the way Clara was. She was the kind of woman that took life by the horns. She didn't back down, even when she should.

His chest constricted. He still didn't know if she was alive or not.

And it was all his fault.

That was why he was so bitter. It wasn't anyone's fault but his own. He had cast the final stone by tossing her to the side per his father's request. Being a half-breed hadn't bothered him in the slightest. She was still Clara.

He should have lifted her up onto his horse. He should have gotten on behind her and held her close. He should have ridden straight home and attended to her.

Instead, he'd cast her aside.

If she were dead, it was all his fault.

The blood of the woman he'd loved his whole life was on his hands.

He was a monster.

He could do better. He would do better.

Opening his eyes again, he studied his wife once more, noting how she was wearing a delicate nightgown, lace trimming the collar and the hem. Much too thin for this kind of weather. She also had a heavy woolen blanket wrapped around her, the blanket a rich burgundy color. Expensive, he decided. The amount of wool and dye used to make that... He shook his head. It wasn't any of his business how much the blanket had cost. She was royalty. Her family could afford such luxuries. But she was right. She didn't want to be here either. The least he could do was treat her better than he had been.

"I'm sorry," he grunted after a few minutes. "I... I've been focused on my men. I hardly thought it fair for me to be sleeping in comfort while they've been in tents on sleeping mats. I would never ask my men to do something that I am not willing to do myself. But that is not fair to you, and I am sorry. I'll try my best to do better. Now get back inside before you freeze further. Please."

Kitty's frown deepened and then she huffed. "You care more about your men than me," she accused him.

Matty flinched again. She wasn't exactly wrong. His men... well, he knew them better. He'd traveled with them, trained with them, and later, he would fight beside them. Kitty... he'd had meals with her and slept with her a couple of times. He barely even knew her if he was being completely honest with himself. He didn't even know when her birthday was, what her favorite color was, or what her favorite food was.

He knew all that about Clara, a snide voice in the back of his mind reminded him.

He had to do better.

He would do better.

"I'm sorry," he repeated, not sure what else to say, feeling a bit like he was being backed into a corner, and he didn't like it one bit. Part of him wanted to rear up and fight, but he knew that would make things worse. The other part of him wanted to scream at the world for being so unfair. How had he gone from planning out his life with Clara not even a year ago to this? No, he didn't need to ask that. He knew. It was his fault. He had let his father get out of hand. He had made his bed and now he had to lie in it. All the consequences that had followed and would continue to follow were on him.

He would do better. He would be better.

Kitty's blue eyes narrowed on him before she huffed again and looked around the camp. Some of the men were getting a fire going and their cook was starting to pull out a large pot to start mixing the morning porridge. An assortment of sausage and rashers of bacon were also being brought out to be fried. Soon, the delightful smell of breakfast being cooked would fill the camp. Matty's stomach grumbled at the thought. He couldn't wait. He was sure Kitty felt the same.

"As soon as the food has been prepared, I'll bring you some," Matty promised, looking back up at Kitty as he started loading his tent and sleeping mat into the back of her wagon. "Is there anything you want in particular?"

"For you to eat your breakfast with me," she stated without hesitation, her blue eyes fixed unwaveringly on him.

"That's not what I meant, and you know it," Matty groaned. Why were women so difficult? He couldn't figure this one out for the life of him.

"Promise me that you'll eat with me first," she pushed back with a determined set to her jaw that he had seen on her father, the king, more times than he'd cared for.

"Fine, I promise," Matty gritted out. "I promise to bring you your breakfast and to eat with you in your wagon."

"Our wagon," she corrected without missing a beat, her delicate hands grasping the blanket closer.

"Fine, our wagon," he conceded, surveying her again, trying to hide his irritation with her. Now was not the time to fight. "Now what do you want to eat?"

"What I want is poached eggs, toast with jam, and smoked salmon," she replied imperiously. "However, I don't imagine you have any of that."

"I can get you the toast with jam, but the poached eggs will have to wait until we get to Springfield. As for the smoked salmon, I'm afraid you won't be having any of that any time soon. We don't have salmon in Springfield."

Kitty's expression soured. "No salmon?"

"Where the hell would we get salmon in Springfield?" Matty laughed at her expression, finding it amusing that she hadn't done her homework on her new home. "Springfield is on the edge of civilization, Kitty. We border a desert on the west, the prairies on the east, and the mountains on the north. We are landlocked. We may have a few streams near us, but all that we get from those is trout."

"No salmon," she repeated blinking. "I... I thought... but..."

Matty shook his head at her in disbelief and amusement. "No salmon. Sorry."

"Then what do you eat for breakfast? Please tell me that this... this slop that we've been eating for the last week isn't what you eat normally," she pleaded, her voice growing desperate.

"Oh, you sweet, naive, little thing," Matty crooned, trying and failing to hide his amusement at the situation. "Do I look like a nobleman to you, sweet Kitty? Do I look like I can afford the lifestyle that you are used to? No, love, I am but a poor farm boy who got thrown into the military and was given a position because of who my father is. You married down, princess, so it's time for you to get off your high horse and join us commoners down here at the bottom. All you'll be getting for breakfast once we reach Springfield is whatever you can cook. And if you can't cook, you best pray my mother will teach you."

"But... you... why can't our cook make our meals?" Kitty stammered, her eyes widening in shock as she paled.

Matty took a step closer to her, looking down at her tiny form. Leaning down so he could whisper in his ear, he pushed the blanket back.

"We are commoners, love. Commoners don't have hired help," he murmured, his lips brushing her ear. "We'll be staying in a two-bedroom cabin on my parent's property until I can have an apartment in town prepared. We will be in the middle of nowhere. Farm country, love. I hope you don't mind getting dirty."

Kitty inhaled sharply, taking a step back from him, her eyes wide. "Take me home."

"Too late for that, princess," Matty stated, crossing his arms over his chest and arching a brow at her.

Anger flared in her eyes. Stepping forward, she slammed her tiny fists against his chest, shrieking angrily. Matty didn't budge, almost laughing at her feeble attempt at hitting him. Tsking, he shook his head at her in warning. When she tried hitting him again, he grabbed her by the wrists.

"That's enough, wife," Matty said calmly, his voice almost cold. "You are making a scene."

"Take me home!" Kitty demanded angrily as some of Matty's men turned their heads in Matty's direction, shaking their heads in amusement, disbelief, and pity.

Noticing the crowd gathering to watch, he shook his head again before he adjusted his grip on Kitty, freeing her wrists, and instead grabbing her by the waist. With a grunt, he hoisted her over his shoulder and carried her into the wagon. If she wanted to cause a scene, she could do so from the inside of her wagon. There was a time and a place for everything, and she would learn that lesson now before she embarrassed him further. He didn't need his men thinking he couldn't control his wife. He was their leader, for gods' sake. If they thought he couldn't control him, would they even listen to him? He didn't want to find out.

"Matty!" she shrieked in protest as the canvas dropped back down behind them, shielding them from view.

"I am a patient man, Kitty," Matty replied sternly, dropping her onto her bed with a small thud. "But even I have my limits. I warned you that you shouldn't come before we left, but you insisted. You made your bed. Now I suggest you stop before I decide to give you an attitude adjustment myself. Do you understand?"

"You... An attitude adjustment? What the hell is that?" she snarled at him, trying to climb off the bed.

Matty studied her for a moment and then let out a deep breath. Reaching down, he undid his belt and tugged it loose, the sound of leather sliding through his belt loops silencing her. And then his lips came crashing down on hers as he shoved her nightgown up around her waist.

CHAPTER 8

WARREN

The fire crackled as Warren rolled over in the fur and opened his eyes to stare up at the ceiling. The wind was still howling outside and he could still hear snow pelting the side of the tent. With a groan, he pushed the furs off and crept over to the entrance of the tent, peering out into the storm to gauge what time it was.

Outside, the world was black and white. The storm continued to rage on, blowing snow everywhere, but the sky was black. Not that it really mattered what time it was if the storm was still going. It wasn't like they could go anywhere. They were stuck in Loch Haven until it let up. But he wasn't complaining. The longer the storm raged, the more time he got to spend curled up with his tiny mate in the warm furs next to the fire.

Stepping back, he let the entrance flap fall back into place before securing it so that the wind couldn't blow it open. Rubbing his hands over his arms, he silently moved back to his spot in the furs, pausing to glance down at Clara. Her dark brown hair was splayed around her, the ends curling gently. Her eyes were closed, her lashes brushing against her rosy cheeks. Her delicate lips were curled down into a slight frown as if she were dreaming of something she wasn't too fond of. Warren's brows furrowed in response, half tempted to wake her to see if that would get her frown to disappear, but thought better of it as he laid back down.

Wrapping his strong arms around Clara's slender waist, he brought her naked body up against his, delighting in how soft and warm she was. A soft murmur fell from her lips at the contact, and she nestled closer unconsciously. A low chuckle rumbled in the back of Warren's throat and then he sighed contentedly.

Four months ago, if someone had told him that he would be head over heels in love with the little barmaid who had saved his brother, Luca, from bleeding out on the floor of her pa's bar, he would have called them crazy. Three months ago, if someone had told him that the little barmaid would willingly come to him, he would have thought the world had stopped spinning. Two months ago, if someone had said that he would have the chance to make up for his actions that had caused her life to turn upside down, he would have broken down and sobbed, hoping that it was true.

Warren buried his face in Clara's hair, breathing in her summery scent. He'd found his mate. He'd fallen in love. Then he'd lost her, but by the grace of the gods, had found her again. And now he was attempting to make up for all the pain he had caused her. He'd never stop trying either. He could live a hundred years with her and that still wouldn't have been enough time to make up for all his mistakes, all the pain he'd caused, all the grief that had been dealt because of his actions.

He didn't deserve her.

But for some reason, even when she'd been presented with an out, she'd still chosen him.

Warren's chest tightened at the thought, a warm feeling spreading throughout his body.

She had chosen him.

He shifted again, drawing her even closer as he felt his body start to heat up. Pressing a kiss to the top of his head, he let out a low groan. He wanted her, but he didn't dare wake her up. She needed all the sleep that she could get, especially for what was to come: an unexpected trip to Reynardsville with her estranged family. Of course, he was going too.

As if he'd let her go alone.

Warren chuckled as the memory of Clara's shocked face when he'd announced his intentions of accompanying her to Reynardsville flashed through his mind. It was like she had never expected him to support her like that. She should have known, though. Not once since he'd claimed her had he not supported her. If she needed something, it didn't matter what it was, he would find a way to get it for her. That's what good mates did.

He shifted again, his lower body grinding up against her, making him groan. Instead of finding relief in the contact, it made his cock throb even more. Cursing under his breath, he untangled himself from her and rolled over, facing the other way. Closing his eyes, he tried to think of something, anything, to get his mind off sinking into the warmth of her body, her wet heat surrounding him as her back arched in order for her to take him deeper, sounds of pleasure falling from her lips.

"May the gods be damned," he muttered under his breath as he sat up and glanced down at Clara's sleeping form. At this rate, he'd have to step outside despite the storm just to cool off.

Scooting over slightly, trying to put some space between himself and Clara, he closed his eyes and took a few breaths, thinking of anything and everything that he could to get his mind and body to calm down. But no matter how hard he tried, his mind kept drifting back to her. The soft swell of her hips, her creamy thighs, the way her hands grasped the back of his shoulders when...

"Fuck," he hissed, reaching down and grasping himself. He'd have to take care of this himself at this point just so he could go back to sleep.

"Everything okay, love?" Clara mumbled sleepily, her eyes cracking open at his curse. Her frown deepened as she raised herself up on her elbow to peer over at him in the darkness, the dying fire not giving off enough light for her to see him clearly.

"Everything is fine," Warren replied through gritted teeth, still grasping himself firmly, his hand beginning to shake as he stroked himself once, twice, then a third time. His breath became shaky. "Everything is just fine."

"You don't sound fine," Clara murmured, reaching out for him.

"Don't," Warren warned, jerking back.

Clara froze, hurt flashing in her eyes briefly.

Warren groaned, catching the look before it disappeared. "It's not that I... Look, if you touch me right now, I will not be held responsible for what will come after."

"What do you mean "what will come after"?" Clara asked in confusion, now sitting up, the blankets that had been covering her falling down to her waist, exposing her bare breasts. She shivered slightly at the cool air, her nipples hardening into soft peaks. Warren licked his lips at the sight.

And then he saw it click in her head, her eyes lighting up.

"Oh," she nodded. "I... okay. I understand. But..." Clara trailed off, hesitating as she bit her bottom lip as if she were debating something. Warren watched her through heavily lidded eyes, fighting back the urge to take her right then and there. And then she leaned forward, grabbed his arm, and pulled him toward her.

Warren's brain went haywire. Within seconds, his hands were wrapped around her waist, pulling her toward him instead of the other way around. Sitting her in his lap, he groaned as she wrapped her legs around his waist. Releasing himself, his hands found her center, his fingers searching out her sweet spot. A low gasp and the arching of her back told him when he'd found it. With a grin, he kept teasing that spot, running his finger over it just the way she liked him to until she was panting. And then he slid himself inside with one quick thrust, making her cry out with pleasure, her fingers digging into his shoulders.

He was home. Right where he belonged.

The entrance to their tent rustled as someone called out for Warren repeatedly. The voice sounded annoyed as they rapped on the canvas, the soft thumping noise barely rousing Warren from his sleep. Peering blearily up at the entrance, he frowned, his hold on Clara's sleeping body tightening as he drew her closer. She sighed in her sleep, her head nestled on his chest, one leg thrown over his and an arm draped over his stomach.

Warren blinked a few times, trying to clear the sleep from his eyes as he continued to peer at the entrance. As his vision cleared and his mind woke up, he realized that it was quiet. The storm had ended. And there was light filtering into the tent through the canvas walls. It was a bright, warm light, meaning the sun was well above the horizon. And that meant that whoever was at the door was someone he really didn't want to see.

Mrs. Reynard.

"Mr. Slora, gods above, I know you're in there. I want an answer. Is my granddaughter coming back with me to Reynardsville or not?" Mrs. Reynard called from the other side of the entrance.

Warren groaned, not answering. He didn't want to deal with her right now. Frankly, he didn't want to deal with her ever. But she was technically the only remaining member of Clara's family. He could be nice for Clara, not that Clara actually liked her grandmother either, but that was beside the point.

And then a mischievous smirk tugged at his lips. Oh, this was the perfect opportunity for him to break the news to Mrs. Reynard. And he would enjoy it.

"There's a tie at the bottom of the flap," he called out to Mrs. Reynard. "Reach down and undo it. You can come in if you'd like. Clara is still sleeping."

"Why the devil is she still asleep?" Mrs. Reynard huffed, her hand grasping under the flap as she searched for the tie. In response, Warren pulled a blanket up over Clara, knowing that she'd have a fit if she was caught naked unawares. And then the tie came loose, the flap falling open, revealing Clara's grandmother. "The morning is half over. She should be..." Mrs. Reynard trailed off as she stepped in, her eyes falling on the two of them tangled up together in the furs. Her face became flushed and her lips pursed. "Why the hell are you two naked right now?"

"We always sleep naked," Warren replied simply. "But that's neither here nor there. I imagine that you're here to hear if Clara has made a decision."

Mrs. Reynard nodded, not bothering to come any closer, instead opting to hover in front of the entrance as if she wanted to be able to make a quick escape if necessary.

"Well, Clara and I discussed that yesterday for the majority of the afternoon and a portion of the evening," Warren began, wondering if he could make Mrs. Reynard sweat a bit and then decided against it. He didn't want to make her start screaming at him. Not yet anyway. Besides, Clara was still asleep. He didn't dare wake her. Not yet.

"And?" Mrs. Reynard demanded.

"You must understand that Clara was raised as a human, and therefore, all her understandings of politics comes from the way human governments are set up. If it collapses, it doesn't matter, there's always something or someone there to pick up the pieces and come up with something new," Warren said, his voice calm as he carefully explained Clara's stance. "Naturally, with that understanding, she did not want to go. Being the good mate that I am, knowing how uneducated she is on shifter ways, gave her a small lesson on pack hierarchy and leadership structure. With that new knowledge, she has agreed to go back to Reynardsville."

"Oh, thank the gods," Mrs. Reynard breathed, practically sagging against the tent, her hand clutching at her chest. But there was a flicker of something else in her eyes. Victory, perhaps? Cunning? Warren wasn't sure, but it made him uneasy.

Clara stirred again, murmuring nonsense under her breath. Warren tenderly rubbed her back, trying to keep her calm enough to continue sleeping. With a soft sigh, she nuzzled her face further into his chest and continued to sleep.

"Well, what are you waiting for?" Mrs. Reynard demanded, watching Warren tenderly soothe Clara. "Get her up. We don't have time to waste. We have to get going."

"About that," Warren smirked, his eyes dancing merrily as he glanced up at her. "Clara agreed to go on one condition."

"She's not really in the position to be making conditions," Mrs. Reynard growled, becoming more aggressive as she became more irritable.

Warren's grip on Clara tightened as he studied Mrs. Reynard for a moment. Trying to remain calm, he took a deep breath before responding once more. "With all due respect, it is you who are in no position to be making the rules. As my mate, she has all the power here while you do not.

With that in mind, I suggest you listen to the condition, or you'll be leaving Loch Haven without your precious granddaughter."

Mrs. Reynard narrowed her eyes at Warren, opening her mouth as if to argue back. And then she snapped her mouth shut and glanced outside, obviously thinking. Finally, she turned back to Warren, clearly uncomfortable. "Fine, go on," Mrs. Reynard grouched.

Warren snorted in amusement, fighting back the urge to laugh. "Clara has agreed to go to Reynardsville under one condition. That condition is that I go with her. She and I both agreed that it would be unwise to let her do something like this alone. She has little to no experience with shifters besides what she has gotten here with my pack. She's also my mate and I would not be doing my duties if I did not come along to protect her."

"You can't be serious," Mrs. Reynard gasped, her jaw dropping as she clenched and unclenched her fists at her sides in irritation and disbelief. "I... You... You are a wolf. You wouldn't fit in. And you don't understand the first thing about foxes."

"I know enough," Warren countered. "Now take it or leave it."

"I..." Mrs. Reynard hesitated. Her body remained tense for a moment as she studied Warren and then Clara sleeping on his chest. "I will need some time to think about this... But... I..."

"The pack tent is still available for you to use while you contemplate all the life choices you have made over the years that have led you to this point," Warren said, his tone a bit more sarcastic than he had intended. "You may stay a few more days. If, by the end of the third day, you haven't made up your mind, I will make it for you. And that decision will be to leave and not come back. Do you understand?"

Mrs. Reynard glowered at him and then nodded, the movement jerky. "I understand perfectly, wolf."

Then she turned on her heel and stalked back outside, heading back to the pack tent, or so Warren hoped. If she caused any kind of trouble, so help him, he'd… He stopped himself from finishing that thought. If she caused trouble, he wouldn't have to do anything. The rest of the pack would see to her.

Now he just had to sit back and watch the show.

CHAPTER 9

CLARA

Clara's cloak swirled around her feet as she walked over the crisp snow toward her grandmother and her entourage. Eyes darting between her grandmother's company, she counted six males, all looking rather rough both in that they looked like someone she didn't want to meet in a dark alley and that they looked like they had seen better days. But she could understand the last part. The journey from Reynardsville to Loch Haven, especially when you didn't know where you were going exactly, was a rather tough one.

Eyeing the three farthest from her, Clara decided that they were only bodyguards based on their positioning. It was strategic, each placed in a position where they could see everything happening around them but still close enough to reach their leader within seconds if the need arose. As they shifted their positions slightly, Clara noticed that their eyes were sharp and alert as they glanced around the Loch Haven camp, looking for any potential threats. All three also had weapons, not that most shifters needed them. But if they were foxes like Clara and her grandmother, then a weapon could mean the difference between life and death when it came to facing larger predators.

Loch Haven was full of larger predators. Wolves, to be precise.

Clara had already learned the hard way that she should have a weapon on her at all times when it came to dealing with larger predators not too long ago. Her "hero", Ronan, a friendly shifter that had saved her from Warren, the Claerys, and certain death a few times, had decided to accompany her to Reynardsville after General Claery had attacked the Loch Haven pack shortly after Warren had kidnapped her. She had thought that she could trust Ronan, had genuinely thought of him as one of the "good ones", but the closer they had gotten to Reynardsville, the more desperate he had become. The night before they were set to make their way into Reynardsville, he had tried to take advantage of her in an effort to claim her as his own, all in the name of protection. Or so he'd said. Desperate, trying to protect herself, she had grabbed the dagger that Ronan had just gifted her and stabbed it into the back of his shoulder, startling him enough to make him roll off her. That's all the time she'd needed to get to her feet, grab her weapon, and make a run for it.

She'd been lucky to make it out of that incident without any major injuries.

Clara's gaze then shifted to the next two members of her grandmother's party. They didn't necessarily look like bodyguards. In fact... Clara's eyes narrowed slightly as she studied the two of them. Like her grandmother, they were older. Both had dark hair and sharp, dark eyes. If Clara didn't know better, she'd say that they were related. Her eyes shifted to her grandmother, trying to figure out who these two males were to her and then it clicked. Their eyes, nose, and mouths were all eerily similar. Her eyes darted back to the two males. They had to be her grandmother's brothers. Her uncles, she decided. Great uncles, to be precise.

Her eyes shifted over to Warren who was walking along beside her. His long auburn hair was pulled back into his signature low ponytail. His brows were furrowed over his dark eyes, his lips curled into a slight frown.

The scar stretching down the left side of his face was stark against his lightly tanned skin, drawing everyone's attention, per usual. Two days worth of stubble coated his jaw.

Clara reached out without thinking and threaded her fingers through his, squeezing his hand gently. She could feel her anxiety starting to skyrocket. This was a stupid idea. But... She paused, not letting herself go down that train of thought, and took a deep breath. Calm. She could do this. Besides, she wasn't alone. She had Warren.

Tearing her eyes away from Warren, who had glanced at her briefly and raised his brow in question at how frazzled and anxious she seemed, she looked over her two great uncles again. Not threats, she decided. But still, she'd need to keep her eyes on them. She didn't trust them. Frankly, though, she didn't trust many people. Not anymore. She'd also learned that lesson the hard way just a few months ago as well when two people she had considered family had tossed her aside and left her for dead simply because she was a half-breed.

Finally, her attention turned to the last male. He was younger. Probably around Warren's age if she had to guess. He stood right next to her grandmother, his dark eyes boring into her as she approached with Warren, his hand on the hilt of his sword hanging off his left hip. His stance was defensive as if he were ready to jump into battle in the blink of an eye.

Her grandmother's personal bodyguard, Clara decided.

Studying him further she noted chestnut hair with hints of red that were noticeable in the sunshine. It was about shoulder length and wavy, neatly combed back out of his face. His brows were thick and furrowed over dark blue eyes. His nose was aristocratic, and his lips were not quite full, but they weren't exactly thin either. A neatly trimmed beard covered his strong jaw.

Clara's eyes drifted lower as she continued to take the male in. He was tall, but not nearly as tall as Warren, who towered over Clara. He was also well built, but not broad, his muscles lean meaning he relied on his agility and skill rather than his brute strength in a fight. And his hands... Clara noticed a few scars curving over the back of his right hand, very similar to what looked like claw marks. She was half tempted to ask him the story but decided against it. He wasn't her friend. They'd never be friends.

Her eyes darted to her grandmother again as her grandmother leaned over and whispered something in her bodyguard's ear. The male hesitated, his hand tightening on the hilt of his sword before he let his shoulders slump slightly as he took a step back, leaving Mrs. Reynard to face Clara and Warren mostly on her own.

"Grandmother," Clara said quietly as she came to a stop right in front of Mrs. Reynard. Reaching up, she adjusted the pack on her shoulder, the strap digging into her skin and making her rather uncomfortable. Not that she'd show how uncomfortable it made her. That would be a weakness, something she couldn't afford to show.

"Clara," Mrs. Reynard replied brusquely with a nod of her head. "Are you all set?"

"I am," Clara replied, her eyes not leaving her grandmother's.

"Good, good," Mrs. Reynard nodded again, her attention shifting to Warren. Her lips pursed as she noted the pack on his back as well. Clara had to stifle a laugh at the obvious disapproval in her grandmother's eyes.

"Ma'am." Warren nodded his head respectfully, though his voice was laced with amusement as well. He was getting just as much of a kick out of tormenting her grandmother as she was.

It became harder to hold back the laugh that was threatening to come out.

When Warren had told her that her grandmother had stopped by earlier that morning to get her response while she'd been sleeping, Clara's jaw had dropped at Warren's response. She had known that he was planning on coming with her, but part of her hadn't really taken him all that seriously. Mostly because she didn't think he would actually leave the Loch Haven pack. But hearing that he had already told her grandmother that he was indeed coming with... Well, that sealed it. And then she had laughed as Warren had recounted the look of incredulity on Mrs. Reynard's face to her once more, finding it just too funny not to laugh.

Mrs. Reynard's eyes snapped back to Clara as she continued to struggle to not laugh. Her brow furrowed and her eyes darkened as she huffed in disapproval, finally setting Clara off. Leaning against Warren to hold herself up, she giggled silently. If this was how their journey back to Reynardsville was going to start, then perhaps it wouldn't be too bad after all. She could do with more laughter in her life. After all, it had been quite a while since she had really laughed. It felt good.

"Is he really going with us?" Mrs. Reynard stated, her irritation evident.

"I told you already, ma'am." Warren cracked a smile as he gazed down at Mrs. Reynard, his eyes twinkling mischievously. "I wouldn't be doing my job as Clara's mate if I didn't go with her. And we wouldn't want that, now would we?"

"She's perfectly safe with me," Mrs. Reynard snapped, her eyes narrowing on Warren before turning her attention back to Clara. "I may not have been the best grandmother in her youth, but I'm here now. I wouldn't do anything to hurt her or jeopardize this new relationship."

"Translation: I won't do anything stupid because I need her, so I can't afford to have her walk away," Warren snorted in amusement, shifting his stance a bit, his grip on Clara's hand tightening. "Look, we all know why you're here. If you didn't need Clara, you would never have bothered to come all this way. And if you hadn't come all this way, Clara and I would be living peacefully here with our pack, working on building our forever home."

Mrs. Reynard let out a long-suffering sigh. "You are infuriating, wolf."

"Don't like the truth, Gran?" Clara piped up finally, tilting her head as she studied her grandmother, finally noting the fine lines that graced her face. Crow's feet lined her eyes. Her forehead was permanently creased. And frown lines seemed to be etched into her skin near her mouth. Silver hair started at her temple and streaked her still mostly dark brown, almost black hair. She really was getting old. But that didn't excuse her behavior.

"Don't call me that." Mrs. Reynard pursed her lips as she studied Clara back. "You look just like your mother. Mara was always a bit of a wild child. Seems you inherited that, too. She would have been a fantastic leader if she had stuck ar..."

"Don't you dare talk to me about my mother," Clara hissed, cutting her grandmother off, her mood changing from lighthearted to dark in a matter of seconds. "You have no right. You could have sent guards to protect her. You could have sent an escort for the whole family, but because my pa was human, you didn't care enough to do that. So don't you dare talk to me about my mother. Get her name out of your mouth, you ungrateful bitch."

Warren's eyes widened in shock as he looked down at Clara as she spat vehemently at her grandmother. Letting go of her hand, he instead wrapped an arm around her waist, stopping her from launching herself at Mrs. Reynard. Pulling her into his chest, he stroked her hair.

"Little fox, breathe," he rumbled, his deep voice low and gravelly.

Clara looked up at him in surprise, and then, feeling his hand in her hair, she let herself relax against him, burying her face in his chest. The pounding of his heart was loud in her ears as she slowed her breathing to match his. But by the gods, she was angry. And it had felt so damn good to yell at her grandmother like that. It had been a long time coming.

Meanwhile, Mrs. Reynard's jaw had dropped momentarily before her face darkened angrily. Before she could respond, her personal bodyguard stepped in, placing a hand on her shoulder with a warning look. Raising her hand as if to smack her guard, Mrs. Reynard spun toward the young male but then froze as the young male raised his brows at her and shook his head, tsking.

"Not worth it," he said, his voice a low bass that startled Clara.

Turning in Warren's arms, she peered at the young male guard again, studying him once again. Who was he really to have such power over her grandmother like that?

The young male, noticing her gaze, turned his attention to Clara once more, his blue eyes piercing. Clara shifted uncomfortably, feeling as if he was staring into her soul with those eyes.

"Who are you?" she finally managed to say with more bravado than she felt.

The young male tilted his head for a moment, pursing his lips. Then he turned back to Mrs. Reynard as if seeking permission to tell Clara. Mrs. Reynard, still huffing angrily, glanced at Clara, her eyes practically shooting sparks with how upset she was. Looking like she wanted to reprimand Clara, she opened her mouth but then thought better of it, and closed her mouth. Taking a deep breath, she worked on composing herself before nodding at the young male, giving him permission before walking over to the two males that Clara had assumed were her grandmother's brothers, leaving the young male mostly alone with Clara and Warren.

The young male watched Mrs. Reynard for a moment before turning back to Clara, his lips still pursed. "Briggs Freisinger," he grunted, his hand playing with the hilt of his sword again. "You can call me Briggs."

"Pleasure," Clara nodded. "But *who* are you?"

Briggs huffed slightly, as if partially annoyed but partially amused at the same time. "I'm your bodyguard. Your grandmother decided that it would be best if you had someone closer to your age protecting you. You are the next leader of the Reynard pack after all. We would hate to see something happen to that pretty face of yours," he stated gruffly, his eyes narrowing again.

Clara rolled her eyes. "I don't need a bodyguard, thanks. Who are you to my grandmother?" If he was going to be difficult, she was going to ask a thousand and one questions until she got the information she wanted. She didn't care how angry it made him at this point. He had successfully gotten her grandmother to back off, the current leader of the Reynard pack. He had power and she wanted to know what kind.

Briggs huffed a laugh, apparently following her train of thought as he flashed her a cocky grin. "Wouldn't you like to know, Kleine?"

Warren shifted behind her, having remained silent until now. Tightening his grip on Clara, he leaned forward a bit. "If you won't answer her, then I'll ask the same thing. Who are you to Mrs. Reynard?"

Briggs sneered at Warren. "I don't talk to wolves," he said, his voice hardening before looking back down at Clara. "You'll find out soon enough, Kleine. But don't worry. I won't hurt you. Much. You'll hate me by the end. But that's okay. I'm not here to be your friend." He sneered again before turning on his heel and stalking over to the other guards. Glancing over his shoulder, he shook his head slightly before raising his voice so the whole group could hear. "It's time. Let's go. Move out."

Grumbling slightly, Clara adjusted her pack once more before grasping Warren's hand in hers. Together, they set off, their boots crunching in the snow as they followed a few paces behind the Reynard pack.

CHAPTER 10

RONAN

Ronan felt Maddox's eyes on him as he paced the bunk room. Back and forth. Back and forth.

Clara was coming.

Back and forth.

Back and forth.

What was he going to do? He could feel his rising panic, smothering him, making it hard to breathe. He couldn't do this.

His chest constricted and a lump rose in his throat.

What was he going to do?

On one hand, he was excited. Despite everything that had happened, the prospect of seeing Clara made him happy. He'd be able to see how well she was doing, if Warren was treating her well. On the other hand, he was nervous, especially with how things had ended between them. He had no idea how the two of them running into each other was going to go. It could either go well. She could forgive him and they would move on. Or… she would still be pissed and could tell him to go kick rocks. The best case scenario, if she was still pissed, would be for her to act as if she didn't know him, ignoring him completely as much as that would hurt him. Less drama that way.

Gods, he felt so out of control. He was spiraling. And that angered him.

Before he could stop himself, he kicked the edge of a large wooden trunk at the foot of one of the beds with a solid thunk. It barely moved an inch. However, pain radiated from his big toe, through his foot, and up his leg. His eyes widened and they narrowed as they watered, his face screwing up to stop himself from whimpering.

Bending over, he grasped his foot, before cursing loudly. "Fuck," he gritted out, hopping up and down on one leg for a moment before reaching over to grasp the edge of the nearest bunk to steady himself. Behind him, Maddox shook his head as Zeke joined him, his eyes wide as he surveyed the scene before him.

"He's not doing well, is he?" Zeke whispered to Maddox, leaning against one of the bunks, his arms crossed over his chest.

"No." Maddox shook his head in response, his eyes never leaving Ronan as Ronan finally collapsed on the bed, hanging his head as he closed his eyes in defeat. "He just keeps saying that he can't see her. And I get that. I think we all get that. They have a history. A pretty serious one if he tried to claim her. But he's... I don't know. It's like he thinks he doesn't have any self-control when it comes to this girl. It's like he thinks that as soon as he sees her, he'll jump her. But we all know that he won't. And even if he tried, we wouldn't let him. He's just... stuck in his head. Overthinking things."

"You can say that again. He's definitely overthinking things," Zeke agreed, watching Ronan closely now as well, his eyes tracking the rise and fall of Ronan's chest as Ronan tried to calm himself down. "But we take care of our own. He's ours. We won't let him mess his life up over a girl he can't have."

At those words, Ronan looked up, his face devastated, his green eyes wide. "I can't have her," he repeated faintly as if that were the worst thing in the world. And then he shook his head before running his hand through his curls.

What was he thinking? He knew this already. He needed to snap out of it.

The long and short of the matter was that he couldn't have Clara. He knew that. He had known it for a long time, and had thought he'd made peace with that, but knowing that she would be coming, that he would be seeing her, that he would have to work with her when she visited their camp… It was too much. He had been operating under the premise that he would never see her again.

This changed things.

Or did it?

He was acting like a spoiled brat. A love-struck moron. An idiot. He needed to get his shit together. Sooner rather than later preferably.

Shaking his head and releasing a soft breath, Zeke moved forward and sat down next to Ronan on the bed, the mattress creaking under their combined weight. Giving Ronan a sympathetic look, he placed his hand on Ronan's shoulder, squeezing it gently.

"I'm sorry," Zeke said after a minute. "I wish things could have worked out differently for the two of you. I think with a little more time and patience on your part, you might have been able to win her back over, even with the mistake you made. However, you said that she grew up human. Something like that for a human is unforgivable if I'm not mistaken. But for us shifters, that's nature. If she'd assimilated to our ways, I believe she would have eventually understood."

Ronan listened quietly and then nodded. "Do you think she would have forgiven me?"

"No," Maddox chimed in, his deep voice booming as he came to sit down on the bed across from Ronan and Zeke. "She was raised human.

They don't forgive those kinds of actions. She may have understood eventually. But forgiveness? No, she would never have granted you that, as much as that may hurt you to hear."

Ronan nodded again, his heart sinking into the pit of his stomach. He knew that, too. But hearing that? Having it confirmed? It was like being rejected by Clara all over again. His stomach twisted painfully as his heart shattered once more. Why was this so painful? He'd spent maybe a month with her. Why was he acting like he'd lost the love of his life? This was ridiculous.

"When she comes..." His voice was shaky as he started talking once more. "When she comes to train with our pack, I am going to hang out in the back. I don't want to come face-to-face with her. It would hurt too much. And if I had to smell her... Gods, she smelled like a summer afternoon. It was heavenly." His body relaxed at the memory, a dreamy look coming across his face.

Maddox watched him, an incredulous look on his face. Looking over at Zeke, he muttered, "Her potential must have been extremely potent for him to be reacting this way."

Glancing over, a serious expression on his face, Zeke nodded. "I've never seen someone react this strongly to a potential before. The fact that it took him almost a month to try and claim her speaks volumes of his self-control. Or it did. I don't know. Maybe once you get a taste of a potential that strong, it leaves you changed. He's like an addict, waiting for his next fix."

Maddox grunted in agreement, concern filling his eyes before reaching over to snap his fingers in front of Ronan's face. "Get it together, man."

Ronan jerked at the loud sound, his head jerking back, startled. Then he blinked a few times and ran his hands over his face with a groan, trying to get his head back in the game.

"Sorry," he moaned. "Just… when she comes to train with our pack, keep me away from her. I don't know if I have the strength to keep myself away, but I'll try. I'm going to stay in the back. Maybe in one of the tents. I'm not sure yet. But I can't…"

"We understand," Zeke said gently. "We'll keep you separated. Or we'll try. No guarantees."

"Is she going to be traveling from pack to pack alone?" Ronan asked as Maddox stood back up and made his way over to his bunk, grabbing his pack so they could head out to their camp later.

Maddox grimaced as Zeke sighed.

"No," Zeke finally said, also getting up to go grab his own pack. "The Reynard pack is so large that they have their own little militia if you will. Not super large, but it's about forty males strong. One of the leaders of that militia is a male called Briggs Freisinger."

"Briggs Freisinger?" Ronan repeated with a frown, never having heard that name before as Maddox shuddered.

"Mhm." Zeke nodded as he went through his pack, making sure he had everything he needed. Satisfied, he sat back down and looked over at Ronan, his lips pursed.

"Tell me about Freisinger," Ronan demanded, though something told him that he would be sorry that he asked as he, too, finally got up and made his way over to his bunk. Pulling his pack up off the trunk at the end of his bunk, he grunted at the sheer weight of it. He'd already double-checked his gear, so he knew that he had everything, but just to be sure… Ronan plopped the pack on his bunk, the mattress squeaking a bit, and opened it.

"Freisinger is… about our age," Maddox answered for Zeke as he rolled his neck, popping it. "And he's got a reputation. The male is absolutely brutal. If he went head-to-head with the king's general, I think the general would finally meet his match. He's a damn good fighter, but he will play dirty to ensure that he comes out on top."

"And this is the male that will be escorting Clara?" Ronan asked, his head snapping up and over to Maddox, his eyes wide with concern. "He'll eat her alive if he's overseeing her training."

"Or he'll turn her into the female version of himself," Zeke mumbled under his breath.

"Look," Maddox groaned as he palmed his pants, looking for his cigarettes. "Foxes have a reputation for being sneaky, clever, liars, thieves, assassins... They aren't the most well-liked shifters out there. And Briggs has taken those qualities and used them to turn himself into a weapon."

"It was like he decided to take every negative thing ever said about his kind and used them to his advantage," Zeke scoffed. "Not that that's a bad thing, mind you. It's served him and his pack well, but it... He's not got many friends, not many people trust him, and by default, not many people trust the pack because of him."

"But he's the one going to be with Clara?" Ronan was quickly becoming more concerned by the second as he closed his pack and looked between Zeke and Maddox.

"I... uh... yeah," Zeke sighed. "From what I heard at the last council meeting, Freisinger is being assigned as her bodyguard and personal trainer. However, I also got the feeling that Mrs. Reynard may or may not be trying to set them up."

"Set them up?" Ronan repeated, his chest constricting painfully again, making it hard to breathe.

"Yeah. The Reynards are aware that Clara is mated to a wolf, and they aren't happy about that. They're elitists. Purists. They like to keep it to the same animal. Every member of the Reynard pack is a fox with the exception of a few coyotes and jackals. They try not to let anyone with an animal bigger than a fox in very often, so even though wolves are of the same family..." Zeke trailed off, letting Ronan finish the thought himself. Wolves were too big. Too strong. Too dominant. They'd take over the pack if they were allowed in.

"And Clara being the heir, well, they'll want to keep their bloodline as clean as possible. She'll only be allowed to mate with a fox, so she'll be forced to leave her current mate," Maddox added. "If she knows what's good for her, she'll stay with her mate up there in the mountains. Less drama. Less danger. No chance of being caught in the war. But if she does come... If her mate knows what's good for him, he'll let her go. There's no way his pack could face off against the Reynards and come out on top, especially with Freisinger leading them."

"That poor girl," Zeke sighed.

"Agreed." Maddox nodded.

"I should have hidden her away when I had the chance," Ronan whispered.

Ronan set his sleeping mat down inside the tent that he and Maddox would be sharing. Zeke would also be sharing their tent with them, but he had simply dropped his pack off and left without saying much. Apparently, a few of the female wolves in the pack, the ones that had begged to come rather than be left behind in the city, were causing some trouble and he'd had to head out to take care of that before it escalated further.

Maddox dropped his pack down at the foot of his sleeping mat with a snigger. "You missed the start of the fight." He glanced over at Ronan, merriment dancing in his eyes. "I swear to the gods, Lena has a chip on her shoulder or something. Constantly getting into some sort of trouble."

"Lena is one of a kind." Ronan nodded in agreement and then grimaced.

Ronan didn't much like the female shifter. But he sort of understood where she was coming from. Like Ronan, Lena had been raised by a rather abusive father. When she'd gotten old enough, she had run away from home and headed to Reynardsville. A rather stupid idea, but she'd succeeded without anything major happening to her, which was a miracle in and of itself. Shortly after arriving, she'd run into Zeke who had quickly taken her under his wing, more so to protect her than because he actually wanted her in the pack, and she'd been a decent pack member ever since. Well, most of the time. She hated most of the males with the exception of Zeke. And the females... She didn't get along well with them either. Too meek for her tastes, or so she'd said. Females should stand up for themselves, and while Ronan agreed, the way she was going about trying to rile them up left a lot to be desired.

"She's going to cause trouble," Maddox continued to laugh. "Watch her be the first one killed when the king's forces finally arrive, all because she can't seem to work with the rest of us. She sucks at following orders."

"I don't want to say that she will be," Ronan agreed, a bit hesitant to wish death upon a fellow pack member. "However, you aren't exactly wrong. I've got a feeling that you, as second in command, will give an order that she doesn't like and because it's you, and because she doesn't like the order, she'll go off half-cocked. I just hope that if she is killed, it's quick. No one deserves to suffer."

"Agreed," Maddox grunted as they both stepped outside, their heads swiveling in the direction of the fight.

Ronan could just make out Zeke holding the wiry female shifter back while he yelled at her. Lena, her face contorted into a deep scowl, yelled back, but they were too far away to be able to make out what they were saying exactly. But they got the gist.

And then...

"You're going back." Zeke's voice boomed across the camp, freezing everyone with the timbre in his voice. Meekly, Lena dropped her head in a sign of subservience.

Ronan's brows shot up in surprise, but then he nodded in agreement. Good. They didn't need Lena doing something stupid and he was glad that Zeke had apparently had the same thoughts that he and Maddox had been having.

"Thank the gods," Maddox muttered behind Ronan.

Turning to face Maddox with a smirk, his eyes landed on the mountains not far from them. And then his eyes landed on a certain copse of trees that he was all too familiar with. Clara had hidden from him in those trees after he had forced himself on her. His smirk fell off his face at the memory, his body tensing.

In just a few days time, he'd be one of the first to see the Reynards come out of the mountains with Clara in tow. He'd be one of the first to see them enter the city through the back gate. He'd be one of the first to see how Clara reacted to being forced to relive parts of that night as she passed by that copse of trees.

Silently, he cursed the city council for placing the Romulus pack right next to the back gate of Reynardsville. This was going to be his own personal hell.

CHAPTER II

MATTY

Matty rolled over on the thin mattress and narrowly fell off the bed. Throwing his hands out, he barely caught himself before careening to the hard, wooden floor of the wagon. Eyes wide, his chest heaving, he lay very still for a moment, attempting to calm himself before deciding on his next move. Beside him, his wife slept peacefully, unaware that he had nearly fallen off the bed and made a major fool of himself.

Finally slowing his breath, he glanced over at Kitty's sleeping form. Her dark hair was splayed out around her on the pillow, and he could have sworn he'd inhaled and tasted some of it sometime during the night. The bed was so small that they didn't have much room, but she had insisted they start sharing a bed. Repeatedly. And after fucking her senseless out of anger, he had felt, well, ashamed of himself. Naturally, he had agreed. Anything to make up for his behavior.

Matty's eyes drifted a bit lower to the dark lashes that were fanned out over her rosy cheeks, her lips pulled into a soft pout and her small hand tucked under her cheek. She was a lovely sight. He would be lying if he said he didn't enjoy looking at her because he did. When she was asleep, that is. She was silent then. She didn't complain or whine or give him that look of sheer disappointment while she was asleep.

He prayed she stayed asleep for a bit longer. Just a bit longer to give him a few more minutes to enjoy the peace and quiet.

He closed his eyes, giving himself a minute to collect himself before he reopened his eyes, his gaze drifting lower. He let out a heavy breath, his face twisting into a grimace, shame and regret filling him.

Kitty would never survive in Springfield, this much he knew. She would struggle constantly. She struggled to get dressed by herself in those ridiculous dresses she had brought with her instead of the more serviceable ones Matty had suggested. She didn't know how to clean beyond making her bed. She had admitted she didn't know how to cook. And Matty was quite certain that beyond her embroidery, she didn't know how to sew. Knitting and crocheting was foreign to her so if she got a hole in her stocking or he needed a button resewn, she would be completely lost.

The thought was anything but comforting. In fact, he was struggling not to panic. What was he going to do with her?

His only comfort at this point in time was that he would be leaving her with his mother during the day while he worked. Mrs. Claery, bless her, was the epitome of kindness. Matty was sure that if he explained the situation to her, his mother would take Kitty in without hesitation. He also hoped that by doing so, when things settled down after helping his dad fortify Springfield, turning it into a veritable fortress for the king's forces, Kitty would be able to do at least the bare minimum. He didn't have the time to teach her himself, nor did he have the time to do all the chores on top of his own. Not with his current position. And definitely not with the farm to run on top of working directly under his dad in the king's army.

Matty shifted as much as he could without falling out of the bed, keeping his arms out to keep himself steady. Slowly, ever so slowly, he sat up, the bed creaking and the wagon rocking ever so slightly. Beside him, Kitty shifted in her sleep, murmuring slightly, her free hand flying out and landing on his chest, pushing him back down. With a grunt, Matty laid back down, biting back a curse. He could hear the camp starting to come to life. He needed to be out there, but no, he was stuck in here with the woman he had foolishly wed.

Gingerly, he lifted her hand off his chest and placed it back down on her hip before slowly sitting back up once more. Again, the bed creaked, the wagon rocked, and Kitty shifted, waking up a bit more. Again, Matty bit back a curse, but before she could fling out her hand and catch him once more, he stood up and moved away from the bed.

Turning slowly, practically holding his breath, his eyes scanned the small interior of the wagon as he searched for his pants and his shirt. Spotting his pants and shirt neatly draped over the small chair, he reached out and snagged them before his eyes flicked back to Kitty to see if she'd woken up the rest of the way. Sound asleep. He let loose a quiet sigh of release, the tension in his shoulders fading.

Turning his attention back to his clothes, a frown pulled at the corners of his mouth before he tugged on his pants. He didn't remember placing his clothes on the chair. In fact, if he recalled correctly, he had tossed them over the wooden chest. His gaze landed on the chest to make sure he hadn't been imagining things, that it was really there. His frown deepened. The chest was indeed there. There also weren't any clothes flung carelessly over the top, but it was open, the contents mussed. He leaned forward to see what was inside, his brows rising sharply. Blankets.

Sitting down in the chair to pull on his boots, he ran a hand down his face with a low groan. He had mentioned that it looked like it was going to be even colder than normal last night during a rather awkward supper with Kitty. He had said it in passing, trying to make small talk because he didn't know what else to talk to her about. She didn't understand military or small-town life, and he hadn't felt like trying to explain it to her at the time.

So the weather, a fairly safe topic, had been his go to. He hadn't thought that she was actually listening, but apparently... His eyes darted to the chest again, putting two and two together. Kitty had pulled out an extra blanket to keep them both warm last night after he had already crawled into bed and, while wallowing in his own self-pity, he hadn't noticed.

He'd been too tired, too upset with himself, ready for the day to end.

She had listened to him.

The thought struck him over and over again, and each time it hit, his eyes widened a bit more. Perhaps... He groaned once more. He had misjudged the girl once more. She wasn't as shallow and selfish as he had thought. She... she cared.

Or rather she had more self-preservation skills than he'd assumed. Caring about him might be a stretch, but he did know that she cared about herself. And apparently, she would listen to him if that meant that she'd be okay.

Kitty put Kitty first. Not that surprising now that he thought about it, but...

Matty leaned back in the chair, stunned.

Maybe, just maybe, she'd be alright in Springfield. Only time would tell, but it seemed like she might just be a quick learner, especially if she was willing to listen. His hopes lifted a bit at the thought. Things would still be rocky, but perhaps it wouldn't be nearly as bad as he had originally thought.

Standing up, he walked the few paces back over to the bed, leaned down, and pressed a gentle kiss to Kitty's forehead before heading out.

Shifting in his saddle, Matty readjusted his grip on Khan's reigns. Even though he was wearing thick leather gloves lined with rabbit fur, his fingers were starting to grow stiff from the cold. His breath came out in clouds in front of his face as he huffed in irritation. He was so done with the cold and couldn't wait to get to Springfield. The thought of sleeping in an actual house sounded like pure heaven at this point in time. And the idea of taking a warm bath was even better. He wasn't sure what he wanted to do more, but then the thought of his mom's baked goods crossed his mind and he nearly groaned, his stomach rumbling.

It was settled. Once he got to his mom's house, he would eat until he couldn't stomach anything else. From there, he would take a nice warm bath before crawling into bed. No doubt, Kitty would join him in bed, but at this point, he didn't even care anymore. Let her join. He would welcome her extra body heat. And... he shook his head, not wanting to admit to himself that he liked having her there. There was something about having her small delicate body next to him, wrapped in his arms. It made him feel strong, needed, and trusted.

He could get used to that feeling.

He shifted again just in time to spot his former mentor, Sergeant Robert Conaway, and one of Matty's few friends, Sergeant Archibald Sinclair, or Archie, coming up to him on their own horses. Conaway, ever the diplomat, nodded politely, addressing Matty by his new rank of lieutenant. Archie, who didn't care about formalities and just liked having a good time, did the opposite.

"Matty, we heard you and the missus "arguing" again last night," Archie teased, his eyes filled with mirth as he grinned at Matty, pulling his horse up next to Matty's so they were level with each other.

Matty felt his face flush in embarrassment that his men had heard him bedding Kitty again last night. But Archie wasn't wrong. It had started as an argument once again, and by the end, Matty had whipped his belt off his pants, the sound of leather sliding through belt loops still fresh in his head. From there, he had grabbed Kitty and thrown her on the bed before yanking her skirts up to her waist.

Not that she'd complained. As soon as she'd seen him go for his belt buckle, her eyes had lit up. This had happened more times than Matty cared to admit, so Kitty knew exactly what was coming.

They both enjoyed it. That's what counted, right?

Matty glanced down at his gloves, flexing his fingers again as his face burned red.

Conaway, noticing Matty's embarrassment, gave Matty a sympathetic smile as if he understood. Then he looked over at Archie with a disapproving look and shook his head as if to tell him to knock it off. Archie, either not seeing Conaway's look or ignoring it, the latter being more likely, continued to rib Matty.

"It sounded like the argument resolved quite nicely. The way she begged you to go harder at the end..." Archie kissed his fingertips and made the motion for a chef's kiss before giving Matty a sly grin. Then he cackled, as if Matty and Kitty's doings were prime entertainment, and slapped Matty heartily on the back.

"Don't you have anything better to do than to listen to me bed my wife?" Matty muttered under his breath, lurching forward at the force of Archie's enthusiastic slaps.

"No, not really," Archie responded honestly. his hand dropping down to readjust his coat before picking up his reins again. "I don't know why you're worried about it, Matty. It's natural. We all understand. If the other married soldiers had their wives with them, I'm almost certain that you wouldn't be the only one burying themselves in their wives every chance they got. It's stress relief, and the gods know that we need every ounce of stress relief that we can get. So, seriously, don't sweat it."

Conaway shifted uncomfortably in his saddle with a low grunt, shooting a look of annoyance at Archie. "I hate to admit it, but I agree with the kid. He's not wrong." Conaway paused and peered over at Matty, his eyes scanning him, assessing. "What was the argument about this time?"

Matty didn't answer right away as he gazed out over the horizon. He could see Springfield in the distance. They would be there by the end of the day. Hope bloomed in his chest.

Taking a deep breath, he glanced toward the end of the wagon train at Kitty's wagon and pursed his lips. "She's spoiled," he grunted in response. "She's not handling the change to this way of life very well. She expects someone to wait on her hand and foot and is throwing a fit when there's no one to do just that. Last night, she was upset that I asked her to take the dishes back to the cook."

"Gods," Archie whispered, grimacing and shaking his head. "You married her why?"

"I didn't really have a choice," Matty grumbled, his face falling momentarily. "It was either I marry her before coming out this way, or I marry her once we got out here. Either way, she was coming with me, no matter how much I didn't want her to. King's orders."

"Do you think that she'll adjust?" Conaway asked next, his voice hesitant.

"I'm not sure," Matty sighed, flexing his fingers, trying to keep them from getting too stiff. "One minute, I think that she'll call it quits on the whole thing and demand to be taken back home to her family. The next, she does something that surprises me and makes me question my assumptions. Usually, they're just small, insignificant acts, but coming from her of all people, they're huge. And seeing that..." Matty paused and shook his head, not quite believing the words that were about to come out of his mouth. "She might take to this life quite well if she'd give it a chance and try a bit harder."

Conaway and Archie both looked at him in surprise, their brows arching.

"I hope that you're right," Conaway murmured. "Not only for your sake, but for yours, the company's, and your parents'."

Matty shuffled from one foot to the other as he watched his mom study Kitty with a critical eye, his stomach twisting nervously. Keeping his hands stuffed in the pocket of his coat, he rubbed the fabric between his fingers, trying to soothe himself.

It wasn't working.

As soon as he had walked in with Kitty, it had become quite evident that his dad had not told Mrs. Claery about Matty's new position, his recent nuptials, or that he was coming home at all. In fact, it seemed that General Claery was still keeping just about everything from his wife. Apparently, he was a firm believer in the saying that ignorance was bliss.

Matty fought the urge to roll his eyes, find his dad and yell at him for being such an inconsiderate ass, and to grab his wife and drag her away to the cabin. This was awkward. Too awkward. His stomach clenched as he watched his mom, waiting with bated breath.

Mrs. Claery, a normally cheery woman, looked anything but as she circled Kitty slowly. As Matty surveyed his mom, he noted that it looked like she had lost weight since he'd left home. Her normally full cheeks were a bit gaunt, and her waist was a bit smaller, her clothes a bit loose. Her eyes were still sharp, though, as they surveyed Kitty, taking everything in. Finally, she reached out and took one of Kitty's hands in her own, turning them over. Running a finger of Kitty's soft palms, Mrs. Claery tsked.

"Such soft hands. Never had to work a day in your life," she murmured her disappointment bleeding through. "They'll be torn to shreds out here."

Mrs. Claery dropped Kitty's hand and turned her attention to Matty. Her face instantly lit up as she cupped Matty's face, her thumbs tenderly stroking his face.

"It's so good to see you again, dear," Mrs. Claery whispered, her voice breaking. "It's been so lonely without you here to keep me company. Not that I'm complaining. Look at you. All grown up finally. A lieutenant. I am so proud of you. I always knew that you were made for bigger things. Just... look at you. And married. I wish you would have written to tell me the news."

Matty's face fell for a second, and then a frown descended as his brows furrowed, knitting together. "I... I did write you. I sent a letter with a rider ahead of the company. You... you didn't get it?"

Mrs. Claery's eyes widened in surprise. "You sent a letter?"

"I've sent dozens, mom," Matty said slowly, his voice full of disbelief. And then he turned away from his mom and glanced at his dad who had just walked in and was leaning against the kitchen door frame, a smug look on his face. His face darkened as he took in the expression on his dad's face and knew instantly. "What did you do with the letters, dad?"

"What letters?" General Claery stated simply, his smug look growing as he lied to Matty's face. "I haven't received any letters from you, the post office hasn't received any letters from you, and your mom has stated that she hasn't received any letters either. Perhaps you wrote the letters and forgot to send them. Or perhaps you're lying and saying you did when you didn't just so you can make your mom feel better."

Matty's hands balled into fists at his side as his temper flared. He could feel his anger bubbling away, just below the surface. As he was about to step forward and confront his dad, a small hand wrapped around one of his fists. Startled, he glanced down to find Kitty watching him closely, a concerned look on her face. She then looked between General Claery and Matty. She had seen Matty write a few of those letters he had sent. She had seen him send them off. She knew General Claery was lying, but wisely, she kept her mouth shut about that.

They both had toxic, manipulative assholes for fathers. That was one thing they had in common.

"Why don't you show me that cabin you were telling me about the other night?" she murmured instead of joining the argument with Mr. Claery. "If I am to stay here in Springfield with you and survive, I will need to get myself acquainted with my new home sooner rather than later."

"Right." Matty nodded his head, turning away from his dad.

"Stay for supper first," Mrs. Claery said hastily before Matty could start leading Kitty away. "I want to hear everything. And…" Mrs. Claery glanced at Kitty again. Taking a deep breath, she nodded, her face softening. "I would like to get to know my new daughter-in-law. I've got a feeling we will be spending a lot of time together in the near future."

"Indeed," Kitty murmured docilely.

"Supper sounds good, mom." Matty placed a hand on Kitty's lower back and guided her into the kitchen, not bothering to spare his dad another glance as he brushed past him.

CHAPTER 12

CLARA

Clouds drifted across the sky, obscuring the sun, and casting the world in shadows every few minutes. As another cloud passed over the sun, Clara shivered, pulling her cloak tighter. She knew it wasn't possible for the temperature to drop that quickly, but in her mind, it got colder every time the sun disappeared. She needed that bright flaming ball of light to warm her up, even if it was just emotionally. And right now, she needed all the help that she could get.

Glancing over at Warren, who strolled a few feet behind her, his sharp eyes scanning their surroundings, she let out a deep breath as her chest warmed, a small smile tugging at the corners of her mouth. A few strands of his long auburn hair had slipped free of its binding at the base of his neck and whipped about in the wind. Every so often, it would fly into his face, and she could see his increasing frustration building in his eyes and in the way his shoulders became increasingly more tense.

"It would be easier to travel in animal form," he had whispered to Clara the first night of their journey back to Reynardsville as they lay cuddled up together for warmth, their sleeping mats not far from the raging fire he had helped put together, the heat from roaring flames washing over them.

"I agree," she had whispered back, nestling closer, his arms tightening around her waist as they both caught her grandmother and her right-hand man, Briggs, watching them discreetly. Not discreetly enough, though. Clara still caught the way their eyes narrowed in disapproving annoyance at the sight of her cuddling up with her mate.

At the time, she hadn't understood their expressions. Now... she huffed, a muscle twitching in her jaw in her annoyance. Purists. The whole lot of them. Her eyes flicked back up to Warren's, meeting his as she thought back to that first night again.

When Clara had caught the annoyance on her grandmother's face, she had narrowed her eyes at her grandmother in return, her body tensing momentarily, before turning her attention back to Warren. Reaching up, she had brushed a few strands of hair out of his face, tucking them behind her ear. And then she had traced her fingers along the rough edges of his scar that marred the left side of his face, the skin red and angry.

"I thought this would fade eventually," she had murmured, tracing the scar once more.

"I thought so, too, at one point in time," he had replied, his voice barely above a whisper. "But it's been years. I've given up hope. I shall be forever ugly." His voice had turned teasing at the end, knowing full well that he was devastatingly handsome in a dangerous way, his eyes glinting mischievously as he had grinned at her.

"Yes, forever ugly," Clara had scoffed, her voice turning teasing as well before pressing a kiss to his scar.

Warren had laughed quietly at her playing along, capturing her chin with his hand. Tilting her head from side to side, he inspected her before pressing his lips against hers in a tender kiss. "And you shall be forever beautiful, my little fox," he had murmured against her lips.

Clara shook her head, clearing the memory of the stolen moment of pure happiness from her thoughts. That had been about a week ago, back when she hadn't started to get to know her grandmother and her entourage. Now, a week in, her patience was starting to wear thin. She glanced at Warren again, reading the same weariness in his eyes. Perhaps, if they could manage it, another night like the first night of their journey would be in order. It would do them both a world of good again. A few stolen kisses, a few whispered reassurances, their bodies touching. She wanted that. She needed that. And she was sure Warren did, too.

Nothing felt better than being wrapped in Warren's arms, knowing that she was safe, that she was wanted, that she was loved.

Offering Warren a tight-lipped smile, she slowed her pace so that she could walk next to him. Slipping her hand out from underneath her cloak, she reached out for Warren's larger hand. Lacing her fingers through his, he tucked both their hands in his coat pocket, not willing to risk her getting chilled. Not that she was complaining. The move brought her closer, their bodies almost pressed up against each other as they walked, the snow making crunching sounds from under their feet as they continued on.

A loud, unruly cough sounded from behind them. Clara clenched her jaw at the sound. Of course, she thought to herself bitterly. Someone was always keeping an eye on her, and it was usually one of her great uncles, Percil or Arik. On occasion, it was one of the guards, but not often. They kept to themselves for the most part, so she hadn't managed to learn their names. Well, almost. She had learned Friedrich's, but that was only because he was the only one who bothered to try and have a conversation with her. The rest of the time, it was Briggs. The asshole, as she had dubbed him not so affectionately. She'd only known the male for a week and she already loathed him.

Briggs was... different. And not in a good way. She couldn't put a finger on why he made her uneasy. He just did. Perhaps it was the arrogant walk that was almost a swagger. Perhaps it was the sharpness of his gaze and how it seemed to lack any warmth. Perhaps it was the way his lips curled up into either a cruel smirk or an angry sneer. Or maybe, just maybe, it was because her own grandmother seemed to care more about him than she had ever cared about her.

The last reason was probably the most prevalent. It shouldn't bother her that her grandmother adored a shifter she had known for years over a granddaughter she had never bothered to get to know. Being flesh and blood did not mean her grandmother was obligated to treat her with any care. Oftentimes, the bonds formed with others you met were stronger than those forged in blood.

Still, it didn't stop it from hurting.

Taking a deep breath, she stepped closer to Warren so that they were practically pressed against each other. She could feel his warmth radiating through his coat and it felt fantastic. All she wanted to do at the moment was step into his arms and lose herself in his warmth, letting it lull her into a peaceful slumber for the night.

"Who's behind us?" she whisper-asked Warren as whoever it was cleared their throat again. None of them liked seeing her and Warren be physically affectionate with each other, especially her grandmother. Her eyes would twitch whenever she spotted her with Warren. If Clara didn't know better, it was because her grandmother was annoyed that Clara had already found someone.

One plan failed.

Well... Clara took a deep breath, biting her bottom lip as she looked ahead at the few members of their party not behind them, squeezing Warren's hand tighter. Her grandmother was one of them, her head held high as she led the group. Technically, and Clara didn't like admitting this to herself... Technically, her grandmother could break her and Warren up. Or she could try. Both she and Warren would fight like hell if it came down to it, she was sure. But... She winced as she bit down harder on her lips, nearly breaking skin. If they tried to kill Warren, she would capitulate almost instantly. She would do whatever they wanted so long as they didn't kill Warren. She wanted... no, she needed him alive.

She'd find her way back to Warren in the end if it came down to it.

The sound came again, closer this time. Her body tensed as she felt hot breath on the back of her neck. Beside her, she felt Warren tense as well.

"Do you have a problem, Freisinger?" Warren asked, finally answering Clara's question on who was behind them. Briggs Freisinger, though she noticed everyone called him by his surname.

Asshole.

"Clara can walk on her own without your help," Freisinger replied, an icy edge to his voice. "You can let her go now."

"I didn't realize that I was helping her walk. Thank you for enlightening me," Warren replied lightly, sarcasm coloring his voice. "Clara, did you know that I was helping you walk?" He glanced down at Clara, amusement and irritation dancing across his face.

Well, that was one way to deal with the asshole, she thought as she decided to play along with Warren.

"I didn't," Clara replied back in the same tone of voice. "Last I checked, we were simply holding hands. Something most couples do. I guess I was wrong. We aren't holding hands. You are clearly dragging me along. Who knows? I might have stopped walking about fifteen feet ago if I hadn't been holding your hand. Oh, the tragedy."

She was clearly mocking Briggs now, a dangerous thing to do. She had seen him knock out one of the guards for mouthing off to him just this morning, and then Briggs had left him behind as he ordered the party to move out. Her jaw had dropped at that move. How cold could one male be? She wasn't sure, but Briggs was showing her new depths to his coldness on the daily, so really, she should watch her mouth. She would get herself into trouble if she continued. But at this point, she didn't really care. She was fed up.

Her nickname for him was fitting. Not that she'd ever call him an asshole to his face.

Briggs stiffened behind her, an icy fury radiating from him that was palpable through her cloak. She fought back a shudder.

"Let. Go. Now." Briggs gritted out the words, his fists clenching and then releasing repeatedly as he breathed down Clara's neck.

"No."

Shit, she thought to herself, her eyes widening at her audacity. Had she really just told Briggs no? She still didn't know much about him, but the rest of the males in the party seemed to fear and respect him. From what she'd gathered, and what she had seen so far, he was cold and calculating. Dangerous. Who better to be her grandmother's right-hand man?

And then it clicked.

"Kleine, so help me, do not make me repeat myself," he hissed from behind her like an angry goose. A very angry goose. One Clara didn't want to cross. If her grandmother didn't need her, she was sure Freisinger would have snapped her neck already. Not the most comforting thought in the world.

Beside her, Warren tensed further, his body coiling as he readied himself for a fight, his hand squeezing hers back.

"And if I do?" she sassed before she could stop herself, groaning internally at her recklessness. What was she doing? She was asking for trouble at this rate. If he clocked her, it would be her own damn fault. Did male shifters hit females? She knew they protected them at all costs, but she was nothing to Briggs. Not yet. When she took over, sure. They'd be partners in crime, so to speak. But until then...

Instead of answering, a large hand gripped her shoulder and yanked her back, causing her to stumble. Throwing out her hands, she barely caught herself before she landed on her back in the freezing snow, her hands and wrists taking the brunt of the fall. Her palms stung in response and her wrists ached.

"Ow," she whimpered quietly.

"I warned you, Kleine," Briggs whispered vehemently, crouching down beside her, his dark eyes boring into hers. "Until your precious grandmother hands you the reigns, you are beneath me. But by then, you will be beneath me... literally. You will always be beneath me. So learn some respect."

Clara's eyes darkened at his words. "Excuse me? Beneath you? I think not," she laughed bitterly. "Here's the thing, Briggs. Or do you prefer Freisinger? Actually, I don't really care. It doesn't matter to me what you want to be called. I will not be forced to do anything that I don't want to do. My father failed to get me to toe the line. My ex-fiance also failed to get me to toe the line. An acquaintance who wanted to be more failed as well. Mark my words, you will be no different either."

Briggs' eyes narrowed. "And this oaf?" He gestured to Warren before his eyes flashed back to hers, his ire growing.

Clara flashed him a feral smile. "He's smart enough to realize I won't be controlled. So rather than putting me 'beneath' him, as you so eloquently put it, he keeps me at his side as a partner. Maybe you could learn something from him."

Rubbing her throbbing wrists, she reached out for Warren's outstretched hand. Briggs promptly knocked her hand out of the way, blocking her.

"I lead your grandmother's army, Kleine. Until you can match me, which you won't, you will do as I say. Now get up on your own. If you expect to lead the pack, prove that you're strong enough to help yourself."

Clara was seething at this point. Help herself? She clenched her jaw so hard, she felt a muscle pop. Around her, she heard the rest of the party stop. She was sure they had caught on to the drama now unfolding and were watching curiously, interested to see who came out on top in this little spat. She wouldn't give them the satisfaction of seeing her give in to Briggs. She was the one in control here.

"Fine," she huffed, dropping her hands down to her side. "You know what? I changed my mind. I don't want to get up after all. This spot is rather cozy. Why don't you go on with the rest of the group? I'll catch up when I'm good and ready. If I catch up at all."

Warren, watching her in concern, looked at her in shock, his eyes widening. And then he nearly doubled over, trying not to burst out laughing at her attitude, before sitting down next to her, stretching out his long legs with a groan. "You know what, little fox? You're right. This is a good spot. Very cozy. Now all we need is a fire and we're set for the rest of the day. Maybe once they move on, I'll get one started for us and then you can whip up some of those roasted rabbits I like so much."

"Mm, perfect," Clara hummed, nodding her head. "I like that plan." Then she turned her attention to Freisinger again, giving him a winning smile. "Looks like we're set. Your move."

Growling, Freisinger reached out to grab her but stopped himself when his hands were just mere inches from her waist. His eyes narrowed dangerously and a muscle in his jaw worked furiously. Swearing, he dropped his hands, stood up, and turned on his heels.

"May the gods damn you, Kleine. I've never met a more frustrating female and I work with your grandmother," he hissed before calling for the rest of the party to set up for the evening.

Watching Freisinger go, a triumphant look on her face, she leaned into Warren. "And now we have a whole afternoon, evening, and night to ourselves, love."

"That we do, little fox. That we do," Warren chuckled, wrapping an arm around her and drawing her close, their bodies pressing against each other once more.

CHAPTER 13

WARREN

The wind whistled through the trees that were surrounding the makeshift camp that the party had set up after Clara's bout of stubbornness with Freisinger. The flames of the large fire in the middle of the camp flickered back and forth wildly, guttering on occasion. It was proving to be a chore to keep the fire going throughout the afternoon and that worried Warren. If they continued to struggle with it throughout the evening as well, there was a good chance no one would be sleeping that night, not unless they wanted to risk freezing to death.

That could be avoided of course, he thought to himself, his inner voice turning bitter as his gaze swept the party of Reynards. And then his attention turned to his mate. Clara's head was tilted back, sunning her face, her long dark hair loose as it cascaded down her back and onto the snow as she leaned back on her hands. Her eyes were closed, her lips parted slightly as she relaxed, or attempted to. Every so often, he would catch her body tense as she sensed one of her grandmother's party eyeing her.

She was more aware than he had realized. Pride bloomed in his chest at the thought. She was doing so well. After taking her from her father in Springfield, he had worried that he and his family would have to babysit her constantly because she'd been raised human. Her shifter senses had been nearly nonexistent at that point in time. But she had proved to have a voracious appetite for learning. Part of him figured that she didn't want to stick out like a sore thumb, so she was eager to learn as much as possible. Another part of him figured that now that she wasn't being restrained and being forced to act normal, or normal for a human, she was reconnecting with the animal that resided just under her skin, losing herself to the instincts that came with being a shifter.

Either way, it didn't really matter. Clara was thriving and happy. That's all that Warren cared about.

Sitting back down on the ground next to Clara, he tilted his head, his eyes narrowing, giving him a wolfish look as he studied her. His eyes landed on her fingers, noticing that they were turning red. His eyes then traveled up her arms and up to her face. Her lips were just tinged with purple. She was cold. His brows furrowed as he scooted closer, wrapping an arm around her and pulling her against him. He wasn't much warmer, but if they shared body heat, they'd be a smidgeon warmer together.

"Why are you always so warm?" Clara murmured after a minute, nestling closer with a contented sigh, her head tilting to rest against his shoulder.

"Um," Warren hesitated, not sure how to answer that question. And then he smirked as a smart-ass answer came to mind. "I'm hot, remember?"

"I thought you said you were ugly," Clara replied back almost instantly, making his jaw drop. Quickly recovering, he laughed and shook his head. He had known she was a spitfire back when they met, but she hadn't let that side out since he'd taken her as his mate. He was glad to see that it was quickly making a comeback.

"There's my girl," he continued to chuckle. "I forgot how witty you can be, my sassy little fox."

"Yeah," she sighed softly, her eyes opening as she peered up at him from under her lashes. "I haven't felt like myself in a long time. Or it feels like a long time. My life spiraled so far out of my control when you stepped into my life, I was left hanging on for dear life, praying that I wouldn't be swept away. Unfortunately, I ended up being swept away in the tides, multiple times over. But I feel like I've come out of all this stronger. And it's taken a minute to get reacquainted with myself, but I am starting to feel like me again. A new version of me. A version I rather like."

"Mm," he hummed, nodding his head in understanding. Clara wasn't wrong when she said that her life had spiraled out of control. Shifters had come into her town, she'd met Warren because of that influx, she'd been kidnapped, claimed, and became his mate, was kidnapped, tortured, and then left for dead, rescued and led to Reynardsville, was taken advantage of, was attacked while in Reynardsville, was found by Warren once more, taken home, moved to Loch Haven to rebuild their pack, and now she was being taken back to Reynardsville. A weaker female would have given up by now, but not his little fox. She was made of tougher stuff than most and he respected the hell out of her for that.

He would forever respect her, no matter what choices she made now. She'd proved herself worthy of being a shifter and his mate. And if she chose to lead the Reynard pack in her grandmother's stead, she'd already proven to him she could be an empathetic leader with how she'd been helping him with the Loch Haven pack. She'd be one hell of a leader. The Reynards would be lucky to have her.

Clara shivered next to him and scooted even closer, turning her face so she could bury it in his chest instead of resting it against his shoulder. He watched her in amusement, noting how she breathed him in, taking in his scent, and how it relaxed her as she did so. She'd never admit that he smelled good to her, that she could smell how appealing his scent was to her as her mate, but he could see it all over her face. If only she'd been able to smell him before he'd claimed her. To see her face when she smelled his potential as her mate would have been priceless.

Wrapping his arm around her tighter, he leaned down to whisper in her ear. "If we can't keep the fire going, you and I will shift so we can stay warm throughout the night."

Clara pulled back, her brows shooting up in surprise, concern, and apprehension. "They'll be pissed," she whispered back. "I can already see it now. My grandmother will have a tantrum and Freisinger will be forced to act. And, I don't know about you, but I don't want to find out what Freisinger will do if we do shift."

"Let him act out," Warren shrugged, unconcerned as his eyes drifted over to Freisinger and Mrs. Reynard. "You're forgetting that I'm a wolf, baby. I'm at least two to three times their size."

"Yes, but there is only one of you and there are seven of them, not including my grandmother," Clara argued, her concern growing.

"Don't tell me that you're scared of that asshole," he teased, not willing to admit that Clara had a point. He was seriously outnumbered if Freisinger decided to get physical and had backup. The only thing he had going for him at that point was his speed and his stamina. He could make a run for it, but by doing so, he'd leave Clara behind, and that wasn't something he was willing to do. Not now. Not ever.

Clara scowled at him. "I'm not scared of him. Just... wary," she huffed.

Pride bloomed in his chest again. She was being cautious, and rightfully so. She could take care of herself, he reminded himself. He was just along for the ride to help her when she needed it. And because he loved her. And because he couldn't stand to be away from her for too long.

He could come up with a dozen more excuses if he wanted to, but it all boiled down to the fact that he honestly didn't think he could live without his fiery little fox. She had him wrapped around her finger so tight that if she ever let him go, he'd feel like he'd be afloat in a stormy sea without a lifeline.

"Good, be wary, baby," he murmured in her ear as he drew her back to his chest, pulling her onto his lap. "Keep your eyes peeled and your ears open. Don't trust any of them."

The flames guttered again, sending the camp into total darkness. Warren glanced up at the night sky, hoping to see the moon or the stars, but was left disappointed when he was met with storm clouds. Another snowstorm was brewing, and from the way the clouds looked, he was willing to bet that this storm would be just as bad as the last one. This time, however, there weren't any tents for them to hide out in as they waited out the storm. They would get hit and they would get hit hard.

Apprehensively, Warren reached out, feeling for Clara's hand. Finding it, he tugged her close, wrapping his arms around her. Leaning down, he brought his mouth down next to her ear. "I think it's time for us to shift, little fox. I don't think we'll be getting that fire going again tonight."

"What? Why?" Clara asked, her brow creasing with concern as she pulled back just enough to meet his eyes.

Tugging her close again, he pressed a kiss to her forehead, smoothing out the creases there. "What do you smell?" he asked, pressing another kiss to her forehead.

Clara tensed up for a minute and then sighed before nodding. She hated it when he asked her to smell for something. It drove her crazy and usually ended with her ranting about how her sense of smell was nowhere near as good as his, so why was he wasting her time asking her to smell something when he could already clearly smell it? Surprisingly, though, he didn't get an argument this time. Instead, she took a second before breathing in deeply.

"Snow," she whispered after a minute. "I smell snow."

"Good girl," he murmured. "And judging by the clouds overhead, it'll hit soon."

"We don't have shelter." Her voice was starting to grow panicked at the thought of being left out in the storm. "Warren, we won't survive a storm. We've got nothing. What are..."

Warren silenced her by cupping both of her cheeks and tilting her face up to look at him. Raising his brows at her, he watched her splutter for a moment before falling silent, a scowl on her lips, but the worry was evident in her eyes.

"Little fox, are we humans?" he asked quietly.

"No," she said, confused. "But what's that got... Oh. Ohhh. That's why... I get it now." Her eyes lit up as she realized why he had suggested shifting.

"Follow me into the trees," he murmured, his voice low so the others wouldn't hear. "We'll sit there and then hunker down there. The trees should block some of the wind. Or so I'm hoping. But it's better than nothing."

Clara bit her lip, glancing over her shoulder at her grandmother. Then her eyes drifted over to Briggs and her great uncles. They were all huddled together, discussing something seemingly important and not paying them any attention. The guards were stationed around them, surveying the landscape, while one worked on the fire, his efforts futile.

"They'll probably do something similar," Warren reassured her, his tone becoming urgent as the wind started to pick up. He laced his fingers with hers again and tugged her toward the trees impatiently.

Upon reaching the trees, he pushed her behind the largest one he could find and started helping her out of her dress. Stuffing her clothes into a burrow at the base of the tree, he watched as she shifted into her fox form, her russet fur blowing in the wind. Stripping his own clothes off next, he stuffed them into the burrow beside hers before placing their packs over the burrow's mouth to protect their clothes and other belongings. Then he, too, shifted.

Where he had stood, a large wolf stood in his place. Giving Clara a wolfish grin, he nudged her toward the tree. Taking the hint, she dropped down onto her belly, huddling against the tree. Once she was situated, Warren dropped down next to her, curling his body around hers, shielding her from the worst of it. Nuzzling his face against hers, he huffed and then closed his eyes, his ears twitching as he listened to the wind pick up even more.

And then the snow started to fall.

Cries and shouts of surprise sounded from the makeshift camp. Warren could hear them scrambling for cover. City shifters, he thought to himself as he opened his eyes and glanced down at Clara. Her eyes were closed and her breathing even, as if she was falling asleep. Good. She needed it. And he'd be right by her, keeping her safe.

The next morning, covered in snow, Warren stood and shook the snow out of his coat. Clara, noticing that he'd moved, cracked her eyes and stretched before also shaking the snow out of her fur. Warren watched her as she moved, admiring how graceful her movements were, before peeking around the corner of the tree. He couldn't see any of their party, meaning that they'd either done something similar to him and Clara, or they were buried under the snow, dead. He hoped for the latter.

Clara, seeing where he was looking, also peered around the tree. As soon as her nose popped into view, an angry yip sounded. Eyes widening, Clara and Warren's heads snapped in the direction of the yip to see a large fox bristling as it stalked into the small clearing, drawing nearer. And then the fox shifted, disappearing from view. In its place stood a very naked Freisinger.

"Kleine, where the hell did you disappear to before the snowstorm? You gave your grandmother a heart attack," he snarled as he marched over.

In a blink of an eye, Clara shifted and marched out to meet him, jabbing her finger into his bare chest, startling him. Warren bit back a laugh at the sight of the two naked shifters: one very taken aback male and one irritated female who stood about a head shorter than the male.

"I did what I had to, no thanks to you. This isn't the first snowstorm I've had to survive in these mountains without shelter. So shut the hell up and let me do my thing," she snarled, her voice echoing through the small clearing.

Warren's eyes widened, trying to think back to when Clara would have had to survive in a snowstorm without shelter, and then grimaced as he was reminded of her time traveling to Reynardsville after being left for dead by General Claery. She'd survived worse alone and it seemed that she was determined to let Freisinger know that.

Freisinger took a step back, his muscles flexing as he moved, his eyes narrowing as he appraised her. His eyes swept over her naked body, lighting up briefly in appreciation before they narrowed in irritation. He leaned down toward her and sneered. "There's no way you could have survived a snowstorm on your own before. You're too soft."

Clara growled. Before Warren could stop her, her fist connected with Freisinger's jaw, sending him stumbling back. And it seemed she wasn't done yet. Stalking after him, she brought her fist back, readying it for another strike.

Sprinting over, now in his human form, Warren scooped her up before she could let her fist fly again. "Not now, little fox. He's not worth it," he crooned in her ear as he carried her back to the tree to grab their bags and their clothes while Clara shrieked angrily, pounding on his chest with her little fists. "Let's get you dressed and then something to eat. You're always a little cranky when you're hungry."

Clara, fuming, snarled over his shoulder, turning her attention to Freisinger instead because she wasn't actually upset with him. Snarling again, she started spewing profanities at Freisinger and her grandmother's party, not caring who heard or if they took offense or not.

Warren bit back another laugh. His little spitfire.

But, even though she was still snarling and spitting at the others, she wasn't fighting Warren. Taking that as a good sign, he set her down, watching her warily to see if she'd take off after Freisinger again. When she didn't, he bent down and dug their things out, handing Clara her clothes.

"You'll get your chance to put him in his place later, baby," Warren murmured as he helped her button her dress. "Patience. Your time will come."

CHAPTER 14

RONAN

Silence. Complete and utter silence.

As Ronan shifted on his perch, a large boulder about five hundred meters from his pack's camp outside the back wall of Reynardsville, his green eyes scanned the area, looking for anything unusual. Not that he would see anything. They'd been out behind the city for over a week now and they hadn't spotted a damn thing. No enemy soldiers, no shifters trying to flee the city and head for the mountains behind them, no city officials coming to check on them. Hell, Ronan was pretty sure they hadn't even seen an animal. He couldn't remember the last time he had seen a rabbit hopping across the clearing between the city and the forest.

It was like the animals knew that something bad was coming and they were making a run for it themselves if they weren't hunkering down somewhere to weather out the storm. Ronan half wanted to make like the animals and disappear. But that wasn't to be his fate. He had a duty to his people. He would give everything at this point to make sure that they were safe. It wasn't like he had anything else to live for at this point, so why not?

But still, it almost felt like they had been forgotten, though Ronan knew that wasn't the case. Zeke went back into the city every other afternoon and came back out with formal letters from the city council. News. Orders.

Requests. Training requirements. And of course, Zeke never forgot needed supplies or requests from the pack.

A frown tugged at his lips as he squinted, scanning the quiet area again, the sunlight bouncing off the sparkling snow, blinding him, his mind drifting to his family back in Everridge. Were they still there or had they fled north to the mountains and the unknown beyond the mountains? Or had they started heading west to Reynardsville?

Sniffing, swiping his nose with the back of his jacket sleeve, he glanced over at the city, the many windows winking back at him in the sunlight. He hoped that his family had headed north, but he had a sinking feeling in the pit of his stomach that Xander and Mirabel had already started heading west. He prayed that they didn't go to Springfield, opting for Reynardsville instead. If they went to Springfield… He didn't finish the thought, shaking his head, trying to shake the feeling of dread that had started to settle over him.

Xander was smarter than that. If anyone could read a situation and get themselves out of it, it was his twin. There was a reason Xander had been their father's pride and joy and not Ronan. Xander could walk into a fight and walk away without a scratch, clearly the victor of the little spat. And he was good with his words. Or maybe it was his charming smile. Or the earnest look in his eyes. Or perhaps it was just how intimidating his brother looked compared to Ronan. If he stepped in and spoke a few words, whatever the issue was, it was usually resolved in minutes.

If Xander and Mira had left already, Xander would keep them safe. He would get them up to Reynardsville. He would know that Springfield was no longer safe.

Ronan would just keep repeating that to himself until he actually believed it. He had to believe it. For his own sanity.

Looking up at the sky, he let out a deep breath. "If the gods are listening, please make sure my siblings don't do something incredibly stupid," he said under his breath. There was no way that Mira, as tough as she was, would survive the Claerys if they got their hands on her. Xander would be fine, as always. But Mira... Sweet, sweet Mira... He shook his head. If anyone laid a hand on her, he hoped that she would have the foresight to shift into her animal, a bear, and take the head off whoever had touched her. And if she didn't, he prayed that Xander would shift into his animal, a mountain lion, and do it for Mira.

Ronan would. He'd already killed for Mira once and he'd do it again in a heartbeat, no matter how much it messed with his conscious. This was war, after all. That meant kill or be killed, and he'd be damned if he let his family die.

Dropping his gaze from the sky where he was watching clouds scuttle across the blue expanse, he peered over at the Romulus pack's camp. He could just make out a few of his pack members moving about. Probably those who had been awake all night, just getting up and going, ready to relieve those who had taken the day shift so they could keep watch while everyone slept once more.

A hulking figure emerged from Ronan's shared tent seconds later, his black shirt straining across his massive back and upper arms. A grin cracked across Ronan's face as he watched his best friend, Maddox, stretch. If he was there with Maddox right now, he was sure that he would hear Maddox groan as his joints and back popped. That would be followed by a few choice swear words and then the demand for coffee, black. Just like his soul, or so he claimed.

Ronan glanced up at the sky again, the sun slowly starting to sink lower in the sky. A few more hours and Maddox would make his way over to Ronan, geared up and ready to take up Ronan's post for the night. Ronan shifted again, his own gear starting to feel heavy, making him uncomfortable. Snorting derisively, he untied the thick leather vest that covered his chest and tossed it down onto the snow-covered ground, the daggers sheathed inside the vest rattling. Sighing in relief, Ronan slipped off the boulder and stretched himself.

Everything ached. His back ached from standing or sitting on a cold boulder all day. His shoulders ached from the weight of his gear. His feet hurt from the boots and the cold he stood in all day.

He couldn't remember a day he hadn't hurt. Not since Springfield, anyway, and that had been months ago.

Glancing down at the vest on the ground, he groaned as he bent down and picked it up, brushed the snow off the leather, and placed it on the boulder where he'd been sitting. He didn't understand why they needed to be as armed as they were when they were stationed behind the city. It was just them, the back wall, and the mountains. And it was boring as hell.

Rubbing the back of his neck, he turned to face the mountains, eyeing them warily. Being stationed here, it almost felt like they weren't even doing anything, like they'd been sidelined. No one was going to make their way around the city to try and breach the back gate. It was impossible, or as close to impossible as one could get. For one, there was nowhere for an army to hide as they tried to sneak around the city. Everyone would see them, which would give the shifters inside the city and the other packs plenty of time to react, cutting the enemy off. For two, if they did try to come around from the back without being seen, that meant they'd have to go through the unforgiving mountains. Ronan wasn't sure how prepared the king's forces were, but he was pretty damn sure that they wouldn't be stupid enough to try and make their way through the mountains in the winter. That was asking for trouble. They'd lose half their troops to either the weather or the hungry predators looking for their next meal. It was only a move the king would make if he was getting desperate and the point of desperation hadn't been reached yet. The war was only starting after all.

Sitting back down on the boulder, using his vest as a cushion, protecting his rear from the cold stone, he sighed, rolling his neck, bored. The downside of having this position, he thought to himself, is that he had way too much time to think. Thinking was dangerous, particularly with his mental state. It led him down the path of different what-if scenarios and they were slowly driving him insane, pushing him to the brink of insanity.

He would snap soon if he wasn't careful. He just hoped it wasn't when Clara finally showed up.

Speaking of Clara, they'd finally received word that she was officially coming, that Mrs. Reynard and Briggs Freisinger had been successful in retrieving her from Warren and his pack. Ronan, not sure how to feel about that, had been rather quiet since his last outburst. He had meant what he had said earlier, that he would stay in the back as far away from Clara as possible when she showed up for training if that was still the plan. He didn't need to make a fool of himself and he sure as hell didn't want to end up with another dagger in his back, even if he deserved it.

"Why our pack?" he asked the silence around him, even though he knew the answer already. Any pack that wasn't directly on the front line, like the Romulus pack, would be helping train Clara. It was something Freisinger had come up with, wanting Clara to learn as many different fighting styles as possible so that when the war finally reached them, she'd be able to defend herself. An ingenious plan but one Ronan still hated, nevertheless. Clara shouldn't have to fight. She should be kept comfortably in a cozy house where she wouldn't have to worry about anything. Hell, he could have given her that.

But this was war.

Comfort went out the window.

Hell, everything that wasn't necessary went out the window. They didn't have the luxury of having luxuries at the moment. Anything that could be used to aid the war effort went to that. If fleeing, anything that wasn't necessary, anything that was too heavy, anything that was just not needed, was left behind for those that stayed to scavenge.

Ronan took a deep breath, running a hand down his face. If he'd learned one thing since she'd rejected him on the busy street of Reynardsville that fateful morning, leaving him crushed, it was that Clara was a Reynard through and through. She was never his to claim in the first place. She wasn't anyone's to claim, for that matter. She wasn't even allowed to make her own decisions. Her life had been planned out for her the moment her grandmother realized that she was still alive.

If only he'd found that out before he'd fallen head over heels in love with her all those months ago in Springfield.

Gods, life sucked. And love was worse. If he never fell in love again, it would be too soon.

"Just make it through the war," he muttered to himself. "After that, we can decide what we want to do."

But the more he thought about what he wanted to do, the more he drew a blank. What did he want besides the one female he couldn't have? Everything that he had envisioned at one point in time no longer felt right. It didn't give him that warm, cozy feeling that he had grown to love, to seek, to want. Instead, everything was cold, dark, and bleak.

Some future.

Letting out a deep sigh, he stood back up and slipped his vest back on, not wanting to be caught without it before returning to his post, surveying his surroundings until it was time to switch out with Maddox.

CHAPTER 15

MATTY

The small cabin was cold. Frosty, even. Matty's breaths came out in puffs in front of his face as he cracked his eyes, shivering slightly in the large but soft bed. Beside him, Kitty huddled up next to him for warmth, her body pressed as close to his as she could manage, the heavy quilt tucked under her chin, still fast asleep. Gazing down at her, he felt a rush of affection, especially after how she'd been handling his parents, but that was it. He didn't love her, not yet anyway, nor was he sure he'd ever really love her. A sad fact, but the truth, nonetheless.

Letting out a deep breath, trying to remain as quiet as possible, he stared up at the slats in the dark ceiling. They'd been whitewashed when his mom had tried to prepare the cabin for when he brought Clara back as his bride. In fact, he remembered helping his mom. They'd talked the whole time they'd painted, Matty spilling his hopes and dreams.

"I can't wait for Clara to see it," he'd said to his mom, his voice loud and exuberant as he'd practically bounded around the room. "She'll love it. Especially next to the window. There's so much light there. I can just picture her sitting in a rocking chair, knitting, while waiting for me to come home for dinner."

His mom had laughed, nodding her head in agreement. For as independent as Clara tried to make herself out to be, she was surprisingly domestic when she got the chance. Or rather, she was crafty as his mom liked to say. Clara got satisfaction out of creating something beautiful and he got satisfaction out of seeing her show it off with pride.

He slammed his eyes closed at the memory, a lump rising in his throat. It should have been Clara huddled up next to him instead of Kitty. He wanted it to be Clara huddled up next to him. He had promised years and years ago that he would marry her one day, that he would love her unconditionally. But, at his dad's request, he had tossed her aside because of her filthy half-breed blood. Not that her being half-breed mattered to him.

He opened his eyes again, breathing heavily from the intense emotions coursing through him. Matty wasn't sure if it was his love for the girl he'd never see again or if it was because of the immense guilt he felt for abandoning her to die, but it felt like he would never be properly happy again. He swallowed thickly, feeling a bit sick to his stomach now.

Was she even still alive?

It was a question he'd asked himself a thousand times and would continue to ask himself until he got the answer to that question. If she was dead... The muscles in his body twitched anxiously as if he was ready to hop out of bed and go hunt Clara down. If she was dead, he wasn't sure he could live with himself. If she was dead, it was his own damn fault. Perhaps that was why he was adamant about her surviving, thriving somewhere to the northwest. At least in his head, she was thriving somewhere. If only that were true, perhaps he wouldn't continue to beat himself up for what he had done.

Matty shivered again as his eyes adjusted to the dark enough for him to make out the dim light filtering in around the heavy curtains that covered the window. It was morning, although fairly early. He hadn't heard one of this mom's roosters yet, so if he had to hazard a guess, he wagered it was probably a little before seven.

And gods, was it cold.

If it was just him, he would have just curled up further under the covers and suffered in silence until it was time to get up. He'd survived worse. He also didn't feel like he deserved to be warm and comfortable when he felt this guilty. But... he glanced over at Kitty. He wasn't alone and he'd be damned if he let her freeze. Her pampered ass wasn't built to handle this kind of weather.

Besides, it wasn't like warming the house up wasn't an easy fix. All he had to do would be to stoke the fire or add some more wood. Maybe both. It would take him five minutes or less, and once he got that done, he could come sprinting back into bed to warm his frozen feet.

Matty huffed as he started to sit up, mentally psyching himself up to get out of bed. Shivering more now that the quilt fell down his chest, pooling in his lap, leaving his upper body bare, he started having second thoughts about getting out of bed. It wasn't wor-... He cut himself off. Yes, it was. The warmth would be glorious. Five minutes, he reminded himself, starting to slip his legs over the side of the bed. But then, a slender arm wrapped around his waist, tugging him back.

"Don't go," a sleepy voice mumbled.

"I need to check the fire, Kitty," Matty said, his voice emotionless even though he was still dealing with a storm of emotions rattling through him. She didn't need to know what he was thinking about currently. It would only hurt her and it wasn't her fault he was feeling this way. It wouldn't be fair of him to take it out on her. The gods knew he took his temper out on her more often than he cared to admit. But, he reminded himself, he hadn't stooped to his dad's levels yet. He hadn't hit Kitty and never would.

He just... fucked her. Roughly. Until she cried because he'd left her a wet shivering mess. Either way, they both seemed to enjoy it and she hadn't asked him to stop yet, so he had no plans on discontinuing that form of punishment anytime soon.

"But if you get out of bed, the bed will get cold," Kitty protested, her grip on him tightening.

"Five minutes," he reassured her. "I'll only be five minutes. The bed won't get that cold that fast."

"Matty," she whined, her hand drifting lower.

Matty caught her hand before it settled in his lap. So she wanted to play dirty, did she? He scowled at her and then shook his head as she pouted at being caught.

"Five minutes and then I'll come warm you back up," he promised, untangling himself and slipping out of bed before she could stop him.

Stepping out of the room, wincing at how cold the floor was against his bare feet and ignoring Kitty's continued protests from the bed, he scanned the main room, noting the dying fire. As he had expected. Stalking over, he crouched down in front of the glowing embers and stoked it with one of the pokers before adding a few small pieces of wood. They quickly caught fire and a wave of heat washed over him. After waiting a few more minutes, he then added a couple larger pieces of wood to make sure the fire continued for a few more hours.

Standing back up, he rubbed his hands over his arms, shivering again. He didn't want to leave his spot in front of the fire, but he had promised Kitty to warm her back up. A slight chuckle left him at the prospect. His body was icy at this point and if he got on top of her, he would bet that month's salary that she would squeal and smack his chest.

He couldn't wait.

Hurrying back into the bedroom, he quickly climbed back into bed and wrapped his arms around Kitty, pressing a hungry kiss to her neck, just below her ear. Kitty, not expecting his body to be so cold, let out a weird combination of a moan and a shriek, causing Matty to erupt into laughter.

"Sorry, princess. It was too good of an opportunity to pass up," he chuckled into her ear before pressing another kiss to her neck, teasing another moan from her lips.

"You said you'd warm me up," she complained between kisses.

"I am," Matty replied, his hand snaking between her thighs, his thumb brushing over her clit, making her gasp. "And it looks like you are quite warm."

Kitty squirmed as he continued to tease her with his fingers, slipping two inside her as his thumb continued to circle and rub. Her breath became heavier, more moans slipping free.

"Matty," she murmured, her hips bucking against his hand involuntarily. "This wasn't what I had in mind when you promised to warm me back up."

"Do you want me to stop?" Matty whispered in her ear, his voice husky.

"I..." she hesitated, still squirming. "No. Don't stop. Please don't stop."

"Then I won't," he promised, removing his hand.

"You... I..." she stammered in protest, her eyes widening at his sudden absence.

"Patience," he laughed under his breath as he shifted over her, positioning himself at her entrance. "I told you I wouldn't stop. I meant it. But you look so much better coming all over my cock than my fingers."

Kitty nodded quickly in agreement, her movements short and choppy. As he pushed inside, stretching her, her eyes rolled back with a loud moan. "Gods..."

"That's a good girl," Matty murmured, his lips brushing over her fore-head as he pressed in further. "If it starts to hurt, just let me know, princess."

Matty stood in front of his dad, General Claery, four hours later, his hands tucked behind his back respectfully. In his dad's office, General Claery wasn't his dad anymore. He was Matty's superior. A position that demanded respect, something Matty wished he didn't have to give his dad period. He still hadn't forgiven his dad for stabbing him earlier that year and then forcing him to go to the capital with him before he'd been healed. He had forgiven his dad for forcing him into the king's army, however. He had met quite a few amazing people because of that so far, a couple of them becoming close friends. And now, because of his training, he could defend himself and his loved ones better. He wouldn't be letting his dad get one up on him again.

The next time his dad pulled a knife on him, Matty would be damned if he let it anywhere near his stomach again. No, the next time his dad pulled a knife on him, he would be shoving said knife into his dad's stomach instead, he thought viciously. Give him a taste of his own medicine. See how he liked it. And maybe, just maybe, he'd let his dad bleed out. It wasn't like he was worth saving. Not anymore.

Gods, that was dark, he thought to himself, blinking in surprise. Since when had he decided his own dad was worth killing? He hid his own gri-mace, not liking the answer to his own question which was multiple times.

It was just becoming more... frequent, more violent. And, he decided, he would do it. Just... when?

"Lieutenant Claery," General Claery barked, his voice laced with irritation. "Are you even paying attention?"

"Sorry, sir," Matty murmured, inclining his head respectfully. "My mind was elsewhere. I apologize. You were saying?"

General Claery narrowed his eyes on Matty, his lips curling down into a frown. "I was saying that you will be leading putting together Springfield's defense system. I have a plan that I would like you to put into effect, but you are free to make changes as you see fit. I have it all here in writing if you'd like to see the plans."

Matty held out his hands for the paperwork, taking it and rifling through them, his eyes scanning the plans. When done, he nodded and looked up at his dad.

"You want my men to build a wall around the city?" he asked, trying his best to hide his incredulity. Was his dad daft? How were you supposed to put a wall around a farming town pretending to be a city? Springfield was too widespread for that.

"Yes, around the main portion of the city," General Claery confirmed with a simple nod of his head.

"And what of the residents outside the main portion? The farmers?" Matty asked, arching a brow.

"They are free to stay where they are at. As of right now, there is no threat to Springfield. However, if a threat arises, hopefully by that time, we shall have the wall built as well as some barracks. We can evacuate them and place them in the barracks temporarily," General Claery clarified, picking up a piece of paper he had been reading and frowning at it. Then, shaking his head, he crumpled the piece of paper and tossed it into the bin next to his desk. "Moronic, he is. Captain Morray needs to get his head out of his ass, or he'll get himself and his men killed."

"Captain Morray?" Matty asked, his voice faint.

General Claery looked up at Matty, a startled expression on his face as if he had forgotten that Matty was there for a second. Either that or he wasn't used to being questioned by someone. It had been a long time since someone under him had asked him questions about his business.

"Captain Morray is the leader of the forces going straight north from the capital. They are set to wipe out the shifter settlements that they come across as they make their way to the mountains along our border with Beris," General Claery explained with a soft sigh. "We are also hoping to cut off the shifters trying to flee into Beris. Dirty shifter lovers, the Berians."

"The Berians accept the shifters?" Matty blinked in surprise. He had never heard that. In fact, now that he thought about it, he didn't know much about the neighboring kingdom at all. Beris was... a mystery. Well, no, that wasn't correct. He knew that Kitty had been set to marry one of the princes from Beris before he came into the picture to be used as a pawn by both his dad and the king.

"Unfortunately," General Claery growled. He leaned back in his seat and eyed Matty critically as if trying to decide whether he should keep talking or not. Finally, letting out a deep breath, he sighed. "The plan is to declare war on Beris once we rid Brunholl of all shifters. We're running out of room in the southeast and our ports are too crowded. If we can conquer Beris, that opens up more ports to bring in more goods from other countries. Brunholl would become one of the wealthier kingdoms in all of Dorroth. Do you have any idea how good that would be for us?"

Matty's stomach churned at the thought of waging war on Beris. The war against the shifters was set to be bloody, more on the shifter's side than the human side. But if they went up against Beris. He swallowed thickly. It would be a blood bath.

"I have an idea, sir," Matty managed to get out as he tried to hide how appalled at the idea he was.

"Good." General Claery nodded, dismissing him with a wave of his hand. As Matty turned on his heel with military precision, General Claery added one last thing. "Your mom has said that your wife, the princess, is coming along in her lessons. So well in fact, that your mom would like your wife to cook us supper this Sunday. Do let that cute little thing of yours know what's expected. We'll see you then."

Matty's heart sank into his stomach and bit back a groan as he hurried from his dad's office.

Great, just one more thing to worry about.

CHAPTER 16

CLARA

"Two more days," Clara sighed, dropping to the ground next to Warren. But she didn't stop there. No, instead, she flung herself back the rest of the way until she was lying in the snow, staring up at the purple-pink sky as the sun slowly descended below the horizon.

"Two more days," Warren parroted, nodding his head in agreement before running a hand down his face, and letting out a low groan. He then looked down at Clara lying in the snow, a look of amusement flitting across his face. "You'll freeze doing that."

Clara looked up at him, her eyes flicking over his face before meeting his eyes. He wasn't wrong. The snow was cold. Freezing. She could feel it soaking through her clothes as it melted underneath her. But she wasn't in the mood to care. Or admit that she was wrong.

She was miserable.

Tired.

Fed up.

She just wanted to go home.

"So?" Clara replied stubbornly. "Better than dealing with this lot. Less painful."

Warren fought back a snort of amusement, failing miserably as a low chuckle erupted from the back of his throat. Clara raised an eyebrow at him in question, confused. Why was he laughing? There was nothing to laugh at. And then it hit her. Here she was, the future leader of the Reynard pack, the mate of a pack leader, acting like a little girl by throwing herself in the snow as if she were having a tantrum. She erupted into giggles herself at the realization. She was being ridiculous, and she knew it. But she had to admit, there was a shred of truth to her words. The icy snow was less painful than her grandmother and her entourage.

Since punching Freisinger in the face after the snowstorm a few days ago, her grandmother's party had been rather cold to both her and Warren, which was understandable. But Freisinger... Clara shuddered. If looks could kill, both she and Warren would be dead right now. She just knew he was itching to get his hands on her to make her pay for getting one up on him.

She chuckled to herself, pleased. She had been able to land a punch on the great Briggs Freisinger. Not something many shifters could brag about. All the ones that had done so were probably six feet under.

"Think we'll be able to escape the frigid bunch once we get to Reynardsville?" Clara asked Warren in a whisper so as to not be overheard.

"Doubtful, but we can try," Warren whispered back before eyeing the rest of the group as he crouched down beside her, brushing a few strands of hair out of her face.

The guards were huddled together, trying to figure out where each of them should stand to ensure the safety of everyone present. Clara's great-uncles and grandmother were sitting down, their sleeping mats already unrolled and cushioning the ground for them, talking quietly amongst themselves about something Clara was sure she wouldn't care about. Freisinger, on the other hand, was the only one not talking to someone. Instead, he was alone, working to get a fire going.

Clara smirked as she rolled over and propped herself up on her elbows so that she could survey the scene with Warren, pleased that she'd caused so much chaos and discord already. Perhaps if she caused enough mischief, they'd give up on their harebrained scheme of making her the leader of the Reynard Pack and send her home. Or so she hoped.

Her eyes landed on Freisinger after a moment, watching as he crouched down in front of a pile of wood arranged into a cone. Optimal positioning for starting a fire, she thought as noticed the dry kindling stuffed into the middle of the cone. Her eyes then drifted over to her great uncles, her brows knitting together. Of course they were just sitting on their asses. Why would they ever help? Not that she cared if they did. Freisinger was more than capable of doing the work alone. In fact, she was glad he was, the smug bastard. But still... It didn't sit right with her that there were other males around who were capable of helping, and yet, they did nothing at all.

Clara glanced at Warren and was about to nudge him to go help when she thought better of it. If she got Warren to help with the menial tasks, there was a good chance that her grandmother and so-called family would take advantage of his generosity, something she was hoping to avoid. Warren was a leader in his own right. He didn't need to be reduced down to the status of a servant for them.

Taking a deep breath, she reached out and placed her hand on his thigh. "When we get to Reynardsville, rather than staying with my family, I think we should find a place to rent. I don't care if it's a room at an inn or an apartment. I don't want to be around them more than I have to," she said quickly, half afraid that her idea would be stupid and get shut down before she got all the words out. But that was stupid. Warren always listened to her. Or, at least, he tried. She couldn't fault him too much when his mind was preoccupied with pack business.

"I think that would be a wise decision," Warren said slowly, nodding his head in agreement, his dark eyes surveying her face. "I don't quite trust your family, to be honest. Space will do us all good."

Clara felt her body relax at his words, relieved. Pushing off the ground, she maneuvered herself into a seated position close to Warren, resting her head on his broad shoulder.

"I miss home," she murmured quietly, a moment of vulnerability slipping through. She didn't dare say it louder, knowing that if Freisinger or her grandmother caught her saying something like that, there would be literal hell to pay.

"I miss it, too, little fox," Warren sighed, reaching up to tug on the end of her braid affectionately. "I miss our tent. I miss snuggling up together in the furs. I miss waking you up with a good romp before heading out to take care of the pack for the day. I miss coming home to see you there waiting for me, eager to tell me all about your day. I miss having you fall asleep in my arms, your soft breathing soothing me to sleep. And now... Now, all I get is you on your sleeping mat a foot or so away. I can't touch you for more than a few minutes. Kissing you is, well, off-limits. If it weren't for your grandmother's pack quite literally falling apart, I would say fuck this, let's go home."

"I'm tempted to say fuck this anyway," Clara huffed in irritation, her fingers tracing patterns into the snow. "I didn't sign up for this. Not one bit."

"I know, baby, but..."

Warren was cut off by Freisinger stalking over and threading his fingers through Clara's hair. With a forceful yank, he tugged Clara to her feet and away from Warren.

"Ouch! Why, you motherfucker! Let. Go. Of. Me!" Clara screamed in agony and frustration, her eyes blazing as her temper flared. Her scalp burned as he tugged her again, yanking her farther away from Warren. She tried to twist so she could reach him, wanting to do some damage. She wanted to hit, to scratch, to tear. Something. Anything.

"I warned you, Kleine. I told you not to touch him. And I told you that you would hate me in the end, that I wouldn't hurt you much. This could have waited, but you, my precious little darling, had to speed my plans up for you the moment you socked me in the face," Freisinger hissed in her ear as his grip shifted so he was holding her hair closer to the roots, making it harder for Clara to move, not paying any mind to her protestations.

Meanwhile, Warren, now livid that Briggs had laid a hand on Clara, jumped to his feet. He was about to follow Clara and Briggs when two sets of hands grabbed his forearms, stopping him. Eyes flashing, Warren glared at Clara's two great uncles.

"Let me go after them," he hissed. "He dared lay a hand on *my* mate. He will pay for that."

Clara's eyes flashed over to Warren, watching Warren get restrained by her great-uncles. Her temper flared even further and she lashed out at Freisinger again. Or she tried to. Her arms fell short and she shrieked in frustration. With a snarl, Freisinger dragged her body against his and slapped a hand over her mouth, silencing her.

"Wolf," Arik said, his eyes darting over to Freisinger for a moment, his eyes hard as glared at Freisinger before softening when he looked back at Warren. His tone was gentle but firm, trying to reassure Warren. "He is not here to hurt her. We would not allow such a thing. This is to teach her. To train her. War is upon us, and she is set to take over one of the largest packs in the northwest during that war. She has to learn to defend herself instead of relying on you to protect her. You have to realize that you won't always be there for her when she steps into this new role. There will be meetings and inspections that you will not be privy to, and while she will have guards, it would be foolish of her and us to expect them to take care of every single threat at all times. It's just not possible. She has to learn."

Both Clara and Warren froze at Arik's words, both contemplating what he had said. Freisinger, noticing that Clara was no longer fighting him, took advantage of the situation, and dragged her further away with little resistance, her eyes still trained on her great uncle as she stumbled a bit, Freisinger the only thing keeping her upright.

Learn how to defend herself instead of relying on Warren to protect her. The words echoed through her brain, stunning her. Of course, she knew that she wouldn't be able to rely on Warren completely. That was a no-brainer. After being taken by General Claery, being taken advantage of by Ronan, and being attacked in Reynardsville, she had already come to that conclusion. She had been planning on asking Warren and his family to teach her how to fight once the snow melted up in their mountain home.

Apparently, life had other plans.

Freisinger stopped pulling her back after a few minutes, stopping them when they were about fifty feet away from the campfire that he had started. Releasing her, he shoved her off him and stepped back, putting space between them.

"Where's that fire I saw a few minutes ago?" he taunted, his blue eyes hard and as icy as the snow around them.

"Stunned silent," she replied without missing a beat. "You do know that I'm not helpless, right? I can and will protect myself when needed. I just didn't expect my own family and their guards to turn on me."

"Rule number one," Freisinger sighed wearily, shaking his head in disbelief. "Don't trust anyone. Not me. Not your grandmother. Not even your *mate.*" The last word was spat, the contempt obvious in his voice. "Being a leader is a lonely position. Get used to it."

"I take it that means you're lonely as well then," she quipped, her eyes meeting Freisinger's.

Freisinger froze, but only for a moment, Clara's statement catching him off guard. "Yes," he grunted. "But that's none of your concern."

"It is," she shot back. "If what you said the other day is true, you'll be trying to place your claim over Warren's, taking me for yourself. Last I checked, mates should rely on each other."

Clara shifted into a fighting stance that she had picked up when watching the men fight in her pa's bar. It wasn't the greatest stance in the world now that she hadn't brawled herself in a while, but it would do in a pinch. Freisinger's brows shot up in surprise, stunned once more.

"I'm going to ignore that last statement," Freisinger muttered as he circled her. "There's no use in talking about it. We both know how this will play out already. I suggest you don't fight it." He kicked at her right foot, pushing it farther out, steadying her further. Then he reached out and placed a rough hand on her shoulder, pulling it back a hair. "Not bad. There's definitely room for improvement. Where'd you learn this?"

Clara glanced up at him in surprise, not expecting something not rude or hostile to come out of his mouth. Coming from him, it was practically a compliment. She'd take it.

"I used to tend my pa's bar." Clara felt her muscles tighten as if preparing for a fight as Freisinger continued to circle her, which was likely.

"Your pa owned a bar and let you run it?" Freisinger asked, his voice incredulous as he paused yet again, seemingly stunned by everything that was coming out of Clara's mouth that evening. "Was he insane? You don't let females run businesses... Not unless it's something she can do out of her own kitchen, but even then..." He shook his head, still stunned. And then he furrowed his brows. "What does learning how to fight have to do with running a bar?"

"I had to break up bar fights," Clara said as if that were the most obvious thing in the world. "You pick up a thing or two when you step between two brawling men. Throwing a punch is one of them."

"May the gods have mercy," Freisinger muttered under his breath. "We have a lot to cover then. You'll have to unlearn half of what you think you know just so I can teach you the proper way to fight. The packs that will be taking you in for a fortnight at a time to teach you their fighting styles will eat you alive if you don't know the basics at the very minimum."

"Then teach me," Clara replied bluntly. "I may not like you at all, but I can tolerate you long enough to learn."

Freisinger snorted. "I'm warning you again. You'll hate me in the end."

"Already do, asshole. Already do."

CHAPTER 17

WARREN

Leaning back against a thick pine tree, his arms crossed over his broad chest, Warren watched Freisinger knock Clara down over and over again. A muscle in his jaw twitched in irritation as he shifted his weight, moving from one foot to the other as he fought the urge to go over there and knock Freisinger on his ass for daring to lay a hand on Clara. But he stopped himself, reminding himself that Clara needed this. She needed to be able to defend herself.

Closing his eyes, Warren took a deep, steadying breath. If they were back in Loch Haven and Clara wanted to learn how to fight, Warren would have taught her, of that he had no doubt in his mind. However, he would have been gentle with her. She was tiny, coming up to the middle of his chest when they stood next to each other. He could snap her in half if he wasn't careful, something he was all too aware of, particularly when he lay with her at night, his body pushing into hers.

Opening his eyes, he instantly focused on Freisinger once more. Freisinger was tall, but not nearly as tall as Warren. Still, Clara only came up to his shoulders, her slender frame looking delicate and fragile compared to Freisinger's well-built, muscular frame. One wrong move and he could accidentally snap her neck and Warren had a sinking feeling in the pit of his stomach that Freisinger knew that but didn't care. If Clara got hurt, so what? One more reason why she shouldn't take over in his eyes.

He unfolded his arms and clenched and then unclenched his fists, forcing himself to remain leaning against the tree. He needed to stay calm. He needed to hold back. As long as he was watching, as long as he was close enough to interfere if needed, this would be okay. Clara would be fine. She had to learn.

Or they could just say to hell with this whole idea and head home. The more Warren thought about leaving the Reynards hanging, the more he liked the idea, his self of duty as a leader of a pack be damned. The Reynards got themselves into this mess, they could get them out. He should just grab Clara and tell Mrs. Reynard that they'd changed their mind and start walking. They could be back in Loch Haven within a couple days if they shifted and ran.

Home. They could be home. But...

Warren groaned internally, his thoughts drifting to the city. They needed a leader, someone to guide them through the war. As much as he hated to admit it, Mrs. Reynard and Freisinger would probably get the city burned to the ground if this was how they treated other shifters. Clara would be the better choice, the better leader.

Still, watching Freisinger train her like this? It was painful. Maddening. He hated it.

"Fuck this," Warren muttered under his breath, his eyes narrowing as he watched Clara land on her ass again with a small whimper, her breath getting knocked out of her from the force of her fall. As she got up, he didn't miss how she winced as she rubbed her backside. That fall had to have hurt. If she wasn't bruised yet, she would be.

Pushing off the tree, he started stalking over to Briggs and Clara. Or he tried. A hand clasped over his wrist, stopping him. Whirling around, his eyes blazing with rage he wasn't allowed to unleash, he came face to face with Mrs. Reynard.

"Let me go," he said, his voice low and dangerous. "I am taking Clara home."

"You will do no such thing," Mrs. Reynard replied, her eyes narrowing with malice as she glared up at Warren. "She needs this."

"And I warned you that if you harmed a hair on her head, I would have yours," Warren reminded her, his voice low and dangerous as he turned the rest of the way to face Mrs. Reynard completely, pulling himself up to his full height as he loomed over her. He knew he was using his size to intimidate her, but he didn't care. He was sick and tired of their treatment of Clara, and their treatment of him was starting to get on his nerves. Not that he would ever admit that out loud to anyone but Clara.

"Is she bleeding? Is she broken?" Mrs. Reynard hissed, gesturing to Clara who was settling back into a defensive stance. "No. Leave her be. Briggs Freisinger is one of the best. His ways may be a bit unorthodox, but they produce results. I wouldn't have tasked him with this if he wasn't the best."

"That's bullshit and you know it!" Warren roared, fed up, throwing his hands in the air before spinning on his heel and stalking away. Turning back around when he was far enough away from Mrs. Reynard so that he wouldn't be tempted to strangle her, he scowled. "She can barely walk without wincing."

"You would be wincing, too, if you were using muscles you never knew you had," Mrs. Reynard replied, flinching slightly and taking a step back, clenching her own fists in frustration. Taking a deep breath, she forced herself to unclench before dropping her hands down to her side where they gathered in her skirts, fidgeting with the material. "You will leave her and Freisinger alone. I am watching them, just like you are. If I feel he is going too far, I will step in."

Warren took another step back, his face clouding with confusion and mistrust. She would step in, would she? Why? It's not like she had ever cared about Clara before. Why start now? No, that was unfair. He knew why she cared, and it wasn't because Clara was her granddaughter. No, it was because the fate of her family and her pack rested on Clara's shoulders. She had no choice but to care, no matter how shallow or fake the feelings actually were. He wouldn't be surprised if, deep down, she despised Clara. However, they would never know, which was okay with him.

"You have my word," Mrs. Reynard continued as she forced herself to unclench her fist and relax. "I will make sure no harm befalls the girl. She means too much for me to let her get hurt."

There it was. Warren shook his head with a scoff as he heard the lack of sincerity in her voice. "And I meant what I said, fox. One hair, old woman. One. I will rip your head from your shoulders so fast that you won't see it coming. She is my everything and I will not stand around idly while you abuse her."

A hand came down on his shoulder.

"Relax, son," Percil's gravelly voice said from behind him, causing Warren to tense even more. "Come. Walk with me. Let's talk, Slora."

Warren's brows shot up. Had the fox just used his name? He had gotten so used to them calling him by his animal that he had almost given up hope that they would ever address him by his name. Granted, it was his surname, but it was a start. Nodding, Warren took a step back and started walking with Percil.

"What did you want to talk about?" Warren grunted after a minute.

"This," Percil said with a sigh, gesturing to the scene behind them. "Freisinger training Clara."

"And?" Warren urged, his expression darkening as he studied the older male, noting the grey in his air, the dark shadows under his eyes, and the wrinkles that lined his face. He may have been a spry male, but his age was rapidly catching up to him. To undertake this journey to retrieve Clara... Warren shook his head. He had to hand it to Percil and Arik. They had his respect. At least partially.

"I understand where you are coming from," Percil said, his voice quiet, meeting Warren's eyes, his voice low. "I really do. My own mate is not a fox either, much to the disgust of the rest of my family. She's a wolverine. Rather feisty in animal and human form, but I would do anything for her. I imagine you feel the same about our dear Clara."

"Obviously," Warren frowned, not sure where Percil was going with this.

"Then let me ask you something," Percil continued. "If you were told that the best way for Clara to survive this war was to be tortured for days on end, but that she would come out of that torture stronger, more confident, and that she wouldn't get hurt later, how would you react?"

"You aren't actually going to torture her, are you?" Warren said, his eyes narrowing as a low growl emanated from his chest in warning.

"Gods, no. I have no such plans. And I would stop my sister from trying such a thing if she brought it up," Percil said quickly, holding his hands up in surrender. "It's just a scenario, son. Just a scenario."

"I don't like it," Warren grumped.

"Neither do I, but that wasn't the question," Percil pointed out.

"I know that," Warren replied, frustrated. Rubbing the back of his neck, he groaned. He felt so out of control right now and he hated it with a passion. "I don't like it. This. Whatever this is. The problem with your scenario is that you are putting her in harm's way, one way or another. You dragged her away from the safety of our home in the mountains and are thrusting her into a situation that could get her killed. No amount of torture will stop a blade from impaling her if she finds herself on the battlefield. No amount of torture will stop her from getting captured and tortured by the other side. And while you may have gone easy on her with your form of torture, the enemy will not. And surprise, she already knows that. If anyone knows that, it's her. The mad general has already interrogated and tortured her once. She made it out, she survived, and she came back to me. If anyone here knows how brutal the general can be, it's her. She knows him personally, and all of you are forgetting that."

"I..." Percil started but stopped, stunned, Warren's words seemingly hitting home.

Out of all of them, Clara really was the only one who was the most prepared for this war. She knew how General Claery thought, how he acted, how he would react. She would be able to help lead Reynardsville's forces to victory if they put her at the helm. The problem, though, was that no one believed her. Why would they when she looked so sweet and innocent, so soft?

"You want her to lead?" Warren growled. "Then put her in a position to lead. She is not a fighter, but she will if she has to, and the rules be damned. She'll fight the way she knows how. You want her to lead, then put her somewhere protected where she can give out orders and advice. Do not put her in harm's way."

"I..." Percil's mouth gaped, opening and closing silently for a moment as he tried to find something to say, anything at all. Finally, he hung his head, defeated. "I understand. I don't know if they will, though." He gestured to the rest of the party. He glanced over at Clara who had ducked down, missing a blow from Freisinger. She was learning quickly, his movements becoming predictable which made them easy to evade. "She is so small, so fragile. But you are right. I will try to get the rest to understand. It'll be an uphill battle, but I will try."

"Thank you," Warren nodded, relieved.

"But... Before I do," Percil hesitated, as if reluctant to continue to tell Warren what Mrs. Reynard had planned for Clara. Taking a deep breath, his face fell, sorrow filling his eyes. "My sister is cutthroat. Bloodthirsty. She doesn't have an empathetic bone in her body. I worry about her sometimes. She was what drove Clara's mother, Mara, to leave. When I'd heard she'd married a human and had a child, I was ecstatic, but Melanie..." He shook his head. "She'd had so many plans for Mara and Mara took them and threw them all back in her face. But now she has Clara. The things she would do if Clara would bow to her."

"What would she do?" Warren frowned as he glanced over his shoulder at Mrs. Reynard, his heart sinking into the pit of his stomach. Whatever he was about to hear, he was sure he wouldn't like. Not at all.

"She wants Freisinger to mate with Clara. The Freisingers are a brutal bunch. A strong line of warriors, but Freisinger is the worst. Mix them with the Reynards, and you'd have a baby born of two strong bloodlines. That child would have the potential to lead the Reynards to new heights. Or so Melanie says. And Freisinger is of the same mind. Clara is nothing but a female to be bred at this point," Percil sighed.

"So her taking over the pack?" Warren frowned, his eyes flashing back to Percil.

Percil laughed bitterly. "Only in name."

Warren's frown deepened. "Explain."

"Melanie will not step down until those two mate. Once mated, she'll hand over the reins," Percil explained, his voice hushed.

"And following shifter culture, as her mate, she would be under his protection. He would make all the decisions for their household. That means..." Warren trailed off as he realized what Mrs. Reynard wanted. "She wants Freisinger to lead, but because they aren't related, she can't hand him the role of alpha without causing an uproar. But if Freisinger is mated to her granddaughter, she could pass the role down to Clara and her mate. In the eyes of the public, they would be leading together, but in actuality, it would be all Freisinger."

"Correct," Percil nodded.

"And you're okay with this?" Warren gritted out, turning on Percil.

"I was until I realized that my great-niece was already mated. You have proven over and over again since I met you that you would do anything for her. In my eyes, you are what she needs, not Freisinger," Percil said quickly. "And I am not the only one here who is of the same mind. Friedrich and the other guards all agree that you and Clara work well together. To see you two goof off, to see you two so relaxed around each other, to see you two have each other's backs, moving in sync with each other... it does the heart good. But, my siblings and Freisinger... They are not of the same mind. Don't worry, though. We'll get them to turn around eventually. Just don't give up, son. Do not let her go. Do not let her out of your sight. Do you hear me? The moment you turn your back for too long, he'll make his move."

Warren's face darkened at Percil's words. He had allies, but their voices were small compared to those who wanted to follow through with Mrs. Reynard's original plan.

"Thank you for the warning," Warren muttered after a minute. "And thank you for telling me this."

"Anytime, son," Percil replied, letting out a relieved breath that Warren hadn't attacked him. Hesitantly, he stuck his hand out to shake Warren's. "To a new era, Slora."

"To a new era," Warren agreed, taking Percil's hand firmly and shaking it.

CHAPTER 18

RONAN

A loud clanging noise filled the air, startling Ronan out of his sleep. With a groan, he rolled over on his sleeping mat and buried his face in his pillow, not wanting to wake up quite yet. He hadn't slept well since coming out to the field in order to set up the scout camp, and his exhaustion was quickly catching up with him. He was sure that if he looked in a mirror, he would find dark bags under his eyes, his eyes red-rimmed and bloodshot, a haggard expression, and enough growth on his face that he could probably almost call it a beard instead of just scruff.

The loud clanging sound filled the air again. With another groan, Ronan forced himself up, shivering slightly as his thick blanket slid down his body, his bare chest pale in the dim light. Glancing down at himself, he noticed smudges of dirt here and there as well as a dark purple bruise on his left pec from when he had been sparring with Maddox on his scheduled day off duty. He'd been so tired that he hadn't seen the hit coming until Maddox's wooden training sword had hit him with a solid thud. He'd fallen on his ass, the air knocked out of him, a surprised look on his face. After that, he had been sent promptly to bed, not that he'd minded. He'd gone willingly.

The tent flap rustled as Ronan stretched, Maddox entering the tent, Zeke hot on his heels. Both males stopped when they saw Ronan sitting up, both inspecting his face with worried expressions on their own faces.

"Good, you're awake," Zeke said after a minute, wiping the concern from his face, though his brows remained raised as he studied Ronan's haggard face. Maddox, on the other hand, crossed his arms over his chest, the muscles in his arms bulging slightly with the movement, the concern only growing more prominent on his face as he furrowed his thick brows. His lips pursed and he let out a huff of air before shaking his head slightly.

"Barely," Ronan grunted as he pushed himself up off the ground, standing and swaying slightly.

"No, no, don't get up," Maddox said quickly, moving forward in alarm. Uncrossing his arms, he put a hand on Ronan's shoulder and pushed him back down as gently as he could, half guiding Ronan back down onto the mat, obviously worried that he would fall flat on his face if he tried to lay back down himself. "I'll get someone to cover for you today. You need more rest. You'll kill yourself at this rate. Rest."

"Gladly," Ronan grunted, letting Maddox push him back down without complaint, his body sinking back into the warmth of his sleeping mat and blankets. "Is there a reason you two are in here other than to check on me? I mean, I know this is your tent, too, so-"

"Yeah..." Zeke grimaced, cutting him off. Avoiding meeting Ronan's eyes, he scuffed his foot against the frozen ground, a nervous tick of his when he had upsetting news or had to talk about something uncomfortable with someone he cared about. Finally, after what felt like forever but was actually only a few seconds, he unlatched the worn leather bag slung over his shoulder. Reaching inside, he pulled out a thick envelope sealed with wax, however, the seal had already been broken, the letter inside poking out a bit as if it hadn't been put back properly. "We… we got some news. We thought it might be best if we told you now."

"News about what?" Ronan asked, sitting back up once more, using his hands to keep himself steady, a frown tugging at the corners of his mouth.

Slowly, Maddox sank down onto his own sleeping mat next to Ronan's with a low groan, as if his body hurt just as much as Ronan's did. Ronan wouldn't be surprised if that were the case. The whole pack seemed to be hurting from a combination of brutal training, the freezing temperatures, and being forced to sit out in said weather for twelve hours at a time without reprieve. It was rough on the body, but nothing they couldn't handle. They were the only pack stationed behind the city, and although they weren't right there on the front line, they took this position seriously. At least for the most part. It didn't stop them from complaining, even if it was up to them to have everyone's back.

No one said they couldn't complain under their breath every once in a while and still do their job.

Zeke took a deep breath, watching Maddox get comfortable on his sleeping mat before pulling the letter out of the envelope. Shifting slightly, as if bracing himself, he then met Ronan's eyes. "It's a training schedule," Zeke answered finally.

"A training schedule?" Ronan's brows furrowed as he gazed up at Zeke, studying his face as if he would find the answer to his question there. "Aren't we doing enough training as it is? Do they want us to do more? Seriously, brother, I don't think I can do any more than what we're doing currently. I already feel like I'm dying, and I'm sure everyone else would agree."

"No, you misunderstand me," Zeke said quickly with a shake of his head as he unfolded the letter, his eyes scanning it, his face grave.

"It's Clara's training schedule," Maddox supplied before Zeke could explain further, watching Ronan carefully, seemingly expecting him to fly off the handle. And truth be told, he wasn't far off.

Ronan felt his chest constrict painfully at Maddox's words. Clara's training schedule? So she really was coming. He knew she was, but a part of him had hoped that it had been a lie, that Warren had put his foot down and kept her with him wherever his pack had ended up. That would have been ideal. She'd get killed out here. He'd have to take her back. There weren't any other options. As soon as they got her for two weeks, he'd sneak her back. Perhaps that would help him win some favor from her again. But...

Ronan tensed, his brows furrowing further as another unbidden thought crossed his mind. From what he knew of the shifter, Warren would never have allowed this. He was sure of it. So if Clara was coming back to Reynardsville with her family, that could only mean one of two things. The first was that Warren had found someone else and had left Clara high and dry. That, however, was the least likely scenario. Ronan couldn't see Warren leaving Clara like that, not after all the trouble he went through to get her.

The second scenario, and the most likely, was that Warren had been killed. How and why, Ronan wasn't sure, but if that were the case, Clara had no one except her family left. His heart sank. He'd step in himself if that were the case, but he already knew that Clara would never see him that way, not after what he had done. But still, he needed to get her away from her family. It wasn't safe here.

As Ronan ran through different scenarios on how to get her away from Reynardsville and her family, he started to hyperventilate. His hands grasped his pillow, clutching it tightly as he brought it up to his chest, holding it close.

"Woah, calm down, Ronan," Maddox said, his voice low and soothing as he reached out and clapped his hand down on Ronan's shoulder again. He then glanced up at Zeke. "I think we might need to take him off duty, send him back to the house with the females. He can keep them in order. It'll give him something to do."

"Don't you dare," Ronan gritted out as Maddox's words registered in his mind, snapping out of it as his eyes flashed in irritation. "I'm staying."

"You're in no shape to stay out here," Zeke snapped in frustration, his, patience starting to wear thin. Folding the letter back up, he handed it to Maddox to peruse. "You keep proving that over and over again. If Clara wasn't a part of the equation, maybe this would be different, but you can't seem to think straight when someone so much as mentions her name. Get over yourself, Ronan. You're going back."

"Give me a chance," Ronan pleaded, watching his chances of getting close to Clara so he could sneak her out slip out of his grasp. He was fully aware that he was now pulling a complete one-eighty on his friends and pack mates, but Clara was in danger. If they couldn't understand that, then may the gods help them. He wasn't just going to sit around and...

"Why?" Zeke demanded to know, breaking him out of his thoughts.

"I... I have a plan," Ronan stammered, struggling to figure out how to explain why he suddenly wanted to stay without giving too much away. He had to keep his budding plans secret if he wanted them to be successful. "I can keep it together, I promise. I... I just have to stay back. In the back. I can't train with her. That's all. Just... Keep me on this schedule. Keep me at that post I've been assigned during the day. It's far back enough. I won't interfere. I promise. And at night, well, I'll be asleep. Can't do anything while I'm asleep."

He was reaching. He knew he was. And he sounded desperate. So very desperate. Gods, he was pathetic. But so be it.

Maddox groaned, scrubbing his face with a dirty hand. "Dammit, Ronan, you are a royal pain in the ass, you know that? Don't get me wrong, we love you like a brother, but pull your head out of your ass. You are not okay right now. Zeke and I agree that sending you back to the house would probably be the best course of action. When she's gone on to the next pack after her two weeks with us, one of us will come get you and bring you back out."

"But..." Ronan protested. And then he sighed, hanging his head. His mind wasn't functioning properly with so little sleep. He was out of ideas and he wasn't about to beg on his hands and knees. Not yet. He hadn't stooped that low. "When will she be here?" His hands grasped the pillow tighter as he asked the question, his fingers running over the rough seam along the edges as he tried to keep himself grounded.

"Um..." Maddox hesitated and then handed Ronan the letter.

With trembling hands, Ronan took the thick parchment and unfolded it. His eyes scanned the letter, his brows shooting up in surprise. Clara would be spending two weeks with each of the packs inside and outside of the city with the exception of the packs which were composed of animals that flew and the two packs on the front line, a pack of panthers and another of squirrels and chipmunks. Squirrels and chipmunks? Did he read that right? He blinked in confusion and then shrugged. A good choice if you needed shifters who were inconspicuous and could blend in with the regular wildlife to spy on travelers. They would probably see enemy scouts first. And panthers? Well, he guessed, they could sneak around unseen as well, but they were large enough to take out said scouts. Whoever had sent them out there had thought out the city's first line of defense carefully. He might have done something similar.

Shaking his head, he turned back to the details of the letter, noticing what packs would have Clara and when. First off, she'd be with the elephants inside the city. Their long memories made them excellent at remembering past conflicts and the tactics used. Typically, they were used as scribes and historians. She'd learn a lot there, or that's what the Reynards were hoping would happen. From there, she'd go spend time with her own pack. Foxes were cunning and sneaky, as well as intelligent. They were the intelligence gatherers in war, and Clara could use all the intelligence that she could get when it came to leading the Reynard Pack and Reynardsville. It would help her make informed decisions, plan battles, and hopefully lead the city to victory. After the foxes, she'd be with the lions. Decent leaders, Ronan supposed, even if they were all a bit arrogant and conceited. They could teach her how to command. And then she'd be coming to the wolves. Them. The Romulus Pack. What would they teach her? Loyalty? How to work as a group? He shook his head and handed the letter back to Zeke.

"So we have six weeks until we have her then?" he clarified.

"Looks like it," Zeke confirmed.

"Do I have to go back to the house until now, before her visit, or can I stay with the pack out here until it's our turn to have her?" Ronan asked, hope filling him. If Zeke and Maddox both agreed to let him stay until Clara's visit, then he had six weeks to show them that he could get a hold of himself. He could prove that he wasn't nearly as mentally unstable as he'd been acting.

"Eh." Maddox shrugged and looked over at Zeke. "I mean, we could use him here until she comes."

"True. True." Zeke nodded before glancing at Ronan, studying him carefully. "There's more, though." He pulled out another letter, not nearly as thick as the first. He then held it out to Ronan.

Taking it, Ronan read through it, feeling like his world was coming crashing down around him once more. So much for trying to get her back to Warren's pack up in the mountains or spiriting her away to keep her safe.

Warren was with her.

How the hell had they managed that?

Pack leaders,

My granddaughter will be accompanied by both Briggs Freisinger and her mate, Warren Slora, to each training. They will both be overseeing her training to make sure that she is learning all that she needs to learn and to make sure that she is not taken advantage of. If I hear of any funny business, both the shifter that caused the problem, and their pack leader, will be answering to me personally.

Thank you for your time,

Melanie Reynard

"I don't think we'll have any problems," Ronan whispered, his mouth dry, handing the letter back. "That sobered me up, real quick."

Maddox laughed quietly. "What? Don't like the idea of getting on the bad side of her mate?"

"No," Ronan replied bluntly. "He'll tear me to shreds. Warren Slora is a wolf and the pack leader of his own pack. An alpha by birth. I wouldn't stand a chance if he caught me looking at Clara the wrong way. I've fought him once before and the only reason I won was because I caught him by surprise when he was trying to claim Clara the first time around."

"Ahh, distracted by his own lust." Maddox laughed harder, finding the situation far funnier than Ronan thought it really was. "Well, in that case, you can stay, Ronan. This should be interesting."

Zeke, trying not to laugh as well, his eyes dancing merrily, nodded in agreement, both eager to see Ronan put in his place by Warren.

"I would pay to see that fight," Maddox continued between laughs. "I'm sorry, Ronan, but this is too good to pass up. No hard feelings?"

Ronan groaned and flung himself back down onto his mat before answering. "You laugh when he hands me my ass, I'll take it out on you," he gritted out in warning.

"Fair enough," Maddox replied, a wicked grin on his face as he rubbed his hands together in anticipation.

CHAPTER 19

ALICE

The wagon creaked to a stop near what looked like the remnants of a barn. Half the walls had crumbled in on themselves and the roof was caved in. Alice looked up at her brother curiously, wondering why they had stopped next to such a dilapidated building. Had they seen something they hadn't? Did they need to hide? What was going on? Beside her, Mira had an identical look on her face, her eyes darting between the barn and the two males in front of them, the same questions running through her head, or at least similar ones.

"Why are we stopping here?" Mira ventured to ask before Alice could ask as a swirl of snowflakes blew off what was left of the roof and settled down around them, making the four of them shiver.

Clearing his throat, Xander pointed one of his gloved hands at a spot on the horizon. Turning their attention to the spot, Alice's eyes widened as she brushed snow off her cloak with frozen hands. Squinting, she studied the spot Xander had pointed to. She could clearly make out the shapes of different buildings from where they were parked. Her heart started pounding wildly in both excitement and anxiety. They had made it to Springfield and this was obviously as far as they could go without getting spotted. The remnants of the barn hid them from view and provided a bit of shelter, at least from the wind anyway.

Now came the hard part: deciding who got to go into Springfield and who would stay behind. Or rather, they all knew who was going. No one wanted to say it out loud. And she was sure that both Xander and Able would argue the unofficial decision a few more times before finally giving up and agreeing. She peered over at Mira to see if she was thinking the same thing. The set of Mira's jaw and the grim determination in her eyes told Alice all she needed to know.

Mira was ready. She knew as well as Alice that it would have to be her that ventured into the human city. And if Alice knew Mira like she thought she did, Mira was currently a bundle of nerves on the inside. She just hid it well, like always.

"We'll settle here for the time being," Xander grunted, breaking the silence, swinging himself off the bench seat and down to the ground, his boots crunching over the thin layer of snow on the ground. "I'm not sure how long we'll be here exactly, but what's left of this barn will provide some shelter for the next couple of days."

Stretching, his eyes scanned the city again, his expression worried as he glanced back at Alice and then over at Mira. He knew who had to go, too, Alice concluded. He just didn't want to acknowledge it yet. Acknowledging made it too real. Something they couldn't avoid. And after years of always protecting Mira, the knowledge that he was about to send Mira in somewhere inherently dangerous had to be driving him crazy.

Or maybe she was just reading too much into the concern she could see filling his eyes. Perhaps he didn't know who to send. Maybe he was just worried about keeping them safe this close to the city.

Gods, she hated this. She felt like she was going insane. She didn't understand what was going on half the time and it frustrated her. And when Able or Xander did explain things to her, she became even more confused. How was she supposed to function like this?

"No fires, though," Able added as he, too, hopped down to the ground with a grunt. Stalking forward, his movements stiff from the cold, he started to check over the horses, inspecting them closely. Alice's eyes tracked his movements, a frown tugging at her lips.

If Alice was the jealous sort, she'd say that Able cared more for the horses than his own sister, but she knew that without the horses, they would be stranded with all their things. Keeping them in tip-top shape was of the utmost importance. That didn't mean it didn't bother her that he checked the horses before he checked on her. She shook her head before glancing down at her hands. She was being ridiculous. She knew she was. They couldn't afford to be soft anymore. This was war. They were essentially refugees on a rescue mission. There was no room to be soft.

"No fires?" Mira repeated faintly, drawing Alice out of her thoughts as she scooted closer to the side of the wagon, her eyes trailing Able. "What do you mean no fires? We've had fires every night since we started this journey. If we don't have some sort of fire, we'll freeze."

Able spun on his heel and glared at Mira, obviously fed up with her attitude. He had been since Mira had confessed that she would have rather seen Alice with Ronan instead of Xander. It hadn't sat well with him, considering Alice knew his feelings about Ronan. The real question was whether Mira knew how Able felt about Ronan, and going off Mira's surprise and the hurt that flashed across Mira's face every time Able snapped at her, Alice would hazard a guess that she had no clue.

"Are you seriously that stupid?" Able hissed, his dark brown eyes darkening dangerously as he drew nearer to Mira, until their noses were practically touching. Shocked, Mira reeled back, falling onto the bench that had been their permanent perch since leaving Everridge.

"I…" she started, blinking, stunned speechless. But before she could continue, Able continued, his voice harsh.

"Do you see the city right there?" He pointed in the direction of Springfield. "Do you know whether they are shifter-friendly or not? Do you know what they would do to us if they weren't shifter-friendly and discovered us out there? No, I don't think you do. If you did, you wouldn't be complaining about a gods damned fire. Three days at most, Mira. That's all you have to suffer through. Three gods damned days. Think you can manage that, princess?"

Mira hissed in response, her own temper flaring to life. "Why you…" she started again before Xander grabbed her and yanked her off the wagon, covering her mouth with one of his hands.

"Shut the fuck up for once and listen," he hissed in a low whisper. "Able is right. If we draw attention to ourselves, they'll be on us faster than flies on stink. And if they catch us, you and Alice could get killed or worse. Do you want to know what it's like to be used as a sex slave for a human man, Mira? Do you? You think male shifters are bad, but human men are just as bad. We have some morals. We'll treat a human woman with some respect because we know we can break them without trying. Them? With a shifter female? Forget it. They see us as nothing more than garbage. The shit smeared on the bottom of their shoe is better than us in their eyes. They will use you without a second thought. That's if they didn't think it would tarnish their perfect reputations. And you best pray that's what they think because if they do, they'll kill you. That's all the mercy you'll get."

Mira turned pale as she listened to her brother in silence, no longer fighting, her body sagging. Alice, listening in, also paled as her eyes widened. Why… why didn't she know any of this? She inhaled sharply as the answer came to her. Female shifters were protected at all costs, guarded like they were some sort of precious treasure. They weren't often given leadership roles. They didn't deal in trading. Why should females know? All females were typically concerned with were keeping their houses clean, looking after their children, taking care of their mates, and avoiding unmated males that were just looking for a good time. This type of thing would never come up in conversation. She would have remembered this if it had. How could someone forget something like this?

"Why are they so bad?" she whispered before she could stop herself, her eyes wide as they darted between Xander and the city.

Xander's eyes flashed up to hers, his face hard, almost unforgiving. And then he sighed, releasing his sister, holding her steady for a minute so she could gain her footing, and then rubbed the back of his neck. Leaning back against the wagon near Alice, he surveyed her for a minute.

"I... I don't want to lie to you, but at the same time, I don't want to scare you," he mumbled uncertainly, his eyes darting over to the city briefly before landing on her once more, his gaze softening.

"I can take it," Alice reassured him, sounding more confident than she felt.

Xander let out a deep breath and then nodded. "The few times any of us have had to leave Everridge to trade with the humans..." He swallowed and shook his head. "The big cities... they live in filth. Their refuse and trash line their streets. Their houses are run-down and dirty. At least on the outside. I never got the opportunity to step inside one, not that I wanted such an opportunity. The human men milled about on the streets, some hawking their wares, others trying to eek a living by begging. The beggars were treated like scum, kicked, beaten, abused. The few women who were brave enough to wander out wore drab clothing. They got what they needed and hurried back. Those who were with their husbands were silenced. I saw one get backhanded for daring to speak her mind once. That was enough for me."

"She was backhanded?" Alice blinked in surprise and then frowned. "That doesn't mean they all treat their women that way."

"Alice, love, that's not..." Xander let out a low groan. "If that's how they treat their women, fellow humans, how do you think they would treat a female shifter? Hmm? Do you think they would let them shift? Do you think they would let them out of their house, out of their sight? No, you would be considered dangerous and would need to be kept close. And then you would be beaten into submission in any way they felt like doing so."

"I..." Alice nodded, finally understanding. "So if they aren't shifter friendly, and they captured us, Mira and I could be kept as... pets? To be used as they see fit?"

"Correct," Able spoke up from the other side of the wagon. "And we want to avoid that. They capture us and we can't protect you. Very likely Xander and I would be killed on the spot."

Mira's eyes widened as she glanced up at her brother, not liking the image that popped into her head at Able's words. Alice had a similar reaction, but then looked down at the ground, nodding. They were in a precarious situation being this close to Springfield. They would have to be as careful as possible if they wanted to survive this.

Suddenly, the unspoken agreement between them to send Mira in to check for Ronan came crashing down around her. If they were in such danger...

"So..." Alice started, unsure how to ask her next question. After all, they had come all the way to Springfield to find out if Ronan was here. But if they were in such danger just being here, why did they come at all? She glanced up at Xander, her brows furrowing as her face darkened, realizing that he had known all along, it had just taken her and Mira until now to fully comprehend. "Why are we here?"

"To see if Ronan is here," Xander replied simply. "I thought that was the plan."

"It was before I knew how dangerous it was," Alice whisper-shouted, her panic obvious.

Xander gave her an amused smile before reaching out and helping her down. Keeping his arms around her, he drew her close. "Would I let anything happen to you, love?" he whispered in her ear. "You and Mira will stay safe here while either Able or I sneak close enough to the city to check, understand?"

"But what if you don't come back?" Alice whispered back, starting to hyperventilate. She didn't know where Reynardsville was. Hell, she could barely drive the wagon on a regular road. Going over snow-covered terrain? Forget it. She'd get lost, stuck, or worse.

"If we don't come back by the end of tomorrow, you and Mira will head northeast." Xander pointed in the direction of a mountain craig just visible over the tops of the clouds littering the sky. "As long as you head toward that mountain, you'll be going in the right direction. Do you understand?"

"I don't like it." She shook her head.

"Send one of us," Mira pleaded. "We won't stick out like you two."

Able huffed in irritation. "You two would stick out just as much. We are on the edge of civilization out here. How many women do you think there are? Not many. You'll attract too much attention."

"But so will you, you giant," Mira shot back as she eyed Able who stood at about six foot four. He wasn't the tallest out of his friend group, but he was still incredibly tall compared to most human men.

"I'm not the giant, he is." Able pointed toward Xander who stood at six foot six. Xander huffed a laugh and then shrugged, unable to deny it.

"Let me go in," Mira pleaded.

The group fell silent as they surveyed Mirabel. Out of the four of them, she was the least conspicuous. She had long golden hair that waved down her back when undone. Her large hazel eyes were framed by long lashes. Her fair skin was clear and flawless but tinged pink from the cold. Her frame was slender and lithe. Girlish almost.

"I don't like it," Xander shook his head. "However..." He trailed off and shook his head.

"She could get close enough without raising alarm," Able muttered. "She could claim that some shifters invaded the village we passed not too long ago and that she fled in fear. They'd take her in without hesitation if she made it sound believable enough. Not that we need her to be taken in. We just need her to get close enough to see if she could spot a shifter or smell if there had been any there in recent weeks. We're all familiar with what shifters smell like, particularly rogues. It shouldn't be hard."

Xander's frown deepened. And then his shoulders slumped in defeat. "Fine," he grumbled. "She can head in. We'll let her ride one of the horses over to the city. That way, if she needs to flee, she can make a quick getaway."

"She can shift though," Alice frowned.

"That would give herself away. And tracking her bear prints would be easier than tracking a horse," Able explained.

"Then it's settled," Mira said resolutely, straightening up and taking a step toward the city. "I'll go."

"In the morning," Xander growled, reaching out and grabbing her shoulder, stopping her. "It's too late to go right now. We need sleep."

CHAPTER 20

MATTY

Standing just outside what used to be the O'Donoghue's bar, leaning against one of the poles on the boardwalk, Matty surveyed the soldiers under his command bringing in lumber for the wall that they had been ordered to construct. Silently, he counted the boards as they were stacked in a dry spot, away from the mud pit that main street had become thanks to the melting snow, the countless horses going up and down the street, the few people that dared leave their houses, and the occasional wagon coming to pick things up from the blacksmith, the general store, or the carpenter.

Speaking of the general store, Matty's eyes glanced up the road toward the store he used to find any excuse to stop by, the place he had spent a few months learning to run while he had waited anxiously for his wedding to Clara to get closer. During his time down at the capital, while he had been surviving training at a nearby army training camp, one of his brothers had come down from wherever he'd disappeared and taken over the store. It wasn't being run as well or as efficiently as Mr. O'Donoghue had run it. Far from it, actually. But it was up and running and Matty guessed that's what mattered. As long as the citizens of Springfield were still getting their supplies, that was what mattered.

He glanced down at the paperwork in his hand, going over his orders once more. Then he flipped over to another page, going over the blue-prints of sorts, if he could really call them that. What it really was, was a hand-drawn map of Springfield with a rough border drawn around the main part of town. That border was supposed to be the wall he was supposed to have his men build. And down in the corner of the paper were the specifications of the wall. Wood. At least eight feet tall. Twelve if they could manage. But they would be hard-pressed to manage any feet given the current state of the ground. It was frozen solid. An impossible task. One he was sure he'd be punished for if he failed.

Closing the file and stuffing it into his pack so as not to ruin them, he looked over at his men again. Today would be focused solely on getting enough lumber to start working on the southern portion of the wall. To-morrow, they would create another pile on the eastern side of town. Then the northern. And finally, the western. They might as well set everything up before the real work began.

A wall... He scoffed. It was such a ridiculous idea. It left most of the town exposed because the majority of the residents lived outside of the city main. As he had pointed out to his dad, this was a farming community. You couldn't just build a wall and exclude half of the residents. Had he even consulted with the town? What did they think? Matty would wager that over half were upset, that they felt like they were being cut off, excluded.

But that was a problem for another day. Right now he needed to figure out how to get the wall started. And while he worked, he decided he would come up with a way to talk to his dad about the wall again. He highly doubted Springfield would ever get drawn into the war. If anything, Springfield would end up becoming an outpost for supplies and that would be it.

His dad didn't think so.

But that was the problem, wasn't it?

Matty shook his head, taking a deep breath before looking up at the sky in exasperation. Studying the winter sky for a minute, he pursed his lips. Was the sky partially cloudy where Clara was?

Dragging his gaze away from the sky, it drifted up to the road once more. A frown tugged at his lips as his eyes landed on a young woman who looked rather lost as she rode into town on a brown chestnut. Both horse and woman looked rather tired and travel-worn. Mud coated the horse's legs and the hem of her skirt. Her hair was wind-swept and coming undone. Grime coated her skin. She'd been on the road for a while if he had to guess.

But where had she come from?

His eyes traveled over the woman, again, taking a closer look. She couldn't be much older than him. Her messy hair was a golden blonde that was falling out of a long braid and her green eyes were wide. He had seen those eyes before. He was sure of it, but he couldn't place where. They were... familiar. He narrowed his eyes, taking in more details like the way her eyes darted around, as if nervous. The way her nose flared slightly as if she'd smelled something unpleasant, which wasn't uncommon on main street.

Was she lost?

Pushing off the pole, he stalked into the street toward her, hiding his grimace as his boots squelched through the mud and the gods knew what else. His eyes remained narrowed on her as he approached. He could see her swallow nervously. Definitely not from around here. So what was she doing here?

"Can I help you?" Matty called, brushing a strand of blond hair out of his eyes, his hazel eyes fixed on her.

The woman startled in her saddle, grasping the pommel to stop herself from sliding off into the mud below. Her eyes widened further as her head whipped in his direction, meeting his.

"Is this Springfield?" she asked, her voice raspy.

"It is." Matty nodded his ascent, noting the bluish-purple tinge to her lips. She was cold. "Can I help you?"

"I…" She hesitated, her eyes darting around the town. Then her eyes landed on the general store, and she sagged. "No. Thank you, though. Mama ran out of supplies and Papa is out hunting. It's been a hard year. I just… I need to head home and let Mama know that there's a store still getting supplies out this way." She backed her horse up a few paces. "I'm not supposed to stay long. Just check and leave. Papa's rules." Her voice became stronger as she talked, but she was still clearly uneasy, her eyes still darting around, taking everything in.

Matty reached out and grabbed the reins before she could back up further. "What do you mean? Do you not have a store near you?"

"Not one with supplies." She shook her head, her eyes landing on his hand grasping her horse's reins. "It's nothing new. Some years are harder than others and with the war…" She trailed off, not needing to say it out loud.

Matty knew exactly what she was trying to say without words. Everyone was struggling because supply routes had been disrupted, troops walking through had damaged fields, and it had been a rather hot year. Crops had withered and died.

"You're a farming family, aren't you?" he asked softly, his gaze softening as he studied her again, specifically her hands. He could see the callouses on her fingers, so much different from his own wife's dainty hands.

The woman nodded. "I best be getting back. I don't want to be away when Papa comes back from hunting. He might need help. And once I give him the news, he'll be right out the door, eager to restock so I'll have to prep the meat." Her eyes darted to his hand rather pointedly.

"Sorry," Matty grunted, releasing the reins before watching her back up a few more paces. "What town did you say you're from?"

Something didn't feel right, but he couldn't quite place it. No one sent young women out to neighboring towns to look for supplies. Not unless they were desperate. But she didn't look like she was desperate. In fact, she still looked well-fed. Either she was lying, or she was running from something and looking for help. That had to be it.

"Are you okay?" Matty pressed. "Everything okay where you're from?"

The woman's eyes flared slightly at the questions, letting Matty know that he was getting closer to the truth. And then she sagged yet again. "I'm looking for my brother. He ran away a few months ago. I'm not sure where he went, and my mama can't go looking for him. She's got health problems. And Papa, well, he won't leave Mama. So I ran away to look for him. He needs to come home."

"Why here?" Matty frowned.

The woman gestured to the mountains behind Springfield. "Where do all young men looking to make a name for themselves go?" she asked.

"You think he went prospecting," Matty stated in a matter-of-fact tone. He didn't need to question it. He had seen plenty of young men come through Springfield over the past year, eager to make a name and a fortune for themselves in the mountains north of the city. But they'd stopped coming through when the first snow hit.

"I do," the woman said softly.

"Well, I hate to break it to you, but anyone that's come through here to go prospecting in the last few months has already moved on. It's all soldiers right now," Matty informed her, his tone apologetic.

The woman nodded again, looking a bit downcast. "Thanks anyway. I'll... I'll be going," she muttered.

Before Matty could stop her, she nudged her horse's sides with her ankles and took off at a steady pace, leaving Springfield behind as she followed the road out. Still standing there, he watched as she disappeared into the distance. And then he sighed. Something still didn't feel right. Stuffing his hands in his pockets, he hurried out of town after her, more to see where she was heading than anything else.

Around ten o'clock that evening, Matty slipped into his little cabin on his parents' property, his mind racing. Closing the door quietly behind him, his eyes quickly adjusting to the dim light coming from the dying fireplace, he couldn't help but think about what he had seen. The woman wasn't alone. There was another woman with her and two men. And the men... Matty shook his head. He should have seen it. Why hadn't he seen it?

The men were bigger than most human men.

Shifters.

That's why he hadn't gotten a straight answer out of the woman. She probably didn't know what to expect in the western towns, the ones on the edge of civilization. None of them did.

It was a smart move, sending one of the women in. They were more easily mistaken for humans than the men. They blended right in.

Matty thought back to how she'd been looking around, the way her nostrils had flared as if she had smelled something terrible. She hadn't smelled something bad though. She had been sniffing for scents, looking to see if there were any other shifters in the area. There was a good chance that she really was looking for supplies before heading further north to join the other shifters. But there was also a really good chance that she had actually been looking for someone. He rubbed the back of his neck wearily. The truth was in there somewhere.

"Matty?" A quiet voice interrupted his thoughts, startling him. Looking around, he spotted Kitty standing in the doorway to their bedroom. "I thought you'd be home sooner than this. Your mother helped me make dinner for you tonight and you weren't here. Your dad didn't even know where you were. He said you should have been here already. What were you doing?"

"I had to check on something," Matty said vaguely, not wanting to give too much away. He may be fighting for the king, but since the whole mess with Clara, he couldn't hate the shifters. He'd let them move on peacefully. This group wasn't bothering anyone. They didn't pose a threat.

"Checking on what?" Kitty pressed, her brows furrowing as she came over and sat in the chair opposite him, pulling her robe tighter around her before stretching her bare feet out toward the dying fire for warmth.

Getting down on his knees, Matty added another log to the fire to keep it going. Once the log caught, he pulled himself back into the chair and looked over at Kitty.

"I thought I saw something outside the city. You know how it is. We can't be too careful these days."

"We're outside the city," she pointed out.

Matty huffed a laugh. "Touche. What I meant to say is that I saw something that didn't belong. But don't worry about it. It was nothing important. Just a family fleeing the countryside for the safety of a city. I don't blame them. The more troops that arrive, the more nervous those out in the country get. They're worried about getting caught in the middle of a battle. But I don't think the shifters will be coming to us to fight. Not anytime soon anyway. They'll only come to us when they've grown desperate. They, like us, just want peace."

"So why are we fighting them?" Kitty asked in confusion.

"Ask your father that. I couldn't tell you that," Matty replied bluntly. The whole war was stupid. Pointless. The loss of life was appalling. How the king and his own dad could justify that was beyond him. If it was up to him, he'd never... but it wasn't up to him. And it never would be. He was just a lowly lieutenant.

And then he froze.

"What did you tell my dad exactly?" he asked.

Standing before General Claery the next morning, two of his men flanking him, he waited for his dad to speak. As he stood there, he maintained the cool façade he had carefully crafted so as not to give away how he was feeling in front of his dad. That, Matty had learned in the last few months, was the key to surviving with his dad. Especially if he didn't want his dad to use his own feelings against him. He wouldn't put it past his dad to use Kitty to get him to comply with something. Or his own mom.

Matty felt a surge of anger at the thought. He better not.

"You left your post yesterday, Lieutenant Claery," General Claery stated bluntly.

"I saw something that caught my eye. I went to investigate to make sure it wasn't a threat," Matty replied as calmly as he could.

"And your men?"

"They continued to do the task that I had set for them. I checked their work when I got back. They finished the task. We did not fall behind on our orders to get the wall around the city constructed," Matty replied, his heart beating loudly in his chest, praying that his dad didn't pry much further. He wasn't sure if that group of shifters was still there, but if they were, they needed to move now. And he couldn't go out there to warn them if his dad decided to inspect himself.

"What was it that caught your eye?" General Claery asked.

"Nothing important," Matty reassured him as one of his men sniggered behind his back.

General Claery raised a brow. "Doesn't sound like nothing important."

"It was a girl," one of his sergeants supplied, a shit-eating grin on his face. "Pretty little thing with golden hair. The lieutenant couldn't keep his eyes off her. Followed her out of the city. Probably made sure she made it home. He's such a gentleman."

General Claery's eyes darted back to Matty, surveying him. His brows raised again as if he saw everything that Matty wasn't saying, but maybe that was Matty's own nerves getting to him.

"Tell me everything," he demanded.

"It was nothing, really," Matty tried to reassure him.

"I will ask one more time," General Claery said, his voice taking on an icy quality.

"It was just a family, I swear," Matty said, trying to keep his voice steady. "A farming family. You know how nervous everyone is."

"Must you lie," General Claery sighed, shaking his head in disappointment. "You'd have thought you'd learned that lesson already."

Standing up, he moved around his desk to stand in front of Matty. Then he sidestepped Matty and shoved a knife into the side of the sergeant who hadn't said anything. Both Matty and the sergeant who had brought up the woman stepped back, their eyes widening in shock and horror.

Yanking the knife out, blood oozing out of the man's side, General Claery let the man drop to the ground. "Kidneys…" General Claery tsked. "He'll be dead soon. I suggest you start talking unless you want your other sergeant to be next."

Matty stood frozen in disbelief and horror as the general stepped over the man and out of the office. Blood gathered on the floor, the puddle spreading to his feet. Dropping to his knees, not caring that he was ruining his pants, he pressed his hands against the wound, trying to stem the bleeding. But it was useless. His dad was right. The sergeant would be as good as dead.

And it was all his fault.

CHAPTER 21

ALICE

The following morning was... warmer? Alice couldn't tell as she stood next to Xander while they waited for Mirabel to come back from scouting Springfield. It didn't feel any warmer. Not by much. But Xander said it was. Stupid living heater. He was always warm, radiating heat. She just wanted to curl up in his arms and forget that they were hiding out in a burnt-down bar a few miles outside of Springfield. Was that too much to ask for?

Frowning and tucking her hands under her arms, she could still see her breath coming out in clouds in front of her. And she was pretty sure that her nose was starting to go numb. But she was warm-ish. Or warm enough thanks to Xander and her cloak. Or maybe that was just the stress. Did people heat up when they were warm? They should. Her heart was racing like it did when she'd been out chasing down one of the animals on her parents' farm. But it was just nerves. She knew it was deep down. Who wouldn't be nervous? Her sister-in-law might have just ridden to her death and all they could do was wait and see.

She shifted guiltily. It was all her fault. If Mira didn't come back, her blood would be on her hands.

It was her fault.

She swallowed down the lump that had risen in her throat. She could feel a panic attack starting. If Mira didn't come back soon...

Reaching out, she sought out Xander's hand. Finding it, she laced her fingers through his and squeezed his hand like her life depended on it while she spiraled. She had been the one who had suggested coming out to Springfield to look for Ronan. She could have suggested heading straight north like everyone else was doing. That would have been the safest option. But no. She was still searching for answers. She had to know what had happened to her former best friend.

And now all they could do was wait and see.

She scoffed to herself. Whose brilliant idea was it to wait and see? She had never been good about waiting for anything, so she knew that it wasn't her idea to wait and see. If it had been up to her, she would have been going into the city with Mira. There was safety in numbers. But she needed to be inconspicuous, so Mira had gone on alone. And now the wait was slowly but surely killing her. If it wasn't freezing cold, she would have pulled her hands out and started chewing on her nails as she waited, just for something to do. She was sure she would have chewed through her nails by now, leaving a bloody mess. It had happened a few times before during less stressful situations.

"How long has she been gone?" Alice asked for what felt like the dozenth time that morning. She could swear it felt like Mirabel had already been gone for hours but she knew that, in all reality, she'd probably only been gone for about thirty minutes to an hour max.

Able coughed a laugh from somewhere inside the dilapidated barn. "You seriously need to relax, little sister. You're going to give yourself a heart attack if you keep stressing like that. And I really don't feel like trying to drag your half-conscious body to a doctor in the hopes that they won't kill you for being a shifter if you do actually give yourself a heart attack. Not my idea of a good time. Relax."

"He's right," Xander said softly from beside her, releasing her hand to wrap his arm around her shoulder, keeping her pressed tightly against his side for warmth. "All we can do right now is wait. There's no point in stressing ourselves out about what may or may not be happening."

Alice glanced up at him, shooting him a look. Since when had he started sounding so wise?

"But you have to be worried," she protested after a minute, deciding that his mask of calm was just that, a mask. "Mira is your sister, for crying out loud. You can't just stand there and tell me that you aren't worried about her."

"I never said I wasn't," Xander stated, glancing down at her, his expression unreadable. "What I said was that there is no point in stressing ourselves out about what may or may not be happening. Am I worried? Of course, I am. I don't like her being in a human city without my protection any more than you do. But it had to be done. If we want to find Ronan, then this is where we have to start. This is where I sent him."

Alice tipped her head back, resting the back of her head against his arm, groaning slightly. Definitely wiser than he normally let on, and somehow she'd missed that. It frustrated her just a bit. "Can I say I hate you right now?"

"If it makes you feel any better, sure," Xander snorted in amusement. "Not that I think it will. And we both know that it's not true. You love me whether you want to admit it or not. If you didn't, you wouldn't be cozied up next to me or put up with my arrogant ass." He looked down at her again, studying her face. "You're cold."

"Am not," Alice protested grumpily, growing grumpier by the second. Wise and aware. How much more was he going to surprise her with this morning?

"Your nose is red and your lips are starting to turn purple," Xander pointed out, tapping the tip of her very frozen nose. "Go shift and warm up inside."

"Can we really call that inside if it's not really enclosed?" Alice grumbled as Xander released her and gently pushed her toward the barn, still complaining.

"It counts for right now," Xander said firmly.

Pulling a face, she turned away and started to walk inside when the sound of horse hooves caught her attention. Glancing over her shoulder, a smile spread across her face as relief filled her, making her feel lighter than she had in days, her grumpiness temporarily forgotten.

"Mira," she whispered under her breath, watching as her sister-in-law slid off the horse, her feet landing on the frozen ground with a crunch.

"Did you miss me?" Mira asked with false bravado, unable to hide her shaky voice as she walked closer, her skin a little paler than usual.

"Of course," Xander said brusquely, trying his best not to show how worried he had been as he grasped Mira by her shoulders and surveyed her, inspecting her for damage.

"So?" Able asked, walking out of the barn to greet Mira. Leaning against one of the sturdier walls, he crossed his arms across his chest and waited for her to tell them everything she had seen.

Leaning against the wagon for support once Xander released her, Mira closed her eyes for a moment before opening them again. She was still pale, but from what Alice could see, she was okay. Or as okay as one could be after being sent into enemy territory.

Alice's heart sank at Mira's continued silence. "He's not there, is he?" she guessed after another minute of silence.

Mira shook her head, her eyes locking onto Xander. "We need to leave. Now."

"What? Why?" Able frowned, studying her before his eyes flicked over to the city in the distance. They could just see movement around the edges. Men carrying lumber. Or that's what it looked like to Alice.

"There are soldiers everywhere. I was stopped by one," Mira whispered in reply as if she didn't want to dwell on the experience.

"And?" Xander asked sharply, his gaze hardening. Alice knew that look. He was preparing for a fight. Gone was her Xander. In his stead stood the one that had dominated the training grounds back in Everridge, the one that was slated to take his father's place on the city council in a few years. "What did he do? What did he ask? What did you say? We need details, Mira. Not just 'we need to leave'. Not that I'm arguing that because we do need to leave if there are soldiers nearby. Hell, even with just humans nearby we need to leave. But we need details. We have to warn any other shifters we come across. We have to keep each other safe if we want to survive this war."

"I'm sorry." Mira quickly apologized as she shook her head, trying to pull herself together. "I don't know what I was thinking, volunteering to go into the city like that. It's not what I expected. I panicked. But I didn't say anything I wasn't supposed to."

"Mira," Xander growled, his patience starting to wear thin as they waited for her to give them more than that.

"Sorry," she said again with a pained expression. "I rode in as planned. I wasn't even in the city yet when I spotted the soldiers. They're the king's soldiers. They're everywhere."

"Are you sure they're the king's?" Able asked sharply, his eyes flashing as his expression turned grim.

"Yes, they all wore the same crest. His crest. The dragon with the flaming crown on its head," Mira explained, twisting her hands together before glancing over her shoulder at the city.

Alice shook her head. Ironic, that, she thought to herself. The man who despised shifters, shifters who were created from the same magic that created the dragons of old, the man who was actively trying to get rid of all shifters, had a dragon on his crest. If she had to guess, she'd say that the king probably liked the power, liked what the dragon symbolized. Back before the country had even been founded, dragons ruled. Their power was absolute. They were the kings. But with civilization, they drew back and eventually disappeared. Now they were nothing more than fairy tales told to young shifter and human children alike in the hopes they'd be scared into obedience. No one wanted a dragon to come eat them for not eating all of their vegetables.

Alice shook her head again, refocusing on Mira as Mira told them about her encounter with a blonde lieutenant just inside the city.

"They're preparing for an attack," Xander said, his voice heavy, after Mira had finished. "Not that a wall could stop us if we really wanted to attack. But they don't have to know that. Let them build their precious walls. All we want is to be left alone."

"He didn't follow you, did he?" Able asked, his gaze sharp as he studied Mira and then the horse before letting his eyes wander to the city once more. Out of the corner of her eye, Alice could see Able tracking the movements of the men carrying the lumber with his eyes, a muscle twitching in his jaw.

He was restless. Nervous. They all were. But Able didn't like being this close to the humans. Not that she could blame him. She didn't like being this close either. She was all in favor of moving on sooner rather than later. If they had to vote on whether to move out now, she would be all in. Just pop her in the wagon and let's go. She was ready.

"No, I don't think so." Mira shook her head, her eyes on the city as well.

Able ran a hand down his face, obviously thinking. "If you're sure... Damn it. I don't want to be here right now. We should move. But I want to give the horses a bit more time before we move. They need a break." He pushed off the wall and walked over to the wagon, running a hand over the buckboard as he glanced at the wheels.

"We need to move now, Able," Xander countered, watching Able. "Just because Mira doesn't think she was followed doesn't mean that she wasn't. You and I both know that if someone has a spyglass, they could have tracked her movements from the city to here. For all we know, we might have just been spotted if we haven't been already."

"True," Able conceded reluctantly. "Fine. Give me a couple hours to do some maintenance on the wagon and then we'll head out. We'll go north. Try and put as much ground between us and the damnable city as possible before it gets dark."

"An hour," Xander countered. "All I can give you is an hour. We don't have time to waste."

"Fine, an hour," Able grumbled, clearly unhappy but not willing to push his luck.

Turning, Xander looked at Alice. "Stay inside until it's time to go. I don't want you spotted. Same for you Mira. I'm going to help Able get everything ready. Sleep if you can. I'm not sure when we'll stop tonight. If there's a road, we might continue after dark. It all depends on how much distance we can put between us and Springfield and how busy the road is. Please... Rest."

Biting back a scathing reply, realizing that now was not the time to argue, Alice ducked behind one of the walls before exploring the burnt building, looking for the warmest spot to hunker down for the next hour. It was just an hour. She could survive that long before crawling under the heavy quilt next to Mira in the wagon.

"Hold on Ronan," she whispered under her breath. "We'll find you."

CHAPTER 22

MATTY

Matty shifted in his saddle, an uneasy feeling settling in the pit of his stomach. This wasn't right. He shouldn't be here. He shouldn't be doing this. But...

Matty looked back at his dad, a sense of trepidation settling over him. He had just watched his dad murder one of his men in cold blood, simply because Matty hadn't told him the truth. His dad knew. How his dad knew was beyond him, but he knew. And he had caught Matty in his lie.

And someone else had paid the price for his lie.

That man's blood was technically on his hands.

It was quite literally still on his boots. And the knees of his pants. Under his fingernails. On the cuff of his sleeves.

He could still see the wide-eyed shock on the sergeant's face as his breath rattled in his throat. Matty had wanted to apologize, had wished it had been him on the floor bleeding out instead. This was his fault. He had done something he shouldn't have and he had lied. Repeatedly. All because he didn't feel like his dad needed to know. The girl and her friends hadn't been a threat. They were just passing through.

And still, someone had died. Knowing his dad, he'd spin it to make it seem like the shifters' fault, too. And everyone would believe him. They had no reason not to.

Matty felt sick to his stomach, clutching the reins tighter in his hands until his knuckles started to turn white. How could he be so stupid to think that his dad wouldn't find out? Most of the men here in Springfield were loyal to his father, whether because they valued their lives or because they abided by the same fucked up values his dad had, Matty wasn't sure. But they were. And at least one had ratted him out.Probably thought he'd get a promotion if he did. Probably had, too.

And soon everyone would know when there was a new officer walking around, barking out orders with a smug look on his face.

Feeling his anger starting to boil just underneath his skin, Matty vowed that he would take him out, just like he would take his dad out eventually. He just needed a plan. Right now, however, was not the time to be contemplating ending his dad and his loyal, mindless followers.

The real question, the important one right now, Matty asked himself, was whether his dad knew that the group of people he had seen were shifters or not. His chest constricted, making it hard to breathe. There was no way that his dad knew. It was impossible. He shuddered, an unshakable foreboding feeling settling deep into his bones, dread filling him.

His dad knew.

There was no other reason for a party of ten to be riding out in the middle of the night to catch this small group of shifters if he didn't know. If they were just normal people, a family of farmers like Matty had tried to play them off as, and if his dad had believed him or at least suspected them to be human, they wouldn't be out here freezing their balls off. He shifted in his saddle, his body screaming in protest at how brutally cold it was.

This was ridiculous. Unacceptable. Inhumane.

It needed to stop.

Matty needed to get rid of his dad, he thought to himself yet again. He had thought so at least a couple hundred times over the last few months, but it was becoming increasingly frequent with each passing day. It happened at least once an hour, sometimes more. Tonight, it was happening every few minutes.

If his dad wasn't around, the king would lose his right-hand man. His army would be reduced to nothing without General Claery leading the troops against the shifters. Perhaps it would get the king out of his dreary castle and onto the fields himself. But even then, it wouldn't make a difference. The tides would turn in favor of the shifters. And from what Matty was coming to realize more and more each day, the shifters just wanted to be left alone. Like humans, there were some bad eggs, but that was to be expected. He couldn't just tar them all with the same brush. It was unfair to all of them.

It was unfair to Clara.

He shook his head as he looked up and stared at the back of his dad's head. He needed to stop thinking about her. She was gone. She wasn't coming back. He was married. He was working for the king. They were technically enemies at this point.

But only in name.

If it came down to it, if he ever saw her again, if she was still alive that is, he would cross that invisible line drawn in the sand and stand before her, shielding her. She was no enemy. Just an innocent girl with a fiery side that he'd fallen in love with all those years ago.

He would take down his dad just for her, even if it was the last thing he did. And then he could die happy, his conscience clear.

His dad's voice interrupted his thoughts as his gruff, cold voice called out to the small party. "Halt," he said. Turning in his own saddle, General

Claery looked back at Matty. "This is where you said you spotted them, Lieutenant?"

"Yes, sir," Matty said dully, trying to keep his face and voice as emotional as possible. He didn't want his dad to see how much this actually bothered him. If he knew, he'd make this much worse for everyone involved.

At times, Matty suspected his dad saw him as a disappointment and this was his way to make Matty know that that's what he thought of him. Other times, Matty suspected that his dad saw him as the son he didn't want. A surprise, and a bad one at that. He'd already had two older boys when Matty had come along. And then he had taken after his mom, sweet and gentle. So now his dad saw this as an opportunity to turn Matty into the man that he had wanted him to be.

Matty dipped his head as General Cleary got off his horse and inspected the dilapidated barn, searching for clues as to where they'd gone – footsteps, scraps of fabric, pieces of food, anything. Another soldier got down and started circling the barn while another started surveying the ground with his lantern.

"Wheel tracks, sir," the one surveying the ground shouted after a few minutes. "They're heading north."

Matty's heart sank as the soldier's words registered in his head. Silently, he offered up a prayer to the gods, begging them to keep the group safe, to keep his dad from issuing the orders to go after them.

General Claery came out of the barn, arching an eyebrow at the soldier. "North, you say?"

"Yes, sir." The soldier nodded and then proceeded to show General Claery the tracks he had found. Walking together, they followed the tracks for about a hundred yards, both talking quietly together, before turning and coming back. "I reckon the tracks are only a few hours old, sir. They can't be too far if they're traveling in a wagon. We could catch up to them within the next two hours. If you want, of course."

General Claery pursed his lips as he mounted his horse, settling into the saddle and rubbing his hands together. Turning, he looked at Matty again, his face a mask of cold indifference. Matty couldn't tell what he was thinking even if he wanted to. There wasn't a hint of anything on his face to go by. Not even in his eyes.

General Claery held Matty's gaze for a moment longer. "We go after them," he said after a minute, his voice cold. "I want to talk to them."

Matty couldn't bring himself to look at the wagon following behind the party as they slowly returned to Springfield. The thought of what had happened when they had ridden up to the small group made him sick to his stomach. Dropping his head, he closed his eyes and swallowed down the bile in his throat.

Sick.

His dad and the troops that willingly followed him were sick.

Monsters wearing men's clothing, spouting how much better they were than anything less than human.

They were worse. Much much worse. The things made of nightmares.

Behind him, muffled sobs barely carried over the sound of the horses' hooves and the creaking of the wagon. If he had to guess, it was the dark-haired female with the curls. She had been hurt and used the most. But she had... Matty didn't want to finish the thought, but it came unbidden. She seemed the most important. When one of the men had grabbed her, fisting his hand in her hair and throwing her down to the ground, both of the males and the other female had both lunged for her. Both males had yelled her name, both sounding anguished. Alice was her name, or that's what it had sounded like. And then the male with the long blonde hair had started swearing violently when the soldier had lifted her skirts.

They had to be a couple. There was no other explanation for the pure rage he had seen in the blonde's eyes. He'd never seen that look before, but he'd felt the way that male had looked when Clara had been assaulted by that red-headed shifter that had been stalking her before he'd kidnapped her. Matty had wanted to kill the male. Still did, if he was being honest. But his dad had beaten him to that with the poison-tipped sword he'd used to run the male through.

The other female, the blonde he'd met in town, had been grabbed as well. But she had not been bent over and used. Not at first. No, his dad had deemed her too pretty. To fix that, he'd taken his dagger and cut her hair off, sheering it short. And then he'd tossed her to his men. She hadn't cried though. Instead, she'd closed her eyes, as if trying to keep herself calm as the men tore off her clothes and used her body, their hold on her bruising.

And the males? They'd been tied to the back of the wagon and whipped, each grunting as the whip lashed across their backs, leaving red welts and then, eventually, blood trickling down as their skin finally split.

He could have stopped it. He should have stopped it. But he had gotten sick, spewing his meager supper of bread and cheese on the ground beside his horse. And then he'd been dragged away after his dad had given him a disgusted look.

He had failed them, just like he had failed Clara.

He slouched down in his saddle. Gods, he wouldn't be able to take down his own dad, he thought, the realization like a punch to the gut.

The shifters would be eradicated simply because he didn't have the mental fortitude or the stomach to stand up to his dad.

He was no better than the rest.

Spotting his parent's house and his cabin in the near distance, he veered off, nodding briefly at his dad as a way to tell him that he would go let his mom and Kitty know that they had made it back safely.

"Tell your mom I won't be back tonight. I've work to do. Tell her to expect me for supper tomorrow instead. If she's even still awake."

Matty nodded again before nudging his horse with his ankles, spurring it into a gallop, wanting to get as far away from the group and the wagon as possible.

He was going to be sick again.

"What did you tell my dad?" Matty demanded, storming into his cabin, rousing Kitty from her sleep as he slammed the bedroom door open half an hour later. He could still taste the bile he'd wretched just outside in his mouth. He felt sweaty and sticky, his whole body shaking. He was a wreck.

Startled, clutching the sheets to her chest, Kitty sat up and stared at him wide-eyed.

"What did you tell him about me coming home late yesterday?" he snarled, his hands clenching into fists, trying to hide how badly they were shaking.

"I... I was with your mom and all I said was that you came home late," she stammered nervously, tugging the sheets closer to her body. "Your dad was there and gave me a funny look before telling me that you should have been home earlier, that all you'd been told to do was start getting the wall around the city put up. So I shook my head and said I hadn't seen you until well after dark when I was getting ready for bed. After that, he just... I don't know. He got this weird look in his eyes and walked out. But I swear I didn't do anything wrong. It was just a conversation."

Matty growled angrily, scrubbing his face with his hand. "Gods damn it, woman. You don't tell my dad anything. Ever. He's a gods damned snake. He will twist everything you say to benefit him and to get you to do anything and everything he wants you to do."

"It's not that bad. Relax," Kitty said in a calm voice, trying to soothe him, even though there was a hint of irritation in her voice. "It was just a conversation. It was harmless."

"Harmless?" Matty scoffed. "No. It was anything but harmless. A man is dead because of that conversation. A good soldier. One that didn't do anything wrong. All because you opened your fat mouth. Two women were raped because of that conversation. Two men were whipped within an inch of their lives because of that conversation. You. Do. Not. Tell. My. Father. Anything."

Kitty's eyes widened in shock. "You can't be serious."

"Do you want proof?" Matty roared, stalking forward and gripping the edge of the bed as he loomed over her.

Kitty shrank back, her eyes widening further. Matty had never yelled at her. Snapped? Sure. Grabbed her hair? More than once. Thrown her on the bed and fucked her when he felt she needed a reminder of where she stood? Most definitely. But yelled? No.

"Get up. Get out of bed. Put some clothes on. I'll give you that gods damned proof," Matty snarled.

Kitty shook her head, her whole body trembling.

"Then keep your mouth shut. Do you understand me? This is war. There are no rules anymore. People can do whatever they want without punishment. And men like my dad? They exploit that in any way they can. So if you don't want to be on their radar, if you want to keep your pampered ass out of trouble and safe, you will keep your mouth shut. Do not say anything to my dad unless it's about the weather, food, or a project you are working on. Do you understand?" Matty said, still seething.

Kitty nodded, her eyes still as wide as saucers.

Matty stared at her for a few more minutes and then turned on his heel and stalked out of the room, kicking the door shut behind him. Heading into the guest room, he grabbed some blankets out of the wardrobe and laid down on the floor, too angry to be anywhere near Kitty at the moment.

CHAPTER 23

Alice

Trying to fix her clothes, wishing that they hadn't been torn, wishing they would cover her better, Alice scooted back into the corner of the freezing cold jail cell, her body screaming at her. She hurt everywhere. Her head. Her arms. Her legs. Her stomach. Her core... Gods, her core throbbed, screaming at her in agony.

Xander and Able had been right. They should have left as soon as Mira had returned from checking out Springfield. Hell, they should have just bypassed Springfield. They would have been halfway to Reynardsville if they had. They would be, well, not warm, but safe. Unharmed with their dignity intact.

Alice shifted again, wincing, unable to get comfortable. Wrapping her arms around herself, she bit back a sob. She was pretty sure she was bleeding. Or she had been. She had seen dried streaks on her legs in the dim light when they had thrown her into this cell with Mira. Right now, she could feel something damp trickling down her leg. If it wasn't blood, then it was something she'd rather not think about. It would make her situation a little too real, a little too bleak, a little too horrific.

She didn't need to think about what it was. Just the sensation of it trickling down her leg made the situation too real. How was she supposed to ignore whatever bodily fluid that was as it dripped down her skin, leaving a trail of goosebumps in their wake, making her shudder and want to vomit?

Her one saving grace at the moment? She had been stronger than those men.

Or she would have been if she had shifted. But in that moment, she had been powerless. There was nothing she, or anyone else, could have done. If she had shifted, they would have killed her on the spot. If Xander or Able or even Mira had shifted... Well, Xander and Mira might have been fine. Xander was a mountain lion and would have been able to do a bit of damage before they would have been able to subdue him. Mira? The small group of soldiers would have been minced meat.

Alice wished Mira would have shifted, but like Alice, she had frozen in shock and fear, not sure how to react.

She pressed herself against the cold wall and looked around the dark cell, trying to get a feel for her surroundings. The cell was made out of wood. The whole building was made out of wood, now that she thought about it. That made things a bit... she rapped her knuckles against the wall next to her. Her heart sank. The planks were thick. Mira, in her bear form, might be able to crash through something thinner, but these? No such luck.

"You okay?" Mira rasped from the other side of the cell, her hands trembling in her lap as she glanced up at Alice, her eyes wide and her face dirty. Her face was streaked with long dried tears that had left tracks through the dirt coating her face, making her look even more disheveled.

"No. You?" Alice responded, still studying the cell.

"No."

Alice turned to look over at Mira, her heart sinking further as she studied Mira's shorn head. Her golden locks were short and choppy, all different lengths. It looked as if a child had taken a pair of kitchen shears to her head and tried to give her a haircut.

"Are you hurt?" Alice asked next, her voice trembling. She already knew the answer. She didn't know why she was even asking.

"Not nearly as hurt as you, I'd reckon," Mira said, her voice broken as she ran a hand over her hair. "They were too busy mocking me to hurt me like they did you."

Alice nodded, knowing Mira was probably right. From what she'd seen from her position on the ground, her face pressed into the dirt as some filthy soldier violated her, Mira had been tossed on the ground and mocked, kicked a few times, and hit.

"We should have left as soon as I got back this morning," Mira whispered, having the same regrets as Alice.

Alice nodded again. They should have done a lot of things. For some reason, they hadn't. They were tired. Dejected. Feeling a little lost. A break had seemed nice. A chance to check things over was necessary. They knew there might be danger, but they had decided to risk waiting a bit longer. And it had cost them.

"Do you know where they put Xander and Able?" Alice asked, reaching up to rub the back of her neck and wincing. She hurt there too.

"We're here," Xander's deep voice echoed down the hall toward them.

Alice sagged in relief at hearing his voice, the sound soothing and reassuring. She wished she could sneak down to his cell and be with him. She needed to be wrapped in his arms, to make sure that he was alright. She wouldn't feel safe until she was in his arms again.

"Are you alright?" Able piped up, his voice gruff, making Alice sag further. Able was there too. It was good to hear his voice. She closed her eyes, trying to calm herself and the storm of emotions swirling within her.

"Do you really have to ask that?" Mira retorted, managing a little bit of her old snark.

"Are you hurt badly?" Able rephrased his question with a long-suffering sigh.

"No," Mira and Alice replied at the same time.

"How are you two?" Alice asked, her voice trembling.

"Bloody and torn to shreds," Xander grunted. "But don't worry about us. Both of us are small enough animal-wise to shift in here. We'll take turns and be healed by morning. I promise. And then we'll figure a way to get out of here."

"Get some rest," Able added.

Alice glanced over at Mira who pursed her lips, not liking being told what to do. But then her face softened, a look of defeat flickering in her eyes. She jerked her head at a cot in the corner. "C'mon. I'm sure we can both fit. And if we huddle together, we'll stay warmer."

Alice startled awake by the sound of heavy footsteps clomping down the narrow hall. Next to her, Mira also startled, shifting to sit up and scoot back into the corner of the bed, pulling Alice with her. Hiding in the shadows, they watched as the General and two guards made their way past their cell. And then their footsteps stopped further down the hall. A key jingled. A hinge squeaked.

"You. The dark-haired one. On your feet," a man's rough voice ordered.

Alice grimaced. They were asking for Able. Then she frowned, her brow creasing in concern. Why did they want him? What were they going to do to him? She wanted to call out, to tell him that she loved him, to make a run for it, to save himself, but the words died in her throat. She'd only make it worse for him if she did.

The footsteps started again. A few seconds later, Mira and Alice watched as Able was led past their cell. He didn't bother looking their way, something that made Alice's heart sink. She knew why, of course. If he showed weakness, they'd use his weakness against him. He, no they, couldn't afford that.

The footsteps died away, leaving them in silence once more.

Settling back down, she tried to get comfortable next to Mirabel once more, but she was too anxious. She needed to see Able return. She needed to see that he was alright before she could rest once more.

And then a cry of pain sounded through the jail, making Alice's heart stop.

CHAPTER 24

CLARA

The sun was still high in the sky when the Reynard group came to a stop at the edge of the forest, almost exactly in the same spot that Clara had stopped with Ronan the first time she had come to Reynardsville. Looking around, she noted that not much had changed since then except that the snow was deeper and there was the stench of wolves everywhere, not that that bothered Clara much. She was mated to a wolf. It was a scent she was more than familiar with by now.

It was comforting.

It reminded her of home.

"We're stopping for a moment," Freisinger called out, his voice echoing through the clearing that separated them from the back wall of the city. Stalking over, he stopped right in front of Clara before crossing his arms over his chest, a stern expression on his face. "I have to go talk to the pack guarding the back gate. You will stay here. You will not try to sneak away and head back to that gods forsaken pack in the mountains. If you do, so help me, I will make your life a living hell when I catch up to you, Kleine." His face darkened as he turned to Warren. "You. I don't care if you stay or leave. But from this point on, this is my territory. I make the calls. So if you try to run off with her, I will gut you like the scum that you are. Do I make myself clear?"

Clara arched an eyebrow at Freisinger as he snarled his warning at them both before glancing at Warren out of the corner of her eye. Like her, he was looking at Freisinger with a look that could only be described as apathetic. But there was a hint of amusement in his eyes. Maybe. Or maybe she was just seeing things. It could have been a trick of the light. But the point of the matter was that she was amused. At least somewhat. As if he could tell her what to do.

Boy, did he have another thing coming. He said she would hate him in the end, but... She laughed silently. It would be closer to he would her in the end. Not that she would lose any sleep over him hating her. In fact, she would prefer it if he did. Maybe he'd stop spouting nonsense such as she'd be under him at her if he did. Maybe he'd finally leave her alone.

But that was a far-fetched wish, one better off bestowed upon a shooting star. She was sure he already hated her, but he loved power, so he'd put up with her for the sake of a more powerful position.

Arrogant asshole.

"We're not going anywhere, Freisinger, so get on with it then. We'd rather not freeze," Warren grunted, bringing Clara out of her thoughts as he stared Freisinger down, not breaking eye contact with him. He shifted and then rolled his neck. "Granted, our animals won't let us freeze, but I imagine you don't want to cause a scene."

Freisinger's gaze darkened at Warren's words, letting Clara know that he had struck home, or at least pretty close. His image was everything.

"We aren't going anywhere," she echoed, just to be on the safe side before she bent over with a small groan, massaging her thighs through the thick folds of her skirt. Since Freisinger had started training her, her whole body felt like one big bruise. She'd started using muscles she hadn't used, well, ever. In fact, she hadn't realized she'd had some of those muscles, but she sure as hell did now.

Freisinger's gaze softened slightly as he watched her bend over and start working on her thighs. "When we get to the townhomes, I'll have one of the maids run you a bath before tonight's meeting. It'll be good for those sore muscles. Besides, you do need to clean up. You smell just as ripe as the rest of us."

Clara frowned slightly. "Thanks," she said dryly. "I was unaware. Just what a girl wants to here, that she stinks."

At the same time, Warren's gaze snapped to Freisinger, ignoring Clara's scathing remark. "Meeting?" he repeated.

"Yes, meeting. One that you aren't invited to, wolf. It's family only," Freisinger said, his words becoming short and clipped.

"Then why are you going?" Clara asked, straightening with another groan.

"I've explained this to you, Kleine. You'll always be beneath me," he said, his eyes darkening as he surveyed Clara for a moment. And then a smirk tugged at his lips, as if pleased with the thought that popped into his head. She didn't have to wait long to hear it either. Leaning in, he brushed a strand of hair out of her face before murmuring in a sultry tone, "Besides, your grandmother likes me more than you. I'll always get the invitation before you."

If he had been expecting a reaction to his words, Freisinger wasn't going to get one. If she had been a lesser woman, perhaps she would have looked up at him, wide-eyed and hurt that he dared say something like that. Clara, however, didn't care who her grandmother did and didn't like. It was all the same to her. After suddenly remembering her grandmother and what a massive bitch she was, Clara had stopped caring for her grandmother at all. Unless you counted trying to see how miserable she could make her grandmother as caring, that is, something Clara had decided was her new favorite hobby.

Freisinger's smirk faltered a bit as he noted her lack of reaction to his words. Beyond that, he didn't say anything more as he dropped his hand and straightened up.

Clara sighed, giving him an unimpressed look, getting right back to business. "Look here, asshole. We're supposed to be a team, remember? So either stop dangling your knowledge about what the meeting is about and tell me, or get lost. You've got a job to do, remember?" She crossed her arms over her chest, knowing full well she was being petty. Not that she cared. If Freisinger just so happened to get hurt during the upcoming war, she wouldn't care. Not one bit.

Freisinger bristled. "It's about what the next few months are going to look like for you," he snapped. "Unless you'd rather not know. I can go to the meeting without you."

It was Warren's turn to bristle. "If the meeting is about her, why am I not invited? I'm her mate."

"For now," Freisinger quipped, his smirk returning and becoming smug. "Just as soon as we can figure out how to get rid of you, she's mine."

"Can we not talk about me like I'm a possession?" Clara piped up, inserting her opinion into the mix.

"You are," Freisinger growled.

"That's right, you aren't," Warren said at the same time.

The two males glared at each other as Clara threw up her hands in frustration. "And male shifters wonder why the women only tolerate them long enough to have a babe or two before skipping off to sleep in a separate room..."

Freisinger's jaw dropped as Warren let out a hearty laugh. "You aren't wrong, my little fox. You aren't wrong. But if you do feel like you should punish me by moving into another room, please let me know beforehand so I can at least try to fix whatever I've messed up."

Clara beamed at him. "Of course. You've always been willing to listen. Or at least try."

Warren grinned back as Freisinger cursed under his breath before turning on his heel. Stomping off, he crossed the clearing, heading toward a small cluster of tents. Nearby, a large male shifter with tattoos up and down his arms and a cigarette in his mouth watched Freisinger stomp across the clearing before turning his gaze toward Clara and Warren.

"You're the Reynard brat," he stated, his voice rough from the cigarette smoke.

"I've never used that name, and I don't plan to anytime soon," Clara replied, her eyes flicking over the male. "You're a wolf."

The male's eyes widened in surprise almost imperceptibly. "My apologies. Maddox." He slipped off the boulder he was sitting on and walked over, extending his hand to shake first Warren's hand and then Clara's. "My pack has been waiting for you and your family to show."

Warren arched a brow at him.

"The Romulus Pack is on duty back here," Maddox explained, taking a drag of his cigarette. "Our job is to guard the back gate. Watching everyone's six."

Warren nodded, immediately understanding. Clara, on the other hand, was completely lost. Watching someone's six? She had no idea what that meant. But watching the back gate, especially now, wasn't a bad idea at all. Not wanting to be left out, even though she only half understood what was said, nodded, too.

"We were told you would be coming from the mountains, so we've kept someone over here to keep an eye out, just to make sure everyone is okay," Maddox continued, noticing the confusion in Clara's eyes. "And..."

he hesitated, glancing over his shoulder at the camp near the gate where Freisinger had disappeared. "Don't trust Freisinger. He's a snake. Brutal. The only person he's loyal to is himself." He stepped back, starting to make his way back to his post. "I'd hate to see a pretty little thing like you get used because you trusted the wrong person."

A frown tugged at Warren's mouth. "I take it you know him personally?"

"No." Maddox shook his head. "But anyone that follows pack politics here in Reynardsville knows what he's like. Be careful."

Warren nodded, a thoughtful expression on his face. And then he met Maddox's gaze. "Thank you."

"'Course," Maddox replied. His eyes flicked over to Clara, his lips pursing as he studied her. Clara shivered slightly, feeling as if the male studying her knew her. But that was impossible. She had never met the male in her life. She wondered if rumors had started spreading through Reynardsville. That had to be the only explanation.

Dropping her gaze, looking down at the snow sparkling in the sun, she waited for him to go back to his post.

Four hours later, Clara was sitting in an over large tub filled with steaming hot water. Bubbles gathered into clumps on the surface and the scent of lavender and chamomile filled the air, relaxing her. Sinking deeper into the water, she closed her eyes and tried to force herself to forget that she had essentially been sent to her room like a naughty child and had been told not to come out until someone was sent to retrieve her.

She was supposed to be at the meeting right now.

She was supposed to be with Warren.

She was supposed to have a say in what happened to her.

Instead, she was sitting in a hot tub with nothing to do because she'd been told no. She'd tried to sneak out, but there were two burly guards standing in front of her door, making sure she didn't do exactly what she had attempted.

She let out a deep groan, dropping her head back against the back of the tub. This was all so stupid. How was she supposed to lead the pack if she wasn't included in any of the meetings? Who cared if the tub was deliciously hot and soothed her over sore muscles? Not her. If she thought for one moment that she could sneak out of here to get into that meeting, she wouldn't be wasting her time in the tub. Oh no. Not one wasted minute.

She groaned again, swishing her hands through the bubbles, watching as they floated away and then back again with the movement.

You're not going to lead, an annoying voice in the back of her head reminded her. *Briggs is supposed to be taking over. Not you. You are the way to the "throne". You are nothing more than a pretty little stepping stool. He will use you. You are nothing more than a means to an end. He does not care.*

Clara hated that that was true. She didn't want it to be true. All she wanted was to be back in Loch Haven with Warren. She should never have come, responsibilities to her family's pack be damned.

A knock on the bathroom door brought her back to reality. Before she could answer, Warren popped his head in, causing her to gasp in surprise. A grin crossed his face as his eyes landed on her, and then his eyes filled with a hungry appreciation as he studied her.

"I thought they weren't going to let me see you," she murmured, sitting up, studying him in return.

"They didn't want to," Warren said, setting some papers down on the floor next to the tub before pulling his shirt off and letting it drop down onto the floor next to Clara's dirty clothes. "Turns out one of your great uncles happens to like me. He convinced your grandmother to let me sit in on the meeting instead of you since I know a bit more about fighting than you, no offense. And..." Warren undid the buttons of his pants and let them drop as well before stepping into the tub, sinking into the hot water behind her. "Your uncle knew that I would tell you everything with in-depth explanations if you needed. No one would take the time to explain anything at a meeting and we both knew that."

"Someone could have told me," Clara protested as she watched him over her shoulder, her eyes raking over his chest. "Here I was thinking that Freisinger had decided to leave me out because I'm useless, just something for him to fuck later so he can get to the top."

A growl reverberated in Warren's chest, his eyes darkening furiously. "Don't talk about yourself like that."

"It's true," Clara countered, a bitter edge to her voice. "That's why they brought me here, isn't it?"

"I don't care if it's true. It's not going to happen. Not while I'm around to protect you. And if I can't, I need to make sure you can protect yourself, hence me being at the meeting instead of you," Warren sighed, wrapping his arms around her and pulling her back against his broad chest. "We didn't make this decision lightly, but after seeing your confusion while talking to that wolf on duty, it became abundantly clear that your family would capitalize on that and force you into something you didn't actually want simply because you didn't understand what was going on. I can't have that. You can't afford that. This war needs you at your best."

"So? What did they say then?" Clara demanded, refusing to relax against him until he told her.

"I took detailed notes. They're all on those papers on the floor. You can..." Warren started but was cut off as Clara leaned forward and reached over the edge of the tub for them. Once she had them in hand, she leaned back against him, letting her body relax as she read through them.

"You're really going to read through my notes now?" Warren huffed a laugh, a hint of irritation in his voice.

"Yes, why?" Clara asked, not looking up from the notes as she rested comfortably against him.

"You have me, naked, in the tub with you. We haven't been able to have any alone time in over two weeks. And instead of taking advantage of that, you're sitting here reading notes. Who are you and what have you done to my little fox?" he said, more irritation bleeding into his voice.

Clara's eyes went wide, having completely spaced that this was the first time in weeks that they had been alone together. They had been counting down the minutes for just this, and here she was, reading notes. Leaning forward, she dropped the notes back down on the floor carefully before leaning back against Warren.

"I'm all yours, love," she murmured repentantly.

"Damn straight you are," he growled, tilting her head to the side so that he could nuzzle into her neck, pressing light but hungry kisses to her skin. "Gods, you're beautiful. I missed having you in my arms."

CHAPTER 25

ALICE

Ropes burned into Alice's wrists as she twisted in the wooden chair she'd been bound to. Blood dripped down her hands from the sores the rough fibers of the rope had created from the amount of times she had already been brought into this gods forsaken room and "questioned". Tortured would be a better word, but the general was very careful in making sure to call those pain-filled sessions interrogations, tiptoeing the line of legal with his words. But if anyone walked in to see what he had been up to, well... all legality would go out the window.

Not that anyone would care if it was legal or not once they found out that Alice was a shifter.

She knew that, too.

Not like anyone would walk in on them to care. They were on the edge of civilization. The people here did what they wanted when they wanted. No one cared if their self-proclaimed leader decided to arrest four unsuspecting "people" and keep them locked in the jail. They could have thrown a child in with them and Alice doubted the people of Springfield would have batted an eye.

The thought made her heart sink down into her stomach. What kind of depraved society would let a man arrest a child simply for existing?

The answer came to her unbidden. A sick one.

The people who ran the Kingdom of Brunholl were sick, like a cancer that needed to be cut out. Perhaps one day it would happen, but at this point in time, Alice doubted that she would live to see it. There was a very real chance that she wouldn't walk out of this jail, but she was trying not to think about that. Seriously admitting it would mean she'd given up, right?

Alice twisted the other way in her spindly seat, the chair creaking as she gasped for air. Water dripped down her cheeks and off her chin, mixing with her tears and sweat. The ropes burned against her raw skin some more, more blood dripping down her hands. The drip drip of the water and the blood hitting the floor slowly driving her insane.

She would not break.

She would not put others in danger.

She would not show weakness.

She would survive this.

"Where did you come from?" the general asked for what felt like the hundredth time.

A soldier stood behind him, holding a freshly filled bucket of water. When she refused to answer, he'd hand it to the general who would then pour it over her face. He would be replaced with another soldier holding another bucket. This could go on for hours.

Alice clenched her jaw, her teeth grinding together as she forced back a sob. They should never have gone searching for Ronan, she thought for what felt like the hundredth time that hour. It had been a stupid idea. The longer she sat in this cold, dark room, the more she realized that he was probably dead. There was no he would have gotten out if he had been here.

The next thought nearly broke her. Had Mira and Xander come to the same conclusion, that their brother was probably dead? That he had been here before them, enduring the same abuse? Had he broken? Had he spilled secrets? Or had he endured the torture in silence until the very end?

She was never going to make it out, just like Ronan probably hadn't. They'd throw her broken body into the same grave as his, or right next to it. Reunited at last in death. The realization wasn't a pleasant one, but until they really started hurting them, she was safe. Or safe-ish. She still had time. Not that it did her any good. She still hadn't figured out how they were going to get out or if they would ever get a chance to get out. There was a chance that by the time they had the opportunity to escape, they would be too broken to escape.

She would leave it to Xander and Able to figure out how they'd make it out of this situation alive, however, they weren't saying anything to her or Mira at the moment. The most she got out of them was a simple good morning, good night, and a question or two asking if she was okay.

Her answer was always the same. No. She wasn't alright. She was hurt. Her body ached. She had bled more in the past few weeks than she'd ever thought humanly possible. She had been used. She felt dirty.

She wanted to die.

She wouldn't admit that out loud. Not yet. It would hurt Xander and she refused to do that. He was in enough pain right now as it was. Just like her.

But death sounded like a nice reprieve. It sounded peaceful. Free of war. Free of pain. Free of misery.

A sharp sting seared across her face as the general slapped her, sending her head flying to the side, the wooden chair rocking slightly. It wouldn't be the first time he'd hit her so hard she'd fallen, chair and all. Had he righted the chair after? No. He had left her there, on the floor, like a piece of unwanted trash because that's what she was in his eyes.

"Answer me," he demanded, smacking her again, sending her head flying in the other direction. More liquid trickled down her face. This time blood from her nose. She could taste the coppery tang of it as some made its way into her mouth. She wanted to spit it out at him, spraying his face with her blood. But she kept her mouth shut, taking deep breaths to help herself remain calm.

He smacked her again, sending her head flying in the opposite direction this time.

She hissed in response, licking her split lips, the coppery tang of her own blood stronger now. "I don't have a home."

"Liar," he snarled. "Where were you born?" He took the bucket from the soldier and held it up, threatening to douse her again.

"A cottage."

It wasn't a lie.

"In my parent's bed."

Also not a lie.

She was going to cross a line she couldn't return.

Maybe he'd kill her on the spot.

I'm sorry, Xander.

A trickle of water started to drip onto her face, causing her to splutter. She tried holding her breath, but she was winded from being smacked around. She opened her mouth. Water filled her mouth. She tried to spit it out but more replaced what she spit out. She gagged and then started choking. She couldn't do this. She needed it to stop. It had to stop. Why wasn't it stopping?

CHAPTER 26

MATTY

The room was dark, the only light coming from the heavily curtained window on the far wall and the single lantern in the corner by the door. In the center of the dark room was one of the shifters Matty had failed to save. In front of her, General Claery stood, a dark expression on his face. Matty had seen that expression once before and that was when he had been stabbed in the gut by his own dad. The general's eyes were cold, icy even. His mouth was a thin line of disappointment. His face was a stony mask, betraying nothing except the irritation and anger he was feeling. And perhaps the disgust he harbored for all things not human, shifters especially.

Matty sat in the far corner on a rickety stool, not that he actually wanted to be there. He had tried to get out of attending these torture sessions, but his dad was insistent. Besides, technically, his dad was his superior. When he gave an order, Matty had to obey. And after what had happened with the sergeant who had died at his feet because Matty had not wanted to give up the shifters, he refused to disobey. He wouldn't have anyone else dying on his watch. Not anytime soon. Not if he could help it.

Checking his watch secured snugly to his wrist, Matty bit back a sigh of defeat. They had been at this for nearly two hours and, as of yet, nothing of any worth had been said. As a soldier for the king, that was infuriating. As a man firmly on the shifters' side, it was a victory. No information meant that the troops had nothing to go on. No information meant that more shifters remained safe, away from any harm his dad and the troops might do to them if they ever caught up to them. Matty could live with that. Not that he could show that. Especially not in front of his dad.

He looked up from his watch and studied his dad, pursing his lips. In the dim light, he could see his dad quickly becoming more agitated. His voice became harsher and colder with each repeated question. He had even started rewording his questions, hoping to trip the shifter up. Nothing. A muscle twitched in his jaw. He was bordering on becoming violent.

It was time to step in.

Matty stood up from his seat in the corner as he watched his dad pour more water over the dark-haired female's face currently sitting in the chair. Alice, if he remembered correctly. Her dark curls were damp and in disarray, her body straining as she tried to endure his dad's current form of torture. Her clothes were dirty. Blood stained the collar and the cuffs of her dress while dirt crusted the hem. As the water increased, she began choking and spluttering, trying to twist away from the water so that she could breathe but it was making her situation worse. Every time she moved, the ropes cut into her wrists further, sending more blood dripping over her hands and onto the floor.

The puddle was tinged red and was quickly growing.

Matty clenched his jaw as he walked up behind his dad and placed his hand on his dad's shoulder. "Let her breathe," he cautioned, a hint of warning in his voice. "You won't get your answers if she dies from asphyxiation."

General Claery growled in response. He hated being told what to do, especially by Matty. He glanced back at Matty, his eyes hardening further.

And then, he tilted the bucket higher, dumping more water on the female as if to spite Matty.

Matty shook his head in disappointment. Was his dad really going to be this hardheaded? What did he get out of torturing this poor female? She wasn't going to give him anything more. It was obvious she didn't have the answers that his dad wanted. But yet, here they were with the female suffering more than was necessary because his dad had to be an asshole.

He could stop now. No one had forgotten he was the current king of the assholes. No one needed a reminder.

Matty took a step back for a moment, thinking. The more time he spent with his dad, the more he came to realize that his dad quite literally acted like an overgrown toddler who had never been told the meaning of the word no. He was spoiled. Or at least he acted like he was. He did what he wanted when he wanted, and if he couldn't, he got violent. Matty couldn't decide if that was a product of his rough upbringing or if that was just part of his personality. Either way, it didn't really matter. It's not like Matty or anyone else could change him. He was past the point of no return.

However, the downside of his dad's personality was that, unlike a toddler, he would get violent when he didn't get what he wanted, and that his violent tendencies could actually do some damage.

Matty wanted to avoid that today.

Somehow, during one of Matty's sessions of self-loathing, he had gotten it into his head that the current predicament he had found himself in was his fault. If he hadn't followed the blonde female and had kept working on the wall, he wouldn't be sitting in this room, watching one of the females being tortured. If he had just gone home on time, Kitty would never have complained, and his dad would never have found out that he had technically left his post for his own little personal mission. If he had never even talked to the blonde, he would never have had to lead his father and a group of men out to where the shifters had been staying and they would be miles away, a safe distance from his dad.

Matty had decided that while he may have failed to save the shifters from his father, he was now determined to get them out of the situation he had put them in nearly a month later. He hadn't figured out how quite yet, but he would do so, somehow, someway. He wouldn't rest until he made this right. It was the least he could do. The shifters had done nothing wrong. They deserved to live life away from this insanity.

He stepped closer to his dad again and gripped his dad's shoulder tighter than the previous time. "Dad," he murmured, trying to get his attention. "C'mon. Snap out of it. You can't kill her if you want answers. That's enough."

General Claery tensed and then shook him off. "Go back to your corner, boy," he growled. "This is my room. I am the general. I do what I want." He looked over at Matty, a manic glint in his eyes. "She will answer me."

"Not if you kill her, she won't," Matty protested, grabbing him again, yanking him back this time. "Besides, think about what she's telling you. She just said she doesn't have a home. That could mean it's been destroyed. They had all their belongings, and when we went through them, there wasn't much. This could very well be a group of shifters that had seen us coming and fled before they were killed in an attack, simply looking for refuge."

General Claery glowered at Matty but didn't say something, meaning that Matty's words were starting to break through. Matty, noticing the change, decided to press his advantage.

"They're young. I bet that they were from one of the villages not more than a couple days from the capital. They probably got the news that the war was restarting and fled. There is a very good chance that her hometown is no longer," Matty continued. "She really doesn't have a home. So drop it. Move on."

"That may be, but we can't know for sure," General Claery growled, his eyes locked back on the female.

Matty grabbed his dad's other shoulder and turned him around forcefully. The general's eyes widened in surprise, shocked that Matty now apparently had the strength to physically move him around. And then his eyes narrowed in anger.

"What the hell are you doing?" he snarled.

"Trying to get you to think," Matty retorted, not letting go. "She is a female. You and I both know that the males don't tell the females anything. The most you are going to get out of her is her daily schedule, and I could probably tell you that. They're housewives. She spent her days cooking and cleaning. That's it. So get a grip on yourself. You are embarrassing yourself, chasing information that she doesn't have."

General Claery took a step back as if he had been slapped, his eyes blowing wide. "Why... You... I..." he stammered.

"Give it a rest," Matty repeated, pushing his dad toward his stool.

General Claery stumbled forward, too shocked at Matty's outburst to do much else at the moment, and sat, his eyes flicking over Matty, studying him. It was as if he had never seen this side of Matty before, hadn't even known it existed. And he didn't know how to handle it.

Matty watched him for a moment, making sure he didn't get back up before crouching down in front of the female. Taking a rag, he gently dabbed at her face, mopping up the excess water and the blood dripping from her nose.

"Alice, right?" he murmured, his voice soft.

She stared at him wide-eyed, her dark brown eyes terrified.

"I'm not going to hurt you. Not interested in that," Matty reassured her as his dad scoffed behind him and started to mutter under his breath. Matty ignored him, keeping his gaze on Alice. "I'm just going to ask a couple questions and then we'll let you go rest. Okay?"

Alice nodded numbly, her eyes still wide and terrified. She reminded him of a puppy that had been kicked and yelled at simply for being a puppy.

"Is your hometown still standing?" he asked, following his gut feeling he'd gotten after listening to her previous answers.

"I don't know," she whispered, her voice so hoarse it made his own throat hurt.

"Why don't you know?" he asked, still dabbing at her nose to keep the blood from dripping into her mouth, his movements slow and gentle. He didn't want to hurt her more than she'd already been hurt. Besides, he'd promised. He'd told her he had no interest in further harming her. He would keep his word.

"When we got word, everyone fled," she rasped, her voice barely above a whisper.

Matty nodded. Not quite what he had thought exactly, but close enough. It was in the same vein.

"Are you mated?" he asked next. This was also a hunch. He had seen how the two males in the little group had lunged for her when they'd been captured.

Alice hesitated and then nodded slowly.

"He was with you." This was more of a statement than a question. He already knew that answer. The question was, which one was it? He sat back on his heels, studying her face. And then it hit him. The tall blonde male. The dark-haired one looked a lot like Alice. They had to be related. But the blonde? It had to be him.

Alice continued to watch him and then nodded again.

"Where were you headed?" he asked next.

"North," she whispered.

"Did you go straight north?" he asked, trying to figure out where she'd come from.

She shook her head. "We had family out this way. We were planning on stopping to see if they were still around before we made our way north."

Matty pursed his lips. That didn't help him much at all. Not really. But it was probably all he was going to get from her, which was more than his dad had managed to get in the last couple of hours.

Straightening, he looked back at his dad and arched an eyebrow as if to ask him silently if that was good enough for now. Running a hand down his face, General Claery gave him a weary but exasperated look. He wanted more, Matty could see it as plain as day, but he could also see that his dad knew he wasn't getting anything else. Not anytime soon. And definitely not from her.

"Take her back to her cell. We're done for today," General Claery finally grunted.

Matty poured a couple fingers worth of whiskey into a tumbler he'd found in one of the cupboards in the old O'Donoghue apartment above the general store. He'd moved back in after the shifter group had been captured since his brother didn't want to stay in the apartment himself. Besides, Matty was too angry with Kitty to stay in the same cabin as her. And there were perks to staying in town besides getting some much needed space from Kitty and his dad. Being in town kept him closer to the shifters. It also allowed him to keep an eye on the situation and step in when needed.

But it also made it a bit too easy to lose himself, drowning in his own doubts and self-hatred mentally while drowning himself in hard liquor physically.

Swirling the contents of the tumbler in his hand, he studied the dark amber liquid before raising it to his lips and knocking it back in one swift go. The whiskey was smooth, a good quality, but it burned as it went down the back of his throat before settling in his stomach, warming him. And then it started to go to his head as he walked over to the sitting room window and looked out.

A month. He'd been in town for a whole month, beating himself up over his own failure. A month where four innocent shifters had been beaten and tortured, being treated like animals when they were just as civilized as normal humans.

A month.

He pulled away from the window and walked down the hall to Clara's old room. Stepping inside, he stared at her belongings he'd unpacked shortly after moving back in, setting everything where they had once gone. It was like she had never left, minus a few items that were missing, taken by Mr. O'Donoghue when they'd gone to "rescue" her.

If the war ever ended...

If she was still alive...

If she ever came home...

Matty shook his head. It was a pipe dream. She was as good as gone. But just to be on the safe side, if she did come back, he'd have a place ready for her. And until then, he would work to make up for his past mistakes, work to make himself worthy of her.

She was his queen and he but her humble servant, begging for forgiveness.

CHAPTER 27

RONAN

The brutally cold morning air made Ronan's bones ache. Spring had to be around the corner. It just had to be. He didn't have a calendar accessible, but he was sure if he had one, it would tell him they were nearing the end of April. However, being nestled right next to the mountains, winter had yet to release Reynardsville from its clutches.

Blowing on his hands and rubbing them together, he walked over to the main fire pit in the center of camp, joining Zeke and Maddox. Both looked tired after having been up on duty all night. He frowned at them as he came to a stop next to Maddox, studying the dark circles under their eyes.

"Why haven't either of you crawled into bed yet?" he asked casually, not wanting to sound like he was prying while testing the waters. Both males had been on edge lately and he didn't want to set them off.

If only he knew what was going on, but they had stopped telling him most things in recent weeks, trying to keep him more mentally stable. He thanked them for that. Most of the time. Other times, he wanted to strangle both men and demand answers. He hated being left in the dark. Out on the field, not having information or being on the same page as his team could get him killed. He knew that. They knew that. And yet...

He dropped his gaze to the fire, watching the dancing flames and the blackened wood crumbling, turning to ash, hoping that they would answer him this time. Or at least hoping they would give him something more than their usual responses.

"I'm tired."

"It's cold."

"Just trying to work out a schedule."

"The news. It's not pretty."

"Politics."

He glanced up before he could stop himself. And then he froze, spotting a folded piece of parchment in Zeke's hands. With a sniff from the cold, Zeke held it out to him, waving it slightly, telling him silently to take it from him.

With a trembling hand, Ronan reached out and wrapped his hand around the thick parchment. It was still warm, meaning that Zeke and Maddox had probably just been reading it while standing in front of the fire. Unfolding what he assumed was a letter, he caught both of them watching him apprehensively. Trying not to let it bother him, he dropped his gaze to the writing. It was a short message. Only a couple of sentences, and not addressed to anyone in particular. But it was signed by someone he'd quickly learned to fear simply from the rumors and stories surrounding him. Briggs Freisinger.

Lions rescheduled their training time with Clara for a later time. Bringing the girl to you later today for your two weeks.

Briggs Freisinger

They were getting Clara two weeks earlier than they had anticipated. Wait... Clara was in Reynardsville? He should have seen them arrive. Why hadn't he seen them arrive? He glanced up from the letter and looked between Maddox and Zeke, his brow furrowing in confusion, trying to keep his emotions in check. He wanted to stay. He had to stay. He had to prove he could handle this or he would be sent back to the pack house before he could even ask them to hear him out.

"When did the Reynards arrive?" he asked, his voice level and clear, making it sound like he wasn't bothered in the slightest that they had arrived without him noticing.

"About five weeks ago," Maddox grunted. "I was on duty that day. They passed right by me. Talked to them all for a minute. Even Clara." He gave Ronan a pointed look as if daring him to ask how Clara was, begging for every minute detail.

"I assume she was well," Ronan said, his voice remaining light and uncaring.

Maddox's and Zeke's brows shot up and then their eyes narrowed suspiciously.

"She was with her mate. And Freisinger. They argued for a minute before Freisinger went to talk to Zeke," Maddox continued cautiously. "The whole group looked as if they were in good health. A bit cold, but given the time of year, that was to be expected. They headed into the city. I imagine Mrs. Reynard reopened her townhomes."

"The Reynards are officially back in business," Zeke snorted derisively. "Or perhaps I should say the Reynards are done using puppets."

"Nah." Maddox shook his head. "Clara is the new puppet. You and I both know that she doesn't know anything about running a pack. She's just going to be their figurehead. They'll pair her with someone who knows what he's doing, and he'll be the real alpha, the real leader."

"I guess that's true," Zeke mused.

Ronan, tuning them out, reread the short letter before handing it back and staring into the dancing flames of the fire once more. Clara would be here today. He would get to see her if they didn't send him packing in the next few minutes.

He clasped his hands behind his back, his unruly curls falling into his face as he continued to stare unseeing into the flames.

He could do this. He had been around her before without making a complete and utter fool of himself. Besides, they'd had more than enough time apart, perhaps he would be able to keep his wits about him when he saw her. And now that she'd been mated to Warren for a few months now, perhaps her scent had dulled to other potential mates. Or rather, perhaps it had mingled more fully with Warren's, giving the potentials a good whiff of the male who had claimed her, a blatant warning to stay away.

But who knew?

Only time would tell.

"Should I pack my bags?" Ronan finally asked after a few minutes of heavy silence only broken by the crackling of the fire and the muffled voices of the rest of the pack moving about in their tents.

"We're short patrols right now," Zeke said slowly, hesitantly. "I can't afford to send you back right now like I had originally planned. Not after the Barker twins' family decided to flee and head north. I can't blame them for following their family."

"So I'm staying then?" Ronan confirmed, his words just as slow, just as cautious.

"You're staying."

The sun was about three-quarters of the way across the sky when a small commotion drew everyone's attention in the camp, Ronan's included. The back gate of the city opened with a loud squeal, making half the shifters wince and cover their ears against the harsh sound. And then there was nothing.

Staring at the now open gate, Ronan frowned. He had a hunch that the gate had opened to let out Clara and Freisinger, but he didn't want to assume. He had to play this cool. No getting excited. No presuming that she wanted anything to do with him. The last time she had seen him, she had made it perfectly clear that he was nothing to her. She'd torn out his heart and stomped on it, leaving him reeling and heartbroken in the middle of a busy street. She hadn't even turned around to see if he was okay. She had just... left.

Dropping his gaze down to the blade in his hand, he ran the whetstone he was using to sharpen it over the sharp edge of the blade again, grounding himself with the grating sound that it caused.

Footsteps sounded close to the gate. About four pairs from the sound of it, but he didn't look up to confirm.

Ronan didn't care.

Not one bit.

Clara was not his. He could whine and pout about that all he wanted, but she was not his. Fate, cruel as it was, had decided that for him years ago. He had just been too stupid to realize it until now. She couldn't choose who she wanted. Even the male she was with now was too stupid to realize that she wasn't really his. She was Freisinger's. It was only a matter of time.

That wouldn't stop him from apologizing though. He had messed up. Committed a crime against her that was unforgivable. He would grovel if he had to. And if she never accepted his apology, so be it. He would never stop paying for his mistake.

Next to him, Zeke sat on the ground, darning a sock, completely unphased. Ronan didn't know how he did it. In fact, he was a bit shocked that the male wasn't up greeting the pack's guests. But that was just Zeke. He may be the leader, but he was, at his core, just another member. He treated everyone the same. He was fair and just. And most importantly, he was down to earth.

Suddenly, Ronan knew why the wolf pack was on Clara's training docket. They were realistic and that was something that a leader needed in a war. Perhaps a bit blunt, but when leading troops, that was necessary. A leader could not afford to beat around the bush. Wasting time could get her troops killed.

He finally looked up just in time to see Freisinger stop in front of Zeke, a sneer on his face. Ronan studied him for a minute. He was tall and lean, much like Ronan. His hair was about shoulder length and pulled back into a low ponytail, his facial hair was neatly trimmed. Freisinger's brows furrowed as he looked down his nose at Ronan and Zeke on the ground.

Behind Freisinger was what looked like a guard, wearing the Reynard's colors of burnt orange, silver, and black. Ronan paid him little mind. He was of no concern to him. He doubted that he'd even speak to the guard.

Behind the guard... Ronan's breath caught in his throat. It was Clara and Warren. Warren looked much the same as the last time Ronan had had the misfortune of meeting him. He was still extremely tall, his long dark auburn hair pulled back into a ponytail, his dark eyes piercing, and the scar down the side of his face intimidating. And he was still just as broad. Solid.

But Clara...

His green eyes studied her for a moment. She had changed. A lot. Not in looks. Not really. It was in the way she carried herself and that changed everything. When he had known her, she had kept her long dark hair pulled back, rarely letting it down. But it had always been a fashionable, or rather feminine, hairstyle. Now it was pulled back into a tight, well-woven braid that went down her back. Her eyes, once kind and warm, were sharp and calculating, not missing a thing as she surveyed the scene. Her dainty mouth was pulled into a frown, her brows furrowed, a look of distaste on her face. And her stance... Gone was the girl bouncing on her toes looking to help and eager to prove herself. In her place was a woman standing with her feet grounded a few paces apart, a fighting stance, ready to go at a moment's notice.

This wasn't his Clara. Not at all.

He looked away, dropping his gaze, not wanting to say anything. He was just going to keep to himself. He'd promised as much. He shifted uncomfortably. He could feel Maddox watching him carefully from a few feet away, trying to see if Ronan would keep his word or if he needed to cart Ronan away before he did something stupid.

He wasn't going to do something stupid.

Out of the corner of his eye, he noticed Warren stiffen. And then Clara stiffened beside him. It was almost imperceptible, but he had a feeling they'd finally either seen him or smelled him. Perhaps both.

But neither said anything.

This surprised him. He had half expected Clara to start yelling at him, to tell him to get away from her, to tell him to get out of her life. He had half expected Warren to lay him out for what he had done to Clara. If he was being honest, he deserved it. And he knew Warren knew. Clara wouldn't have kept that from him.

Ronan looked up, trying to keep the shock radiating through him from showing. His eyes landed on Freisinger, determined not to look at either Clara or Warren. He was with his pack. He was minding his business. Everything was fine.

"Darning a sock? How low could you be?" Freisinger finally spat at Zeke.

"Unlike you, I am outside the city and do not have the luxury of having someone knit me a new pair," Zeke said calmly.

Behind him, Clara's face softened almost imperceptibly, a hint of her old self trying to shine through.

Ronan's heart pounded in his chest.

Freisinger scoffed. "Well, put it away. We've much to discuss now that we're here. Clara is to train with your pack. I am to oversee."

"And the other two males?" Zeke asked even though Ronan knew he knew that answer already. He was just probing to see what Freisinger would say.

"The wolf is yours to do with as you please. He hasn't gotten the hint to go home back to his own pack yet. Perhaps you'll have more success than I in that department. And the guard is here to watch Clara when I cannot. She is the heir after all and we simply cannot have anything happen to her," Freisinger responded.

"Yet," Ronan added to Freisinger's words silently. He couldn't have anything happen to her yet. He had yet to mate her, and until then, she held a slight advantage.

Zeke stood, putting his sock back in his bag. "Come, we can talk in my tent."

As Zeke started to lead the small group to the tent, they started to pass by Ronan.

That's when things went south.

As she neared Ronan, Clara visibly stiffened. Everyone could see it. And Ronan made the mistake of speaking when he should have kept his mouth shut.

"I won't hurt you again, Clara," he murmured just loud enough for her to hear.

Smack!

Clara's fist collided with his face, hitting him square in the jaw and knocking him onto his back.

Ronan's eyes widened in surprise. He had not been expecting that. And he had not expected her to pack that powerful of a punch. She had gotten stronger than he had realized.

Before he could sit up to confront Clara, wanting to know what that was for, Freisinger whirled on her, grabbing her arm and dragging her over to him. Behind her, Warren growled low in his chest, an audible warning for Freisinger to get his hands off of her.

Not looking up, Freisinger grabbed Clara's chin, digging his fingers in as he wrenched her face up to his. "You will behave," he hissed.

Without warning, he released her face and spun her around. Another audible smack rang through the camp as his hand slammed into her ass making her shriek.

Ronan's eyes widened further.

Freisinger had just publicly spanked Clara.

Freisinger had just publicly spanked a female that wasn't his.

Chaos erupted.

Shit.

CHAPTER 28

WARREN

*S*mack.

A shrill cry of surprise escaped Clara as Freisinger's hand made contact with her rear end through the trousers that she had been given for the purpose of training. Long skirts that were the usual day-to-day wear for females only got in the way when sparring. She jerked forward, her eyes widening. The pack surrounding them started talking, their voices getting louder, protesting. A few moved forward to help Clara but then paused, looking uncertainly between Warren, Clara, and Freisinger, not sure if they would be causing more problems if they helped.

Warren took a step forward as Clara's eyes met his. Her cheeks pinked in embarrassment as Freisinger's hand came down again.

Smack.

Another cried pain escaped her lips, followed by a soft whimper as she squirmed, trying to get away. Freisinger's grip tightened, yanking her closer, bringing his mouth down to her ears and hissing something at her, too low for Warren to make out.

The camp fell silent. No one talked. No one moved as Clara whimpered again. Her eyes met Ronan's, anger and hatred shimmering in them. But there was also embarrassment and shame. And then her eyes darted back over to Warren's, pleading now.

Meeting her eyes, Warren saw red. How dare this male touch his mate. Clara was not Freisinger's. She never would be if he had anything to say about it. He'd held his tongue up until now, not wanting to cause any problems. But no longer. He was done. He had warned Mrs. Reynard what would happen if she was harmed, and he had meant every word. It was time to live up to his promise.

Jerking to life, Warren lunged forward, wrapping his large hand around Freisinger's throat. With a growl, he yanked him back away from Clara. Eyes wide, Clara watched him yank Freisinger further back before scrambling back herself, away from Freisinger, away from Ronan, away from the rest of the wolves. Her eyes darted warily to the guard who had quickly darted away, running toward the city. Warren followed her gaze to the guard, his heart sinking. He should go after the guard, should stop him before he got to the Reynards and told them about what had just happened. But he couldn't get himself to release Freisinger.

With a snarl, he turned back to Freisinger, his dark eyes blazing as he took in the smug look on the male's face that was quickly fading to anger, hatred, and a bit of fear.

"What the hell do you think you're doing, fox?" Warren demanded with a low growl that resonated from the depths of his chest. "She is not yours to touch."

"She stepped out of line," Freisinger snarled back. "If you will not reprimand her, I will."

"That is not your place!" Warren yelled into his face, spittle flying in his anger.

"It is not my place. Yet," Freisinger corrected, trying to maintain his cool façade, trying to show that he was unbothered by the situation. But Warren knew better. He could see the male's pupils dilating in fear as he realized that he was in a rather precarious situation. Warren was bigger, stronger, and an unknown. A wild card. Freisinger had made the mistake of not paying more attention to Warren. He had no idea how Warren would react, and he was regretting it now.

Warren relished in his fear.

"It will never be your place," Warren countered, his eyes narrowing. "I do not plan on going anywhere anytime soon. I survived death for her. I'll survive you and everyone else that thinks they can take her from me, too."

Freisinger scoffed, his eyes narrowing. His body tensed in Warren's grip as Warren tightened his hold. He could feel Freisinger's pulse fluttering under his thumb. He was more nervous than he was willing to let on, hiding it from everyone surrounding them.

He wasn't as unphased as he led everyone to believe. Warren could work with this.

"Apologize," Warren demanded, dragging him closer so that they were nearly nose to nose.

"Why?" Freisinger said, sounding more like a petulant teenager than the fearless military leader he was reputed to be.

"You were out of line," Warren hissed. He glanced up at Clara to see her still standing a few paces away, keeping her distance from everyone, her arms wrapped around herself as if she were trying to hold herself together. Warren's heart ached at the sight, wanting to toss Freisinger off to the side so that he could sweep her up into his arms and comfort her. But that would make things worse right now. She didn't need him stepping in to comfort her. She needed to maintain her image as the next leader of the Reynard pack.

Not like Freisinger hadn't just ruined that by spanking her in front of an entire pack. The bastard. No wonder called him The Asshole when it was just the two of them. Perhaps he would have to steal the name from her and use it himself.

But still, it this was the treatment she was going to get, why'd they even bother coming?

He looked back down at Freisinger, releasing him and shoving him away from Clara. "Stay away from her today if you aren't going to apologize. You've made things worse than they needed to be. You've done enough damage."

Freisinger massaged his throat, glaring at Warren for a moment before straightening up, and fixing the hair that had slipped out of his neat ponytail. A muscle in his jaw twitched, his face hardening as he stared down Warren. And then his gaze shifted to Clara.

"Your grandmother will hear about this," Freisinger stated, his voice flat but cold.

Clara bristled slightly. "Is that supposed to scare me?" she asked, her voice just as cold as Freisinger's.

"It should," Freisinger countered.

Clara sneered at him. "You're forgetting, I hold the power here. Not you."

Freisinger's eyes widened at her statement, obviously flabbergasted. Warren's eyes widened as well. What was she talking about?

"Little fox..." Warren said cautiously.

"No." She shook her head. "It's true. I have the power. I can walk away. I can go home. I don't have to take this."

Warren's eyes widened further before they softened, pride filling his chest. She wasn't wrong. Huffing a small laugh, he walked over, wrapping an arm around her like he'd been dying to do since he'd seen Freisinger lay a hand on her. "Let's get our tent set up for the night while Freisinger hashes things out. It's about all he's good for."

He glanced back at Freisinger with a smirk, but then his eyes flitted over Ronan. Memories of Clara telling him what had happened before he had been able to come after her after the attack on their camp by the general and his men flickered through his mind. His eyes hardened. This must be the male that had helped her. Clara wasn't one for violence, so that would explain the punch. And... He sniffed the air tentatively, his gaze hardening further. He thought he recognized the scent.

The rogue from Springfield.

But he wasn't a rogue anymore.

Warren wondered if his new pack knew what Ronan had been up to before joining them. Not that it was any of his business. He needed to focus on Clara.

"Let's go," he murmured quietly to Clara, leading her back to the horse and small cart they'd been using to haul all their gear and tents, courtesy of Mrs. Reynard.

Warren watched as Clara circled the small tent in her agitation. Her cheeks were still pink from Freisinger's very public spanking earlier. He couldn't even fathom how agitated and humiliated she must feel. Part of him still wanted to go murder Freisinger. Part of him also wanted to go murder the rogue. Hell, if he could take out both in one shot, half their problems would be solved. But violence wasn't the answer.

Yet.

"Little fox, how bad did he hurt you?" Warren asked, his voice low and soothing.

"Physically? My ass stings. Emotionally? I want the earth to open up and swallow me whole," Clara responded, her voice trembling slightly.

With a sigh, Warren stood up and walked over to her, pulling her against him, caging her in with his arms. Leaning down, he pressed a kiss to the top of her head before burying his nose in her hair, breathing in her scent. He would never get tired of how she felt in his arms. He would never get tired of how she smelled. This felt right. It was right. And he'd be damned if he let anyone take her away from him again. He'd rather die first.

"You'll be alright, love," he murmured into her hair as he felt her rest her head against his chest, her body slowly relaxing with each breath they took together. "It was one moment. In front of just one pack. And they didn't seem to be on Freisinger's side. They won't hold it against you or think any less of you."

"I hope you're right," Clara whispered into his chest, her breath warm against his skin, even through his shirt.

"When am I wrong?" he asked, teasing her.

"Uh, all the time," she said, matching his tone of voice.

He scoffed playfully. "You wound me."

"I do believe you'll live," she countered.

"I do believe you're right," Warren chuckled, running his hand up and down her back soothingly. "Let's get you into bed. I need to go have a word with the pack leader myself. I don't trust Freisinger to give us all the information we need."

"Fair enough," Clara conceded, pressing a kiss to his chest before stepping back. "It won't have been the first time he has willingly held information back. He thinks he's the most important, the only one that deserves to know everything that's going on. He couldn't be more wrong. He'll get someone killed."

Warren suppressed a smirk. Clara had definitely been paying attention to the elephant shifters and the other fox shifters during their endless hours of history and intelligence lessons. She was already starting to see patterns in behavior, noting how Freisinger led and how those of the past had led. She would be a fabulous tactician. Not that he was going to tell her that. Not yet. The time wasn't quite right.

Reaching forward, he swiped his fingers through the laces securing her shirt, loosening them all at once. "Arms up," he said gruffly before tugging her shirt over her head.

Dropping the shirt on the ground, his eyes swept over Clara's bare torso, the way her nipples peaked in the chilly air. Huffing a laugh, fighting the urge to strip her trousers next and sink into her warmth right then and there, he turned to her bag and fished out a nightgown for her. Bunching it up, he held it open and waited for her to slip her arms through before letting it flow down over her body.

"Do you need any more help?" he asked, watching as she hooked her thumbs into the waist of her trousers and pushed them down over her hips before they, too, dropped down to the ground.

"No." Clara shook her head. "I'll get the bed made up. You go do what needs to be done before they retire for the night."

Warren nodded before pausing to press a tender kiss to Clara's lips. Then, ducking, he slipped out of the tent and made his way to what he assumed was the leader's tent. However, when he got there, it wasn't the leader he found. It was the male that had greeted them before entering the city, Maddox, and the rogue. If he remembered correctly, Clara had said his name was Ronan or something like that.

"How can we help you?" Maddox asked, a hint of sympathy in his eyes as he studied Warren.

Pointedly ignoring Ronan, Warren met Maddox's eyes. "I was looking for your leader. I wanted to go over the same information with him that Freisinger did."

"Zeke?" Ronan's brows shot up in confusion. "Why do you..."

Maddox cut him off, holding up a meaty hand. "He's still meeting with Freisinger. Is there a reason you want to speak to him as well?"

"Freisinger has a habit of leaving Clara in the dark," Warren grunted. "He doesn't tell her anything, even when the plans involve her."

Both Maddox's and Ronan's mouths popped open into a surprised "O".

"That'll do it," Maddox grunted. "As soon as he gets back, I'll send him your way unless you want to wait."

"No." Warren shook his head, his eyes flicking to Ronan again. Maddox, catching the quick look, glanced at Ronan, too, quickly putting the pieces together.

"You know what he did," Maddox said in a way that was more of a statement than a question.

"Yes," Warren grunted. "I heard it all. What he did, how she reacted, how she felt, how she still feels..." His gaze locked on Ronan again.

Ronan bristled, shame darkening his cheeks a dark ruddy red.

"You are no better than I," Ronan retorted after a second.

"I never claimed I was," Warren returned coldly, taking a step back, desperate to get away before he pummeled Ronan for his past actions against Clara. She still woke up crying on occasion, clutching her neck, her whole body trembling. He knew he was responsible for some of her nightmares, but so was Ronan.

Ronan, noticing his retreat, narrowed his eyes at him. "That's right, go run, just like you always have. Go live in your shadows. As if you deserve her," he scoffed, taking a step forward, causing Warren to back up another pace.

Maddox's brows shot up in surprise at Ronan's bold behavior. And Warren...

"You're right. I don't deserve her," Warren admitted, his voice low as he stopped his retreat. "But for some reason, she has stayed with me even though I have given her ample opportunities to leave me behind. And because of that, I will spend the rest of my life trying to become the male that she deserves. If that includes burning the kingdom to the ground to make sure that she is safe and happy, to make sure she gets the future that she desires and deserves, I will gladly do it."

"You wouldn't," Ronan retorted. "You didn't even have the balls to confront her in person. You didn't have the guts to talk to her father, to explain that you were interested, to ask for her hand. You just took."

"As if you were any better?" Warren arched a brow at him.

"I saved her," Ronan retorted.

"We both did," Warren corrected. "But I have continued to protect her and that's more that you ever did and ever will do."

"But..." Ronan tried to counter, now thoroughly pissed, his whole body shaking.

"I may have done things the wrong way when it comes to her," Warren admitted readily. "Hell, I hurt her more times than I can count, but I have owned and apologized for my mistakes. And even though she has accepted my apologies, I will continue to own them and try to make up for them. I will do everything in my power to make up for my mistakes with her because she is perfection. She is the air I breathe, the reason I exist. She is my queen, my goddess. I will gladly serve and worship her until I breathe my last breath. Can you say the same?"

Ronan took a step back, his eyes widening. And then he disappeared back into the tent, leaving Warren with Maddox.

"Holy shit," Maddox breathed. "I'm getting the feeling that there's more to this story than just Ronan trying to claim your mate."

"There is. And maybe one day you'll hear that story. But tonight is not that night," Warren grunted. "I'm going to go back to Clara, keep an eye on her. When Zeke returns, please..."

"I promise to send him your way," Maddox said solemnly. "You have my word."

CHAPTER 29

Clara

Clara's footsteps sounded against the tile floor of the foyer of her grandmother's townhome. She hadn't been here since the night they'd arrived a little over four weeks ago. Warren had insisted on renting a small apartment away from her family. Naturally, she hadn't complained. It gave the two of them time away from the harsh demands being thrust upon her, the disgusted looks when they saw her with Warren, and let them decompress. Alone. But now that they were moving to the packs outside the city for training, it was starting to feel like a waste of money. She made a mental note to talk to Warren about that later, but right now she needed to focus.

Not even an hour after Warren had left her to go talk to Zeke, leader of the Romulus pack, her guard, or rather Freisinger's guard, had returned with a summons from her grandmother. She needed to meet with her grandmother and the council at eight o'clock exactly the next morning. Grumbling, she had begrudgingly agreed to go and then had whined about it to Warren when he'd returned. He didn't like that she was being summoned any more than she did, but he had assured her that it would be fine.

She wished she had her mate's confidence. Even just an iota of it would be nice right now. Alas, she was stuck with her own meager confidence at the moment. It would have to do. She could put on a brave face. She could pretend that none of this bothered her. And when she returned home to Warren, she could let it all out. He would listen. He would hold her. And then he would reassure her.

Everything would be alright.

Maybe.

The sinking feeling in the pit of her stomach that she couldn't quite shake told her exactly what this meeting was about. It was about her punching Ronan in the face as soon as she'd seen him. Not that she could help it. She had just sort of... done it. Without thinking. One minute, she had seen him. The next, she'd felt her heart freeze, memories flashing through her head. How he'd shifted and approached her. How his approach had forced her to shift herself. How she'd run, grabbing the dagger he'd gifted her. How he'd caught up to her and they'd both shifted back, leaving them both naked. How he'd grabbed her and started to force himself onto her. How she'd stabbed him and fled.

That should have been the end then and there.

But no.

Ronan had followed her into the city to "keep her safe". And for that, she was grateful.

Sort of.

Mostly.

She wanted to be.

Ronan had kept to himself after that, making sure she'd had room and board for that first night, offering to help her find her family. But after being attacked in the old city hall, she'd come to the realization that she didn't need him, that her family wasn't there, that she needed to get out, to go home, to find Warren. And that's what she'd done.

Once the memories had faded, all she'd felt was white-hot anger flowing through her veins. It was all his fault. He had led General Claery to Warren's pack. He was the reason she'd been captured and tortured. He was the reason her pa was dead. He was the reason her grandmother had figured out where she was. If only he'd left well enough alone.

But it was too late for that now. She couldn't change the past. Nor could he.

That didn't stop her from being mad, though.

She had intended on walking past him. Had planned on not even acknowledging him. But then she'd caught his eyes. They were such a pretty green.

That thought alone had sickened her. Why was she admiring her attacker's eyes? And before she knew it, her fist was colliding with his face. God's had it hurt. Her knuckles were bruised now and very sore.

She wouldn't lie, though. It had been satisfying, watching his eyes widen in surprise as she'd punched him. It had been even more satisfying watching him wince in pain.

Her satisfaction had been short-lived, however. All because of Freisinger.

Clara didn't hate many people. It was a short list, reserved for only those who had grievously wronged her. General Claery was on the top of that list. Ronan was right under Claery, tied with Matty. Freisinger, though... Oh, he was contending for spot number one at this point. And not because of what he had done so far. No, he was contending for spot number one because of what he was planning on doing. If he got his way... She shuddered. She would rather die than let him claim her as his.

Living as Briggs Freisinger's mate would be a living nightmare.

If she could punch him for every little snide comment he'd made in the last few weeks about how he'd have her under him, he wouldn't be able to use his mouth anymore. Soon, though. She would get her revenge soon enough. Then he'd see that she didn't belong under him, that he would never have her under him. She was above him in every single way.

She'd prove it.

Clara came to the end of the hall, stopping just in front of a pair of massive double doors. Oak, she thought, though she wasn't sure. Her hometown, Springfield didn't have many trees. Any and all lumber was brought in from the towns to the north, closer to the mountains. They were reliable trade partners. They got wood and wool from them. Springfield gave them wheat and meat in return. She wondered idly if that partnership was still going with the war now going.

Raising her hand, she knocked on the oak door, her knuckles smarting from the contact. Wrong hand. She should have used her left. Too late now.

The door creaked open and a butler in a ridiculous outfit ushered her in. Clara stared at him for a moment, her eyes wide as she took in the sight, biting back a laugh. Gods, her grandmother was pretentious. Shaking her head, she tore her gaze from the butler and stepped inside, her eyes sweeping the room before landing on her grandmother. Her great uncles stood behind her and Freisinger stood off to the left. Her cheeks flushed as she noted Freisinger standing there, the memory of him spanking her in front of the wolf pack still very fresh in her memory. Her ass still stung. Hiding a grimace, she met his gaze coolly. She wouldn't let him see how much his punishment had affected her. She wouldn't give him any more power over her.

Arching a brow at her, he met her gaze, his face impassive. He wasn't giving anything away either.

The bastard.

"You wanted to see me, grandmother?" Clara asked politely, hovering by the door, unwilling to step further into the room as she turned her attention to Mrs. Reynard.

"I did." Mrs. Reynard nodded, pursing her lips in distaste. "I was told, by your guard, that you have resorted to violence to solve your problems. And I had such high hopes for you. Your mother never..."

"Don't talk to me about my mother," Clara cut her off, a muscle in her jaw twitching.

Mrs. Reynard's eyes narrowed. "Very well. Since you are so insistent that we never talk about your mother, we won't. But the issue remains. You attacked that wolf unprovoked."

"It wasn't unprovoked," Clara stated bluntly. "There's history between that male and me. I warned him the last time that I saw him that it wouldn't be pretty if we ever met again. At the time, I wasn't sure what I'd do if I saw him again, but I did warn him. He was well aware he'd probably get hit. If not by me, then by Warren. Besides, he was lucky it was me. Warren would have killed him."

Freisinger's brow arched as he studied Clara, her response apparently taking him by surprise. Crossing his arms over his chest, he responded before Mrs. Reynard could get a chance.

"History? What kind of history?" he grunted.

"The kind that involves trying to claim someone without their consent," Clara replied, not looking at him. Instead, her gaze was focused on her grandmother.

"When did this happen?" Freisinger asked, his voice growing darker as his eyes zeroed in on her neck as if looking for signs of a second claim mark.

"A few months ago," Clara said, crossing her arms over her chest, trying not to let it show that him scrutinizing her like this was bothering her. She would not show weakness in front of him again. It was a good way for her to get publicly spanked again and she didn't care to repeat the experience. Ever.

"I take it he was not successful," Percil, her great uncle, chimed in. Like Freisinger, he was busy studying her. Unlike Freisinger, his gaze wasn't judgmental. Only concern and curiosity lingered there. Clara felt her heart warm just a bit. Perhaps she wasn't as alone as she thought. She had an ally. Or so she hoped.

"No," she answered her great uncle.

"Did that strapping young wolf save you then?" Percil asked, earning himself a dirty look from both her other great uncle, Arik, and her grandmother.

"No."

Freisinger's gaze snapped to hers, his brows furrowed in confusion. "Who saved you then?"

"I did," she replied simply. It was the truth. Not one that she expected him to believe. But still, she had no reason to lie. It would do her no good. He could take it or leave it for all she cared.

"How?" he demanded, his tone growing colder and darker by the second, causing both her uncles to stiffen, their gazes landing on Freisinger, a hint of warning in their eyes. He needed to back down or they would step in. They would always choose a female family member over a male that could protect himself.

Clara watched the interaction with interest, but she kept her facial expression neutral, not wanting to give anything away. It wasn't often she got to watch the dynamics between her family and Freisinger without prying eyes. It was one thing as they traveled. Freisinger was in his element there so they all deferred to him to keep them alive and on the right path. In the city? That was a whole different story. This was her family's territory, and they knew it. Freisinger was supposed to defer to them.

Her brow twitched slightly.

The keywords being: "was supposed to".

Freisinger wasn't deferring. His ego had apparently become so large with the promise that he would be leading the pack once he mated her, he no longer cared it seemed. He was going to do what he wanted when he wanted. And that made him dangerous.

Clara took a step back.

"How did you get away without being claimed?" Freisinger demanded, taking a few steps toward her.

"I stabbed him in the back. Quite literally," she said coldly. Let him do with that information what he will, she thought to himself. It wasn't every day that a female shifter fought back. And it was rare that a female won when she did.

"You... you stabbed... him?" Arik said slowly, his voice choked as he blinked at her as if he wasn't sure he had heard her right.

"Yes, I stabbed him." Clara nodded, her eyes locking with Freisinger's even though she was responding to her great uncle. "The wolf in question, Ronan, was accompanying me to Reynardsville after helping me escape from General Claery. Or rather, he didn't really help me escape. He gave me instructions on how to survive until he came back for me after the general finished torturing me for information. When he returned, he made sure I was alright for the night and then left for a week or two. He returned again and then accompanied me the rest of the way. The night before we entered the city, he gifted me a dagger. I accepted it. And then he lost control. He was on top of me and I had the dagger in hand, so he got stabbed. From there I fled. End story."

Freisinger's eyes widened as he studied her. Behind him, her family had gone unnaturally still.

"What? Did you think I was helpless?" she asked, a hint of bitter amusement in her voice. When no one answered, she continued. "I grew up with humans in a remote town on the edge of civilization. I didn't grow up a lady. I grew up learning how to survive. I worked and I worked hard. I know how to grow food. I know how to butcher meat if needed. I can cook. I can clean. And I can fight well enough to get myself out of most scrapes. I have survived being kidnapped twice. I have survived being tortured. I have survived being claimed. And I have survived being taken advantage of. If you thought you could walk all over me, that I was some meek, timid girl, then you were and are so very wrong, and I feel sorry for you."

Silence.

Clara gazed at each of them for a minute, her gaze challenging.

"I know what you have planned. I am far from stupid. I have heard enough snippets of your conversations and the snide remarks thrown at me to piece your plans together. You will not get that. Not from me. So try to tell me to leave Warren. I dare you. You won't like what happens when you do," Clara continued, needing to say her piece before walking out the door. "If you try and force me to be with someone I do not want nor love, I will walk right out those doors and I will not look back. I have better things to do with my time and my life than be a puppet for you. Things change now."

As she finished, she turned on her heel and shoved the double doors open, stalking out of the room and down the long foyer.

CHAPTER 30

ALICE

Alice shifted on the small bed being careful not to disturb Mira, who was finally getting some sleep. Neither one of them had been sleeping much since being captured what felt like a lifetime ago, so when one managed to fall asleep, the other kept watch. Down the hall, in their own cell, Alice knew Xander and Able were doing the same.

Wishing she could curl up with Xander, wanting to seek out the comfort and safety of his arms, she resisted the urge to call out to him. She didn't want to attract any attention to herself or Mira. She also didn't want to get Xander or Able into trouble.

Communication between prisoners was apparently strictly forbidden.

She'd learned that the hard way already, she reminded herself, rubbing the raw skin of her wrists, the memory of getting dragged out of her cell and beaten for trying to check on the males still fresh in her mind even though it had been weeks ago. But it still stuck out, probably because it had been one of the instances that showed her just how cruel the human men were.

Ropes tied around her wrists.

Being yanked out of the cell by the rope.

The rope cutting into her wrists, burning, tearing, ripping.

Blood dripping down her hands and her arms, the steady *drip drip drip* on the wood floor beneath her seared into her memory.

The rough voices of the guards as they yanked her along.

Tripping over her feet, stumbling, nearly landing on her face.

Alice shook her head, trying to clear the memory from her mind as her heart started to race and her breath came out in short, quick bursts. She didn't need to hyperventilate. That was a weakness, and if anyone heard, they'd exploit it, using it against her.

She had to be strong.

It's hard to be strong, though, when it feels like the whole world is against you, especially when you didn't do anything wrong.

Alice slipped off the bed slowly, still moving carefully so as to not wake Mira, and tiptoed over to the bars of the cell. Positioning herself just right, she was able to see down the hall to Xander and Able's cell. Her heart ached and her chest constricted when she couldn't see either of them. They, like Mira, were probably resting, saving their strength for whatever fresh horrors the morning would bring. Not that the general or his men cared what time of day it was. Any time was a good time to show them just how worthless they thought they were all because they were shifters.

Dirty.

Filthy.

Barbaric.

Unworthy.

Monster.

Animal.

Heathen.

Creature.

The list went on as Alice's mind played the list of insults she'd had hurled at her. Some she could ignore. Others... were harder. Each was as untrue as the next, but they still hurt. And when that's all she heard, it got harder and harder to remember that they weren't true, that she wasn't those things.

Gods, why wouldn't it end?

As quiet as a mouse, she retreated to the bed, perching on the edge, not wanting to lay down but wanting to rest at the same time. Sleep was her only reprieve, but she wouldn't fall asleep. Not while Mira was sleeping. She could take her turn later.

If there was a later.

Leaning forward, she buried her face in her hands with a low groan, wincing as her face brushed the abused skin on her wrist. She wasn't sure which was worse, her wrists or her face. Both were in bad shape.

Footsteps sounded near the end of the hall, making Alice tense. No, no, no, no, no... This could not be happening. Not right now. It was the middle of the night for crying out loud. Couldn't they give them a break? They could only take so much. But Alice was painfully aware that they didn't care. Why should they when they didn't even see them as human?

Dirty.

Rotten.

Inhuman.

Whore.

Filth.

She shook her head again, lifting it slightly, her eyes trained on the hall, shrinking back. Reaching behind her, her hand found Mira's shoulder. Squeezing her shoulder, Alice shook Mira gently, not saying a word, praying that Mira wouldn't wake with a start. She had to stay quiet.

Mira groaned.

Alice's heart stopped.

The footsteps paused.

And then keys jangled and the footsteps resumed. Alice's eyes widened in fear as she watched a guard approach, his keys in hand. Fuck, they were coming to her cell. She wasn't ready. She wanted to stay in the cell. Praying silently to the gods, wishing they would listen and answer her, she begged them for a reprieve of some sort. This was too much.

The guard stopped in front of her cell, his eyes searching as they swept the small, enclosed area. Huddling further back, shielding Mira from sight, Alice prayed he wouldn't see her, that he would miss her in the dark.

But that was just wishful thinking.

The guard flipped through the keys, searching for the one to her cell. Finding it, he slid it into the slot, the metal clanging against each other, making Mira stir further. Opening her mouth to ask what was going on, Alice slapped her hand over Mira's mouth, preventing her from talking, her eyes never leaving the guard.

The door creaked open, the hinges squealing, making both Alice and Mira wince. And then the sound of footsteps sounded again as the guard drew nearer, each clomp of his boot sending terror racing through Alice's veins.

Stopping in front of the bed, the guard's eyes flickered between the two, hesitating, deciding. And then he reached out, grabbing Alice by the hair, yanking her off the bed. She whimpered in shock and pain as she found herself flying to her feet. She would not cry. Not here. Not now. Not in front of him.

Twisting just enough, she shot Mira a look that said she would be alright. And then she let the guard drag her from the cell, down the long hall, and to the room she had come to despise.

Opening the door, the guard shoved her inside, sending her sprawling to the ground. Before she could get up on her own, two sets of hands grabbed either arm and hauled her into the chair, setting her down roughly. Her hands were dragged behind her back and secured, the rope used to secure her already battered wrists cutting into her skin. The torture hadn't even started yet and already she could feel blood dripping down her hands. And sure enough...

Drip.

Drip.

Drip.

Her blood was staining the floor once more.

CHAPTER 31

MATTY

Matty winced as the dark-haired female, Alice, was shoved into the room so forcefully that she fell, a sharp exhale leaving her as her knees collided with the wooden floor. A low groan followed as she braced her wrists against the floor, as if she was getting ready to get up on her own. His eyes widened at the sight. The sheer amount of strength this female had was astounding. It was commendable and the respect he felt for her grew, just like it did every time he saw her brought in.

Moving forward to offer her a hand, he was stopped as two other guards stepped in front of him and grasped her upper arms. With a grunt, they lifted her off the floor and dropped her onto the chair, another groan escaping her, her back arching. Matty was sure that hurt her lower back. It hurt his just watching her land.

Midnight interrogations. The general's newest idea or trick or whatever you wanted to call it. Matty simply called it a giant pain in the ass. It wasn't like dragging the shifters in at midnight was suddenly going to get them to talk. They were just as tired now as they were during the day. If they hadn't said anything of particular importance yet, Matty doubted they would say anything at this ungodly hour.

Unless...

Matty shook his head as he watched them bind the Alice's hands behind her back per usual. And then he grimaced as he watched fresh blood start to drip down her hands just from the rope cutting into her already raw and fragile skin, the blood landing on the ground with an audible drip, the sound ominous.

His dad was sinister, sure. And his dad was an asshole, no question about it. Devious was also on that list.

There was no strategic reasoning behind bringing already exhausted shifters into the interrogation room in the middle of the night. It would be one thing if they were normally well-rested. It would be one thing if the troops, the guards, and his dad were treating them well and then threw this into the mix. But they weren't. They'd played their hands. They had nothing left except for straight-up killing them. But that would defeat the purpose of keeping them as prisoners to get information out of them. Right?

Matty tilted his head as he surveyed Alice. She had been thin to begin with. But now? He could see the toll that little to no sleep and food was taking on her. She looked half dead, and he had a hunch that she probably wished she was actually dead. If he was in her position, he was sure he would feel that way. Hell, his dad had stabbed him and then taken him, half-healed, all the way down to the capital before throwing him into the army. That had been literal hell on earth, and still, that was nothing compared to what the shifters were going through right now. If he had wanted to die then... He shook his head.

How they hadn't broken yet was beyond him.

Sitting back on his stool, he waited for his dad to show up to begin the usual questioning. It wasn't like him to take this long to show up, but maybe he was banking on building up the tension in the room. If he was, it was working.

Tilting his head while he waited, Matty surveyed Alice again, watching as she dropped her chin down to her chest, her eyes closed. She was the very image of broken, but he knew that once his dad walked in the room, she would raise her head, a hint of defiance in her eyes. She wasn't finished, not by a long shot.

That fire...

Matty sighed and shifted in his seat. And then he cleared his throat.

"I know you don't want to talk, but I'm curious," he began, his voice low and soft. "Where did you grow up? I've not seen this level of strength in someone in... well, never, to be frank."

Alice lifted her head, her eyes guarded as she surveyed him. Matty felt a shiver run down his spine under her gaze. It almost felt like she was seeing right through him as she searched his face, trying to decide if he was trustworthy or not. Finally, she sagged, her chin dropping back down to her chest again.

"A farming village," she rasped. "On the outskirts of a forest."

Matty frowned. A farming village? There was no way a farming village would produce this kind of courage. But... he shook his head. There was a good chance she was lying, but he had a feeling that she wasn't. She'd already proven repeatedly that if she didn't want to answer, she just wouldn't talk. For her to be talking... He pursed his lips.

She was telling the truth.

"How'd a farming village turn out a girl like you?" Matty asked after a minute. "Springfield is a farming village, as you put it, and not once have I ever met a girl like... No. That's a lie. There was one girl. She's gone now though."

Alice looked up, shock registering in her eyes for just a second before it was gone. "What happened to her?" she rasped.

Matty let a small smile tug at the corner of his lips as he thought back to Clara. "She was a friend. We grew up together. We were engaged. Should have been married back during the winter solstice, but plans changed. She was kidnapped by a male shifter and when I went to rescue her, I found out she was half, herself. We... we left her there. If she's still alive, she's with the man that had been running the bar for her father. Starting to think he wasn't human either with how quickly he disappeared."

A frown graced Alice's face. "You left a female shifter, your friend, all because..." She cut herself off with an angry huff. "Humans..."

"Yeah, you don't have to remind me," Matty muttered under his breath. "I beat myself up for that every day."

Alice's eyes snapped to his, shock registering in her eyes again. Calmly, he met her gaze. He had nothing to hide. Not from this group of shifters. And if he had his way, he'd be letting them walk right out the door with an apology and enough supplies to get them up to Reynardsville where they'd be safe for a little while.

"Who was the man who disappeared?" she asked after she'd composed herself.

"Some fellow named Ronan. I didn't like him much. He kept making eyes at my fiancé. I'm not too proud to admit that I was jealous. I was worried she'd take more interest in him than me. He was a good-looking fellow. It was hard not to be jealous," Matty explained, leaning back on his stool, his back resting against the wall.

He was about to continue when she let out a choking sound, her eyes wide and still very much trained on him.

"Did you say Ronan?" she asked faintly, almost looking like she was going to be sick.

Matty nodded, concern creasing his brow. If she was going to be sick, he was going to take her back to her cell so she could rest, his dad's plan to question her be damned.

"Did he have green eyes and curly black hair?" she asked in the same tone of voice, though now it was trembling a bit.

Matty nodded again, puzzled as to why and how she knew that. And then the realization dawned on him. She knew Ronan. Those green eyes… the blonde male had the same eyes. They were family. If he had to hazard a guess, Matty would wager that they knew Ronan had been out here and had headed this way to collect him before heading farther north. It's what he would have done.

"Are you alright?" Matty asked cautiously, leaning forward now, ready to untie her at the drop of a hat.

"I…" Alice pursed her lips, taking a deep breath through her nose as if to calm herself down. "You said he disappeared?"

"I did." He nodded.

"So he was alive the last time you saw him?" she clarified.

"Yes."

"Would you know if any shifters have been captured in the area besides us?" she asked.

"I would," Matty hedged. "You've been the only ones to get close enough to a human settlement in the last few months. No other shifters have been spotted or been brought in."

Alice sagged in relief. "Thank you," she sighed.

Matty was about to reply when the door banged open. Almost instantly, he slid back on his stool and slammed his mouth shut. If his dad caught this poor female talking to him openly, if he caught on to the fact that she knew Ronan of all people, then he would know that she and the rest of her group had been holding back, that they knew more than they were letting on, because now that she'd told Matty that, he was very keenly aware that all four of them were keeping a lot to themselves. But how? Why weren't they talking? Ronan was gone. Disappeared. And if his suspicion about their hometown was true, it was gone, too. What were they trying to protect? Or was it a someone? Matty chewed on the inside of his lip in frustration, trying to figure it out without giving anything away to his dad.

General Claery, not paying any attention to Matty, locked his eyes on Alice who had dropped her head back down onto her chest, her breathing ragged. Matty watched him survey her closely, noting each rise and fall of her chest. She seemed nervous now after her brief conversation with Matty, and he knew his dad could sense that.

Shit, he thought to himself. *She's going to break finally. She's going to give everything away. And once she gives that information to him, he'll kill the lot of them.*

Closing his eyes for a moment, he prayed she'd keep her mouth shut. He still had to get them out. He had promised himself he would get them out. But if she opened her mouth, it would all be for naught.

He opened his eyes again just in time to see his dad walk back over to the door, talking just loud enough for Alice to hear him, his voice low and menacing.

"I've given you plenty of opportunities to talk, and you haven't taken a single one. This is your fault. You could have prevented this. All you had to do was tell me what I wanted to know, and then maybe I would have made your death quick and easy. Nothing about your end will be quick and easy now. I will make you pay."

Matty swallowed, his eyes widening for only a second before he schooled his face into a mask of composure. His dad was... done. He was done trying to get information out of them. Well, sort of. Matty had no doubt in his mind that while his dad was slowly killing each and every one of the shifters currently kept in the jail, he would be listening for any little juicy tidbits that they might drop.

He doubted his dad would get anything.

He wasn't going to let his dad get that far. He was going to get them out. And soon.

The door creaked open further and one of his dad's men stepped inside, a hot iron with a cattle brand on the end in his hand. The door snapped shut behind him. And suddenly it felt like all the air in the room had disappeared.

Matty's eyes widened again as his eyes darted from Alice to the brand. No. This couldn't be happening. His dad wasn't that sadistic, was he? His heart sank. He knew the answer to that question and he didn't like it.

Alice's eyes had widened, too, raw fear and panic filling her eyes as they locked on the brand.

Matty looked over at her again, and for a brief moment, they locked eyes. *Close your eyes*, Matty tried telling her with his eyes. If she didn't look, he reasoned with himself, then perhaps the pain wouldn't be nearly as great. Or so he hoped.

By some miracle, she did just that, squeezing her eyes shut and clenching her jaw. She knew it was coming, that it was inevitable. She couldn't get away even if she wanted. And as much as Matty wanted to stop his dad and his men, there was no way for him to. He would be overpowered and thrown out of the room faster than he could ask them to stop. He also risked putting more lives at stake by crossing his dad. He couldn't risk it.

His eyes widened further as his dad yanked her collar down. Alice shuddered, her whole body shaking. The man with the brand came closer, and then, with a hiss, the brand was pressed against the sensitive skin just above her left breast, a strangled scream escaping her as the smell of burnt flesh invaded the room.

Matty gagged as did the guard at the door, his eyes just as wide as Matty's.

Turning away, he made up his mind. He needed to talk to Archie and Sgt. Conoway as soon as possible.

If anyone could help him get these shifters out and not say a thing about it, it was those two.

CHAPTER 32

RONAN

For the next few days after getting punched in the face by Clara and then watching her get spanked rather publicly by Freisinger immediately after, Ronan decided to keep his distance, not wanting to irritate Clara further or provoke her to attack him again. If she was out training, he was at his post or he stayed in his tent. If she was in her tent resting, he allowed himself to wander or train. If she was eating, he was nowhere to be found. If she was meeting with Zeke or Maddox, he steered clear.

Simple enough, even though it drove him crazy.

Ronan also tried to stay clear of Clara's mate, Warren. While Ronan didn't know Warren very well, the few times they had come in contact had not been pleasant. The first time, Ronan had knocked Warren flat on his ass for trying to claim Clara in the middle of a dark alley back in Springfield before she'd even known that she was half shifter. The second time had been from a distance when Ronan had been in wolf form. He'd followed Warren after he'd kidnapped Clara and taken her back to his pack where he'd claimed her. At the time, he'd thought that Warren was just using her, but come to find out, he'd been attempting to get her away from the Claerys, something Ronan would have done himself if he'd known what was going on sooner rather than later.

The last time Ronan had come into contact with Warren, Ronan had led General Claery right to Warren's pack which resulted in the death of Clara's pa, Warren getting run through with a poison-tipped sword, and more than a handful of deaths. To say that Ronan still felt guilty was an understatement.

If that wasn't grounds enough for Warren to hate him, then the fact that he had tried to claim Clara and forced himself on her while she was under his care was enough. Ronan knew that Warren knew all about what he'd done while he'd been traveling with Clara to Reynardsville. He had seen the look in his eye after Clara had socked him, had seen him put two and two together, his eyes flashing dangerously. If Freisinger hadn't stepped in to discipline Clara, Ronan was sure that Warren would have come after him next. His ire, however, had been redirected to Freisinger the moment his hand had come in contact with her rear.

Livid was an understatement.

Ronan never wanted to be on the receiving end of the look that Warren had fixed Freisinger with. It had made his blood run cold. If looks could kill, Freisinger would have been skinned alive and flayed in front of everyone, and even then, Ronan was almost positive that Warren wouldn't have been satisfied and would have kept torturing the male.

In terms of power, however, Freisinger was one of the big dogs. Shifters that had animals much larger and stronger than Freisinger's fox feared him. He had a commanding presence that demanded and expected respect. His word was law. He wasn't used to being told no and he got what he wanted fairly easily. When he couldn't get it, he'd work for it and he wouldn't stop until he got whatever it was he was trying to obtain.

Warren, on the other hand, was more laid back and preferred to keep to himself and his pack Ronan decided after watching him with Clara over the past few days. When he got the chance to watch him anyway. But that didn't mean Warren was weak. No, Ronan had an inkling that he had more power than Freisinger. There was just something in the way he held himself, the way he moved, the way he talked. It all screamed power.

He just wasn't an asshole about it like Freisinger was.

When Freisinger realized that Warren was the stronger opponent... Ronan shuddered. There would be hell to pay, and Freisinger would probably pay with his life trying to one-up Warren.

He'd pay to see that fight. He wanted to see the look on Freisinger's face when he realized he'd been beaten. But the chances of that happening any time soon were slim, but not zero.

Ronan rolled over on his sleeping mat to bury his face in his pillow as he contemplated the impending fight between Warren and Freisinger. As much as he wanted to see it himself, the little voice in the back of his head said that he wouldn't want to be there because he was next on Warren's list of reckoning. He'd need to get the hell out of town, hide somewhere, flee. He knew his pack would protect him, but that would only get him so far.

Ronan wasn't necessarily a coward. But he sure as hell wasn't a fighter either. Not unless he felt that someone he cared about was in danger. In fact, he prided himself on being smarter than the average shifter. He liked to read, to gain knowledge. He was, by no means, stupid. He knew he wouldn't win. Not by a long shot. That was a fool's dream. He had to flee.

Until that time came, though, he'd bide his time and enjoy having a pack while it lasted.

Cursing himself, his father, his sister's late fiancé, his brother, his sister, the general, and the Claerys, he rolled back over, unable to get comfortable. Staring at the canvas top of the tent, he wished he could go back in time to stop the events that had led him here. He should be home, in Everridge, with his brother and sister. Or his cabin. He should have been at his cabin that he had spent so much time lovingly building, preparing for a better future.

He should have been cozy in the small living room, sitting in front of the fire, working on his next little project. And if he'd been lucky, he should have had a cute little mate sitting across from him, working on her own little project. Or perhaps, if she liked to read as much as he did, he could have had her reading out loud to him.

He shook his head, sending his daydream scattering into nothing. It would do him no good to get caught up in the destructive cycle of what-if's. Sighing, he rolled back over and then furrowed his brow as voices drifted through the canvas.

"Again," Freisinger's voice demanded.

Clara's voice, softer and sweeter, but sounding exasperated, responded. However, her voice was too low for Ronan to make out any of the words.

He sat up as Freisinger cursed at her, letting Ronan know that Clara was either sassing him or she was just done and told him no more. Of the two options, Ronan was leaning toward the latter. They'd been training since before breakfast. He knew that Clara had to be exhausted, her body sore. The male just wouldn't let up.

And Warren...

Ronan shook his head again. He'd heard Warren step in multiple times, but that just seemed to make the situation worse. Freisinger would get mad at Warren for interfering, they'd argue, he'd storm off for the night, heading back toward the city, and then he'd return in the morning with a vengeance and take it out on Clara.

"Again, Kleine. Damn it, again," Freisinger barked.

"I'm done," Clara snapped, her voice rising enough for Ronan to hear now. "I need a break."

"You don't get breaks during war," Freisinger snapped back.

"This isn't war," Clara argued. "This is training."

"For war," Freisinger tacked on.

Clara's voice became indistinguishable again, though Ronan was sure that she was cursing under her breath.

A snarl followed and then a sharp smack and a cry of pain.

Ronan bolted off his sleeping mat and out of his tent in response. Darting around his tent, he skidded to a halt. Clara was standing a few paces back from Freisinger, her hand clutching her face, her eyes wide in shock. Freisinger was standing in front of her, his chest heaving, one hand clenched into a fist. The other hand was up, but restrained by Warren who was towering over Freisinger, murder in his eyes as he glared down at the other man.

Had Freisinger just... hit Clara? Across the face?

Ronan's eyes widened and his jaw dropped before he scowled, his hands clenching into fists. By the gods, he had hit Clara.

Maddox and Zeke, having also apparently heard Clara cry out in pain, skidded to a stop behind Ronan, taking in the scene. Shaking his head, Maddox let out a low curse, stalking forward to help Warren pull Freisinger away from Clara. Zeke, not wanting Maddox to get into trouble followed after, leaving Ronan by himself.

Watching his fellow packmates and friends for a minute, he turned his attention to Clara. Taking a deep breath, he shook his head and stalked over to her. He could do this. She needed help right now. All he was doing was making sure she wasn't seriously hurt.

"Are you alright?" he asked, his voice cracking from nerves. He shouldn't be talking to her. He knew how she felt, and yet, here he was. However, he needed to know that she was okay.

Clara looked up at him, her eyes widening for a millisecond before darkening. "Why do you care?" she retorted.

"Because I don't like seeing you hurt," he sighed, running a hand through his hair nervously. "And before you say I have no right to say that after what I did, I know. I messed up. Royally. And I don't expect you to forgive me. I don't know what I was thinking when I did what I did, and I know that's no excuse, but it's true. I'm usually fairly levelheaded and I'm sorry you didn't get to see that side of me. Instead, you got the side of me that was ruled completely by my instincts and hormones. That was unfair to you, and I'm sorry. But I do care if you're hurt."

Clara's scowl deepened and then she sighed, relenting just a bit. "Against my better judgment, and because I don't know anyone in the gods forsaken city besides Warren and my so-called family, fine. I'll trust you. On one condition. You keep your distance. I don't want you close enough to touch me unless I'm hurt and need help. Understand?"

Ronan's eyes widened in shock. This was more than he had been expecting. More than he'd hoped for. And he was beyond grateful. There would be no complaints out of him.

"Understood. Now can I see? Please?" he pleaded, his voice soft as he gestured at her face.

With another sigh, she dropped her hand from her face, revealing a bright red cheek that was starting to swell. Ronan could see the outlines of Freisinger's fingers across her cheek, starting near her ear and going almost all the way across to her nose. Her bottom lip was also split near the corner of her mouth, a bit of blood welling up. He grimaced as he led her over to the campfire and sat her down on a log.

"Wait here. I'll go get some medical supplies to treat your lip," he said, his voice quiet. This felt familiar. After spending a few weeks with her, traveling to Reynardsville, he had played doctor a few times. This was normal. It felt normal. It felt right.

Clara nodded numbly, her eyes darting over to where Zeke was talking to Freisinger, his voice low so the rest of the pack couldn't hear what he was talking about. Ronan followed her gaze to watch Zeke for a minute, recognizing the look on his face. He was giving Freisinger a talking to, and going off Freisinger's face, he wasn't pleased. Nor did he look remotely guilty for what he'd done. Off to the side, nodding his head in agreement with what Zeke was saying as he paced was Warren. Every few seconds, his eyes would dart over to Clara, relief and anger warring across his face. And then his eyes would land on Ronan and the anger would win for a moment before going back to Zeke and Freisinger.

Ronan swallowed nervously before darting into his tent to get the medical supplies. Patch her up and then give her space. That's all he needed to do right now. That's all he could do right now.

Not even a minute later, Ronan crouched down in front of Clara. Gently, he took a damp cloth and dabbed at her lip, causing her to hiss in pain. Apologizing under his breath, he took some salve and dabbed that on next. Then he took a towel and filled it with some of the remaining snow on the ground and pressed it to her cheek.

"The cold should help," he said, taking her hand and placing it on the snow-filled towel where his hand was so she could hold it there herself.

Clara raised her brows at him and then shrugged, not bothering to argue with him. Either she was too tired, too sore, in too much pain, or she'd done something similar before. Ronan didn't care which as long as she was getting the care she needed.

"I'm not sure if it'll bruise yet, but I imagine it probably will. It won't be pretty for a while," he said cautiously, warning her as her eyes closed.

One of her eyes cracked open after the words registered and she peered up at him. "A bruise is the least of my worries right now."

Ronan frowned, not liking how ominous that sounded. He was about to ask why when he thought better of it. It wasn't his business. She didn't trust him enough to discuss personal matters with him. She was allowing him to help and that was it. He could not afford to step over the boundaries she had just set.

Closing his mouth with a snap, he nodded and then disappeared back into his tent where he let out a deep breath. Making his way back over to his sleeping mat, he collapsed onto it, feeling like the weight of the world had just been lifted off his shoulders. He may not have gotten what he wanted completely, but he had gotten something.

He'd been forgiven, even if it was conditionally.

CHAPTER 33

CLARA

Clara watched Ronan back up a few paces, almost stumbling over his own feet as he hurried to give her space. If she didn't hate him as much as she did, she would have found the sight rather comical. As it was, she did still hate him, so all she could muster was finding the sight pathetic instead.

She had wanted to like him.

Had grown to trust him.

And then he had done what she'd come to realize was almost second nature to male shifters. He'd given into his biology, his instincts, against his better judgment.

Even the best of people had a dark side, secrets they wanted to keep hidden away from prying eyes. Just like the worst of people had a good side that was rarely seen. Why try to be good when everyone already assumed the worst?

Ronan was one of the former people. He was good, kind, intelligent. She was foolish to think that he was free from having any weaknesses or darkness in him. That was on her for trusting a male she barely knew, even if the main reason had been for survival.

She wouldn't make that mistake again. But right now, she needed allies. She knew he would protect her if things got ugly, knew he'd stand up for her if she needed an ally. But that's all he'd ever be. An ally. One she couldn't fully trust.

She scoffed softly. What was the saying again? Keep your friends close and your enemies closer. That's exactly what she intended to do with Ronan. She wouldn't give him a chance to turn on her again. Not like that.

Glancing over at the gaggle of men surrounding Freisinger, she felt her temper flare. He had actually hit her. Across the face. Her cheek still stung, and her lip... Gods, it was swollen. She could still taste a hint of copper from where her lip had split. It made her want to gag. She couldn't stand the taste. But no matter. She could rinse her mouth out once she made it back to her tent, whenever that was.

Clara studied Freisinger for a moment, hoping against hope that they were done for the day. She wasn't sure how much more she could take. Her body hurt. When she stood, her knees felt like they were going to give out and her leg muscles felt like jelly. And that was just her lower half. Her upper half was just as sore. Lifting her arms more than halfway made her groan as her shoulders protested the movement.

What she needed was a good soak in a hot tub. She yearned to slip back into the city to the room she had been given to stay in. The tub there was luxurious.

Clara shook her head. She shouldn't think about the tub. Not right now. It would make her more miserable than she already was at the moment simply because she couldn't have it right now.

Her eyes returned to Freisinger. His eyes were dark, his brows furrowed over them. His jaw was clenched so tightly that she could see a muscle twitching. He was angry. Angry that he was getting reprimanded by the leader of the Romulus Pack, Zeke, if she remembered correctly. Angry that he was being held back by that Maddox fellow. Angry that Warren had intervened.

She'd end up paying for this later. She could feel it in her bones. Her body already ached at the thought.

Standing up, she swayed slightly as her legs protested holding up her own weight. Gritting her teeth and clenching her free hand into a fist, she glanced over at Warren. His eyes were fixed on her, a flicker of worry dancing through them. He had seen her sway. She was surprised he hadn't already hurried over. At the same time, she wasn't. There was no way he was letting Freisinger out of his sight at the moment. Not until he was certain that Freisinger wouldn't come after her in a fit of anger for not getting his way.

Meeting Warren's eyes, she jerked her head in the direction of their tent, silently telling him that she was headed that way for now. She needed to lay down, needed a minute to compose herself, needed a chance to gain her wits about her before she had to face Freisinger again.

Warren, glancing in the direction she had jerked her head, spotted the tent and then looked back at her. He didn't move for a minute, giving Clara pause. Was he going to tell her no? Her stomach clenched at the thought. She'd been humiliated enough for one day. Please just let her go. She didn't think her pride could suffer falling in front of everyone simply because her body had given out.

Finally, his eyes raking over her body, taking inventory of every little bump, bruise, and scrape, Warren nodded slowly as if he was reluctant to let her out of his sight but knew she needed some space.

Sagging in relief, Clara slowly made her way over to their tent, already imagining stripping off her sweaty, filthy clothes and laying down on the sleeping mat with a soft blanket wrapped around her.

A few painstaking steps later, Clara entered the small tent. Dropping down to her knees with a groan, she started working on the small fire in the center of the tent to warm the space up. A few pieces of wood, some lint, and... she hit the flint with the striker. Sparks flew. One landed on the lint and instantly lit up. Bending down, she blew on it gently, helping it spread to the other pieces of lint until it grew large enough to catch the wood on fire.

Sitting back on her heels, she let the warmth wash over her, warming her and the space before she pushed herself back up off the ground to undress. Once she'd risen to her feet, she undid the laces of her pants and let them slip down to the ground. Then she undid her vest, pulled her shirt over her head, and flung her clothes into a corner where they lay in a crumpled heap. She knew she should straighten them, but she was too tired and sore to care. Moving stiffly, she walked over to the other corner of the tent where she kept their blankets folded neatly, grabbed one, and wrapped it around her. And then she sank down onto the sleeping mat.

Laying down, making sure she was completely covered, she stared at the dancing flames until her eyes grew heavy and closed of their own free will.

The tent flap rustled, rousing Clara from her nap. Blinking blearily, she instantly went on the defense before she realized that it was Warren who had entered the tent and not Freisinger. Releasing a small breath of relief, she relaxed back down into her spot, her eyes drifting closed once again.

"Don't go back to sleep quite yet, little fox," Warren said, his voice low and soothing. "Can you sit up for me? I want to take a look at your face."

Clara groaned in protest but sat up anyway, wincing as she did so, her whole body aching. Meanwhile, Warren tugged off his boots and then walked over to his pack. Rummaging through it, he found what he was looking for before coming over to Clara. Sinking down onto the mat next to her, he tugged her into his lap and pulled her against his chest.

"How are you feeling?" he asked, his voice still low, making his chest rumble underneath Clara's ear.

"Like I've just barely managed to survive being caught in a stampede," she muttered dryly. "I've never been so sore in my life."

Warren half laughed, half groaned in sympathy. "I am sorry, little fox. Freisinger, the bastard, is working you too hard. We don't even train young male shifters this hard. I don't understand what he's thinking."

"This is war," she quoted Freisinger bitterly.

Warren rolled his eyes. "Smart ass."

"Yes, my ass is very smart, thank you. But it's also very sore," she quipped.

Warren huffed another laugh. "You know what I meant," he said, running a hand through her hair, pulling her even closer. "Yes, we're preparing for war. It's coming whether we like it or not. But that still doesn't excuse his current behavior. He's being an ass simply because he can."

"I thought that was obvious. I'm pretty sure jackass is his middle name," Clara continued, feeling extra sassy at the moment, partially because she was tired, partially because she hurt, and partially because she was still upset with Freisinger for a multitude of reasons. It felt like her list of reasons to be upset with him grew longer every day.

"You know, I think you're right." Warren shook his head with another laugh. "I don't know what's come over you, but this side of you is absolutely glorious. Perhaps you should give him a bit of this sass. He might just lose his mind."

"I might just get hit again," Clara said darkly.

That thought sobered both of them up.

"I'm going to kill him," Warren declared.

"I know," Clara replied simply.

"Tonight."

"No. Not yet. We need to make sure there's no one worse that will take his place once you off him," Clara reasoned.

"True," Warren grunted, not sounding very happy that he had to wait to tear the shifter limb from limb. Dropping his head down, he buried his face in her hair. "Seeing him hit you..." A low growl built in his chest.

"I know," she grumbled.

Straightening, Warren sighed heavily and then he gently grabbed her chin and tilted her face up to his. Angling her face so that the light could illuminate it, he pursed his lips as his eyes surveyed the damage to her face. Reaching over for the items he had grabbed before sitting down with her, he carefully cleaned her face again.

"You've got a hand-shaped imprint on your face," he murmured as he dabbed some ointment onto her lip, numbing the area. Then he leaned down and gently pressed a kiss to her lips.

"Don't..." she tried to protest, not wanting to get the ointment all over his lips, too.

Shushing her, he deepened the kiss, his tongue flicking over her bottom lip, seeking entrance. Against her better judgment, she parted her lips and let him in, her tongue meeting his as it slid into her mouth.

"I need more," he whispered a minute later, readjusting his hold on her. "I need to feel you, need to hold you..." he dipped back down, pressing a gentle kiss to her split lip, and then trailed more kisses down her jaw, each one feather-light so as to not hurt her tender skin.

"I know," she whispered back, her breaths coming in short bursts, heat pooling in her lower belly. It had been a while since they'd had time to themselves like this.

But she was hurt, she chided herself.

But she needed this, she reminded herself at the same time.

Recapturing his lips with hers, she reached in between them to undo his pants, freeing him, hoping that this was indeed what he had wanted. Wrapping a hand around his length, she stroked him, earning a growl of approval. Nipping her bottom lip, his own hand dipped in between them to palm her center. Letting out a soft moan against his lips, her hips jerked forward against his hand. She had been right. Thank the gods. She needed a release, needed to forget everything. At least for a little while. And this was the perfect distraction.

Her hips jerked forward again involuntarily and one of his fingers dipped inside, another breathy moan escaping her.

"Please," she whispered against his lips.

"Patience, little fox. Tonight's about you. You'll get what you want. I promise," Warren murmured back, adding a second finger.

The next morning, Clara stood bundled in her cloak as she sipped on some coffee with some of the other members of the Romulus Pack. As she sipped the bitter liquid, she felt multiple pairs of eyes on her, surveying her face. She knew what they were looking at. She had a nasty bruise now. She'd caught a glimpse of it in the handheld mirror she'd brought to help her do her hair. But that hadn't necessarily bothered her then. Not when Warren had kissed it so tenderly and had helped her do her hair, calling her beautiful in the process. But now...

She shifted on her feet self-consciously. She didn't want their pity or their judgment. She wanted it to stop. However, if she asked them to stop, she'd draw even more attention to herself and that was something she didn't want. At all.

Taking another sip of her coffee, she spotted Ronan with Maddox and Zeke. The three were huddled together, talking in hushed whispers. Her brows furrowed slightly, curious to know what they were talking about and hoping it wasn't about her. It was none of her business though. Zeke ran a whole pack. Maddox, if she remembered correctly, was the second in command. And Ronan? She wasn't sure where Ronan fit in the Romulus pack, but suffice it to say, she knew he was friends with Zeke and Maddox, so she figured that meant he had a decent enough standing here.

Just as she was about to look away, Ronan glanced over and caught her eye. His eyes studied her for a moment, his eyes lingering on her cheek. A flash of something flickered through his eyes, though what it was she wasn't sure exactly. After, he nodded and turned back to Maddox and Zeke who were also watching her. Maddox and Zeke were easier to read. Maddox looked upset and Zeke looked a bit guilty as if he thought that if he'd stepped in sooner, he could have prevented the incident. Warren had been there though; they all knew that. If he hadn't been able to stop Freisinger before he'd lost control and hit her, then Zeke wouldn't have been any more successful than Warren.

She took another sip of her coffee and turned away, waiting for Freisinger to exit his tent. It wasn't like him to start their training this late in the day.

She frowned as she surveyed his tent, and then she glanced over at the city. Instantly, she regretted that decision as she saw Freisinger striding toward them looking fresh and well rested.

She hated him, hated everything about him.

As he neared, he motioned for her to follow him. "We have a meeting, Kleine. Get moving."

With a groan, she drained the rest of her coffee and then started after him, glancing back at Warren with a look that said, "wish me luck".

Two hours later, freshly bathed, wearing clean clothes, her hair braided back, Clara stood in front of her grandmother. Glancing around the room, she noted that the rest of her family and her grandmother's council were missing.

It was just her, her grandmother, and Freisinger.

A feeling of dread settled low in her stomach like a lead weight. She took a step back without thinking about it, her eyes still looking around the room. She swallowed nervously. Shit, she was about to get in trouble. For what, though, she wasn't quite sure.

"Would you mind telling me why you told Freisinger that you were done with training yesterday?" Mrs. Reynard asked, sounding like a disappointed parent.

Clara's eyes flashed up to her grandmother's and then over to Freisinger who looked overly smug. Her eyes darkened at his expression. What had he done?

"We'd been training nonstop since the sun rose yesterday," Clara said, her eyes drifting back to her grandmother, plotting the various ways she wanted to murder Freisinger on the spot in the back of her mind. "I simply said I was done, that I needed a break. I hadn't eaten. Hadn't been able to sit. Nothing. It wasn't an unreasonable request."

"That's not what Briggs said," Mrs. Reynard said, her lips pursing.

"Seriously?" Clara's brows rose as she glanced over at Freisinger again. "Why would I lie about what happened?"

"To get out of trouble," Mrs. Reynard supplied.

"By the gods," Clara cursed. "I didn't realize asking for a break would get me in trouble, so why in the world would I lie to get out of trouble? That's not something most people are punished for. Do you hear how asinine that is, getting in trouble for wanting a break after almost eight hours?"

Mrs. Reynard and Freisinger both faltered for a moment at her words. Clara knew she wasn't wrong, that what she said was more logical than what her grandmother had suggested. But then Mrs. Reynard's face darkened.

"Watch your mouth. That was unladylike."

"Yes, let's not curse because it's unladylike, but let's train her how to fight in a war because that's peak lady behavior," Clara muttered under her breath.

"That's enough, Clara. You will behave. And you will listen to Freisinger. He is training you. Not the other way around. If he says to keep going, then you keep going," Mrs. Reynard snapped.

"Are you fu..." Clara started.

"I think a little punishment as a reminder to hold your tongue is in order. Perhaps you'll remember this the next time you decide that you have a say at the moment," Mrs. Reynard said, her face darkening even further. "Freisinger, if you will." She gestured at Clara, giving him permission to dole out the punishment. "I shall be in the parlor when you are done. Take her back and then come find me. We have some reports to go over and discuss."

"Of course, ma'am," Freisinger said respectfully. Turning to Clara, a dark smirk tugged at his lips.

He continued to watch her as he waited for Mrs. Reynard to leave the room. As soon as the door snapped shut behind her, he rubbed his hands together and then walked over to a door on the far wall. Opening it, Clara could see some sort of dark storage room, but for what she wasn't sure.

"Turn around," he ordered as he disappeared into the room and then reappeared with a whip and some rope. "This is going to hurt."

CHAPTER 34

WARREN

Pacing back and forth in front of their tent, Warren found himself continuously looking over at the back gate of Reynardsville, waiting for Clara to reappear with Freisinger. She'd left with Freisinger around nine that morning for a meeting with her grandmother, or that's what Freisinger had said she was needed for. Warren knew that she had probably been retrieved early to clean up after being outside the city for a little over a week and that the meeting would probably take an hour or two, depending on what was being discussed. That would put her return somewhere between eleven and noon, or so he hoped. There was an off chance that Clara's grandmother would request that she stay for lunch, and Clara being Clara, would probably oblige, simply to get out of training for the day. Warren didn't blame her.

Pausing, he rolled his neck, trying to relieve the building tension there, but to no avail. He hated waiting. He hated being away from Clara. No good things came of them being separated.

Blowing out a breath, he stalked over to where Maddox and Zeke were standing near the fire, both looking tired and anxious.

"Would either of you happen to know the time?" he asked gruffly, wanting to get a read on the time so he could gauge how much longer Clara might be. If she wasn't back by supper, he would go into the city to search for her himself. He didn't care if the Reynards didn't want him around. Her safety came first.

"It's a little after one, why?" Zeke replied, glancing down at the pocket watch he kept attached to his belt and tucked into his front pocket.

"Clara should have been back by now," Warren grunted. "After yesterday, I don't like her being alone with Freisinger. Or her grandmother. She's been gone too long."

Maddox grimaced at Warren's reply, nodding in agreement. "What he did was uncalled for, I will give you that. He's a nasty piece of work. The Reynards should have cast him out when he started rising through the ranks of their militia the way he did. But oh no, they couldn't possibly do that. No, instead he got the Reynards' stamp of approval, and he became their golden child, if you will. In their eyes, he can do no wrong."

"That's what I was afraid of," Warren muttered. "He could do anything to Clara and her grandmother would look the other way all because of who he is. She doesn't give a damn about Clara. She's just a means to an end."

"Unfortunately," Zeke agreed, spitting into the fire, the wad of saliva sizzling as it hit a log. He shook his head as he, too, glanced over at the back gate. "The old man himself before he died wasn't too bad from what my family told me back in the day. He passed when I was young, so I don't remember much myself, unfortunately. After his death, though, Mrs. Reynard..." He shook his head again. "She seemed to go off the deep end, especially when Mara took off, fleeing the city, and didn't come back. Can't say I blame her. The stories my family told about how Mrs. Reynard used to treat her daughter..."

"Terrible," Maddox cut in, adding to the story. "Apparently she handed Mara off to nannies most of the time. Didn't spend any time with her own daughter. Too busy. But then Mr. Reynard got sick and suddenly all her attention went to Mara, trying to prepare her to take over once Mr. Reynard passed. I heard she had a whole slew of male foxes lined up. And when Mara decided she was having none of it, Mrs. Reynard would have her punished."

"So it's not far-fetched that she'd punish Clara in the same way," Zeke concluded. "Unfortunately, your fears are justified, so if you want to head into the city in a bit, by all means, we won't stop you. We'll even send someone in with you if you'd like."

Warren shook his head, stuffing his hands into his coat pockets. "No. I don't want your lot to get into trouble on my account. The Reynards hate me. Don't need to drag you into that spat. Wouldn't be fair to you."

"Of course." Zeke inclined his head respectfully. "Still, if it's all the same, let us know when you want to head in. We'll send someone into the city with you to keep the gates open if you want to return to camp tonight."

"I can do..." Warren started but was cut off as a messenger from the city with a heavy leather satchel thrown over his shoulder hurried out of the city and over to the camp.

"Mail!" the male called, holding up the heavy satchel. "A couple weeks' worth for you lot from the looks of it. Your mailbox at the post office was so full, we decided to deliver it to you. Went to Romulus house first and delivered the mail to the lovely females there. Or at least half of it. They told me to bring the rest out here, so here you have it."

He came to a stop in front of Zeke and held out the satchel as if expecting Zeke to take it from him. Zeke raised his brows at the male for a moment and then sighed. Taking the bag, he started fishing the mail out and handing it to Maddox to hold. Once emptied, he handed the bag back.

"Thank you, that'll be all."

The mail carrier stuttered for a moment and then nodded before backing up a step. Turning on his heel, he hurried back to the city, his steps quick and light.

"You could have let him ask if we had any mail to send out," Maddox huffed a laugh, surveying the pile of letters in his arms.

"Damn it," Zeke grumbled, shaking his head. "My mind is so scattered... You know what? Never mind. If we have mail to send out, I'll take it into the city myself tomorrow morning. And apologize to the mail carrier. It's the least I can do."

Reaching over, he pulled the top letter off the stack in Maddox's arms. Clearing his throat, he called the pack members not on duty over and began reading names. As the owner of the letter raised their hands or let out some sort of noise to claim it, they stepped forward and Zeke handed it over. He was halfway through the pile when his brows shot up in surprise. With a low chuckle, he handed the letter straight to Warren.

"Seems your pack knew where to send your letter," he said in amusement.

"Seems like it," Warren agreed, pulling a pocketknife out of his pocket and slicing one end of the envelope open. Sliding the letter out, he unfolded it and glanced at the name on the bottom. Marcus. He should have known.

Shaking his head, he took a step back, away from Zeke and Maddox. Before turning around to head to his tent to read the letter, he glanced over at Maddox.

"If, by chance, I reply to this letter, could I get someone from your pack to take my reply to Loch Haven?" Warren asked cautiously. "I'd send it via the post, but I'm afraid they wouldn't know where Loch Haven is. My own pack has to send our own carrier out to bring mail here and to gather supplies."

Maddox hesitated for a moment and then shrugged. "I don't see why not. We're allies, or in my eyes we are. Your people deserve to know what's going on just as much as ours. Just let me know when you've got a reply ready to go. I've got a few people who can make that journey without an issue.

"Thank you," Warren breathed in relief before taking another step back.

Maddox nodded in response. Glancing down at the letter, his fingers trembling, anxious to hear the news, he turned and hurried to his tent where he could read it in privacy while he continued to wait for Clara.

Sitting just outside of the tent, leaning against a boulder, Warren reread the letter from Marcus. Most of it was just normal pack doings and what was going on with him and the family.

Normal.

The letter was so calm and relaxed, peaceful even, that it made his chest ache. He wanted to feel that sense of peace again, but being out here in the field outside of Reynardsville, dealing with Clara's family that seemed to want to use and abuse her, finding that feeling was nearly impossible.

Tilting his head back, he let the sun warm his face and neck. Letting out a deep breath, he groaned. The sun felt nice even though it was still chilly outside, the breeze nipping at his nose, the tips of his ears, and his fingers. He'd put up with it for this moment, though. It was worth it.

The only thing that would make this moment better would be if Clara was sitting there next to him, enjoying the sun too. She probably would have complained about the cold, getting up to go grab a blanket from inside the tent. When she returned, she would have spread the blanket out on the ground and then sat down, providing a thin barrier between her bare hands and the still frozen ground.

Warren would have laughed. Teased her a bit.

But no, she wasn't here. She was still in Reynardsville. It was driving him insane. Where was she? What was she doing?

Something felt off, but he couldn't place the feeling. He needed Clara. He needed to see her, touch her, make sure she was okay. Until he got to do that, he would feel unsettled and restless.

He was going to drive himself insane waiting.

CHAPTER 35

CLARA

The marble felt cold under her cheek. And wet. The amount of tears she'd shed as she held onto the pillar as if her life depended on it was astonishing. She'd cried more than she'd ever cried before in her life, although it had been mostly silent. She hadn't wanted to cry, but the tears had come unbidden and she didn't have the mental fortitude to stop herself. Let the tears come. Let Freisinger see what he'd done to her emotionally.

All because she'd ask for a break.

She swallowed back a wave of nausea as she hugged the pillar that she was still using as support, her legs trembling underneath her, barely holding her up. She would not fall. She would not collapse. Not in front of Freisinger.

Not that it would matter if she did. She was already crying. how much more embarrassing and shameful could this situation get? She wasn't sure, but she felt like she was at her lowest. She'd hit rock bottom. She was nothing. She was completely at their mercy.

Why had she ever thought that she'd had any control? She'd been delusional and they, her grandmother and Freisinger mainly, knew it. Clara was sure that this whipping was part of their plan to remind her of her place. They'd wanted to take her down a peg or two.

She wouldn't lie, they'd been successful. She'd never felt more humbled in her life.

Why hadn't she stayed in Loch Haven? She would regret leaving for the rest of her life.

She closed her eyes, feeling more tears leak down her face. Breathe, she reminded herself. She just needed to breathe. She could get through this. After, she would go back to Warren and he could comfort her.

She froze.

Warren.

How was she going to explain this to her mate? He would go ballistic when he saw her back. That would lead to him possibly doing something stupid. Forget possibly, she corrected herself. He would do something stupid. She winced. The next question was would that something stupid be killing Freisinger or her grandmother? She knew the answer before she'd finished asking herself the question. Her grandmother, who had ordered the punishment, would be the first to go. Freisinger would follow, but Clara wasn't sure how soon he would meet the same fate as her grandmother.

Clara jolted as the whip cracked across her back again, a cry of pain leaving her unbidden. She'd been doing so well with being silent up until that point. However, with each subsequent crack of the whip, a searing, tearing, blinding pain lanced through her back. She was sure that he'd broken skin at this point. Her back felt wet, as did her now sticky clothes, clinging to her skin. She'd lost count of how many times he had whipped her at this point.

She wasn't sure how much more she could take at this point. She was done. She wanted to be done. If the gods were listening, she prayed that they would intervene by making Freisinger grow a heart or something along those lines.

If only he would put the whip down and untie her.

She could hear him breathing heavily behind her, just a few paces away. She could hear how he readjusted his grip on the leather handle, how the end dragged across the floor as he shifted and prepared to strike. Her body tensed as she heard the hissing sound of the whip dragging across the floor. She squeezed her eyes tight, preparing for the inevitable pain, trying to keep her body loose. That was harder said than done, though. She knew, however, that if she stayed tense, it would hurt more.

Relax.

She swallowed anxiously, but the strike never came. She cracked open her eyes and peered over her shoulder to see Freisinger winding the whip up, blood dripping off the end. His face was guarded and dark as he did as if he had locked up all his emotions behind an impenetrable wall. Did he even feel bad for this punishment that was so out of proportion for her supposed crime that it would be funny if it wasn't as serious or as painful as it was? Clara doubted it. She'd come to realize that Freisinger just didn't... He didn't feel. Not like a normal shifter.

If she didn't despise him as much as she did, she'd probably wonder why he was closed off, what had made him that way, and how to get through to him. As it was, she did hate him and, at this current point in time, she would rather throw him into the depths of the nearest volcano and call it a day. He could burn in the depths of one of those raging infernos for the rest of his days for all she cared.

She dropped her head onto the pillar and released a shaky breath, not daring to relax in case Freisinger had something else planned for her. It would be just her luck.

And then she heard something that was like sweet music to her ears. Freisinger's footsteps were retreating, heading toward the closet where he'd retrieved his whip. She heard the door creak open, his footsteps disappear inside, and then return, the door creaking closed once more. From there, instead of walking in her direction, he headed for the locked double doors. Tugging one open, he paused, his dark gaze burning into her.

"You are done for the day, Kleine. Let's *not* repeat this anytime soon. It was just as unpleasant for me as it was for you."

Clara's body tensed again, her eyes shooting open in surprise. She peered over her shoulder at Freisinger just in time to see him disappear through one of the double doors, the door closing softly behind him. Had he just said that he hadn't enjoyed whipping her? That's what it had sounded like, but she must have misheard him. There was no way. If it had been nearly as unpleasant as he had indicated it was, why had he lashed her so many times? Surely a couple strikes would have sufficed, not that disobeying his order to continue training warranted whipping anyway.

She held herself up for a few more minutes before sliding down the column, landing on her knees with a thud. A low groan escaped her throat followed by a choked sob. She was loathe to admit that she may have begged him to stop. Thank the gods she hadn't promised to do anything she couldn't or wouldn't do, like leave Warren, though that pesky voice in the back of her head decided to chime in to remind her that there was probably a part of Freisinger hoping she would promise that. She was almost one hundred percent certain that if she had, he would have stopped whipping her almost immediately and then whisked her away.

She shuddered at the thought.

Sure, he wasn't bad looking. He was handsome, in an arrogant, asshole-ish way. But because she knew who he was and what he was like, she wouldn't touch him with a ten-foot pole. Being tied to him was not her idea of a good time.

Pushing off the pillar, she tried to stay upright, but soon found that she didn't have the strength to remain sitting and slid down onto the floor, her cheek pressed against the cool wood. She swallowed, squeezing her eyes shut as she noticed the drops of blood on the floor around her. Her blood. And then her stomach twisted and she heaved, emptying the contents of her stomach onto the floor. With a groan, she pushed herself away from her own vomit and laid back down on the floor.

She'd get up. Soon. She'd definitely get up. Head back to her room. Clean up. Grab something to eat. Head back to Warren. Yes, she'd do all that. As soon as she could move without her head spinning.

She closed her eyes, trying to focus on her breathing and the nausea that threatened to overtake her again. But before she could count to four, she was unconscious, the pain and blood loss winning.

Stumbling into the bathroom of the townhome, Clara turned on the bathtub, watching the steaming water as it filled the tub. Standing, or attempting to stand, she started to pull her clothes off and then froze. With a low groan, she sank down to the floor. This was going to hurt.

As much as she wanted to get into the tub, it would hurt more than she was willing to endure at the moment. She didn't want to black out in the tub and potentially drown. And her clothes... She glanced down at herself. She didn't have any spare clothes here. She would have to put these filthy things back on if she did manage to get them off and into the tub.

Feeling put out, she turned the water off and then drained the tub.

She couldn't do this alone.

CHAPTER 36

WARREN

Unfolding the letter he had received from Marcus earlier that day, Warren reread the small message yet again. His rough fingers glided over the parchment, over the ink, as if he could get a sense of home by doing so. He sighed after a second, his heart aching. He should be home, with Clara, preparing to help the pack plow fields for spring planting and building more homes. He should be starting on their home. He wanted to be building their home up on the hill he had dragged her to shortly after they'd arrived at the lake.

Loch Haven.

Home.

He read the words again, wondering if he should show Clara when she got back. He knew she was dying for news of home, worried about the pack. She had a few good friends within the pack already. Not being able to just be herself, doing what she enjoyed, with the company that she enjoyed, was killing her inside. He could see it every morning when she forced herself off their sleeping mat to get dressed for the day. He could see it in the firm set of her jaw as she braced herself to face Freisinger.

He'd made a mistake in convincing her to come back out to Reynardsville for the sake of her family and her family's pack. They didn't actually want her here. They were more concerned with what she could do for them, which was to put Freisinger in an even greater position of power.

Clara was a pawn and nothing more.

The thought stung.

As her mate, Warren should have protected her from this. It was his duty. That was why he had insisted on coming with her after all, right?

Frowning, Warren stretched and stood up, tucking the letter into the breast pocket of his coat. Stepping out of the tent, he surveyed the setting sun. Only a small portion was left, just barely visible over the horizon, an inky blue and black following in its wake. No stars were out yet, but it wouldn't be long.

Clara should have been back already. It was late and she'd been gone all day at this point. Nearly twelve hours. What in the world was she doing? Only the gods knew at this point, but he was about to find out.

Glancing back at the tent briefly, he turned in the direction of Zeke's shared tent. Stalking over, he rapped his knuckles against the thick canvas.

"She's not back yet," he announced as Maddox popped his head out, his voice rough with emotion and worry. "I'm going to go look for her."

Maddox simply nodded and disappeared back inside the tent. Before Warren had taken more than a couple dozen steps toward the city gate, Maddox stepped back out, his own heavy coat on and a blade on his hip. Picking up his pace, he hurried after Warren.

"I'm coming with you, simply so I don't have to listen to Ronan worry himself sick over her. He's not a silent worrier," Maddox mumbled, his voice low. "Between you and me, I like the male. He's one of my best friends, but gods alive... He's got the temperament of mother hen."

Warren huffed a laugh, accepting Maddox's company as they started toward the gate together. "I don't know much of the male, but from what Clara told me, I don't want to know him. I might kill him."

"I don't blame you." Maddox nodded in agreement, surprising Warren. "If I had someone like Clara and I'd found out someone had tried to place their claim over mine, among other things, I would be furious."

"Furious is an understatement," Warren murmured.

It was Maddox's turn to huff a laugh. "Either way... I understand. Just, whatever you do, don't kill him, yeah? We need everybody we can get right now with the war coming, and Ronan is a decent fighter."

"I know." Warren's mind went back to the first time he'd met Ronan, how the slightly smaller male had rammed into him, sending him to the ground in an effort to save Clara from him. Noble, but stupid. It had only made him want Clara more, his desire for her growing with each hour that passed without her.

Maddox, not knowing the story, arched a brow at him. Not wanting to relive the embarrassment and rage he'd felt that night in front of a male he still barely knew, shook his head. "Perhaps another time. Or ask Ronan. I'm sure he'd be happy to tell you. He's quite fond of playing the hero."

Maddox chuckled under his breath and was about to respond when the city gate creaked open, cutting him off. Both males froze in their tracks, their eyes focusing on the dark opening, their hands instinctively going for their blades.

A small figure appeared in trousers and a white shirt with a vest over the top. A cloak was draped over the figure's shoulders, but not clasped. Their arms were wrapped around their middle, their face bowed down to the ground as they moved slowly.

"Clara," Warren breathed, not quite letting himself relax yet. Something was wrong. He could see it in the way she was moving, in the way she was behaving. His brows furrowed as he moved forward, quickly closing the distance between them. Coming to a stop in front of her, he dropped down to his knees and peered up at her, taking her hands in his. "Clara? Little Fox? Where have you been?"

Clara's eyes widened as she looked at him. Her face was pale, and her expression was a bit pinched as if she were in pain. The bruising on her cheek was a dark purple, a stark contrast against her normally fair skin. Her lips were also chapped and slightly parted, and her breathing labored.

"Grandmother needed me," she whispered, her voice barely audible to his ears.

Warren frowned. "And...?" he pressed.

She simply shook her head. "Not here. Not now." Her eyes flickered to Maddox nervously and then back to Warren.

Warren opened his mouth to argue further and then closed it with a snap, taking the hint. Something had happened and she didn't want to talk about it in front of Maddox. She wanted privacy. Standing, he wrapped an arm around her shoulders, not missing the way that she winced at the contact, and started leading her back to the camp.

"Let Zeke and Ronan know that she's back." Warren raised his head and looked at Maddox as he spoke. "Let them know that if they see Freisinger, to keep him away from Clara for the next couple of days."

Maddox nodded, surveying Clara himself. Warren was sure he had also noted Clara's behavior and the way she had winced judging by the way his eyes had darkened, and his hands had clenched into fists at the mention of Freisinger. Concern also flickered across his face, but then it was gone as he looked back up at Warren. "Consider it done." And then he picked up his pace, leaving Warren alone with Clara.

"What was the meeting about?" Warren asked as soon as Maddox was out of earshot.

"Disobeying Freisinger. I got quite the lashing for it," Clara said, her voice bitter.

"What did she say?" he asked, glancing down at her.

"Not much, but it was plenty," she said before falling silent, not offering up anything else on the matter until they reached their tent. Even then, the only thing she said was that her grandmother had made it clear, under no uncertain terms, that she was to not disobey Freisinger again. As she talked, Warren noted that her voice still had the same bitter tone to it that she had used to answer him before.

A sinking feeling in his gut told him that more than words had been done. Something that had left a lasting impression that she wasn't keen on repeating. Something that had left her reeling, shattering her self-confidence. She was a shell of what she had been this morning before she had left.

What had happened?

"Are you tired?" Warren asked as he put a kettle over the fire to heat.

"Very," was her one word answer.

"Let me help you undress," Warren insisted.

"No, I've got it," she replied, her voice soft, weary, lifeless.

She turned away from him as he watched and started to reach up to pull her cloak off her shoulders, but then she hissed in pain, tears filling her eyes.

Warren hurried over, turning him to face him, concerned. "Clara, what in the world...?" he started, and then froze, his hands hovering over her shoulders as his eyes landed on her back. Her white shirt was stained red. Dark red. And it was wet, sticking to her back. Blood. " What happened?" His voice came out harsh and demanding, making her flinch.

"I told you," she whispered faintly. "I got quite the lashing for disobeying Freisinger."

"Lashed you with what?" Warren asked, his stomach twisting, making him feel sick. At the same time, an indescribable rage took over him. Someone had laid their hands on Clara with the intent to harm her. They had harmed her. And here she was, standing before him, her back bleeding so much that it had soaked the back of her shirt.

"A whip."

"Who?"

"I think you know who," she murmured, dropping her head, tears dripping from her eyes in defeat.

"Hey... Hey... It's okay. I'm here. Let it out," Warren said, his rage taking the back burner as he spotted her tears. Gathering her in his arms, careful not to touch her back, he pulled her to him, letting her bury her face in his chest as she started to sob.

"All I wanted was a break," she sobbed. "I shouldn't have been whipped for wanting a break."

"No, no you shouldn't have," Warren agreed, appalled.

The punishment should match the crime. What they had done was so grossly unjustified, that it made him physically sick. And even angrier if that were possible. He would kill Freisinger with his bare hands, rip him limb from limb if it were the last thing he ever did. He would do it for every ounce of pain he had inflicted on Clara, and he would enjoy it.

"Let me clean you up, my little fox," Warren requested, his voice low and smooth, soothing.

Mutely, Clara nodded and let Warren pull her shirt over her head, careful to unstick it from her back piece by piece so he didn't hurt her further. When he got the shirt free, he guided her down onto the mat, laying her on her stomach so he could see the damage done. Surveying her back, he cursed under his breath. Her skin was shredded and raw. Blood oozed from the lacerations, coating her back.

Taking a deep breath, he poured the now heated water into a bowl, grabbed some supplies to clean her back, and got to work, mopping up the blood. Each time the cloth came in contact with her tender skin, she hissed or let out a strangled sob.

"I know, baby," he whispered each time, his heart breaking with each sob. "I'm so sorry. I know it hurts. I promise I'll do my best to make it feel better. Just a little longer."

When he finally managed to get the last of the blood, he grabbed another salve Marcus had sent them with. He shook his head in amusement, grateful that he had let Marcus pack their bags and thanking the gods that Marcus had the forethought to pack healing salves in them. This one, according to Marcus's hastily written scrawl, would numb the skin. Just what Clara needed for relief. Hopefully, it would also allow him to wrap her without causing too much pain.

Unscrewing the lid, he dipped his fingers into the cool gel and slathered it onto her back. She winced and then gasped as the cool gel hit her skin, crying out as he smoothed it out over each laceration. The salve was good, but the effects weren't instant unfortunately, so by the time he was done, she was sobbing, her breaths coming in quick pants.

"I'm done, baby. I promise. You'll feel a bit better in just a few minutes. Do you want some tea while we wait? Or maybe some food? Have you eaten? Are you hungry?" Warren rambled, trying his best to soothe her.

Clara lifted her head and looked at him with tear-stained cheeks. "I..." she hesitated, as if unsure how to answer that question.

"I'll make some tea and some porridge. That should be easy on your stomach. Does that sound alright?" he asked quickly. Gods, he sounded like his late mother when he had been sick growing up. She had fussed constantly and now look at him. He bit back a smile. Now was not the time to reminisce over his late mother, but he allowed himself two last thoughts as he started preparing the tea and porridge. One, his mother would be proud of him for taking care of his mate in such a caring manner. And two, he was sure she'd adore Clara.

An hour later, Clara had been fed, bandaged, and put to sleep. She was uncomfortable, that much was evident in the way her mouth was twisted into a small grimace, but there wasn't much else Warren could do for her at the moment.

Now that she was asleep, though...

Warren stood and made his way out of the tent, hurrying over to Zeke's shared tent. Rapping on the canvas once more, he was again greeted by Maddox, concern shining in his eyes.

"Is she alright?" he asked.

Warren grimaced and then looked around, not wanting any prying ears to hear. What could he say that wouldn't alert the whole camp to the fact that Clara had been whipped for a minor infraction? Any trust in their leadership would be dashed at the news and that was the last thing they needed going into war.

Noticing his look, Maddox ushered Warren into the tent where Zeke was curled up on his sleeping mat, paperwork strewn around him. Ronan, on the other hand, was sprawled out on his sleeping mat, staring at the top of the tent, his eyes unseeing. As he entered, both males' attention turned to him.

"What's going on?" Ronan asked, his voice rough with worry.

Warren cleared his throat, trying to figure out how to word what had happened to Clara without going into too much detail. Finally, he settled on being blunt and honest without any embellishments.

"Clara was taken to her grandmother this morning because Freisinger told her about Clara asking for a break from training. They saw it as disobeying orders. She was whipped for it. Her back is completely torn up."

Ronan shot off his sleeping mat, his eyes blazing in fury. "They what?"

Warren nodded grimly. "I'm going to go talk to her grandmother. Tonight. Alone."

"You can't go alone," Zeke said calmly, but there was an angry glint in his eyes.

"I have to. I need someone to look after Clara while I'm gone. I don't want Freisinger anywhere near her." Warren shook his head. "There's no telling what he'd do now that she's weak and can't fight back. I don't want her alone. And I can't let this go. I warned her grandmother of what would happen if she got hurt before we left Loch Haven. It looks like she needs a reminder..."

"I'll go guard her," Maddox grunted before Ronan could volunteer. Ronan, put out, shot Maddox a brief glare, but it lacked heat. Ignoring Ronan, Maddox hurried out of the tent and made his way over to Warren and Clara's tent, planting himself firmly in front of the entrance.

Satisfied, Warren turned toward the city once more.

The door banged open as Warren strode into the townhome he knew Clara's grandmother lived in when she was in the city. The house was dark, telling him that everyone was asleep. Good. Let them be woken rather rudely. It served them right.

Just as he reached the stairs, Mrs. Reynard appeared at the top, her face white. Spotting Warren, her face twisted into an angry sneer.

"Why in gods' names are you here?" she demanded.

Warren, seeing red, climbed the stairs quickly, taking three at a time. Stopping just in front of her, his hand darted out and wrapped around her throat, squeezing. Her skin was thin and delicate and he knew she'd have a bruise in the morning from his rough handling. Good. Someone needed to teach her a lesson.

Eyes widening, Mrs. Reynard opened her mouth to protest, but all that came out was a squeak and a hoarse gasp. Her hands lifted, her fingers digging into his hand, trying to get him to loosen his grip. He only tightened it in response.

He wanted to kill her.

He should kill her.

She'd deserve it.

He had warned her.

He leaned in, his mouth mere inches from her ear. "I warned you when you first showed up in Loch Haven," he whispered, his voice low and dangerous. "I told you that if you harmed a hair on her head, I would end you. And I mean to do just that. However, considering the circumstances, I shall give you one last chance. You will not use her like that again. She has been through enough in this life already. I can not bear to see her go through more shit, especially at your hands. I do not want to see her hurt more than she already is. If you must hurt someone, hurt me. Take me in her place. I can take it."

He released Mrs. Reynard. Stumbling back, she glared up at him, and then a snide smile tugged at her lips. "I shall do just that."

Warren gave her a funny look, his gut telling him something was off. Before he could turn around to head back out of the house, he was slammed into the wall, a picture hanging nearby coming loose and falling to the ground, shattering, glass going everywhere. He could feel hot breath on the back of his neck and his ear.

"I never wanted to hurt her," a low voice said from behind him. "But she needs to learn. If she wants to live, what I say goes."

Warren opened his mouth to protest, recognizing the voice as Freisinger's, but before he could make a sound, his arms were yanked behind him and cuffs were snapped onto his wrist. His eyes widened in shock. And then he swore.

"Fuck

CHAPTER 37

RONAN

Sitting in front of the large fire in the center of camp, on the side closest to Clara's tent so that Maddox could join them, Ronan looked at the cards in his hand and groaned internally. He was going to lose this round. Silently, he thanked the gods that they weren't betting money and were using dried beans from their dried good stash as poker chips. If they had been using money, Maddox would have cleaned him out. Not that it would be the first time. The male was unnaturally good at playing a round of poker. In fact, Ronan had yet to see someone beat him.

Beside Ronan, Zeke set his hand of cards down. "I fold," he grunted.

Maddox, a wide grin stretching across his face, glanced at Zeke. "Are you sure?" he taunted. "You've only got a few beans left. Why not throw them in the pot?"

Giving him an unamused look, Zeke rolled his eyes. "I don't want to be out yet, that's why, you smug bastard."

"Me? A smug bastard?" Maddox snickered. "Why, I would never."

"Yeah, yeah. Laugh it up," Zeke responded, setting his cards down.

"How about you, Ronan?" Maddox grinned at him. "You going to wimp out?"

Ronan didn't answer right away. Studying his cards, he sighed. He already knew how this would play out. Maddox would lull him into a false sense of security, making him think that he had a shot at winning a hand. This would then lead to Ronan putting more in the pot. And then Maddox would strike. It just wasn't worth it. Besides, he was already in a bit of a shitty mood from not being able to watch over Clara himself. He'd wanted that position, and instead, it had gone to Maddox. Not that Ronan blamed Warren for preferring Maddox. Maddox hadn't tried to claim his mate. Still, though... It stung.

Looking up at Maddox, Ronan pursed his lips and then sighed. "I fold, too," he said. "I already know how this works, Mads. I'm not falling for it. Not this time." He set his cards down and leaned back, reaching for his cup of coffee. Taking a sip, he shook his head at Maddox as the hot, bitter liquid scalded his tongue.

"Oh, come on," Maddox groaned, glancing down at his hand and then back up at Ronan, his eyes pleading but still full of mischief.

"No, I know that look," Ronan laughed, unable to help himself. "That's the look you give me every time you've got something up your sleeve, and it always goes in your favor."

"Well, of course." Maddox nodded, as if that were the most natural thing in the world for him to do. "Why wouldn't I put my own interests first? I love you, Ronan, but I love me more. No offense of course."

Zeke snorted in response, almost spraying his own coffee all over the ground as he tried to hold back a laugh. "Damn that was cold," he gasped, his voice hoarse as he wiped coffee off his chin.

"It's the truth," Maddox said in a matter-of-fact tone. "I put myself first. That's not to say I don't consider the interests of the pack and whatnot. I do. I won't jeopardize their safety or their health but in things like this? It's all about me."

"Mhm," Ronan hummed dryly, setting his cup down. Before he could say anything else, though, the sound of approaching footsteps greeted their ears. His brows furrowing, Ronan turned in the direction of the sound, his eyes narrowing as he scanned the darkness, searching for the source. Behind him, Zeke got to his feet and Maddox shifted back into position in front of Clara's tent, ready to stop anyone from getting to her. Realizing he was the only one still seated on the ground, Ronan hurried to stand, too.

Brushing his curls out of his face, he braced himself, not sure who to expect but praying it wasn't Freisinger. One glance at Zeke and Maddox told him that they were hoping the same thing. Ronan wasn't sure he could stop himself from murdering the male on the spot for what he had done to Clara. He'd deserve it. No, actually, he deserved worse, but if given the chance to take him out, Ronan wouldn't complain about how it got done. One less pompous male to worry about.

"C'mon," he murmured under his breath as the footsteps drew closer, his eyes straining. He wished it wasn't around midnight. He felt like he was at a disadvantage. Whoever was coming could clearly see him and his two friends while they couldn't see shit.

Just then, an elderly male came into view. His clothes were a deep, rich, navy blue made out of a finely woven fabric. His dark hair was slicked back. And his eyes... Ronan recognized those eyes. Or, at the very least, they looked familiar. Why did they...? Clara. Those eyes were like Clara's. That must mean...

"Who are you?" Ronan's voice was sharp as it cut through the still night air.

Flinching, the male held up his hands in a sign of surrender, slowing his pace as he approached them. "I mean no harm. I promise. I came to warn you... to warn Clara..."

"Who are you?" Maddox growled from his place in front of Clara's tent, his eyes darkening, the male's words putting all of them on edge.

"I am Percil Vivak. I am Melanie Reynard's older brother, Clara's great uncle," he said, his voice cautious as he took a few more steps closer to them and the fire. "I mean Clara no harm. None at all."

"Right..." Ronan said slowly, his voice full of disbelief as he shifted positions, his arms crossing over his chest as he glowered down at the male who only came up to his shoulders. Ronan wasn't much of a fighter, but if push came to shove, he felt like he could quite literally snap the man in half if he wanted. But he didn't want to do that. Yet.

"I know you don't believe me, but let me speak, and then you can judge all you want. I would not blame you," Percil pleaded, dropping his hands and rubbing them over the front of his jacket. "I beg you. Let me speak. For five minutes."

Silence. Finally, Zeke shifted, taking a deep breath.

"Fine," Zeke said. "I may not trust you, but I pride myself on being fair. We will hear you out. But if I feel that you are lying..." Zeke shook his head, a dangerous glint in his eye.

Percil, noticing the look, took a step back, his eyes widening. "I understand. I do. I understand."

Maddox chuckled darkly. "You've got five minutes, fox. Start talking."

"Warren came into the city tonight. I am sure that you know that already, otherwise the three of you wouldn't be blocking me from what I assume is my niece's tent," Percil started, speaking quickly so that he could get everything out that he wanted to say. "He went straight to my sister's residence to talk to her. However, his version of talking was a touch more violent than the usual version of talking. He choked her. And he was rather threatening. Anyway, I don't think he realized that my sister has guards in her house. He was quickly taken into custody for his assault. He's in jail, and I'm not sure they're going to let him out anytime soon or at all. In fact, as loathe as I am to admit this, I wouldn't put it past my sister to have him put to death. Once the city finds out what he's done..." Percil shook his head. "The city will be demanding his head on a spike. Either way, he's now out of the picture as far as my sister is concerned. She'll be having Freisinger make his move. Soon. We have to warn Clara. We have to get her out of here. Send her back to Warren's pack. She'll be safe there."

Silence fell again. This time, Ronan and the others were stunned. Warren had been arrested. Ronan could hardly believe his ears. He had known going in to talk to Mrs. Reynard had been a rather stupid idea, but he had assumed it was stupid because he had been almost one hundred per-cent certain that she wouldn't have entertained him. He would have been shouting at a closed door, demanding she treat Clara better. To hear that he had gotten into her house before assaulting and threatening her... Ronan sighed. What had Warren gotten himself into?

"Is she that paranoid that she needs guards stationed in her house?" Maddox snorted, breaking the silence.

"My sister is... cautious. Overly cautious." Percil frowned. "She does not feel safe anywhere. Perhaps, if she had not made so many enemies within our pack and the city, she would have no need to guard herself so heavily, but as it is, she has. There are more than a few who would love to hurt or kill her if they could."

"Stupid fox," Maddox huffed, partly in humor and partly in disgust.

Percil's frown deepened at the insult but said nothing.

Zeke, not wanting to goad Percil, studied the male, his lips pursed. "Do you know where Warren is being held?"

Percil shook his head. "There are at least a dozen places throughout the city she could be holding him. I could find out and try to let you know, but

I am afraid that if you tried to get him out, you'd find yourself in a similar predicament."

"Right." Zeke nodded his head, a thoughtful expression on his face. "Thank you for letting us know."

"Of course." Percil took a step back, his eyes darting to Clara's tent and lingering there, the worry in his eyes visible to the three of them. "Keep her safe. Don't let Freisinger near her. If you do... she won't ever be able to leave."

Ronan nodded himself as he watched Percil take one last look at the tent before turning and hurrying back toward the city, disappearing into the darkness with a quiet, "I must go."

"Well... Shit," Maddox groaned.

Shifting from foot to foot, Ronan stuck his hands in the front pockets of his pants, his eyes shifting nervously from Maddox and Zeke to Clara's tent and then to the rising sun that was just peeping over the tree lines, making the city wall cast a long shadow over the camp. He shivered before looking at Clara's tent again. Any minute. She'd be awake. And she'd wake up alone.

Fuck.

When was the last time Clara had woken up alone? Ronan didn't have the slightest clue, but he imagined it was about the time she'd left him in the city street, heartbroken. He knew that there had been a day or two between her leaving him and when she'd left to meet back up with Warren. That was... months ago.

He shifted anxiously again, his hands clenching into fists in his pockets. Part of him was angry that Warren had done something so stupid. It hadn't just cost him his freedom, but it had put Clara in more danger. However, Ronan had to give the male some grace. Warren hadn't known that he'd be arrested. Hell, none of them had. Sure, they had known that it had been risky for Warren to go talk to Mrs. Reynard. They had known that he could possibly make things worse than they already were. But for him to get arrested?

Rolling his neck, Ronan looked up at the sun, squinting as he did so. It was going to be warm for a spring day. Not that he was complaining. He was tired of freezing his ass off. But it would do nothing to deter Freisinger if he showed up to continue his training with Clara. In fact, it would probably further encourage the male. Ronan would be surprised if he didn't show up in the next few minutes. His eyes shifted to the gate, waiting with bated breath. Any minute now...

His thoughts were interrupted by a groan from Clara's tent, the sound pained and miserable. His heart clenched at the sound, and he grimaced before glancing over at the tent. His muscles spasmed as he started to take a step toward the tent, but then forced himself to stay still. She didn't want him. And she would be beyond upset if he showed up just as she was waking up. It was highly likely she'd attack him and then demand to know why Warren wasn't there.

Ronan didn't want the unfortunate task of breaking the news to her.

Next to him, Maddox also shifted, his eyes locked on the entrance to the tent, waiting. "She's going to be pissed," the male muttered, the muscles in his arms tense.

"Ten coins says she'll launch herself at whoever breaks the news," another male whispered with a snigger from somewhere behind Ronan and Maddox.

"Fifteen coins says she'll storm into the city and get arrested herself," yet another male added.

"Good riddance," one of the females muttered.

Ronan tensed, stopping himself from turning around and snapping at the female.

"Both her and her mate are good for nothing nuisances," another female quipped. "How dare he threaten the Reynard leader."

More hushed mutters and whispers broke out among the rest of the pack gathered around the main fire. Some were exclamations of surprise, scandalized or surprised Warren had the gall to do something so bold and so reckless. Some were more negative, condemning Warren, and by default, Clara. Very few defended Warren. Those few were the ones that had gotten to know him or had mates themselves. They knew what it was like to want to protect their mate, how angry seeing them hurt would make them. To them, Warren's actions were understandable.

More rustling came from Clara's tent and all eyes shifted to focus on the entrance. Zeke took a deep breath in through his nose, his nostrils flaring. He then glanced at Ronan and Maddox before pursing his lips. He nodded. Then he stepped forward, closing the gap between him and the tent. He rapped his fist on the entrance flap, calling out to ask if she was decent.

"Come in," Clara's voice called out, rending Ronan's heart further.

Clara's voice was quiet, weary, and dejected. It sounded... It sounded like she'd given up. But... Ronan shook his head. He knew why. It was one thing to get punished. It was another to be whipped to the point where she'd lost consciousness, her back torn to shreds, and have her own grandmother sanction the act. He'd want to give up, too. But she couldn't. Not now.

Zeke glanced back at Ronan, giving him a look that told him to stay put, and then gave Maddox a look that told him to make sure Ronan stayed put before stepping into the tent. Straining his ears, he tried to overhear what Zeke was telling Clara, but the male had dropped his voice too low for Ronan to make anything out. Glancing over at Maddox, Ronan could tell that Maddox was struggling to hear just as much as he was.

And then silence fell.

Ronan could feel his heartbeat pounding in his ears, the sound deafening.

Clara shrieked. "Over my fucking dead body!"

There was a collective gasp from the pack and then a few chuckles. Ronan himself chuckled. There was that fiery spirit he knew. He knew it hadn't disappeared. It was still there. And maybe it had been struggling for a moment, but the news that Warren had been arrested had been the kick in the ass she'd needed apparently because seconds later, she stormed out of the tent, her eyes ablaze.

"Where the fuck is Freisinger?" she demanded.

"Not here," Maddox's deep voice said calmly.

"Good. If I see him, I'll kill him. And then I'll kill my grandmother. To hell with them. To hell with them all," she snarled.

CHAPTER 38

MATTY

The sounds of the bar floated back to Matty as he sat at his desk in what used to be the storage room for the bar but had been turned into his dad's office after Mr. O'Donoghue had passed and his dad had taken over O'Donoghue's assets. Matty, being just under his dad, shared the office space. His desk, not that you could really call it that, it was more of a small table, had been pushed back against the wall in a corner. A spindly wooden chair was tucked in at one side, usually kept there for when someone came in to talk to him. Matty sat in the other, his legs cramped and feeling a bit claustrophobic.

In the center of the room was General Claery's desk. The large, rather grand piece of furniture took up most of the space. A comfortable looking leather chair sat behind it, pushed out just a bit. The leather was a bit worn on the seat and the armrests, telling Matty his dad sat there quite often. There were no chairs on the other side of the desk, a move meant to discourage the general's subordinates from getting too comfortable around him. Files and papers were strewn across the desktop in a haphazard manner. And the general himself? Matty had no clue. If he had to hazard a guess, Matty would say he was out in the bar getting a beer or eating some lunch with his men.

For someone as psychotic and as cruel as his dad, he knew how to turn on the charm and play the friendly but charismatic leader. Perhaps that was why most of the men looked at Matty like he was insane when they found out the Matty and the general didn't get along. "But... He's your father?" "How can you not like him? Have you heard his jokes?" "He's always got our backs. He's dependable. Are you sure you're not the crazy one?" And so on and so forth.

Matty rubbed a hand down his face wearily. He could handle the questions and the snide jabs at him for not getting along with his dad. He understood that not everyone saw the general for what he truly was. A few had, and those men where currently the men he'd trusted enough to let into his inner circle. Connaway and Archie were two of them, just to name a few. There was also a man named Gunnar, another named Bena, and another called Fitzwater. All good men. All trustworthy. He'd die for them if he had to, just as sure as they would do the same for him.

Hopefully it never came to that.

Matty dropped his hand down onto his desk and picked up the file he had been attempting to go through. It was a report from one of his men obtaining wood in the mountains for the wall since they had run out just trying to put the wall up on one side of the city. The sheer amount needed was mind boggling and made his head hurt and there weren't any cities close enough that they could ship more wood in. So that left sending a team up to the mountains to get more.

It made him uneasy.

It made the general uneasy.

However, they were uneasy for different reasons. Matty was uneasy because the shifters had gone north to the mountains. He had no reason to believe that there were any shifters hanging out in the foothills at this point in time. It had been a few months since the war had been announced publicly. He also knew that the shifters weren't exactly keen on fighting back. They just wanted to be left alone, which hopefully meant they'd fled so far north that he could safely assume his team would have no problems collecting enough wood to build some more of the wall.

His dad, on the other hand, was uneasy because he didn't like sending that small of a group to the mountains. He, like Matty, knew that the shifters had gone north. And he, like Matty, was hoping the shifters had gone further north. Sort of. Well, not really. It was complicated. On one hand, the general wanted the team to get in and get out with the wood they needed. On the other hand, if the shifters had indeed gone that far north, then they were wasting their time reinforcing Springfield. The city was in no danger. What they needed to be doing if the general really wanted to exterminate the shifters was to follow after them, bring the fight to them.

Leaning back in his seat, Matty set the report down. He'd read it later. Just as he was closing the file, the bell on the front door of the bar tinkled and the ruckus out front quieted down. Matty frowned. There wasn't much that made the men quiet down and behave, which meant a woman had just walked in. He grimaced. The only women that ever came into town anymore, if they didn't already live in town, were his mom and, well, that was it. And the only women that came into the bar was... He groaned, standing up.

Pushing his chair in, he started making his way to the office door when it swung open, and his dad walked in. General Claery was wearing his uniform pants and a button-down shirt, his uniform jacket thrown over the back of his leather chair. His sleeves were rolled up, exposing his forearms. He was talking jovially as he held the door open for who Matty assumed was his mom. However, instead of his mom walking in...

"Kitty?" Matty's brows shot up as he watched his wife walk into the room.

Since he'd brought Kitty with him to Springfield, her attire had changed drastically. Gone were the fine gowns she'd worn back home in Rotmuth. Instead, she wore something similar to what his mom wore. Long full skirts, a blouse tucked into the skirt, and an apron over the top, tied tightly around her waist with a... was that a giant bow? And were those frills on that apron? Matty blinked in surprise. His mom didn't do that, which meant... Kitty had made these clothes herself. He knew she could sew, but he'd thought it had been limited to embroidery. He had been terribly mistaken.

"Husband," Kitty crooned, arching a delicate brow at him as she swept in, a bit of an amused smile quirking up her lips as she studied the flabbergasted expression on his face. "You haven't been home very often in the last few weeks. I was getting lonely. And since you weren't coming to me, I figured I'd come to you."

"I... I... Kitty... I... You see..." Matty tried to speak but found himself speechless, unable to spit out what he wanted to say. How could you tell the woman you were married to that you thought marrying her was a mistake? How could you tell your wife that you didn't like her? And how could you tell her that you were angry with her for complaining to his dad? He knew, deep down, that she had meant well. He knew, deep down, that she'd had no idea that her complaining would lead to a good man's death. But yet... Matty swallowed thickly. He couldn't get over it. It festered and burned, making him angry.

General Claery also arched a brow at Matty, though whether he was amused or trying to figure out what was going on, Matty hadn't decided yet.

"What's going on, son?" the general asked, his voice firm. "Why haven't you been home?"

"I've... um..." Matty struggled some more, trying to figure out what to say that wouldn't land him and his friends in more trouble than they could handle at the moment. Finally, an idea struck. "I've been staying in the apartment above the store. So I can be close to the jail. In case there was an issue. With the shifters."

"I've got guards for that," General Claery said, his voice unamused as he sat down in his chair, the leather squeaking as he settled.

"I know that," Matty said quickly, stuffing his hands in his pockets as he leaned against his own desk, trying to act calm and relaxed. "But if you're at home with mom, I can be there quicker if something big happened. It's purely a precaution. That's all."

General Claery narrowed his eyes at him before letting out a deep huff, his hands clenching the armrests of his chair in irritation. Matty could see it in his eyes that he wanted to argue, wanted to tell Matty to suck it up and go home to Kitty, but he couldn't deny that Matty had a point. At the same time, Matty could also see a hint of suspicion in his eyes. He didn't trust Matty any more than Matty trusted him. Matty could see the cogs working, trying to figure out what Matty was really up to. Matty bit back a smug smirk, knowing that unless one of his men was a snitch, his plans were safe. For now.

"But I miss you," Kitty whined, breaking the awkward silence.

Both men turned to look at Kitty as she stomped her foot and pouted at Matty.

"I don't like sleeping alone," she continued on. "It gets lonely in the evenings and at night. Not that you seem to care."

"I have work, Kitty," Matty sighed, rubbing the back of his neck. "The moment the shifters are no longer a problem, I'll be home. I promise. But right now, someone has to watch them."

"Why can't your dad watch them?" she argued.

Matty glanced over at his dad just in time to see irritation flash in his eyes. He felt his chest tighten in annoyance and worry. If she kept this up, she'd get to see how his dad really was firsthand, and he didn't want her to see that. Ever.

"Kitty," he said before his dad could respond. "Look, dad has served his time. He's put in the work. He deserves to go home and sleep in his bed. I'm not going to take that away from him..."

"But..." Kitty cut in, trying to argue further.

"No buts, Kitty." Matty shook his head. "You agreed to marry me. You knew I was a farm boy. You knew I was a soldier. That life isn't easy. Not on me. Not on you. But those were the cards we were dealt. You'll have to suck it up. When the war is over, I'll be home every night. But until then, I'm sorry."

Kitty's eyes widened and her jaw dropped for half a second before she regained her composure, her eyes flashing angrily.

"Admit it, you don't want me," she shrieked.

"For gods' sake, woman," he groaned.

"That's enough," his dad said at the same time, his eyes fixed on Kitty, a disapproving expression on his face.

Matty and Kitty both froze at General Claery's tone. Matty, not bothering to look at his dad, already knowing what expression he would see there, kept his eyes on Kitty. Kitty, on the other hand, turned to look at her father-in-law. Her eyes widened and her face paled at the expression there. And then she swallowed nervously.

"This is not your father's court," General Claery continued, a hint of danger in his voice. "I am sorry that life here in Springfield is not up to your standard, but this is what you are stuck with. You can complain all you want, but it will not change your situation, do you understand me?"

"I..." Kitty's voice trailed off as she nodded slowly, her eyes still wide. "I want to... I want to go home."

General Claery's face hardened further. "Then go home."

"Not... I want to go *home* home," she clarified.

General Claery scoffed. "I do not have men to spare to take your spoiled ass back to your father and neither does your husband. You're stuck, princess."

Kitty, swallowing again, looked like she was on the verge of having a major tantrum. Her bottom lip trembled as her eyes grew glassy. Turning to look at Matty, her expression turned pleading. Hating himself for what he was about to do, Matty kept his face impassive as he looked at her.

"Go back to the cabin, Kitty," he said, his voice gruff. "If I have time, I'll stop by for supper before coming back to keep an eye on things."

Kitty stumbled back, as if she had been slapped. Letting out a choked gasp, she turned on her heel and stumbled out of the office. A few seconds later, Matty heard the bell over the front door chime followed by the noise in the bar returning once more signaling that she'd left.

Looking down at his feet, he slumped slightly, hating himself for being so cruel. He couldn't let her in though. He'd only hurt her more in the end if he did.

After a few seconds of a tense yet awkward silence, General Claery cleared his throat. "Mind explaining what the hell is actually going on, Matty?"

Matty sagged in defeat but didn't look up. "I don't love her, okay? I don't hate her, but... I don't... She's hard to be around. So when we captured the shifters, I saw a chance to get a bit of a break from her. Not that me being here hurts. We need one of us here anyway. Just in case."

General Claery rolled his eyes. "Suck it up, kid. She's your wife."

"I didn't want her to be my wife. It's not like you or the king gave me a choice in the matter. If I hadn't married her back at the capital before we'd come here, I would have had to marry her here," Matty pointed out.

"True," his dad conceded. "She wasn't your choice, not your first pick. That filthy little half breed was who you wanted. And that would have been fine. I liked the girl well enough. But then those male shifters started hanging around and I knew... just like her mother. I'd been hoping she'd have taken after her father, but those shifter genes... Just too strong I guess."

Matty, looking startled, looked up sharply, not having heard this part of the story about Clara's family.

General Claery huffed a cold laugh. "Guess I should have told you sooner, boy." He rubbed the back of his neck ruefully. "The short and long of it is this. I got word back when you were just boy that the Reynard heir had left Reynardsville, that the heir had married a human and was living among them in plain sight. And then I learned that the heir was a female shifter, that they were here in Springfield. So I packed us up, decided that it was time to try farming so I could keep an eye on things, and moved here."

"You knew..." Matty said faintly, not quite believing what he was hearing.

"I liked the O'Donoghues. I really did. Mara wasn't half bad. She kept to herself. Didn't cause trouble. As much as I didn't like shifters, I could tolerate her. For her husband's sake. But then her mother, Mrs. Melanie Reynard herself, kept getting involved. The woman is unhinged, Matty," his dad said gruffly. "In my eyes, she was dangerous. And that meant Mara was dangerous. I had to take her out. For the sake of the city. So I did. And things were good for a while. At least until the land north of us, the mountains, opened up, became part of our kingdom. Shifters and all sorts of trash started flocking that way and we got hit. I thought we'd be good, but Clara started attracting attention. A little too much attention. She didn't know what was going on though, bless her little heart. So I decided I'd marry her off to you and get you both the hell out of dodge, get you somewhere safe."

"You would have let me marry her?" Matty asked, astounded.

"As long as she remained ignorant to what she was, why not? The girl couldn't even shift, for gods' sake," General Claery snorted in amusement. "In my eyes, any kids you two would have had would have been as good as human. I'm not that bigoted, Matty."

"But…"

"That damned redheaded shifter, that massive one I killed… He signed her death warrant. If you're to be mad at anyone, be mad at him," General Claery continued. "He told her the truth. He turned her against us humans. And since he marked her? She was no longer safe to be around humans."

"I…"

"I'm sorry, son," General Claery said, sounding sorry for the first time since he'd stepped back into his role as general, surprising Matty. "I didn't want it to go this way. But it did. And there's no use dwelling on it."

"But all those people you had killed?" Matty frowned at his dad.

"Collateral, Matty. Collateral. There's always collateral in war. The sooner you learn that, the better off you'll be."

"But…"

"Go home to your wife tonight, son," General Claery cut him off. "I don't care that you don't like her. Learn to like her. You're stuck with her."

"But…" he tried again.

"Matty, don't piss me off," his dad warned.

Matty gulped. And then he nodded

CHAPTER 39

CLARA

Clara's back ached. No, scratch that. It throbbed. It made her want to tear herself apart, scream, and cry. She hurt so bad that she wanted to lay down and give up. She could feel a couple of the welts on her back that had broken skin reopen start to leak blood down her back, soaking the bandages Warren had so carefully wrapped around her before putting her to bed as she paced in front of her tent angrily.

Gods was she angry.

She wanted to rip, to hurt, to kill.

And as soon as she saw Freisinger...

She paused, blinking in surprise. Who was she right now? When had she ever wanted to hurt someone before? This was a new feeling, one she wasn't quite sure she liked, but she knew she didn't hate it either. What she did know was that someone had taken something that was hers and hers alone, her mate, her other half, her husband. May the gods help whoever had laid a hand on Warren, she'd... She stopped herself before finishing that thought. She needed to calm down. Breathe.

Jamming her hands in her pockets to hide the trembling of her hands from the sheer amount of anger coursing through her, she glanced up at the three males standing in front of her. The closest to her was the leader of the Romulus pack, Zeke.

Zeke was a tall slender male who was good looking, but he didn't stand out much. He didn't have a face that you could pick out of the crowd, but that was okay. Clara didn't think that he wanted to stand out. Hell, she didn't even think he wanted to be the leader of the pack. Rather, he'd been forced into the position and had taken on his new role in life in stride, which was very much like what she'd come to expect from him in the short amount of time she'd come to know him. He was laid back, relaxed, which made her like him well enough. He reminded her a bit of Warren's cousin, Richard, because he was also levelheaded, easy going, reasonable.

Gods, she missed Loch Haven and her pack. She missed the Sloras, her family. Soon, she told herself. Once she figured out how to get Warren back, they were leaving. She was done with the Reynards. She didn't want to lead the pack, or rather, she didn't want to be a pawn for her grandmother and Freisinger. And she was done with the idea of going to war. The humans wouldn't track them through the mountains, of that she was certain. They'd be safe in Loch Haven. They could live, unbothered. Start a new life. If only the rest of the shifter population could get on board with the same idea and start their own villages up in the mountains or past them. Away from Brunholl and the king.

She glanced at Zeke again, a flicker of irritation rising in her chest once more. Part of her was angry that he had told her that Warren had gotten arrested. Part of her was angry that he hadn't stopped Warren from going into the city in the first place. But, she reminded herself, trying to stop Warren when he'd made up his mind to do something was like trying to stop a stampede of wild animals. Impossible. Besides, Zeke had to protect his pack first, which meant that stopping Warren from going on a suicide mission probably wasn't high on his list of priorities. Still... She shook her head slightly. Even though she knew that, the irrational part of her was still angry.

Next to Zeke stood Maddox. Clara didn't mind the massive shifter. In fact, she wouldn't admit this out loud, especially right now, but she actually liked him. He was more on the quiet side. A bit moody but not grumpy, he just liked being left to his own devices. He didn't have any patience for drama and the other bullshit she'd seen come up in the different packs she'd already visited. But, from what she'd seen, he was a good friend, loyal, and had a wicked sense of humor. He was, however, a bit intimidating with his size and the tattoos that covered his body. In spite of that, she felt safe with him. She didn't know why, didn't understand it, but she wasn't about to question her gut feeling. Maddox was someone she wanted on her side, wanted to watch her back.

And then, next to Maddox there was Ronan. Her stomach soured as she glanced at him for all of a second before turning her attention back to Maddox. Yes, she had decided to put up with him for now because she needed allies while here, but by the gods, she still hated him. What was worse, she could see the hint of hope in his green eyes every time she looked at him, all because she'd said he could stick around. She'd put that pesky bit of hope there. And she hated it. Hated every little bit of it because she knew that she'd hurt him again later when she managed to find a way to leave and go home.

She wouldn't look back.

There was something else there, too. Something she hadn't expected to see. And it bugged her. What was it? Was it... Her body stiffened and her chest constricted, making it hard to breathe. Was that... pity? No, it couldn't be, because if it was, he knew something about this situation that he wasn't telling her. And it was bad. It had to be.

He'd always been terrible at hiding things from her.

Taking a shaky breath, she looked back over at Ronan, trying to hide the fear that was steadily creeping over her.

"Ronan?" she whispered. "How bad...?" She couldn't finish the question, couldn't make herself say it. If she said it, it would be too real.

Ronan's eyes widened as she turned to him, a bit of surprise and uneasiness flashing across his face. Then, like flipping a switch, a mask of calm descended over his face.

"Clara... dear..." he said, his voice low and soft, hesitating as he took a step toward her. He reached out a hand, as if to brush a strand of hair out of her face but thought better of it and dropped his hand to his side. "Your uncle came to talk to us last night. He, uh, he said that there's a good chance they'll put him to death. He's trying to convince your grandmother not to, but..."

Clara's eyes widened further. No. No. That couldn't be right. It wasn't. There was no way that her grandmother would do that to her. Was there?

"You're joking, right?" she whispered, her eyes pleading with him to be joking. She wanted him to crack that crooked smile she'd come to adore during their time traveling together. She wanted him to flash her a wink. Something. Anything.

Instead, his face twisted in an apologetic grimace.

It felt like someone had dumped a bucket of ice water over her head as her eyes widened and she stumbled back. Pain seared across her back as she opened more of the wounds on her back from her clumsy movements. This couldn't be happening. She was dreaming. That's what it was. It had to be. But no...

Her foot caught on something, she didn't know what, and suddenly the ground was rushing up to meet her. She could hear her heart pounding in her ears, could feel her lungs seizing, could feel her eyes stinging. And, oh gods, her back. Her back killed. The pain needed to stop. She wanted it to stop.

A pair of warm hands caught her, hands she didn't recognize. She looked up, her vision blurry from the unshed tears filling her eyes. Was that...? Yes. Her body relaxed as she recognized Maddox, his large hands circling her waist.

"There you go," he murmured, his deep voice deep, calm, soothing. "Take deep breaths. I've got you."

Clara sucked in a breath, the sensation painful. She blinked furiously, trying to clear her vision. Spotting Ronan, she noticed his face was twisted up with remorse, guilt, and concern. Her heart clenched. She couldn't be mad. Not right now. He was just trying to help. Besides, she had asked. If she hadn't wanted to know, she should have kept her questions to herself. This was on her.

Turning her face away, her heart threatening to break, she closed her eyes and tried to take another breath. She needed to breathe. Maybe when she opened her eyes again, everything would be back to normal.

If only life worked that way.

"Let's go take care of your back, yeah?" Maddox murmured as her eyes flashed open again, concern filling his eyes as he met hers. He was still holding her gently but securely, trying not to hurt her worse than she already was but still trying to make sure she wouldn't go down the rest of the way.

Numbly, her body trembling from the pain, both physical and emotional, Clara nodded and let him lead her back into her tent where he helped her undress and lay down. Once she was laying back down on her mat, her back bare so Maddox could work on her wounds, she heard Zeke and Ronan come in, both taking sharp breaths as they spotted her back. Not wanting to talk to them, she closed her eyes again, burying her face in her pillow as she listened to Maddox quietly shush them, warning them not to say anything.

She still listened though, not wanting to miss anything in case they decided to start talk about getting Warren out. Much to her displeasure, however, the only thing they talked about was who would keep an eye on her so they could keep her away from Freisinger. Letting out a small, disgruntled huff, she tried to rein in her temper.

If they weren't going to rescue Warren, she'd do it herself.

A couple of days later, Clara sat on a wooden stump in front of her tent, watching Maddox who had become her designated babysitter. Wherever she went, he was sure to follow. Currently, he had a little chunk of wood and a knife in his hands. Every so often, a small piece of wood would fall to the ground while tiny flakes fluttered slowly through the air. Her eyes tracked one such flake, watching as it caught the bit of sunlight currently trying to peek through the overcast sky.

Clara looked up at the clouds, studying them. Back home in Springfield, before everything had gone wrong, or before the Claerys as she liked to refer to that time, she'd stand out in the back garden and watch the sky in the morning, trying to get a feel for what the weather would be like that day. Her pa, if she wasn't back inside by the time he finished his breakfast, would come down with a cup of tea for her while he carried a cup of coffee. Together, they'd stand there and watch the clouds or watch the sun rise above the city and color the morning sky.

She missed that. She missed the simplicity of those mornings, missed spending time with her pa, missed how quiet life was then. She'd give anything to go back.

Clara glanced at Maddox again, wondering what his family life had been like. Had he grown up in Reynardsville like Zeke or had he grown up in a shifter village like Ronan? She doubted he'd been raised with humans like she had. Her case was special. She hadn't yet met another shifter like her, though she was sure there were a few out there, but like her, they were probably hiding in plain sight like she had been.

Clara opened her mouth to ask Maddox but then stopped when she spotted Freisinger across the camp, watching her. She closed her mouth with a snap and met Freisinger's eyes, trying not to be sick. The smug look on his face was enough to make her want to scream and cry in frustration. He looked like a cat who had cornered a mouse and was just waiting to eat them for dinner.

Pushing off the stump she was sitting on, she glanced at Maddox again. "I'm heading inside for a bit," she murmured just loud enough for him to hear. She didn't want to be here when Freisinger was staring at her like he was. It was unnerving. And she didn't want the reminder that it was just only a matter of time before he could step up and claim her as his.

Her stomach twisted violently as she stepped into the tent, ignoring the concerned expression on Maddox's face as he offered her a hand for support. Letting the tent flap swing shut behind her, she dropped down to her knees, gasping for breath as she let her panic overtake her. Would she know when they put Warren to death? Would she feel it through the mating bond she shared with him? Or would she be left in the dark, only finding out what had happened when someone came to tell her the news?

Clara dry heaved and then winced, feeling the healing welts on her back strain and sting. She had to do something. She needed to go save Warren herself. No one else was going to, or that's what it looked like. She hadn't seen any sign that anyone had any interest in finding out where he was, how to get him out, or where to hide him when they did.

She had an idea though. She had a feeling that her grandmother was keeping him close by because Clara was sure her grandmother was anticipating a rescue attempt. Or at least, if Clara was in her grandmother's shoes, that's what she would do. But if she was right, and if her grandmother was keeping him close, that meant he was either under town hall or being kept in a room at her grandmother's townhome. If she had to guess, she'd wager he was at town hall. There were cells there. That meant that her grandmother wouldn't have to focus most of her guards on keeping Warren in a spare room. The cell could keep him contained well enough.

But how would she get him out?

Clara straightened as she made up her mind. She'd head into the city to go talk to her grandmother. She hadn't spoken to her since the day Freisinger had whipped her back raw. She hadn't wanted to. Frankly, she never wanted to talk to the female again, but she was technically family. Clara could play the role of a concerned granddaughter for a few minutes if she had to. Just long enough to take a glimpse at the basement windows surrounding the building. That's all she needed to do. It would only take a few minutes to figure out which cell they were keeping Warren in. And then she could come back and tell Zeke and the other.

What they did with that information... Clara sighed. She didn't have high hopes. She had a sneaking suspicion that they wouldn't do anything. Zeke would thank her for the information. Maddox would humor her and say he'd see what he could do. And Ronan? Ronan would look at her with his eyes full of pity. Like Maddox, he would also tell her he'd see what he could do, but those were just words. They wouldn't disobey Zeke. If he said they shouldn't get involved, she'd be out of luck.

Slipping out of the back of the tent, she took a deep breath.

Just sneak into the city, find Warren, and then come up with a plan to get him out. She could do that. She would do that. She needed him back.

CHAPTER 40

WARREN

The holding cell in the basement of the town hall Warren was quickly coming to despise was made of a rough brown stone he'd seen make up most of the city's building foundations. Sturdy. Strong. Not prone to breaking. Which meant, much to Warren's dismay, that trying to break the stones surrounding the small window in order to escape would be a waste of time. He'd be more likely to hurt himself trying to tear through the stone and that was something he was keen on avoiding.

The rest of the cell was rather bland. It looked like a normal room, probably meant for storage, but instead of a normal wooden door, a cell door had been fixed to the stone, the hinges secured by screws drilled deep enough that it would take more force than he could expend to pull the door loose.

Not that he hadn't tried.

There was a narrow bed on the far wall, just under the window, that creaked every time Warren sat on it, the mattress bowing a bit under his weight. It made him anxious every time he sat or laid down, worried that it would break and send him crashing to the floor. This bed was not meant for full grown shifter males. A child perhaps. He'd been tempted to pull the mattress off the frame a few times already and throw it in the corner so he could curl up on the floor. He'd be able to actually turn in his sleep without fear of falling on his face if he did that, but ultimately, he had decided against it in favor of not making a scene with the guards. They were already irritated with him for moving the chamber pot to the corner nearest the door so they wouldn't forget to take and empty it.

Besides the bed and the chamber pot, there was a small wooden table about the size of a standard nightstand with an equally small lamp on it that the guards lit for an hour or two once it got dark in the evening. Nice, but not necessary, Warren decided. There was nothing of interest in here that he needed to see after it got dark. There were no books to read, no little trinkets to study, no pictures to stare out. And he could count the stones during the day. Why drive himself mad counting them again at night?

Eyeing the bed, Warren took a deep breath and lowered himself down onto the chilly stone floor, his back against the wall. He could feel the rough texture of the stone through his shirt, grounding him.

He'd fucked up. Big time. And now Clara was alone.

Warren dropped his head into his hands with a groan. He felt like he had failed the one person he had sworn to protect, the one he claimed he loved most. She was now alone, nearly defenseless, with no one to protect her against Freisinger's advances or her grandmother's machinations. If he didn't get out of here soon, they'd eat her alive and he wasn't sure there would be any pieces for him to pick up.

The thought was disheartening.

How long had he been in this cell now? Two days? Three? It hadn't been long, but it felt like it had been forever already. But that's what happened when you were stuck in a room with nothing to do but count the stones that made up the floor and the wall. What was she doing? Was she safe? Had Zeke and the Romulus pack taken her in? Or had Ronan tried to get her away from the city? He had a sneaking suspicion that the wayward shifter would jump at the chance to get her alone if only to convince Clara to give him another chance, however, at the same time, Clara's right hook had definitely sent him a message. Perhaps the shifter wouldn't push his luck, but he'd definitely keep his eye on her.

Warren raised his head again and let out a deep breath. He hated this, hated being locked up, hated being kept away from Clara, hated being unable to touch her and make sure she was okay. Hell, how was her back? Had it become infected because she couldn't disinfect herself? Or had she caved and asked for help? A low growl sounded in his chest. May the gods help whoever had helped her if they touched more than her back.

The sound of the front door upstairs sounded above his head with a loud thud, signaling they'd been thrown open. Warren's brows furrowed as he looked up at the ceiling. What in the god's name...?

And then he heard her as clear as day.

"Where the fuck is my mate?" Clara's voice rang through the townhouse, the sound shrill but angry. No, angry was an understatement. She was furious. Livid.

Warren's heart sank. He had caused this. But he had warned the old bat. If she harmed Clara, he'd take her head. He had meant every word. He should have killed her grandmother as soon as he'd seen her, before she'd been able to call for back up. If he had, he could have gotten away, grabbed Clara and fled, but no. He'd had to say something, had to tell her why he was there. He'd wanted to see the fear in her eyes when she realized he was coming for her. Damn his ego.

More yelling came from the main floor, though this time it wasn't just Clara yelling. There were a few deeper male voices and then the shrill voice of her grandmother, all trying to be heard over the other. And then there was silence as one final statement was said.

"You are as pathetic as your mother was," Mrs. Reynard sneered, her voice cold. "She thought she had a say in her future, just as you do. But let me tell you something, you little whore. You have no say. Your opinion, your thoughts, your feelings? They don't matter. Your future was decided for you the moment you were born and then it was set in stone once your stupid human loving mother got herself killed because she couldn't see that staying with your filthy human father would be her death sentence." A loud scoff sounded. "She got what was coming for her. And you'll get yours too if you don't shut the hell up and start behaving. I have no problem having Briggs whip you again. Shall I call for him?"

Warren's blood boiled as he shot to his feet and slammed against the iron cell door, trying to get it to budge. He needed to get to Clara. He needed to protect her. He needed to make sure she was okay.

More silence followed as he rammed into the cell door again, feeling it shudder under the impact but not budging. And then the front door slammed open again followed by the sound of heavy footsteps retreating. Shit, guards were being sent to go get Freisinger. If that male touched her again...

Warren panicked, ramming against the cell door again and again.

A soft knock sounded against the glass of the window above his bed. He almost didn't hear it. When it came again, he frowned and turned, his breathing heavy, his eyes wide. And then his heart stopped when he saw who was at the window.

Crouched down in front of the window, her brows knitted together as she peered in, was Clara. A small smile tugged at her lips as he turned his attention to her and then she waved and blew him a kiss. Warren sagged against the cell door in response, his face twisting in grief and remorse. Surging forward, he climbed on top of the bed to get closer to her. Wrenching the window open, he stuck a hand out, grasping hers.

"Clara... Little fox..." he rasped, his voice thick with emotion. "Are you alright?"

"Upset. Pissed. Furious. The works," she whispered.

He let out a choked laugh. "What are you doing here?"

"Coming to rescue you," she replied in a matter-of-fact tone. "Or would you rather be executed?"

Warren's eyes widened further, his body tensing. Executed?

Clara grimaced, realizing he didn't know. "Percil...," she started to explain. "He's on our side. He's been feeding us information since you were arrested. Or rather, he's been feeding Zeke information. I've been left in the dark. Mostly."

Warren blinked at her, trying to make sense of what was going on. Then he shook his head, trying to get his brain working. Letting out a huff of breath, he met her eyes. "You won't be able to get me out. Not by yourself. I couldn't break through this stone even if I wanted to and the door is too sturdy for me to break through."

Clara's face instantly fell. "Well..." She sat back on her heels, her lips pursing as she turned to look at the busy street for a moment before looking back at him. "I'm not sure if Zeke and them would be willing to help, but I'll ask. It's our only shot."

Squeezing her hand tighter. "Clara... If you can't... If you can't get me out, go. Go home. Benji and Luca will take care of you. Do. Not. Stay."

"But..." Her voice became pained as her eyes filled with tears. "I can't. I've lost too much already. I can't leave you."

"Little fox, you have to. For me," he whispered. "Now go. Before someone finds you here talking to me. I love you. More than life itself. Now go."

Clara squeezed his hand, her smile strained. "I love you too."

"Go."

Clara nodded and stood, giving him one last look before she hurried out to the street and lost herself in the crowd, tugging the hood of her cloak over her head to hide herself.

Warren stared after her for a few minutes before closing the window and sinking down onto his bed, his mind reeling. What had he gotten himself into?

CHAPTER 41

Ronan

The camp was buzzing. Everyone was talking about one thing or another, but the common theme was Warren. They hadn't stopped talking about the male since the news broke that he had attacked and threatened Mrs. Reynard and was later arrested.

It wasn't as if the news was anything out of the ordinary. There was a reason the Reynards were so heavily guarded. No one... well, there were a few... but almost no one liked them. It wasn't uncommon at all for there to be a story in the city's paper about an attempted murder or an attack on one of the Reynards. Mrs. Reynard was usually the target, but her family, both immediate and extended, were often targets as well. Before Clara had come back with them, Ronan was sure he had read that a certain Bartholemew Reynard, a second cousin to Clara on her late grandfather's side, had been jumped and beaten on his way out of the city to the cabin he usually stayed at in the foothills.

No, what caught everyone's attention was that Warren was an outsider. He came from outside the city. He wasn't a resident of Reynardsville. Never had been. Never would be. And this left most of the residents of Reynardsville with a bit of a bad taste in their mouths.

Currently, from what Ronan could hear, half the camp was of the mind that Warren should be executed. How dare an outsider come in and mess with their city? He had no right. He should have left well enough alone and let the Reynards do what they wanted with their granddaughter. Some even went so far as to say that he should have never come to Reynardsville, that he should have given up his claim on Clara the moment her family had shown up for her. Others were of the mind that Clara should have stayed away as well, but that was a whole different topic that Ronan didn't particularly like to think about.

The other half of camp that wasn't part of the Execute Warren club were thrilled that someone had the guts to come that close to killing the Reynard matriarch. They claimed that all she'd done since her husband had died was cause trouble, that they lived large and were waxing fat off the taxes they collected from them, that the city would be better off without the Reynards. They applauded Warren for doing what so many of them had been dreaming of doing themselves. And they were more than a little upset that he had been jailed. Ronan had heard more than a few ideas on how to go break him out of jail so that he could finish what he had started. He'd even heard a few willingly volunteer to help him finish the job.

Sticking his hands out over the main fire to warm them, he scoffed at the idea of any one of the Romulus members actually helping Warren. Sure, they were all wolves and wolves had a tendency to stick together. They liked to take care of each other, pack or not, but this... It left a bad taste in his mouth. This was straight up premeditated murder, and he wanted no part of it. Not really. He'd killed enough to last him a lifetime, though he knew with the war he'd have to kill again. The difference, however, was that during a war it was kill or be killed. This time? It would be cold blooded, just like it had been when he'd killed his sister's mate, Michael. He was done. He was swearing off murder.

Ronan huffed a bitter laugh, finding his last thought humorous even though it was dark. Who would have thought that he would be swearing off murder? Not once while growing up had he ever thought in his wildest dreams that he would be capable of killing someone, let alone deciding he wouldn't do it again unless to defend himself. How far he had sunk.

Turning to look back at Maddox who was still sitting in front of Clara's tent, whittling away, Ronan studied him for a minute.

"You ever kill someone?" he asked Maddox after a minute.

"What do you mean?" Maddox's brows furrowed as he answered Ronan, but he didn't look up from what he was doing.

"Have you ever killed someone outside of a fight? Like, gone into a situation knowing you were going to kill someone or gotten so mad that you lost control and just snapped?" Ronan clarified, hoping that he wasn't alone in his poor self-control.

"Uh," Maddox hesitated before clearing his throat and setting the little carving that looked like a tiny eagle down. "Yes. I think most of us have. It's a shifter thing, I think. At some point, most of us have lost control and snapped as you put it. Probably why there aren't as many shifters as there are humans. We're too busy losing our tempers and fighting each other when you crowd us together. We like our space, like to keep what we see is ours only to ourselves. Or within our packs, I guess I should say. We have a tendency to be more lenient about sharing within our packs. Especially us wolves."

"What happened?" Ronan asked, coming over to sit on the stump that Clara had vacated when she'd gone inside the tent, presumably to rest, though Ronan had a feeling it was to avoid him and the rest of the camp and their whispers and looks of pity.

"The usual." Maddox shrugged. "Someone threatened what was mine and I reacted accordingly."

Ronan nodded, realizing what he'd done with Michael wasn't so extreme for shifters after all. Or at least for wolf shifters.

"Who were you protecting?" Ronan asked.

"Family," Maddox grunted. "You?"

"Same." Ronan looked at the tent behind him. "She taking a nap?"

"Nah." Maddox shook his head. "Freisinger showed up and she noticed him staring at her, so she disappeared inside to avoid him. I don't blame her. But if anyone else asks, yes, she's taking a nap."

Ronan huffed a laugh and nodded his head in agreement. He'd lie to protect Clara, especially from Freisinger. "When are we going to tell her we're taking her home?"

Maddox gave him an annoyed look instead of answering. "I'd like to wait for the official edict on Warren before we decide anything. Zeke is leaning toward taking her home now because we can spare a few shifters, but he knows she deserves to know what's going to happen. He knows she deserves a say, or at least the chance to voice her opinion."

"And if she doesn't want to go?" Ronan asked hesitantly, realizing he was treading on thin ice with this line of questioning.

"We'll keep her safe until she decides what she wants to do," Maddox replied, his voice gruff. "Or at least I will. She's a good one who's been through a lot. She deserves some peace of mind."

Ronan blanched slightly, catching the look Maddox shot him as he spoke, understanding the unsaid warning in Maddox's statement. Maddox wasn't going to let him anywhere near Clara, not when she'd already made her feelings for him clear. He was serious about keeping her safe.

"Would you claim her yourself?" Ronan asked even more hesitantly.

Maddox shot him an unamused look. "No. I have no reason to." And then he paused before continuing. "She reminds me of my sister. I can't help but see her every time I look at Clara."

Ronan nodded in understanding before leaning back to peak inside the tent. His eyes scanning the darkened area, he froze. "Uh... Mad?"

"What?" Maddox asked, his tone still gruff and unamused.

"Clara isn't in the tent. She's gone."

Sitting in front of the tent with Maddox and Zeke, Ronan kept his eyes trained on the city gate, waiting for it to open. Any minute now, he was sure of it. It always opened around this time. Or it used to before Freisinger started coming and going whenever he pleased. But with Freisinger and the Reynard messengers, the gate only opened enough to let someone out instead of all the way to let wagons, carts, and horses through.

Ronan glanced over at Maddox to see the male sitting rather stiffly, a muscle in his jaw twitching in irritation as he watched the gate intently, not missing a single thing. Zeke, next to him, looked worn out instead of irritated, as if he was done with everything Clara related. Ronan didn't blame him. This whole situation was exhausting.

As he was studying the tired lines on Zeke's face, a small dark figure appeared at the gate, slinking forward almost unseen. However, since they had been waiting for just that, both Zeke and Maddox noticed immediately, their bodies tensing further, their muscles coiled and ready to spring into action to go grab Clara.

Noticing their reactions, Ronan turned and noticed the small figure and shook his head with a small chuckle. She was getting better at being a shifter, he'd give her that, but she still lacked the subtlety of her animal.

That would come with time, but for now, she was as obvious as a small child trying to sneak a cookie out of the kitchen right under its mother's nose.

Standing, he moved forward to intercept her, Maddox right behind him. As he approached, Clara froze, her hood falling back as she peered up at him, wide-eyed.

"What in the gods' names are you doing?" Maddox asked, his tone reminiscent of a disappointed parent.

Clara winced. "I, uh, had to go talk to my grandmother."

"Really? I don't remember getting any summons or seeing someone coming to fetch you," Maddox pointed out.

Clara winced again. "I went by myself. I needed to see... needed to see if what Ronan had said was true. No one was telling me anything," she whispered, sounding defeated.

Maddox's face softened as Ronan grimaced, mentally kicking himself for not keeping Clara in the loop. He should have. Warren was her mate, she deserved to know what was happening. If he was in her shoes and his mate was locked up while awaiting execution, he would have gone mad and done just this... sneaking off to see what was going on and if he could get them out.

"What did your grandmother say?" Maddox asked gently.

"I'd rather not repeat what that foul female said," Clara muttered bitterly, looking down at her feet, but not quick enough for Ronan to miss the grief that flashed through her eyes.

"Clara..." Ronan started, debating on whether he should pull her in for a hug or not. He was sure she wouldn't want one from him, but she looked so broken. He half hoped that if he held her close and tight enough, he could keep her together.

"I know where he is," she whispered, cutting him off. "I could get him out... I could get him out if I had help."

Ronan froze and then looked over at Maddox. Maddox raised his brows at Ronan before shooting a look back at Zeke who shrugged wearily, as if giving in. Wrapping an arm around Clara's shoulder, Maddox started guiding her back to her tent.

"I think we need to talk."

Rolling his neck, Ronan stuffed his hands into his front pockets as he fought the urge to look back at Maddox who was standing next to Clara, a hand on her shoulder, restraining her. Or, no, restraining wasn't the right word, Ronan decided. Discouraging was probably the better word. Clara wasn't fighting to go with Ronan, Zeke, and the two other males who had jumped at the chance to go break Warren out. Rather, she was standing there as calmly as she could manage, which was a feat in and of itself. He could see the longing warring in her eyes. She wanted to be there when they got Warren free, wanted to be there to make sure that he was okay and unharmed.

He didn't blame her. Not one bit.

And since Maddox was the only shifter that she seemed to actually like rather than tolerate, he had volunteered to stay with her. It was probably for the best.

Losing the battle, he looked back at Maddox and Clara, his face impassive as he surveyed them standing there. Clara looked like she was in more pain than she cared to admit. It was evident in her eyes and in the way she was holding herself. It was like she was worried that if she moved to quickly or bent funny, she would rip her scabs open on her back, which wasn't too far-fetched since it was a possibility. If she'd just shift...

Ronan

Ronan rolled his eyes, knowing exactly how that conversation would go. She would argue that she was healing just fine, that she wasn't comfortable shifting with anyone but Warren, and that would be the end of that conversation. He wasn't going to argue, let alone try to convince her. It wasn't his place.

His eyes shifted to Maddox right before the group walked through the gate. Maddox's face was stoic, but there seemed to be a fire burning in his eyes. He was jonesing for the fight that might happen upon breaking Warren out just as much as the two males who had volunteered were. He was restless, judging by the twitching of his fingers. But he wouldn't say a word. Not when he was needed at the camp to watch Clara.

Slipping through the gate, they picked up their pace as they made their way to the town hall, Clara's words echoing through his mind. Someone needed to distract the guards in front of town hall so that they wouldn't walk around to the side of the building and spot those who were trying to get Warren out. Zeke had volunteered to do that. He needed to go to town hall anyway, so it made sense for him to stop and chat with the guards about the current war efforts before heading inside to talk to the council member in charge of coordinating the war effort. Meanwhile, Ronan and the other two would go around to the side and work on removing the window and the stones around it so Warren could squeeze through.

Ronan glanced at the paperwork held loosely in Zeke's hand, idly wondering what they contained, but then shook his head. It wasn't his concern. If Zeke wanted him to know, he would tell him. Until then, he'd mind his own business. Or rather, he'd focus on the task at hand and then mind his own business after.

Reaching the town hall, Ronan and the others bid Zeke goodbye, making it seem like they were going on to the pub down the road as they continued walking. Once they had gone down a couple streets, they slipped into an alley and doubled back, coming up to town hall from the back roads.

Entering the alley between the town hall and the high-end apartment next to it, he decided to stand watch as the other two knelt down in front of the window to the cell Clara had said Warren was in. His head swiveling back and forth between the two ends of the alley, he kept his eyes peeled as the others discussed how to get the window out. Finally, deciding to pry the stones out by digging out the mortar between them, they pulled out some tools and set to work. Ronan, cringing at the noise, went on high alert.

"We're fine. No one knows we're here. We're okay," Ronan muttered to himself under his breath before peering over his shoulder at the two males working on the window. Beyond the glass, he could see Warren watching them, a wide-eyed look on his face as he glanced between them and his cell door. Shit, was it noisy in there? Ronan hoped there weren't any guards stationed right outside his cell. If there were, they were done for. All of them.

Starting to pace, he kept his eyes on the ends of the alley between periodically checking to make sure no one had rushed into Warren's cell. This war, this city, and this gods damned male were going to give him grey hairs at this rate. Some days, he wished he'd never left Everridge. But then again, he was glad he had. He'd found a family of sorts, his pack, something he had been dying for back in Everridge. He'd never go back.

A soft thump sounded. His head snapping up, he looked over at the window to see the first stone on the ground and the second one being hauled out by one of the males while the glass pane was being held up by the other. Biting the inside of his cheek, he hurried over to help the one holding the glass pane. Carefully removing it, he jerked his head at Warren.

"Try and climb out."

Warren didn't need telling twice.

Ronan watched as the male climbed onto a piece of furniture that he couldn't see before starting to shimmy through the small hole. It was a tight fit and a few grunts and pained gasps left Warren as he shoved his broad shoulders and chest through.

"Gods damn it all," Warren grunted as his fingers scrabbled against the ground, looking for purchase as he tried to continue scooting forward.

The male not holding the glass, seeing his struggle, leaped forward, grabbed his hands, and pulled. With a few heaves, Warren was through the window and the group was putting the window back together. This time, however, they didn't care how quiet they were. What mattered was that they got out of there and fast. As soon as the last stone slid into place, they nodded and took off.

"Here," Ronan muttered, shoving a cloak at Warren before they stepped onto the main street. "Hide your ugly face."

Letting out a bark of a laugh, Warren took the cloak and pulled it on before tugging the hood up over his head.

"Let's get the hell out of here," Warren suggested, his voice urgent as they melded into the crowd on the street and started making their way out of the city.

CHAPTER 42

CLARA

T ime moved... slowly. Too slowly.

Pacing back in forth in her tent, Clara peeked out to see if Maddox was still standing watch outside her tent. Sure enough, as if he knew she'd get antsy and try to go into the city to help out the rescue party, Maddox was sitting in his usual spot, his knife out, working on one of his many little projects. Not that she blamed him. She was grateful he was there and that he remained level-headed while she was not. Someone had to keep her in line.

Scanning the rest of the camp, she spotted the male that usually tailed her and Freisinger, a fox named Dante if she remembered correctly. And just like usual, he was standing in his usual spot, just outside camp, near his own little fire and bedroll. He had declined a tent for some reason Clara hadn't figured out yet. How he hadn't frozen was beyond her, but to each their own she guessed.

Narrowing her eyes at the male, she studied him for a minute. He wasn't looking in her direction, but she knew by the way he had stiffened that he knew she was there. He wasn't fond of her, or that's what she was guessing if she had to go off his physical reactions to her being around. He always tensed up and kept his eyes on her until Freisinger came and took over. It was as if he was treating her like she was some sort of wild card, which, fair. She was to them. They didn't know her well enough to know what she would do if push came to shove. They didn't trust her as far as they could throw her.

The feelings were mutual.

Stepping back, she let the flap swing closed most of the way, but she kept her eyes on Dante. If Dante was here and standing guard, then that meant Freisinger wasn't around.

Her stomach sank.

If Freisinger wasn't around, then that meant he was in the city. If he was in the city, that meant he was probably at either the townhome or town hall. If he was at town hall, if he thought something was going on, then the rescue team risked getting caught, and if they got caught… Clara swallowed nervously. She was going down a dangerous road with that thought process. A very dangerous road. One she didn't like. At all. It set her on edge and made her even antsier. She needed to do something. Anything.

Stepping further back, the tent flap closed the rest of the way, hiding her away from the rest of the world. Looking around the tent, she searched for something to keep her hands busy. Knitting, crocheting, sewing, mending… Something. But there was nothing. She had packed as light as possible before following her grandmother and her entourage to Reynardsville with Warren, thinking it would be a short trip. Yet here she was a few months later with nothing to show for it except a messed up back, her once flawless skin marred forever.

Clenching and unclenching her fists, she looked around again. She could clean but there really wasn't anything to clean beyond refolding her blankets or rolling up her mat. She could make herself some tea, but she didn't think her hands were steady enough to pour a kettle of boiling hot water. She'd only end up hurting herself further than she already was.

With a huff, she turned back around and opened the flap again. Her eyes quickly landed on Maddox. "How long has it been?" she whispered, fidgeting with the edge of the canvas.

"Relax, Clara," Maddox said, his deep voice soothing. Looking up at her, he surveyed her with his dark eyes. "I know it's hard to wait when you're so close to getting what you want, but you have to wait. Do you understand me. If you do anything suspicious, it could draw attention to you and possibly Warren. We can't risk that right now."

Clara huffed but then nodded. She understood as much as she hated to admit that she did. She felt like it was a lesson she'd learned countless times over the years.

"Do you want to sit out here with me and talk or would you rather stay in your tent?" Maddox continued, still studying her face as he set his knife down on his leg.

Clara shook her head. "I think I'm going to go lay down if you don't mind. My back hurts and laying on my stomach seems to make the pain seem less than it is when I'm standing."

"Understandable. I'll let you know when they get back. Get some rest." Maddox nodded at her, gesturing for her to close the tent flap again.

As Clara closed the tent flap once more, she glanced in Dante's direction and grimaced. He was watching her, his eyes narrowed as he studied her every move. And then he turned away when he caught her watching him, his shoulders stiffening and a scowl on his face.

Laying on her stomach, her head propped up on her arms, Clara watched the small fire in the middle of her tent that Maddox had come in to start for her. There was nothing better to do and the flames were mesmerizing. The way they twisted and twirled as they reached for the sky, dancing. They were so free, able to do as they chose. She wished she were able to be that free, but for now, she had to deal with the complications that came with man and shifter kind.

Blowing out a breath through her nose, she closed her eyes, wishing for sleep but her mind just wouldn't shut off. It had been hours since the rescue team had gone into Reynardsville to rescue Warren, and they still weren't back yet. It was causing her anxiety to spike, and she hated it. Had they been caught? Or were they simply taking their time coming back, making sure that they didn't raise any suspicion coming back to the camp? Had they been waylaid by something? Or were they dawdling, stopping by Zeke's home to get more supplies for the camp? Each possibility was highly likely, so it was hard to rule anything out. The sheer fact that she was no closer to figuring out what was keeping them was maddening. She needed to know.

Squeezing her eyes shut, she forced herself to focus on her breathing. In. Out. In. Out. Release the tension. In. Out. In. Out. Relax.

Footsteps sounded outside her tent, reversing what little progress she had made in attempting to relax, not that she would really call it progress at all. Pushing herself up onto her elbows and wincing as her back arced in a way her skin protested, she peered over her shoulder at the entrance.

"Please be them. Please be them," she whispered to herself.

Perhaps if she said it enough times it would come true, she thought to herself, her eyes never leaving the entrance. Quieting her breathing, she strained her ears, listening for any sign of who it was. She needed to know. If it wasn't Warren... She swallowed the lump that had started to rise in her throat.

"Breathe," she reminded herself, closing her eyes again. "Breathe in for four. Breathe out for four. One... Two..."

"Look at you," a warm, deep voice chuckled as the flap was pushed open.

Clara's eyes flashed open. Standing before her was Warren, his long red hair a bit disheveled, and wearing clothes that were a bit too small for him. Her eyes widened as she surveyed him. A choked sob got caught in her throat. Her eyes became glassy and suddenly her vision was blurry.

Warren's eyes widened as he caught the strangled sound and quickly dropped down to his knees in front of her. "Shh. Shh. It's alright, little fox. I'm just fine. You don't need to cry. I wouldn't leave you, not on my life. You can bet on it."

Very carefully, he wrapped his arms around her, scooping her up off her sleeping mat and tucking her against his warm chest. She let out another strangled sob, burying her face in his chest and breathing him in. Wrinkling her nose, she almost drew back. He didn't smell... right. No... she moved her nose up to his neck and breathed in deeply, her body relaxing. He smelled fine. It was the clothes. Whoever they belonged to, she didn't like their scent at all. And she didn't like them on Warren.

"No more crying," Warren continued, gently cradling her head against his neck as she buried her nose further into his neck. "I'm not going anywhere. I promise. It's you and me for life. And even then, I'm not sure I could leave you in death. I'll always find you. Just breathe. Relax. I've got you."

Clara took in a shaky breath. "I was so worried," she finally managed. "I was starting to think that you had gotten caught and that the whole pack was in trouble and that they were going to come for me and that I would end up with Freisinger by the end of the night and..."

Warren silenced her by placing a finger over her mouth, a chuckle rumbling in his chest as he listened to her ramble about how she'd spiraled. "Let's not finish that train of thought. None of that happened. I'm safe. You're safe. Let's relax for right now."

Clara nodded mutely, closing her eyes as she snuggled closer, wishing she could melt into him because she wasn't nearly close enough. Another chuckle rumbled through his chest, sending a shiver down her spine as it sounded under her ear. Shifting her carefully, he laid her back down on her mat and curled up around her, tucking her body against his.

"I can't stay in here with you all night," he whispered in her ear, his stubble tickling. "I have to hide for now. They'll be looking for me by morning."

"Where will you go?" she whispered back, her body tensing once more.

"Ah, no. No worrying about that, little fox," Warren chided. "And if I could tell you, I would. But I can't. They'll come to you first. The less you know, the better. Understand?"

"Unfortunately," she grumped. "But once they stop questioning me, you better tell me."

Warren huffed a laugh. "As you wish, love."

Clara wasn't sure when she'd fallen asleep. All she knew was that she slept like a log, curled up safe and warm in Warren's arms. She never wanted to leave.

However, all good things must come to an end.

When the sun was just starting to rise above the horizon, a loud angry voice startled her out of her sleep. Jerking, she nearly smacked Freisinger in the face as he bent over her and hissed in her ear.

"Ah, now you're awake, Kleine. I thought I'd have to drag you out of your little nest and dump you in a snowbank," Freisinger sneered, catching her hand with his before it connected with his face. "Now, where is he?"

Groggily, she peered up at him. "Where is who?" she slurred, only half awake.

"Your gods damned mate. The wolf. What's his name? Warren?" Freisinger snapped, his cheeks a ruddy red in his anger.

She frowned at him. "You should know exactly where Warren is." She gave him an unamused look like it should have been obvious. "Didn't my lovely grandmother lock him up somewhere?"

"Yes, she did. And now he's not there," Freisinger grumped. "And I think you had something to do with it."

"Of course, blame the female with the wrecked back. How the hell would I get him out when I don't even know where my grandmother was keeping him?" Clara grumped back, pushing him back so she could sit up. Grimacing, she tried to hold back a groan as she moved, her back killing her, but she was unsuccessful.

Freisinger arched a brow at her. "Are you still in pain?" he asked, his cold eyes looking a little less cold.

"Obviously," she said dryly.

"Why haven't you shifted to heal?" he asked as if that should have been the most obvious thing in the world for her to do.

"Wouldn't that be cheating?" she asked, her brown knitting together as she looked at him in disbelief. "You were punishing me for something that I still don't think I should have been punished for, but that's neither here nor there at the moment. It was a punishment. Doesn't that defeat the purpose of whipping me until my back is in ribbons if I shift to heal?"

Freisinger looked at her, dumbfounded, his mouth hanging open slightly. "By the gods," he whispered. "I knew your grandmother said that you were rather ignorant of shifter life, but this..." He pinched the bridge of his nose. "This is worse than I thought. You should have shifted. It would have saved you from all this pain. Why are you still punishing yourself?"

"You... want me to shift so I won't be in pain?" Clara blinked at him in confusion. "If you didn't want me to be in pain, why did you whip me so hard?"

It was Freisinger's turn to look confused again. "We are getting nowhere with this conversation," he sighed finally, still pinching the bridge of his nose.

"No, we aren't," she agreed.

"Fine, first things first, is your back still torn to shreds?" he asked, his voice low and even though Clara could hear a hint of concern bleed through.

"Yes." She nodded.

"I need you to shift then."

"I will in a few minutes."

"Can you not be difficult for five minutes?" He raised his head at her and shot an angry glare at her that made her shiver.

"I'm not saying no," she protested. "I just want to hear the rest of your points here. That's all. And then I'll shift."

"You are the most frustrating female I have ever met," he growled at her.

"Thanks, I think?" she grimaced at him.

"Why you… No. I'm calm. We're just having a conversation," Freisinger said, trying to calm himself down. "Next, can you walk?"

"Yes, but it hurts. A lot."

"Can you make it into the city?" he asked.

Clara narrowed her eyes at him, seeing where he was going with this line of questioning. He already knew that answer and it was yes, she could. He was going to pin Warren's escape on her and then he'd take her back to town hall where he'd punish her again.

"Answer me," he growled.

"No, how's this for an answer," she growled back. "Ask your little goon, Dante, if I left camp at all between the last time the guards saw Warren and when the guards realized he was missing because I'm assuming the guards were the ones that sounded the alert."

"I will ask him."

"Good, because when you do, I already know what he'll tell you."

"What's that, smart ass?" Freisinger glared at her.

"That I was in my tent all afternoon and all night. I haven't left the tent except to go relieve myself. He'll also tell you that the Romulus pack has me under lock and key, too. Maddox doesn't let me out of his sight. I'm being babysat by more than one shifter."

Freisinger rolled his eyes at her before standing abruptly. Grabbing her arm, he hoisted her up. "Alright. If that's the game you want to play, then let's go talk to Dante. And then I think your grandmother would like a few words with you. It seems to me that she thinks you're responsible. You better pray that Dante's story lines up with yours," he whispered in her ear before shoving her out of the tent.

CHAPTER 43

WARREN

Waiting was murder.

Warren didn't mind hiding out in one of the tents with some of the other wolves of the Romulus pack. The males he was bunking in were nice enough, but the space was small and cramped. He barely had enough room to roll out his borrowed sleeping mat and lie down. He was also getting bored. He wasn't allowed to leave the tent for any reason, especially if Freisinger and his watchdog, Dante, were around. Which was almost always. Dante was always keeping an eye on things for Freisinger.

Groaning, Warren tucked his hands behind his head as he stared up at the top of the tent. The canvas was a dark tan that let the light from the sun outside in, brightening the inside of the tent. On occasion, a shadow would flicker across the surface, either from someone walking past or a bird flying overhead. He almost wished that the top opened up so that he could stare at the sky instead. At least that way, he would have the clouds to watch during the day and the stars at night. He'd make do without though. He had to.

Rolling onto his side, he looked in the direction of Clara's tent. What he wouldn't give to be over there, curled up with her in their sleeping mats, taking care of her. That was his job, for crying out loud. She needed him. He wasn't much help to her from here, hiding like a coward.

His mood souring, he rolled back onto his back with a huff. He'd sneak out tonight to go see her, one way or another. He couldn't be faulted for that. As long as he went around the back and he borrowed someone's cloak, he should be able to get away with that. Or so he hoped. Warren knew for a fact that Dante didn't pay much attention to the Romulus pack. His eyes stayed on Clara and Clara alone. That was his job, after all. So, in theory, if he looked and acted like another regular pack member, he wouldn't raise suspicion, so long as Dante didn't get close enough to scent him.

His mood lifting a bit at the prospect of seeing Clara in a few hours, he closed his eyes. He might as well get some rest while he could. He had no plans on sleeping. Not when he would have Clara in his arms.

Wrapping the cloak he had snagged from Ronan around him, Warren wrinkled his nose. It smelled like the other shifter, and to him, the scent was awful. It wasn't that the male smelled terrible because he didn't. It was more that the smell reminded Warren of his and Clara's past encounters with him. Mainly Clara's encounters. It still made his blood boil that the male had tried to place his claim over Warren's and had tried to take advantage of her. Ronan had more than deserved the dagger in his shoulder for that move.

Straightening up and readjusting the cloak so that the hood covered his head, Warren slipped out of the tent, pausing to let his eyes adjust to the darkness. Looking up, he glimpsed a few stars in the overcast sky. Perfect. There wasn't enough natural light available for anyone to get a decent look at him. They'd have to get in his face if they wanted to see who he really was. Smirking to himself at the thought, his eyes shifted around the camp, noting where everyone was.

At the main fire, Ronan, Maddox, and Zeke stood in a small group. Ronan had his hands out, his palms facing the fire to warm them. Maddox had a cigarette dangling from his lips, one hand in his pocket, the other tapping an unheard rhythm onto his leg. Zeke had his arms crossed as he talked, his brows furrowed. Every so often, Maddox and Ronan would nod, the only signs that they were listening to what their leader was saying.

Around the fire, a few other males were gathered, all doing much the same as Ronan: warming up. Some were trying to warm their frozen hands before heading to bed after a day spent on guard. Some were trying to trap some warmth, relishing the bit of heat, before heading out to spend the night keeping watch. A few other males moved between the tents, either getting ready to go to sleep or to head out. The camp was alive, always restless, never completely asleep.

Finally, Warren's gaze landed on the tent on the outskirts of the camp. Dante's. A frown tugged at his lips. There wasn't a light inside meaning Dante hadn't lit a fire to keep warm while he slept. That wasn't too unusual, but... Warren tilted his head, scanning the area around the tent. Dante wasn't out keeping watch like normal either. That meant one of two things, either Clara had gone to bed already, so he had too. Or Clara wasn't in camp. But that wasn't possible... he paused, his eyes flickering back to Ronan, Maddox, and Zeke, his heart sinking. If Clara was here, Maddox would be sitting outside Clara's tent, keeping an eye on her. The fact that he wasn't meant that she had probably been summoned by her grandmother.

"Shit," he cursed under his breath, hoping he was wrong. The last time Clara had gone to see her grandmother, that he was aware of anyway, she had come back with her back torn to shreds. She wouldn't survive another beating like that. But… He paused, stopping himself from going down that path. Clara hadn't done anything wrong in the last few days that he knew of. She had mainly stayed in her tent, trying to heal, milking her injury for as long as possible to get out of training with Freisinger rather than shifting to heal faster. He bit back a laugh. He would have done the same if he was being completely honest with himself. As petty as that move was, he would have done the same, no questions asked. It was clever, and he applauded her for it. But when Freisinger found out, he'd be… "Shit," he muttered again. That's what would get her in trouble.

Hurrying over to the tent, praying that Clara would be sleeping soundly inside, he crept around the back and slipped in through the front. Pausing just inside, he let his eyes adjust again before letting his eyes sweep over the small interior. It was just as he had left it last night, minus Clara. The fire was out, but the kettle of water was still on the grate over the small firepit. The bedrolls were still rolled out, the blankets a mess on top of them. Their packs were open, their clothes and belongings spilling out over in the corner, the first aid supplies sitting precariously on top.

Warren's heart sank like a rock.

She wasn't there.

From the looks of things, Warren gathered that Freisinger or Dante had come to fetch her before she was even fully awake. Clara never left things a mess like this. She was tidy, keeping things organized and well-maintained. It was one trait that he admired greatly. He would never have to worry about their things falling apart or into disrepair because she was always on top of it. And if she couldn't fix it, she let him know that something needed fixing.

With a groan, trying not to let his worry eat him alive, he started straightening up the tent to pass the time.

"She'll be back soon," he repeated to himself over and over again as he cleaned. "And she'll be in one piece. She won't be hurt. She'll be just fine."

He had just finished refolding all of their clothes in their bags and putting them carefully away when the tent flap rustled and Clara stumbled in, clutching her stomach as if she were going to be sick, her face pale and a light sheen of sweat covering her skin, making some of the loose strands of her hair cling to her face. Dropping the socks he was holding, he rushed over to her, catching her before she fell flat on her face.

Lowering her down to the sleeping mat gently, he could feel her whole body shaking in his hands, could feel the sweat coating her body seeping into her clothes.

"There you go. You're alright. I've got you, my little fox," he whispered, his voice soothing as he pressed a gentle kiss to her damp forehead. "It's alright now."

He pulled his hand away from her back, covering her with a blanket before turning to start the fire and get some tea started. Reaching for the kettle, he paused, noticing how dark his hand seemed. Bringing his hand closer, he peered at it, his eyes widening. What he had thought was sweat wasn't sweat. It was blood.

Whirling back around, he yanked the blanket back off Clara, causing her to protest feebly. Carefully, he rolled her onto her stomach so he could get a look at her back. As soon as the light from the small fire washed over her, he felt bile rise in his throat. The back of her shirt and vest were soaked through, turning the dark fabric almost black. And there, on the sleeping mat where he had laid her, was a perfect imprint of her back in blood.

"Fuck, baby," he whispered, horrified. "What did they do to you?"

"They… they…" she started but then stopped before leaning forward and retching.

Jumping slightly, Warren's hands flew out to steady her. "It's okay. Let it all out. I've got you," he whispered, brushing her hair out of her face.

"They… they thought I was the one… the one that got you out of… out of…" she retched again as Warren's face darkened. She'd been whipped because they blamed her for him escaping.

"I'm so sorry, my little fox," he whispered, wanting to rub her back but refraining, knowing it would only make things worse. "I should never have entertained your grandmother when she showed up at Loch Haven. I should have sent her away as soon as she told us who she was. And I should have never suggested we come here; your family's pack be damned. They don't really want you. You're just a means to an end. I should have seen it then, but I…"

"Stop," Clara rasped. "It's not your fault. We thought they had more honor than this. This is on both of us for being so gullible as to believe they would treat us fairly. We should have known after what they did to my mother all those years ago, but it never crossed our minds."

"We can leave if you'd like," Warren murmured, pressing another kiss to her forehead. "Just give the word and I'll get us out of here tonight. We'll head home. Our family and pack would be thrilled to see us again."

"I'd… I'd like that," she responded quietly, her voice faint as he sagged against him, her body still trembling from the pain and the effort of trying to remain sitting up. "But if we go home, who will feed the war news back home to our pack?"

"Damn it, Clara, you aren't supposed to be reasonable right now," Warren huffed after a brief pause. "But you're right. Of course, you're right. We need someone to relay news so if the king and his forces do start to make it through the mountains, we have time to pack back up and head further north. Not that I particularly want to move further again."

"None of us do," Clara agreed, resting her forehead against his chest. "The war is just barely starting and we're all already so tired."

"That we are, my little fox. That we are," he murmured, kissing the top of her head, holding her close as gently as he could. "Now let's get you fixed up so you can get some sleep."

Pulling his arm out from under Clara's head, Warren guided her head onto one of the pillows and set the other behind her in his place. Praying that she'd keep sleeping, knowing that it wouldn't take much for her to wake with how much pain she was in, he gently finished untangling himself from her sleeping form and eased himself off the sleeping mat. Stretching, he tiptoed over to his clothes and pulled them on, his eyes landing on Clara's bloodstained clothes as he finished dressing.

Anger boiled his blood. He was furious. How anyone could beat someone that brutally for something she'd had no hand in... He shook his head, his hands shaking as he tried to finish lacing his boots.

This was going to end.

Tonight.

Grabbing his own cloak, Warren tugged it on and pulled the hood over his head, casting his face in shadows. Then, heading to his bag, he rummaged through it, looking for the dagger he knew Clara kept on her. It was the one that Ronan had gifted her, the one she had used on her. It was only fitting that the first weapon she'd owned and used to defend herself, would take its revenge on the shifter ordering this level of abuse.

Melanie Reynard's time was up.

Slipping the dagger into his boot, Warren stepped out into the cold night air. Now that spring had sprung, it was no longer freezing at night, but it was still cold here next to the mountains and he could live with this kind of cold. In fact, he was grateful that winter had finally relinquished its hold. The trees had budded, the leaves filling out the bare branches. The bushes had filled back out. There were more hiding spaces, something he needed, especially if he succeeded.

Glancing back at the tent, he swallowed, an uneasy feeling settling over him.

"Forgive me, my little fox," he whispered before turning and hurrying toward the city, following the wall around to the front gate that remained open for travelers and merchants.

Joining the small crowd still lingering at the gate, most of them drunk merchants heading back to where they had set up camp with their wares, Warren noted where each of the guards were. When he was sure that none of them had noticed him, he slipped into the city, making his way through the dirty and unused allies as a way to avoid the main streets where he ran the risk of being recognized. He knew people were looking for him. He wasn't stupid. And if he wanted to succeed, he could not be seen.

Avoiding a rank smelling puddle, Warren stepped around it and came up behind the Reynard's townhome. His eyes ran the length of the building, starting at the bottom and going up to the very top, noting the entrances and the exits.

He could do this, he reminded himself as he hyped himself up.

Eyes drifting back down to the third-floor window he knew belonged to Mrs. Reynard's bedroom, he contemplated how to get up there. He couldn't go through a door. He'd be caught as soon as he walked in the door. That left climbing up to the window, but how? He scanned the surrounding area, looking for anything that would help get him up there. Spotting a trellis on another building, he hurried over and tugged on it, testing it. It wasn't heavy, but it seemed sturdy. It would do.

Crouching, he gripped the bottom and tugged it out of the ground with a low grunt. Correction, it was heavy. Blinking in surprise, he turned it on its side before carrying it over to the Reynard's townhome, trying to decide where to set it up. Hoping it would reach, he placed it off to the side of the windows to avoid risking being seen. Taking a step back, he surveyed the area one last time to make sure he was alone before placing a foot on the trellis, testing it.

Closing his eyes as he felt it shake, Warren took a deep breath. It was now or never.

Reaching a hand up, Warren made his way up, going as fast as he could, worried the trellis would break under his weight if he stayed in one spot for too long. At the top, he reached over and gripped the windowsill, wiggling his fingers into the crack between the window and the sill.

"C'mon," he grunted, reaching down to pull the dagger out of his boot and wedged it between the window and the sill when his fingers weren't getting anywhere. The window budged as he dug the blade further. "Thank the gods," he whispered as he finally wedged his fingers under and lifted the window, re-tucking the blade into his boots.

Climbing into the room, he surveyed his surroundings. A slow smile crossed his face as he spotted Mrs. Reynard sleeping soundly in her bed. This was going to be easy. Too easy. He almost wished she was awake. He had so many things to say to her before he killed her. But beggars couldn't be choosers. He was out of options. It was now or never.

Tiptoeing over to the bed, he stared down at the face that was so like Clara's but was so different at the same time.

"Family," he whispered, shaking his head. "You should have done right by them."

With those final words, he pulled the dagger back out and slid the blade across her throat, cutting deep. Blood spilled from the wound, soaking the pillow and the sheets behind Mrs. Reynard. Her eyes flashed open, and her hands came flying up, grasping at her throat, horror twisting her face.

"Don't worry about Clara. She's in good hands," Warren murmured before stepping back and scrambling back out the window before Mrs. Reynard's panic could rouse the guards.

CHAPTER 44

CLARA

Clara shivered as the cool morning air washed over her, reminding her that she was alone instead of curled up with Warren like she had been when she'd fallen asleep, her body aching and sore. Her body was still aching and sore and her back itched from where the wounds had scabbed over. Freisinger's words echoed in her head as she stretched and winced, trying to be careful not to reopen her wounds.

"Why haven't you shifted to heal?" he had asked before looking shocked and horrified at her answer.

It made sense, though, she thought to herself. She now knew why he had punished her so harshly, tearing her back apart with his whip. He had expected her to shift and heal when she had regained consciousness. The pain from the whipping was her punishment. The pain from healing? That was self-inflicted at this point. But for Clara, it was a reminder not to trust her family, not to trust Freisinger.

She hated them all.

And soon she'd be rid of them all.

A slow smile spread across her face as she finally opened her eyes and looked up at the sunlight filtering through the canvas of the tent. She and Warren were leaving today as soon as it got dark. They were going home to

Loch Haven where he would resume his position as alpha, as leader, and she would be his equal, helping him take care of their pack and making decisions. By this time next year, perhaps they would have their house built and she'd be waking up beside him in a comfortable bed instead on a cold, hard sleeping mat.

Clara rolled her neck as she listened to the sounds of camp filtering in. There was the usual chatter, the words too silent for her to make out. But... her smile fell and was replaced with a frown as she sensed the hint of panic behind the chatter. It wasn't the usual lazy or casual chatter she was used to. No, something had happened that had caused the wolves of Romulus pack to panic. Had the king's forces made it to the city finally? Were they being attacked? Or... She shook her head. She wasn't sure what else would make the pack panic like this, but she was going to find out.

Rolling off the mat, she slowly stood and stretched again, muffling a cry of pain with her hand. This wouldn't do. If the enemy really was attacking, she needed to be at full strength, not hobbling around because she was worried about opening the wounds on her back. Cursing silently, she tugged off the shirt Warren had given her to sleep in and closed her eyes, willing her body to shift.

It started as a tickle in her toes and her fingers and then she felt her body start to rearrange. It was a disconcerting feeling, knowing her bones were breaking and reforming, that her hair was swapping out for a ruddy fur. However, before she could think too much about it, she found herself on all fours, her little black nose twitching as she continued to listen to the sounds around her.

As a fox, her hearing was better than when she was in her human form. It was a bit disconcerting, she had to admit, but in this instance, she was grateful for it. It allowed her to listen in without having to leave her tent, giving her time to process what was being said.

Padding over to the front of her tent, she paused just before the entrance and laid down, resting her chin on her white paws, her amber eyes trained on the flaps as she listened.

"He's missing," someone whispered. "He was supposed to be in our tent and he's just... gone."

"Is he with his mate?" someone asked in response.

"No, I checked," someone that sounded like Maddox said. "I've been standing outside her tent all night. She came back torn to shreds again. He never stopped by her tent. I would have smelled it."

"Are you sure?" This voice sounded like Zeke, worry filling his voice.

"Positive," Maddox replied.

"Is she still in there?" Another voice. This one sounded like Ronan.

"Yes," Maddox responded. "I think she just woke up, though. Her breathing pattern changed."

"Should we tell her what happened when she comes out here?" Ronan asked anxiously.

"If she comes out, yes," Zeke said in a tone that said that his decision was final. "I don't want anyone going in there to bother her. This news is... No. I don't want anyone but one of us breaking it to her. And if she's locked herself in there, she's in no state to be told what's going on right now. If she found out that her grandmother was murdered last night and that Warren has now gone missing before she's ready, it would wreck her."

Clara froze, her heart stuttering to a stop, her breath catching in her throat as the panic coming from outside her tent suddenly made sense. Melanie Reynard, leader and alpha of the Reynard pack, had been found murdered. And Warren was missing. However, that last tidbit was probably only known by the Romulus pack, and now her. The city, as far as they were aware, thought Warren was already missing, having gone into hiding after his escape from captivity. Would he still be a suspect to them? More than likely, she decided, but she highly doubted he'd be the main one. But to the Romulus pack? He was the only suspect.

Covering her face with her paws, she worked on steadying her breathing, her mind racing. What would that mean for her plans to leave tonight? Would she have to sneak away on her own? Would she meet Warren somewhere in the woods or in the mountains? Or would he find her? Probably the latter, she decided. She was terrible at tracking, something she'd yet to figure out how to do at the level of a normal shifter. It all had to do with following scents and that was something she struggled with.

Uncovering her face, she went back to listening in.

"What do we do if Freisinger comes for her?" Ronan asked.

"Let him take her. She's more trouble than she's worth," someone she didn't recognize said, their voice harsh.

A chorus of voices seemed to agree.

"She's no longer welcome her. We only agreed to watch her because her mate's a wolf. But he killed Mrs. Reynard. He's no wolf. He's a traitor, come to tear our city apart from the inside out," someone else shouted.

"Get rid of her!"

"We don't want her!"

"Enough!" Zeke shouted.

Silence.

"As of right now, we don't know that Warren Slora killed Melanie Reynard. Is it likely? Highly. But she is innocent in this. She was raised human. She came here to learn how to be a shifter. She needs our protection more now than ever. We would not be doing our jobs if we threw her out because we've decided to blame her for her mate's actions," Zeke proclaimed, his voice firm and steady. "With the death of Melanie Reynard, her family will come for her. They will take her into the city, and I have a feeling that by the end of the week, she will belong to Briggs Freisinger. That is not a fate I wish upon her. You may not agree, but I will continue to protect her until we can get her back to her pack."

"I second that," Maddox said gruffly, his deep, gravelly voice carrying through the camp. "I will continue to guard her as I have done for the past week or so."

"I third that," Ronan chimed in, his voice grave. "I may have wronged her in the past, but I do care for her still. I will continue to ensure her safety."

A few other wolves Clara had interacted with also agreed, their deep, hoarse voices solemnly saying, "We stand by Clara."

The rest of the pack, however, grumbled, unhappy with the decision.

Clara's body sagged against the hard ground where she lay. She felt limp. Her heart raced. Her mind was a whirlwind. How much time did she have before her family came for her? She needed to get out of there as soon as possible.

Shifting back, her back still tender but mostly healed, she stalked over to her bag and started dressing before repacking both her bag and Warren's. She needed to be ready to go at a moment's notice. There was no other option.

She was going home.

Grasping both her bag and Warren's tightly in one hand, Clara peaked out of her tent to see if the coast was clear. She had stayed inside all day, avoiding everyone who might have something to say to her. She knew she only had a few people who had her back. Meanwhile, the majority wanted her gone and she knew that if she had gone out, she would have been assaulted with all manner of insults. She didn't need that. She just needed to focus on the task at hand. Going home.

Her eyes scanned the camp as she poked her head farther out of the safety of her tent.

"Please don't let anyone be there," she whispered to herself.

Near the fire, Clara could see Maddox and Ronan. Both had a steaming cup of something, coffee if she had to guess, and both were facing the fire. Neither had their eyes on her tent, though she was sure they could hear her by how their shoulders had tensed infinitesimally. She ducked back inside before they could turn to look her way to see if someone was trying to sneak into her tent or if she was coming out.

They would stop her from leaving. She was sure of it.

"Think she knows?" Ronan's voice floated over to her as he made conversation with Maddox.

"I'm sure of it," Maddox replied, his voice solemn. "The pack hasn't been exactly quiet. She'd have to be deaf to not hear what they've been saying, and we all know she has some of the keenest hearing out there. No, she definitely knows, and I don't blame her for hiding in her tent all day. Not one bit. I would, too, if I was her. She doesn't know who to trust, who she can turn to, who might stab her in the back."

"I hate this," Ronan grumbled as Clara found herself nodding along to Maddox's words from the safety of her tent. "I hate seeing her in this position. If I... No, I'm not going there. I shouldn't think like that."

"Good, you're learning," Maddox huffed a laugh, a hint of pride in his voice as well as a bit of relief. "Leave her alone. If she wants you, she'll come to you."

"Yup," Ronan sighed.

Clara rolled her eyes. Oh, Ronan. What was she going to do with him? No, she wasn't going there. She knew. She was leaving him and the Romulus pack behind. Nor was she ever going to come back. This chapter in her life was closing. She was moving on.

A gruff cough from outside her tent caught her attention, forcing her to pause.

"Is Clara here?" a voice that sounded like her Uncle Percil queried.

"She's in her tent," Maddox replied, his voice taking on a dangerous edge, warning her uncle to mind himself or things would get ugly. "Why?"

"Does she know? Has she heard the news?" Percil asked, his words halting, as if he was scared to ask.

"No one has told her directly," Maddox replied. "However, she knows. The pack hasn't been quiet."

"How... how is she doing?" Another voice asked. This one belonged to her Uncle Arik.

"She hasn't come out of her tent, if that tells you anything at all," Ronan cut in, his tone angry and annoyed. "So why don't you cut the bullshit and tell us why you're here or you can turn around and leave. No one wants you here, least of all her."

"I..." Arik faltered, stunned.

"We came to collect her. For a meeting," Percil supplied.

"A meeting?" Ronan repeated, getting angrier. "You mean you've come to collect her to get punished. She'll come back to us, her back torn apart because you and your cronies think it's acceptable to punish a shifter that was raised human as a purebred who knows what shifter life is like."

Clara covered her mouth, her eyes wide as she continued to hide in the tent. She hadn't expected Ronan to come to her defense like that. Not really. She knew he would protect her, but this...? She shook her head. No, she was not about to go soft on him. She could appreciate his actions without liking him. Besides, she was leaving. She had a mission: to go home.

"No, you misunderstood me," Percil continued, panic lacing his words. "With our sister dead, she's the new leader. She's now the head of the Reynard pack. We... there's a meeting to catch her up to speed on what's going on with the city and the packs around the city. If she does not want to be the leader, she needs to state her intent to step back at the meeting so we can elect someone else, though I'm sure the council has already decided that. They just..."

"Wait," Maddox interrupted, his gruff voice silencing Percil. "You're saying you'll let her go?"

"Yes," Percil said quickly. "We just need her to formally announce her decision to step aside so we can elect a new leader, a new alpha. Granted, we had hoped... But no matter. It is not important at this point who leads the pack. What is important is that we keep the city safe from the king's forces. We need a strong head. And unfortunately, as much as I hate to admit this, that's not Clara. She is too sweet. Too soft. And that is perfectly okay. That is what a female shifter should be. Melanie was foolish to think that Clara could be as cutthroat as she after only a few months when Melanie had years."

"You'll let her go," Ronan repeated faintly, stunned. "So after this meeting, you'll send her back to Loch Haven? With an escort?"

There was a moment of silence where Percil and Arik hesitated. And then a sigh followed. "As much as we would like her to remain where we can keep an eye on her since her mate has gone missing, we would understand if she chose to go back to Loch Haven if that is where she is more comfortable."

Clara, still stunned as she hid in her tent, set the bags down and lowered herself down to the ground slowly.

She was free.

Or so she thought.

A little niggling sensation at the back of her mind told her not to get too comfortable. Something was off. But what?

"Can we retrieve her now?" Arik prompted Maddox after a few minutes. "We realize that you've grown close to her as she is your charge. We do not wish to overstep, but it is imperative that…"

"Yes, yes," Maddox huffed. "You can "collect" her and take her to this meeting. But I am going as well."

Clara's eyes widened as she quickly stood back up and put the bags back where they normally sat, not wanting to give her plans to leave away. Unrolling her mat, she threw the blanket down in a hurry and quickly laid down on it, face down. Resting her head on her arms, she stared at the cold fire pit, waiting.

"Act normal," she told herself silently.

The tent flap opened and she heard a soft chuckle. "I know you're not asleep, Clara," Maddox murmured.

Clara sat up and turned to look at Maddox, scrunching her mouth off to one side as she did so. "Blast your hearing," she muttered.

Maddox chuckled again. "C'mon. We have somewhere to be. I'm assuming you heard."

Clara hesitated, debating on lying but decided against it and nodded. "I heard. That's all I've done today is hear this and hear that. I almost wish I could turn my ears off."

Maddox gave her a sympathetic look. "I'm sorry," he replied softly, extending a hand to help her up. "Let's get this over with so we can get you back home, yeah?"

"Yeah," Clara whispered.

Two hours later, freshly bathed and wearing a dress for the first time in what felt like months because it was, Clara was led into a large room with a high ceiling and arched stained glass windows depicting what Clara thought was the history of Reynardsville. She had to admit, it was impressive. She had yet to learn much about Reynardsville, and if she was staying, she would have asked for a book or two to find out more. But she wasn't, so she decided that it didn't really matter anymore.

Dragging her eyes away from the windows, she noticed a large table in the center of the room. It was rectangular with chairs lining the sides. At the head of the table were two chairs that Clara assumed were for the alpha, or leader, and their mate. There were no chairs at the other end of the table. Instead, there was a platform placed a few feet back. She furrowed her brows as she studied it, confused.

A hand grasped her elbow, and hot breath caressed her ear. "That platform is where those seeking an audience with us stand and present their case, Kleine."

Clara froze, instantly recognizing the rough voice. Freisinger.

"What are you doing here, Freisinger?" she whispered as he led her to the head of the table, pulling the chair out for her.

Freisinger glanced down at her, his eyes hard and unfeeling as he waited for her to sit. "Your mate is missing, no?" he asked, ignoring her question.

"I don't see what that has to do with anything right now," she replied tartly. "I am asking you what you're doing here?"

A few heads swiveled in her direction at the harshness of her voice, a couple eyebrows rising in surprise, not having expected Clara to have a backbone. Clara, noticing this, stood next to the chair and arched a brow at Freisinger. They had underestimated her. Good. She had the advantage. Now she was going to put it to work.

"Sit. Down. Kleine," Freisinger hissed under his breath, leaning in so that his nose was nearly touching hers. "I am not having this discussion with you here. And it's Briggs to you now, not Freisinger. Do not call me by my surname again."

Her face hardened. "I will call you whatever the hell I damn well please," she snapped.

More eyebrows rose. Even Maddox, who was standing by the door, looked surprised. And then he sighed, shaking his head. Hurrying over, he placed a hand on Clara's shoulder. "Clara, not now," Maddox murmured in her ear as he guided her into the chair. "Freisinger is here because he's the one the council is going to elect to lead the Reynard pack. When you formally step aside, you will be passing the torch to him in a way."

Clara stiffened for a second as she processed Maddox's words and then nodded, relaxing. That's all this was. Passing the torch. She straightened in her seat, surveying the others that had been watching her in surprise, missing the grateful nod Freisinger had given Maddox before pushing her chair in.

"Are you calm now, Kleine?" Freisinger whispered as he sat next to her, leaning back in his seat.

"Why would I be calm?" she murmured back, not glancing over at him. "I don't want to be here."

"This is the last meeting you'll have to attend," Freisinger replied in an attempt to reassure her. "I am sure you'll have other things to attend to that will make it difficult to attend another."

Clara scoffed. "Precisely. I shall be home. Not here."

A faint smile with a cruel edge tugged at his lips. "Precisely. You are learning. Such a good girl, Kleine."

Clara shuddered slightly before rolling her eyes. "Pig," she whispered.

Freisinger chuckled but didn't respond. Instead, he turned his attention to Arik and Percil who were seated to his left. Arik, taking the hint, stood and called the meeting to order.

"As you are all aware, my sister and our leader, Melanie Reynard, was murdered in her sleep last night. We are here now to discuss the future of our pack and to give our new head a chance to get caught up to speed on what's going on." Arik glanced over at Clara and took a deep breath, a hint of regret flashing through his eyes. "However, I do believe that our new head is not feeling up to the task of leading our people, so she has come to respectfully decline the position. In her place, Briggs Freisinger will step into the role. For all those who are in favor of this change, please raise your right hand."

Clara's eyes swept over the table, watching as hand after hand was raised. It was unanimous. None of them wanted her to lead. Her brows furrowed slightly, surprised to feel a bit hurt by this decision. But then she reminded herself that she didn't want to be there. She didn't want to lead.

"Very good," Arik continued, nodding, seemingly satisfied. "Briggs, the floor is now yours."

"Thank you," Freisinger murmured, leaning forward in his seat to pick up a stack of paperwork sitting on the table in front of him. As he leaned back, his right hand landed on Clara's thigh, squeezing it gently, the cruel smile widening a bit. "As you all know, in order to take the position as head of the Reynard pack, you either have to be a Reynard or elected. You have all chosen to elect me, and I thank you for that. However, we also all know that in order to gain the favor of the pack, you have to do as they want, and in this instance, they want someone of Reynard blood. That presents a problem. To counter that problem, I would like to present Clara as my mate. After this meeting, I shall be taking her home and claiming her as mine. If you need to reach me over the next few days, I would advise leaving a message with either Arik or Percil. Anything that needs to be discussed in the next few days, I highly suggest bringing it up now."

Clara froze at Freisinger's words. And then it made sense why Arik had looked at her regretfully. He'd known he was going to turn on her. He'd known what was coming. He'd promised her an out and then stabbed her in the back.

Freisinger's hand curled around hers, holding it tight as if to say he wasn't letting her go anytime soon as the males around the table congratulated him on his new position and on his eminent mating.

She'd been betrayed.

Long live the pack.

The End
For now...

ALSO BY

Twisted Fates Series:

Twisted Fates

Darker Fates

Tempting Fates

Savage Fates (coming fall 2025)

The Vampires of Chicago:

All In My Head

Til Death Do Us Part (Coming January 2025)

Stand-alones:

Caught Under The Mistletoe

Check out Mspaidbooks.com to sign up for my newsletter to stay in the loop, get exclusive sneak peaks, and bonus chapters.

Don't forget – Reviews are like hugs, sometimes awkward and a bit weird, but very much appreciated. And needed.

About the Author

Meagan started writing as a teenager, trying to stave off summer boredom. No, seriously. She grew up in one of those houses where she wasn't allowed a gaming system. Boring! So, she turned to reading and writing. However, she was too shy and self-conscious to try and publish anything then, carefully hoarding her written babies away for safe keeping.

A decade or so later, Meagan finally gathered the courage to start sharing her stories. Not sure where to start, she stumbled across a web series app, Stary, and put out three web novels with them. (They're terrible, not gonna lie. Don't read them.) Realizing that her writing style was more suited to writing actual novels than web novels, she decided to dip her toes into the self-publishing game. After a lot of self-doubt, hesitation, and encouragement from her husband, she finally published her first book, Twisted Fates.

Meagan lives in Utah with her husband and three children. When she isn't writing or reading, she's busy taking care of her children and pursuing one of her many hobbies.